FALLING SHADOWS

BONNIE L POPE

Books Academy LLC
112 SW H K Dodgen Loop, Temple, Texas 76504
Hotline: (254) 800-1189

Ordering Information:
Quantity sales. Special discounts are available on quantity purchases by corporations, associations, and others. For details, con-tact the publisher at the address above.

Printed in the United States of America.

ISBN-13:   Softcover   978-1-968807-08-5
              eBook   979-1-968807-09-2

Library of Congress Control Number: 2025916502

Chapter 1

An autumn evening in mid-September settled over the small cemetery, casting its muted red glow over ancient stones and moss-covered crypts surrounding an open child-size grave. The small group of mourners crowded silently together as a wintery breeze whipped brown leaves into swirling dry eddies around their ankles. One particular mourner stood apart from them, oblivious to the cold, to their pitying glances, to pretty much everything except the gaping hole which looked like an open maw that had recently been fed.

Ashlon didn't feel the chilling wind rise around her and dry the tears on her face. Her eyes glazed over during the final prayer, watching as a small, hyacinth-colored casket was lowered into its final resting place. She stooped and picked up a handful of dirt piled neatly around the gravesite and threw it into the open grave, grimacing as it hit and scattered across the smooth lid. The other mourners stepped up to perform the same ritual until everyone had given their final of-fering and moved away, leaving Ashlon standing alone once more. The rabbi intoned his final prayer and benediction, but Ashlon paid little attention to the words, closed away from the people around her as she blankly stared at the open gash in the earth while the mourners' voices sing-songed the final prayer.

She tightly closed her eyes, blotting out everything; only her lips moved as she silently offered her own prayer for Emma. Beautiful Emma, sweet Emma, her Emma. No more pain, no more medicines, no more hospitals. The battle had been waged, and the ultimate loser had been her little girl. No more, Emma. Ashlon's throat ached from holding back her own pain, crying to be let out.

But, not here, not now. She barely noticed when the service finally ended.

Rabbi Summerson rested a consoling hand on Ashlon's shoul-der, disturbing her reverie. His smile was gentle and inquiring. "Is someone going to be with you tonight?" he asked. "You shouldn't be alone at this time. I could arrange for someone from the temple ..."

Ashlon wearily shook her head as she glanced up at him. "A friend is putting me up for a few nights, Rabbi," she said with a wan smile. "I was ordered to take a bag to her place before we came here." Ashlon tipped her head in the direction of a short, intense-looking woman with long dark brown hair waiting by the stone bench at the foot of Emma's gravesite.

Janey Ramirez, Ashlon's best friend and confidant, had helped take care of Emma during her last admission at Children's Hospital in Boston before Ashlon brought her home to finish her final struggle in comfortable, beloved surroundings. Janey and the hospice nurses had been Ashlon's patient-loving supports during that death watch, crying with her, talking sometimes deep into the night. Always there for her and Emma.

Both women had lived in this community for several years now, calling it their haven from the real world. Both divorced, they had pooled resources to survive the many crises their status entailed. And they both loved what they did. Janey worked in the nurses' pool at Children's, and Ashlon worked for a home health agency. Their close bond became a critical factor when Emma became ill this last time. Unlike many of the regular staff involved in Emma's care, Janey knew when to tell Ashlon to back off if she became too aggressive—that was the real blessing of having such a good friend. She rarely pulled her punches.

It had been just such a sunset like this evening's when Emma, so tiny and wasted from her long downhill battle, had sighed softly and turned her head toward her mother at her bedside. One long breath, and then she smiled as if surprised by something breathtakingly beautiful, half-whispering only one word: angels. And then, she was gone.

With this in mind, Ashlon looked up at Rabbi Summerson again, tears beginning to fall, but maintaining her composure. "You asked me once if my daughter knew she was dying. I never kept anything from her, Rabbi. Janey and I would answer her questions as honestly as we could. But I think she already knew once we came home.

She often told me my grandmother was there, watching and waiting. At the end, my Emma saw something beautiful as she slipped away from me. Death held no terror for her, and for that I'm thankful."

She squeezed his hand one last time, then quickly left him, making her way over to the diminutive Janey, who was looking at something beyond Ashlon's approach with a tight, suspicious gaze.

"Who the heck is that?" Janey pointed into the distance toward the deepening dusk. The sun was only a scarlet and purple glow above the far mountains' silhouette as Ashlon turned, shielding her eyes and searching the direction in which Janey was pointing. Her gaze fell on a shadowed figure barely discernible from the deep shade of a wide canopied pine spreading its lush, eternally green foliage over the top of a black marble mausoleum set above them on the gently sloping hillside under the ancient pine's spreading protection.

"He's been standing there the entire service," Janey observed, her tone low and suspicious.

"So what?" Ashlon bleakly shrugged her indifference, only half-trying to make out some kind of detail from the shadows in the distance. "He's watching. Maybe he was visiting and became interested in the service. There aren't too many Jewish burial services in this part of the country."

Janey sniffed and turned to her friend, her expression skeptical. "Okay, meja." She grabbed Ashlon's arm and immediately pulled her away from the graveside, down the hill toward the parking area outside the gate. "It's sundown, and a total stranger watches a child's burial service just out of curiosity? Uh uh. I know he was watching you and every move you made. You ask me, he's doing something for that worthless ex of yours. C'mon, before he makes any moves of his own."

"Janey!" exclaimed Ashlon, a little irritated by this sudden departure from Janey's usual reasonable behavior, but maybe also a little concerned. Would Wyatt have actually sent someone to the funeral instead of coming himself? Was he that much of a bastard he couldn't even attend his own daughter's funeral? Sure, he was, she angrily decided. And hadn't he flat-out disappeared when they first learned of Emma's cancer? Hadn't he cleaned out their joint checking account of the little there was in it? He couldn't get away fast enough. Thank heaven she'd had the foresight to open her own account, the worthless shit couldn't touch.

As Ashlon climbed into Janey's car and buckled in, she took one last long look up the hill at the unmoving tall figure under the tree. A chill coursed through her and bit at her angry, grieving spirit, destroying what little meaning she had tried to salvage from this heartbreaking day. "He can rot in hell for all I care," she spat as she slumped into the Volvo's passenger seat and fixed her eyes out the windshield on the road back to town. *I won't shed one more tear because of him,* she vowed silently as Janey wheeled out of the emptying parking lot and steered the little Volvo back into town in a spray of dust and gravel.

He watched from the depths of the shadows under the tall pine at the top of the hill as the two women quickly followed the other mourners out of the cemetery to the parking lot and drove away. She had seen him standing there, only dismissing his presence as incidental. In fact, she hadn't much cared. The other, the shorter dark one, had become angry. He could sense it. She had bowed to her friend's apathy and departed with her. He had felt the deep anger in her friend's suspicion concerning his presence there. Someone had hurt the short one very badly, he decided, and the wounds were still fresh. No pity to the one who had crossed her!

He stepped out of the shadows into the open as the glow from the setting sun disappeared behind the distant mountains, and gentle night settled over Lloyds Corner. The taller woman was the object of his attention. How fortunate he had decided to linger here instead of heading directly into town.

It was her. The moment he set eyes on her, he recognized her image, her face so clearly. And he heard her name on the lips of the mourners, her lady friend, and the man who had presided at the graveside.

Ashlon. An unusual name, as lovely as its owner. As lovely as he had imagined her, but so pale, so terribly sad.

He gazed into the depths of the distant town as its street lamps came on one by one, various businesses illuminated to shut out the autumn darkness, which came sooner and sooner each evening. He would go into town soon enough to visit the lawyer who had handled the details of his home with the town council and developers, and then plan its renovation to make it habitable again.

What a fuss they had made when they had learned he desired the estate again as a private dwelling! He had had to engage a solicitor—a lawyer they called them here—to intervene and handle the legalities of certain historical documents he had presented to the town officials, which plainly and simply stated that if any living descendant existed who could stake proof of inheritance, the estate must be returned to that rightful heir. He had to smile to himself at this. Rightful owner! He had arranged for this many years ago when he had been compelled to leave by certain unfortunate circumstances. If they knew the truth of it, they would all be in their own graves by now. He would not risk discovery again, forcing him to flee back across the Atlantic to his home country until anyone who knew of him had long since passed into the dust of time.

The night embraced him as a cold moon glowedbrilliantly in a clear, starlit sky, the rising wind sweeping the branches of the pine tree against the walls of the silent black crypt. Rich pine scent spilled into the air around him and into the solitude of the cemetery. He closed his eyes, wanting to erase this loneliness that haunted him. The emptiness of each night grew more profound with the passing ages until his longing had become an insatiable hunger no amount of hunting could satisfy. His need, his overwhelming desire, had no outlet, no resolution until he had sensed another soul like his own, tracking it to this place, to the one who was searching for the same resolution he desired but had considered unattainable.

He had seen its reality by that tiny gravesite down the hill from his family's resting place. She was real and resided here in this small isolated town he had once cursed for its very existence, those shrouded years ago. Strange that he had heard the calling even across a vast ocean, and that it had pulled him back here. But, then, maybe not. Their kindred souls had found each other again through some common bond, and had touched in a minute place between darkness and dawn; a mere blink in time, but it had been enough. Would she be accepting, allowing him to show her a world of unimaginable beauty between darkness and light, of real and only perceived at the edge of human reality?

As a contemporary of his, William Shakespeare had written in a play he particularly favored, '... t'is a consummation devoutly to be wished.' For the present, he would content himself with the knowledge of his discovery and its eventual fulfillment. Now, it was time to satisfy another hunger away from this place.

He turned from Lloyd's Corner in the distance, and in the space of a random thought, vanished.

Ugly realization hit Ashlon like a runaway truck once she and Janey arrived at Janey's studio apartment on one of the side streets off the main circle in town. Emma was gone; she'd done all the right things to make her daughter's passing as pain-free and peaceful as possible. She was so sure her acceptance would be easier when it happened.

She was so very wrong.

A strange inertia paralyzed Ashlon's legs, numbed her thoughts. Janey had to keep pulling on her to keep her moving; first out of the car, then through the secure doorway held open by a worried doorman who offered to help her get Ashlon upstairs to the second-floor landing. Between the two of them, they hauled her, oblivious to their efforts and moving her legs mechanically, until she was low-ered into a large overstuffed chair in Janey's comfortable living room.

Janey thanked the doorman—what was his name? Leon? Nice gentleman, really, Ashlon thought without much caring why he'd been there. But, as soon as the door to Janey's apartment closed, all of Ash-lon's defense mechanisms crumbled into a dirty pile of emotional de-bris. The tears began to fall fast and hard. Then, she just collapsed into an agonized crying spasm that tore at her heart; the utter helpless-ness and anger she had suppressed for too many long weeks breaking loose and dropping her into a pit of such bottomless despair everything around her turned black and chaotic.

Janey rushed to her and sat beside her, gathering her close into her stocky arms and rocking her gently, comforting her with hushed tones, unabashedly crying with her. Janey held her firmly against her ample, cushioning bosom until Ashlon utterly exhausted herself and was nodding off.

Janey pulled her to her feet and then practically dragged her across the large living room/dining area to an alcove partitioned from the rest of the apartment. She helped Ashlon onto the daybed behind a folding screen, sat her on the bed, and pulled off her shoes. She helped Ashlon lie down and turn onto her side, then tucked her in.

Ashlon was only hiccupping at intervals now, blinded by her still-falling tears, her head turned away from her friend. The worst was over with for now, Janey decided, as she clicked off the small reading lamp on the table by the bed. She bent over Ashlon and wiped her face with the tail of her blouse, then gently kissed her on her forehead.

"You earned this one," Janey spoke softly into Ashlon's upturned ear. "Crap has to be gotten rid of somehow, or it eats you up alive. Doesn't beat chocolate, but it's a close second. Get some sleep now, sweetie. I'll see you when I get home tomorrow afternoon."

Janey stood wearily and moved back around the partition, heading for her own room down the hall, running off the back of the living room. She smiled when she heard a muffled, thick voice call out from behind the screen, "Thank you for being there."

"Like you've always been for me, sweetie," Janey said with a deep sigh, and then went on to her room. She changed into a long sleep t-shirt, leaving her clothes in a pile on the floor, hastily washed her face and brushed her teeth, then collapsed exhausted into her bed and a dreamless sleep.

Ashlon woke late the next morning with a throbbing headache, a dry mouth, and a very empty stomach. It rolled and rumbled as she turned over and sat up blearily on the edge of the bed, trying to lick the slimy stickiness from the inside of her mouth. She felt like she'd been rolling around in a mud and grease pit after sleeping in the clothes she'd worn to the funeral.

Emotionally, she felt marginally better than she had through those last days up to Emma's funeral. At least the pain in her chest was only a dull ache now, and not trying to wrench her heart out of it. Yeah, yeah, it's supposed to get better in time as you reconcile with the loss and yadda yadda. How many times had she mouthed those same refrains to family members as they'd coped with their own losses and looked to her for some kind of comfort as they tried to make sense of it all? Ashlon wondered if those same words had as much effect on them as they did on her and concluded: nope, probably not. In the light of reality, they proved to be only widely uttered generic platitudes passed around for countless ages by the medical establishment and clergy simply because they were safe and convenient. It was all only a load of pink-colored crap the living used to distance them from the bereaved by being blankly conciliatory. Ashlon vowed she would never utter such worthless things again. The bereaved deserved better.

With this resolution in mind, she stood and wobbled her way into the bathroom, which happened to be in Janey's bedroom, the only bathroom in her apartment. September sun blazed boldly through the window curtains and gleamed off a mirror on the opposite side of the room, temporarily blinding her. She groaned as her head pounded even worse. Painfully covering her eyes with one hand, she groped her way into the bathroom and closed the door, leaving the light off. She fumbled with a zipper on the side of her dress and finally pulled it off, throwing it to the floor and using her foot to jam it against the bottom of the door where the sun tried to invade her dark refuge. Oh yeah, that was a lot better, at least for the time being.

After clumsily shedding her sticky underclothes and stockings, she stepped into the shower, felt around for the faucet and the handles, turning on a spray of pulsating warm water. She moaned with sheer delight as she stood beneath it and allowed it to run from her hair down to her toenails until she was thoroughly soaked. She groped for the washcloth on a bar above the faucets and the scented soap Janey always kept on the soap dish, and soon was covered with its lovely scent and oodles of suds. After a long rinse under that delightful, relaxing shower spray, she stepped from the stall feeling at least like a civilized human again. She toweled off with a bath sheet and wrapped herself with it like a toga, then hurried back through Janey's room, covering her eyes again against the blinding glare off the mirror. Janey really had to move that dresser to another wall, Ashlon decided as she fumbled her way back to the hall with its subdued light.

She returned to the living area and crossed it to the kitchen-ette. Where the hell did Janey keep the drugs? She kept them some-where in the kitchen, but just where Ashlon had no idea. After a desperate search through all the cupboards, she finally located several bottles in a wooden bread box set next to the microwave. Note to self, she thought as she downed several ibuprofens and the last dregs of a still warm pot of coffee in the dripper on an opposite counter: get a breadbox and move all her meds to the kitchen in her house. Great idea, really. She returned to Janey's bedroom to dress. But first, she pulled the shade over that blasted glare from the autumn sun on the mirror!

Later, she sat heavily on one of the benches set around a small trestle table that served as both dining and activity areas, a second cup of coffee steaming between her hands from a fresh pot she'd brewed.

Now what, she wondered bleakly? Her head was feeling a little better, and the daylight had started into its afternoon path, glaring less through the wide living room windows. Ashlon glanced up at the clock above Janey's sink. Hmm. It was almost 12:30. Janey would return in about five or so hours and be dog tired from her shift. She was a dedicated floater now, which meant almost never being in the same unit two days in a row. Ashlon was tired of feeling inert, even if Janey felt she deserved to be at this time.

I should do something for Janey, she thought with the curve of a smile on her lips. But first, food, and then, get busy. She knew exactly what she wanted to do to fulfill her resolution.

Janey dragged in close to 6:00 pm, noting that there was only one lamp shining in the living room. She slowly, wearily pushed the door closed to the apartment with her with one foot and moved with heavy shuffling steps to her overstuffed sofa. She dropped her purse and canvas carryall on the floor and plopped back heavily onto the large pillows, groaning wearily as she pulled off her white Reebocks, now soiled with flecks of blood and spew, and peeled off her socks, dropping them into the shoes. Her nose wrinkled in disgust at the sour smell embedded in them.

The living area was semi-dark with both windows' curtains drawn full shut to block out the evening's dull lamp light glowing from below on the street, and Janey was grateful for this. It smelled nice in the place, too. Homey. Her eyes were heavy with fatigue, and she just wanted to lie down for a moment before checking on Ashlon, who, she supposed, was still sleeping after yesterday's emotional wear and tear. Yeah, that's a good way to put it, Janey considered with a fatigued smile, her eyes feeling suddenly very heavy and sleepy. She took a deep breath, stretching out on the firm pillows and nestling into a plump throw pillow gathered in her arms. She relaxed into its puffy softness, letting her weariness take over for just a little while before getting up to check on Ashlon and maybe make something for them to eat. In a moment, she was fast asleep.

"Janey," a soft voice called from far away. "Janey, wake up."

Janey's eyes refused to open as she stirred, turned stubbornly to her other side, curled up with a snort, and refused to move.

"C'mon, sleeping beauty. Dinner's ready." A hand gently shook her.

Dinner? Janey stirred again and opened one eye, yawning widely as she rolled onto her other side and tried to pull herself into an upright position.

What was that amazing aroma, she wondered as she opened both eyes. She found herself staring into the mischievous, glowing orange grin of a Jack O'Lantern greeting her from its place on the coffee table.

"What the fuck ...!" she swore with surprise, launching off the sofa and sidling around the table as she shook her head to clear it. She also looked around the room searching for the source of that heavenly aroma that was making her mouth water. The lamps were shining on either end of the sofa, and a table lamp glowed from the depths of the alcove across the room. Lit pillar candles set on shiny copper plates on her trestle table were waving a welcome to her as Ashlon ladled something from a Dutch oven into two deep bowls. She looked up with a broad smile as she placed the bowls on opposite sides of the table and sat behind one, motioning to Janey.

Janey's mouth dropped open as she stared around at her

apartment in bewildered amazement. Now that more lights were turned on to chase away the evening gloom, she could see the place was—clean! So, clean it seemed to sparkle! Floors washed and polished, not a speck of dust in sight, kitchen polished and gleaming; the appliances, which had suffered some benign neglect due to her work schedule, were shining without a speck of crud on them. Funny, she hadn't noticed any of this when she'd schlepped in earlier. But then, she usually couldn't see much of anything anyway when her brain was in shutdown mode and her eyes were slamming shut.

Ashlon was grinning as she motioned again for Janey to join her. "I take it you like what I did," she said with an air of satisfaction as her friend shuffled to the table, delighted disbelief in her expression. "I needed to do something. Work therapy." Ashlon served up a butter-slathered slice of fresh, hot, crusty Italian bread, setting it on a saucer next to Janey's bowl of stew. Then, she poured a frosty beer into a chilled mug and watched the head of foam form to her approval before setting it in front of her friend. She lifted her own mug and held it in front of her. "I guess the pumpkin was a bit much, though," she admitted sheepishly. "But I couldn't resist it. You know how much I love Jack O'lanterns. Anyway, to you, my dear friend, and for all we do for each other." She tipped her mug and then took a long draw off the nearly black lager.

Janey lifted her beer and took a sip of the bitter brew, then another when it met with her approval. "Sometimes you amaze me, Ash. Yesterday, I would've sworn you were down and out for at least a week. You know you can hold on for only so long before the dam has to break. I guess that's what happened yesterday. But, I hope you're not pushing it like you always do." She smiled. "For now, thank you ... for all this. But yeah, ditch the gourd, okay?" She reached over the table and ruffled Ashlon's short, scruffy black hair with a meaty hand. "By the way—you look like crap."

Ashlon laughed back at her and then dove into her stew with a large spoon. Janey took one more swallow of her beer and proceeded to down her stew with equal appetite.

Chapter 2

The cemetery was quiet that afternoon. A few visitors were scattered at other sites, tending to their usual neatening rituals, and placing flowers or more personal keepsakes by monument stones and plaques marking the occupants sleeping within their depths.

Ashlon cleared dust and mud from the purple marble teddy bear that bore Emma's name and the usual things found on a standard gravestone, except hers also bore a tiny silver Star of David on its chest below Emma's name with a blessing, V'shalom—Rest in Peace. The bear had been placed two days after the burial, when most of the grave fill had started to settle a little.

Ashlon sat straddling the stone bench above the gravesite and sorted the flowers she'd bought to place on it because it was so barren of any grass or other greenery it desperately needed. It still looked too fresh, too new. Ashlon pressed several lavender cuttings into the soft soil, scattered some winter grass seed, and placed the flowers near the teddy stone. Then she took a large bottle of water from her oversized canvas bag, in which she had carried everything, and poured it over the ground, thoroughly soaking the small bare patch. After putting the empty bottle back in her bag, she sat back, quietly meditating as she watched the sun over the western horizon.

It was so peaceful here. The ache in her heart lost its edge as the golds and reds and oranges played over the grass and stones around her, inviting her to drink them in and warm her soul by their fire-like brilliance before they faded once more into the inevitable purples and indigo blue of nightfall. She wouldn't stay to watch the disappearing sun, wanting to be back at Janey's before it got dark.

These days, it was no longer safe to be out after the street lamps came on. There had been attacks on several ladies who worked tending a bar several miles out of town, heading in the direction of the interstate, a place known as the Scupper. The first reported attack was on a barmaid as she got out of her car late one night after work at an apartment building which had been built between the bar and Lloyds Corner, only a 2-mile stretch between the two. It had been between 2 or 3 am, and the girl recalled being approached by a tall, good-looking, dark-haired man with a strange accent, asking questions about the town and what it had to offer since he was new to this part of the country. He'd touched her arm and looked into her face with a gentle smile. She wasn't afraid, but mentioned he had 'weird eyes'. Then everything went black. She had awakened in the backseat of her car, the sun was up, her clothes were still intact and undisturbed, but she felt weak, barely able to sit up and find her purse with her cell phone to call the police.

At first, the police thought she was just being silly and trying to justify getting a little drunk after work. The girl swore she wasn't a drinker. She even took a blood alcohol test, which showed zilch, forcing the investigating officer to take her report of an assault very seriously.

Then, a second attack, and a third several days later, convinced the police that these were not unrelated incidents. They echoed with similar details: the victims unable to give an accurate description of their attacker other than being very handsome, very charming, a gentle, albeit weird smile, strange eyes, and then blacking out for a while, waking a few hours later so weak they could barely walk. The last two attacks had occurred right outside the bar after it closed, and these ladies—one of the bar maids and a bartender, respectively—were the last to leave each night of these attacks. Again, zilch blood alcohol. Drug screens had also been done on the last two victims. They, too, were negative. The town newspaper ran these stories with a warning to the town's women about the risk of being out after dark, even suggesting in an editorial rant that a temporary curfew was in order until the perpetrator was apprehended. Janey and Ashlon marveled with frank disgust that the editor even knew how to spell 'apprehended'.

"The guy's a chauvinistic moron," Janey spat as she crumpled the paper and threw it into her recycle container. Ashlon gently grimaced, only half-listening as she finished folding the last of her laundry, then sat back on the sofa and sighed as she looked around for any missed items.

"Well, that's the last of it, Janey," she said with a resigned sigh. "Time to go home and face the inevitable." She'd been at her friend's apartment far longer than she'd planned to be and knew that even a good friend could wear out a welcome after too long.

"At least I got some new clothes out of it," Ashlon commented, trying to sound upbeat but falling flat. She quickly turned away and busied herself with stuffing the clean things into a grocery sack so that Janey wouldn't see the tears beginning to fill her eyes at the thought of being alone in her own home for the first time in several years. In fact, it absolutely terrified her. Janey had tried to talk her into staying just a few more days, but Ashlon only waved her off. This had to be the next step in picking up the threads of her life, and she was the only one who could do it. However, any help would not be refused.

Janey squeezed her shoulder and reached over it to grab the bag. "C'mon, Meja. Let's go get some lunch, and then we'll go there together. I'll help you get Emma's things sorted, okay?"

Ashlon managed a small, bleak nod and allowed Janey to lead her downstairs to the street, where she stood silently watching while Janey stashed the bag in the back seat of her car and locked the doors again. It was colder since Emma's funeral, Ashlon idly thought as she closed her eyes and turned her face into a chilly wind wafting down between the buildings lining Mason Way, a short street off the circle in the middle of Lloyds Corner. Janey's building was located at the end of this street. The original brick paving first laid sometime in the early 1800s still existed, and for the most part, was pretty much in good condition. The cobbled effect hadn't roughened too badly, and the original material had endured in contrast to all the repaving that had been done over the years to the roads running around and out of town. The entire town was set up somewhat like a wagon wheel with four main roads meeting in the center, correlating to the four points of the compass. It had been deliberate and proved to be convenient planning in the middle of nowhere at the time it was constructed. Getting lost would be more difficult even if the sun was cloud-covered. She suspected, too, that the town founders may have had some mystical motive in mind to appease the local natives who had traded in town for necessary supplies.

Ashlon closed her eyes and inhaled deeply as the breeze

whipped up swirls of dead leaves to dance along the street's length. It cleared her head temporarily of the dread she had been experiencing all morning, temporarily lifting it. She looked at Janey and was able to smile. "Where to?" she asked.

Janey thought for a moment. "There's a new tea room I've wanted to try forever," she eagerly replied. "It's on the circle just around the corner there." She pointed up the street toward the end of the road, where it opened onto the main town circle. "It's called 'A Moment in Thyme'. Irma Robert's daughter opened it in May after she quit as chef at that hotel where she started at in Framington. Said they crimped her style."

Irma was a third or fourth generation native who occupied an old farmhouse several miles outside of town. It was surrounded by a towering ancient forest that was protected from development by the state game commission. The fields had long since gone to native seed and supported an astounding variety of wildlife that the old woman protected with a ferocity equaled only by that of her son, who administered the game lands for the state as a parks and wildlife ranger. He worked half a day north at the edge of the parklands and made a visit to his mother once a month to make sure she was alright. When he couldn't visit, he called regularly.

Then, Irma's daughter, Mineau, had returned home and moved back in with her mother, much to Irma's consternation. The old lady had flat-out enjoyed her independence and made no bones about letting Mineau know it at every opportunity. This seemed to be every time the two of them were together. It was a wonder they could live together without killing each
other.

Unfortunately, Irma was also dependent on Mineau due to the fact that one day, while Mineau was still shopping for a place that would be her new tea room, she had come home one late afternoon after picking up some wallpaper samples and found her mother semi-conscious on the kitchen floor with a large, bleeding laceration on her forehead.

Irma was hospitalized for over a week, and Ashlon had been contracted to visit the old lady at her farmhouse. That's when Ashlon had learned all the details leading up to Mineau's moving in.

The old lady proved to be a fighter, determined to take back a measure of independence. She worked with Ashlon with a ferocity the nurse wished her other clients had. Ashlon even suggested some minor adaptations to Irma's kitchen to allow her to cook again without risking a fire or injury to herself. Her client had been delighted with the results and had rewarded Ashlon's efforts each time she came out to the house with treasures from her cooking efforts. As Irma grew stronger, Ashlon tapered back her visits to once a week; then, every two weeks with phone consultations to stay in touch; then, finally, to once a month until Mineau finally convinced her mother that she was staying, like it or not.

After that, Ashlon went out to the house only when Irma wanted her to try some new concoction, or complained of what the old lady stated as 'feeling a little peaked'. More like piqued when Mineau got on her nerves. Ashlon sometimes took Emma on these visits, which absolutely delighted the old woman. Then, Emma had relapsed for the last time. Ashlon notified her agency to send another nurse if Irma called for her again. The old lady had asked only once more after that, and then refused the services of another nurse. She didn't call the agency again, either.

Ashlon felt a guilty conscience coming on as she reflected on Irma's past devotion to her, and for a moment, considered suggesting she and Janey go somewhere else for lunch. However, the limited choices of good dining spots reminded Ashlon how far out of civilized territory Lloyds Corner actually was. That's what had drawn her and Janey to this area to begin with, and their instincts were proven correct insofar as looking for a small town rural enough for privacy, but within a reasonable driving distance to a major interstate or a large city. Right now, however, Denny's or The Scupper just didn't tip her cup of tea.

With Janey leading the way, she trailed after her friend to the main street on the circle. They crossed the street onto the center island with its wide-trunked Wye maple trees sporting their autumn colors like a riotous multitude of pointed palettes, circling around it to the other side, and crossing the street to the opposite side of the circle. The shop front they approached was painted a clean winter white with dark green shutters flanking a bay window. It had been a private residence many years ago, undergoing several disastrous revisions until Mineau had rescued it and restored it to its more or less historical beginning as a town colonial storefront. The entrance way was flanked by black iron railings set on either side of a solid concrete step up. The deeply recessed wooden door was painted the same dark green as the shutters and sported a pewter knocker and European-style door latch. A custom inn sign hung off the sofited entrance, its ornate script lettering proclaiming the inn's name over the face of a rustic clock, its hands pointing at the 12 o'clock hour. Ashlon immediately liked the looks of it. The women went inside and were immediately surrounded by comforting warmth and the rich, tantalizing aromas of fresh coffee, and the subtle fragrances of cinnamon, ginger, and vanilla hanging in the welcoming atmosphere.

"Oh yeah," Ashlon sighed happily as she and Janey were led to a table by a bored-looking young woman clad in tight black jeans and a deep green tunic top, a carpenter's apron tied to her waist. The table was adjacent to the bay window with its full view of the circle. The waitress had just handed menus to her customers when a familiar voice called out shrilly from behind a short, glass-enclosed refrigerator counter set off next to the kitchen entrance at the back of the dining area. "Oh my lord and butter! If it ain't my favorite nurse!"

Ashlon turned too late and was immediately scooped into the wiry, strong arms of Irma Roberts, who bent close to place a warm, dry kiss on Ashlon's cold cheek. Ashlon recovered her voice as Irma hugged her tightly.

"How are you, Irma?" she managed to gasp, amazed at the strength in those embracing arms and more than relieved by the old woman's greeting.

"If I was any better, sweetie, I'd be twins!" the old lady exclaimed, patting Ashlon's cheek affectionately with flour-covered hands. "Found a calling when I thought I was permanently out to pasture. Working for my daughter here has made me happier than I've been for a long time. And you know what made me do it?" She poked Ashlon with her bony elbow and grinned knowingly when Ashlon only shook her head and looked at her questioningly. "Why, it was you, darlin'!" Irma again exclaimed, glancing over at Janey with a wry grin.

"How do you figure?" Janey said, winking knowingly at Ashlon.

Irma gave Ashlon another hug and a firm pat on the back, leaving a floury handprint on Ashlon's sweater. "My girl here helped me get my independence back after I had that blasted stroke," she proudly declared, not just to Janey and Ashlon, but to the entire dining area, where several other customers stopped eating to listen. "I gave her hell the entire time about it, too, because I was convinced that it was time to hang it up and just go to seed. But the nursery here wouldn't let me. No siree. I don't think I've worked so hard as I did with her fightin' with me and doin' things to get me going. Got me to thinkin' that maybe there was still some good to this bag of bones. So, I asked my daughterif she'd mind my helping out here a few days a week after she opened this lunchroom of hers. And you know what? Minnie actually hired me to do what I do best: baking some of the best goods this town's ever tasted."

She actually asked her daughter? Not demanded or bargained her way in, Ashlon wryly thought, biting her lower lip and trying not to laugh. "Irma, I think that's wonderful," she said instead, genuinely pleased. "I'm really happy for you. And complemented! But, I was only doing my job."

"Piffles, child!" Irma exclaimed. "You did all that for me while still taking care of that sweet baby of yours, Lord rest her. And because you and your friend are my special guests today, lunch is on the house. Anything you want! Just let Maggie know, and it'll be up in no time." Irma wouldn't hear any refusals from Ashlon or Janey, as she gave Ashlon one last big hug and motioned for the young waitress to get their order, then happily returned to the kitchen, giving them a hearty wave as she disappeared through the swinging doors.

Ashlon was shaking her head as she finally relaxed in her chair. That lady's a fighter, alright, she reckoned as she brushed the floury deposits out of her sweater.

Janey leaned over the table and examined her with a curious expression. Ashlon frowned at her. "What the hell do you think you're doing?"

Janey gave her a sly grin. "Looking for a big red 'S'," she replied.

Ashlon groaned and rolled her eyes as she shook her head and laughed. "Left it my suitcase with my magic wand".

Janey snorted as she proceeded to happily stuff a thickly buttered piece of warm French bread into her mouth from a basket Maggie had set in front of her. "Smartass," she mumbled through the crumbs.

Their lunch arrived and put an end to any casual banter as the two women dined hungrily on what proved to be a most excellent meal. They heartily agreed that Mineau and Irma had themselves a solid winner if all their food was the quality they enjoyed that afternoon. Afterward, they sipped on large coffees laced with just a touch of Bailey's Irish Creme (courtesy of Irma) and a dollop of whipped cream. Ashlon sighed with deep contentment as she studied the thick steam from her cup as it tendrilled upward to condense on the nearest fogged panes of the bay window. Janey was lazing back in her chair as well, stuffed and satisfied as she hummed over the edge of her mug and let her eyes drift around the homey decorations on ledges around the walls and hanging from supports securely fixed to the exposed ceiling beams.

Their peaceful after-lunch interlude was abruptly and loudly disrupted by the appearance of two large moving vans rumbling onto the far side of the town circle directly across from the restaurant. With a loud grinding of down-shifting gears to slow their progress, and carefully negotiating the narrow street, they proceeded around the circle. Their large diesel engines grumbled, shaking the large bay window in its frame as they slowly, carefully negotiated the narrow street, heading in the direction of the residential district. Irma suddenly appeared from the kitchen entrance. She rushed up to the table and excitedly watched the behemoths move by, smiling and laughing with excitement as the large vehicles rolled by one by one. They were followed by a smaller van with the logo of a fine furniture store out of Boston.

"The old McAnders House's been taken by its new owner!" Irma declared excitedly.

Ashlon nearly dropped her coffee cup. She looked up at Irma with surprised chagrin. "The town council sold it?!" she gasped. "They can't do that, can they?"

Irma shook her head vigorously. "Not sold, sweetie. Surrendered! You can't sell what you don't own. And who shows up but a descendent of the original builder with papers in hand as proof and his lawyer with him to help make his point! Mayor Tisbee's secretary told me yesterday at the grocery store. The council is seething mad, and Alice is positively pissing in her overpriced underwear!" Irma smiled wickedly at Ashlon and Janey with this piece of gossip.

Ashlon laughed out loud and looked over at Janey, her delight copied in her friend's wide grin. "Well, all I can say is it's about time someone claimed that beautiful old house. Now maybe they'll fix it up and chuck all that butt ugly furniture and fixtures the historical ladies were passing off as real period pieces."

Janey snorted in agreement and took a sip of her coffee. "Ecch!" She wrinkled her nose. "How about a warm-up, Irma?"

Irma motioned Maggie over with a fresh steaming coffee pot and then pulled a chair up to the table. Once the coffee had been poured, she looked at Ashlon with a wry smile. "I sense a story here, nursey. C'mon! Spill it."

Janey chuckled and pointed at her friend. "You are looking at a fanatic, Irma. She's dragged me up to that place so many times and made me go on the tour with her, I could probably find my way around it blindfolded. Ash could conduct the tours herself with everything she knows about that house."

Ashlon smiled sheepishly. "Yeah, I suppose so." She shrugged and took a distracted sip of her coffee. "I know I got carried away at some point. But, you know, I feel a kind of connection with the place. Maybe because it's been so messed with by former renters over the years, and all the misplaced efforts to use it as a tourist attraction by the council and the historical society. They didn't do their homework at all if you ask me or Mr. Stanley."

"What do you mean?" said Irma. "It's just an old 19th-century relic, isn't it? Simple enough to fix even for those pea-brains."

Ashlon slowly shook her head, thoughtfully studying the table surface. "Would you believe it's older than that?" she said. "Say, a 17th-century relic?" She cast a sideways glance at Irma and was rewarded with the old woman's widened eyes and slightly dropped jaw.

Irma glanced questioningly at Janey, who confirmed this information with a slow, gleeful nod. "You are in the presence of a genuine China Bayles when it comes to the history of that house," she said, pointing at Ashlon.

Ashlon only shrugged. "It's one of those mysteries from early American history," she said. "The early settlers were more concerned with surviving day to day with the usual births, deaths, weddings, baptisms, and occult dealings. Believe me, it was a bear to trace."

They were interrupted by a shrill, exasperated voice calling from the kitchen at the rear of the restaurant. "Mother! Where are you? You let the dough dry out!"

Irma grabbed Ashlon's arm and pulled her closer to her. "Come out to the house tomorrow evening, about fiveish," she whispered. "You can finish your story for me over goodies and coffee. Bring your friend, too!" Releasing Ashlon's arm from her iron grip, Irma hustled back to the kitchen with a laugh and a wave as she disappeared through the swinging kitchen doors.

Janey grinned at Ashlon. "I'm going for the goodies and coffee with or without you," she declared as she stood, pulling on her jacket. She quickly grabbed the bill from under Ashlon's hand and headed for the checkout, tearing the paper in half and dropping it into the waste can by the checkout.

Oh well, Ashlon thought as she stood and slipped into her fleece jacket, snapping it up to her neck. She dug into her pocket and left a tip on the table for Maggie's efforts. She'd go out to Irma's tomorrow evening with Janey just to get away from her lifeless house for a while. And not just because of the promised goodies she knew would be nothing less than her favorite savories. Nothing like the company of kindred spirits to make one feel a part of this world. And, frankly, she was tired of feeling so dull and aimless. She supposed that meant healing had begun. Only time would tell. But how to deal with the loneliness now that she wasn't at Janey's anymore? Even during Emma's final days, there had been someone at the house filling up the space as her daughter was being taken away from it.

How could that hole be filled now?

Chapter 3

Well, here she was.

Janey had helped her get her things up to her bedroom and then had stayed for a short while before her pager went off and she had to leave. She'd squeezed Ashlon's hand, given her a firm hug, and told her to call her if she started getting overwhelmed by what Janey called the 'onlyness' of the house, and then quickly departed with a reminder she'd help with Emma's things.

Ashlon sat in her kitchen, staring out the window at the widow's walk of McAnders House is just down the easement from her back fence. Everything in her house was clean and dust-free, just as her neighbor had said she'd keep it. The place really wasn't that big anyway—just a two-bedroom garden home in the residential district off the main circle in town, and only a stone's throw from the McAnders House. This was her first house after Wyatt had left her those long years ago, with a small daughter to care for and her new shattering diagnosis of cancer. Ashlon had used all of the small inheritance her grand-mother had left her to pay for her new refuge.

Ashlon nearly had a breakdown during the following years, working two jobs to keep up her health insurance, buy food and gas, pay utilities, and keep her old car running, in addition to the countless doctors' visits and hospital stays. Many nights, she couldn't afford to pay for a decent room at the motel next to the hospital while Emma was being treated with another round of chemo or for another infection because her immunity was so depressed. This was before the Fisher Houses and the Ronald McDonald Houses had finally opened. Thank heaven they finally had during Emma's battle with a killer they'd fought into remission, as temporary as that turned out to be. Before these places existed, she spent the nights either in the hospital chapel or in her old car, going to Emma's room to clean up each day before trudging exhausted off to work. More help had also come with better insurance coverage for Emma, so that Ashlon could back off her brutal work schedule and stay with her daughter through her hospitalizations and outpatient visits.

Then, her old car had finally died, and she'd found this great used Jeep Wrangler, its former owner had painted it deep sienna. It was only a little faded now and had small rust spots here and there, but the frame, engine, and trans- mission were sound, the rag top was still intact, and it had four-wheel drive, which made it the ideal vehicle for her rural visits on those cow paths passing for access roads to her clients' homes. In the winter months, it had never stranded her like her old vehicle had. Ashlon swore she'd be buried in it first rather than trade it for anything else.

But she'd accomplished all these changes without Wyatt the rat bastard, the coward, her officially ex-husband, a year after his disappearance, when she'd signed the papers presented by his lawyer in the presence of her grandmother's lawyer. Naturally, Wyatt hadn't been present for this. Never present, never there.

Ashlon screwed up her face with disgust. What in the name of heaven had she seen in him? Did she buckle because her grandmother had wanted to see her married before she died? Or was it because he was such a good liar, presenting himself as someone who could be depended upon, a man of means, someone who could really love her and wanted to spend his life with her? In the end, Ashlon was the one who had paid a very painful price for not being able to say no to either him or her grandmother despite her own misgivings.

He hadn't worked two months in a row in the time they were married, always with an excuse for why he quit a job, or pretending to be job hunting when he left their small apartment each day, but really hanging with 'friends' he had known before they were married. Sometimes he disappeared for days at a time and then returned with fistfuls of money he claimed he'd been owed, or from jobs he'd done out of town. Ashlon's beloved grandmother had died during one of his disappearances, and Ashlon went alone to the memorial service and reading of the will. To her surprise, her bubbe had left a small inheritance to her. A codicil to the will made days before the old woman died contained in it an apology to Ashlon for urging her to marry Wyatt. The money left to Ashlon was in trust and untouchable by Wyatt, to be released to her only when she got rid of him. After Wyatt had finally left, never to return, and Ashlon filed for divorce, she had quickly and quietly moved with Emma to this small community which was near enough to drive Emma to the Medical Center for her weekly outpatient visits. Ashlon had loved this small town from the very beginning and the easy pace of its daily routine. She'd fallen in love with her house, which was fronted on the street by well-established spreading maples and oaks; there was even a weeping willow in the tiny backyard. Plus, the houses on either side appeared well-kept, too. But it had been that widow's walk she had seen out her kitchen window across and down the easement that had intrigued her and started her on her love affair with the old McAnders House.

During Emma's hospitalizations over the last three years, and late at night when her baby was in bed at home, Ashlon surrounded herself with books and a second-hand laptop while Emma slept. Ashlon compiled reams of notes as she slowly uncovered the remarkable history of that mysterious house. This research was the only thing that kept her mentally intact during those weeks and enabled her to be present for Emma when she needed her mother the most.

She'd carried on her research even while making those tiring trips back and forth to Boston every week. She and Mr. James Stanley, who was the caretaker of the McAnders House, her good friend and collaborator, had pooled their collective research and presented their findings to the historical council of Lloyds Corner and were subsequently made honorary members (they couldn't be full members until their research was verified by the state.)

Big fat hairy whoop, she glumly remembered. Something about a budget crunch, funds unavailable, or some such other excuse. The town's historical council, chaired by the present mayor's wife, claimed it would cost too much for the town to renovate the old house and buy new furnishings. Ashlon and Mr. Stanley resigned their honorary titles and put their research away, warning the council that one day they'd regret not taking action on their recommendations. And, oh, how that day had arrived and bitten the council hard on their collective butts!

Ashlon sighed with disheartened resignation, knowing her thoughts were going in too many directions, deciding she'd put off the inevitable long enough. She reluctantly stood and slowly moved through the living room, climbing the stairs to the second floor. Turning right at the top, she passed a long mirror still covered with a sheet and headed to the end of the short hallway, stopping just outside a hardwood door painted with red roses and yellow daisies against a bright violet background. Placed at child's eye level, a sparkling rainbow sign proclaimed 'Emma's Place' in shiny flecks of color.

Ashlon took a deep breath, hesitantly fingering the door handle before pushing it down and opening the door into a room still glowing warmly in the dwindling early evening light. She stood in the doorway, letting her eyes wander around the now uninhabited interior. There was the small hospital bed, neatly remade with the sheets and blanket that Emma had loved because they had ponies on them; the bedside table with its Tinkerbelle lamp and Peter Pan clock; a multitude of toys neatly stacked into three laundry baskets set in the open closet across the room left of the doorway. Small pants, shirts, and dresses hung from the rack on purple kid-size hangers (Emma liked things neat, hung where she could see them, and purple was her favorite color). On the opposite side of the room, to the right of the entrance, was a kid-size chest of drawers Ashlon had purchased from a raw furniture discount store. She'd finished it in dusty hyacinth with round blue knobs on the three drawers, just big enough to fit small hands.

The carpet was splashy with alphabet letters and numbers in all the primary colors. Ashlon had found this at a carpet outlet and knew it would fit the room like a glove. It had the padding already attached to it, and laying it had been so easy. And, yes, it fit like a glove. Emma spent hours upon hours sitting on this carpet when she couldn't go outside, happily playing with her many 'My Little Ponies' and singing all her favorite songs. There had been many naps on this beloved carpet as well as picnics attended at various times by Ashlon and Janey, the hospice nurses, and sometimes one or more of the neighbors if they stopped by to say hello.

Love had designed this room to fit its former occupant. And Ashlon had delighted in each and every detail as her daughter had, pulling into reality a child's imagination and creativity with a determined mother's wherewithal. Silent tears ran down Ashlon's cheeks as she turned and left the room untouched, gently closing the door behind her. Not today, she decided. Not yet. She just couldn't face it.

She quickly walked away down the narrow hallway to her own room on the other end of the hallway, and dug a pair of shorts, an old t-shirt, and a sleeveless faded fleece hooded pullover from the depths of her dresser. She knew what she had to do next, or she'd fall apart, or worse, start destroying something. The evening was calling, and the cool air would clear her head and help her decide what course of action she should take next.

Ashlon changed her clothes in a heartbeat, dug her beat-up running shoes out of her closet, clipped her house key to a pocket inside her shorts, and, after going out to the front stoop and locking the front door, inhaled deeply the gathering twilight with its cool, comforting embrace. Turning left as she stepped off her low porch, she took off at an easy lope away from her house as the sun began its descent behind the mountains in the distance.

Chapter 4

Dusk. He rose from a secret room in his recently acquired home and made his way to the bedroom where the old caretaker had just built a fire in the large stone hearth and set out a fresh set of clothing for his new employer. The caretaker nodded silently and turned as he entered, leaving the room.

The new house master decided that he had made a very good decision in retaining the old man's employment with him. Everything he'd moved into the house had been placed exactly to his instructions by this gentleman, with only a few adjustments for size or space. If any place could truly be thought of as home now, he had accomplished it with his personal effects. After several nights of settling in, the house felt like it was his again.

The old man rather liked this new owner, especially since he'd been kept on after the house had been yanked from the town's historical society by a descendant claim that was several hundred years old. And, to be working for an actual McAnders family member who possessed the original contract documents drafted by the colony's first settlers—well!

This new McAnders certainly had tabbed the character of the house accurately when he'd moved in, Mr. Stanley mused, smiling to himself as he departed the room and closed the door behind him. Master Bowen had disposed of everything cluttering up the place (he had asked Mr. Stanley who would likely benefit from all those mismatched pieces, and the old man had gladly taken charge and saw to the dispersal of them to several families in the area, as well as to a second-hand furniture store that gave its profits to the area Red Cross). Lord McAnders had then moved in several truckloads of furnishings and fixtures brought from his native Scotland, and dated about the same time the house had been built. Priceless antiques, ornate framed pictures, and a 16th-century spinet which had been a gift from none other than Elizabeth I, a token of loyalty to an ancestor for performing outstanding services for the crown. It had been lovingly restored to a playable condition and set by a large window in the music room to catch the afternoon sun. Several hand-written pages of music were opened on the instrument's music holder. The old man suspected the music had been composed by Lord McAnders himself, as fresh and new as the pages appeared.

Lord, or Laird, Bowen McAnders spoke very little to his caretaker, but was kind and explicit with his instructions when he did. Puzzling that his business always took him away during the day. Stranger still that the old man could never remember hearing his employer return in the evening. Lord McAnders would simply quietly appear, change his clothes, and then disappear into his study. But, he always wished the old man a pleasant evening, or to remember to lock the door when he departed to make his way home to wife and dinner.

Oh well, the caretaker brushed off his musings with a shrug as he gathered his coat and hat from the front hallway closet and bundled himself against the evening chill. He looked down a side hallway to the study's half-opened door. "I'm leaving now, sir," he called out as he opened the heavy oak entrance door. "Good night, Mr. Stanley," McAnder's deep voice called from the depths of the study. "Have a pleasant evening."

"Thank you, sir," the old man replied and stepped out onto the porch, pausing to secure the lock before he adjusted his scarf and hat, and pulled up the collar of his long coat. Hearing rapidly approaching light footsteps out on the street, he looked up to see a young woman as she rounded the block and trotted past the iron fence surrounding the house. She slowed for only a second when she spied the old man on the wide porch above the yard and waved at him, shouting a breathy "Hey, Mr. Stanley!", as she disappeared down the street. He quickly waved back and smiled with delight.

Oh my! Miss Ashlon must be home again! He very much liked her and had missed their long discussions. The countless times she had toured through the house were always so enjoyable, too. He had spoken to his wife about the young woman with the sick child, and she had visited Miss Ashlon a number of times. However, these past few months, Miss Ashlon had been strangely absent, and he had missed her terribly. This had chagrined him somewhat, the old married man that he was. Then again, Ashlon had a way of making one feel like a most cherished friend with that husky sparkle in her voice. And she was easy on the eyes as well, with that short, ragged cut, black hair shining with natural blue highlights, and intelligent probing green eyes with their thick fringe of dark lashes.

Then, Master Bowen had appeared, shaking things up to the old man's relieved satisfaction. Mr. Stanley had been well prepared due to his and Ashlon's endless discussions of the house and her in-depth research into its history. Master Bowen had been very impressed. That was probably why he had been kept on. Mr. Stanley decided he would visit his young friend now that she was back and thank her properly for all those pleasant hours she had willingly passed with him at McAnders House. But now, to home and dinner.

As Mr. Stanley walked down the stoned path to the gate, the new master of McAnders House watched silently from the widow's walk atop the house. So, his caretaker had a close association with this young woman, who had collaborated with him to keep the integrity of his house from being compromised. How advantageous!

The night surrounded him with a blanket of stars folding him in its soft, cool embrace, an unclouded moon rising in the distance. He gazed over the rooftops of the quiet town and wondered where she lived, what had befallen her that she was in the cemetery that evening he had first seen her. He needed desperately to find her and begin his campaign of winning her over.

It was like a madness to feel like this! He, who had not felt much of anything other than his unnatural hunger for untold centuries, was now at someone's complete mercy to satisfy this deeper yearning creating a dark pit in his existence. What would she do if he revealed his identity too soon? The possibilities made him shudder involuntarily because he knew too well the answer to that loaded question! He knew the terrible consequences of being discovered inadvertently by the day walkers or purposefully hunted down by a desperate community when one of his kind became too brazen and careless.

Bowen shook his head and stiffened his resolve, pushing away the pain of doubt and once more setting his sight again on the one thing that had drawn him to this place. He spread his arms to the sky, closing his eyes. The night circled in around him, enveloping him in its cold embrace and lifting him into the northern breeze until he heard the fall of running footsteps below him. Looking down, he spotted her as she moved swiftly, her feet pounding the pavement from one street lamp to the next, and then rounding the next corner again, down from his front gate. She seemed to become one with the wind as she lengthened her stride, moving swiftly along his fence line, turning the corner one more time. She sprinted full out halfway down the length of the next block, finally slowing and then stopping beside a faded orange vehicle parked under a lone street lamp. Her face was shiny with sweat, she was breathing heavily and holding her side as she walked around the vehicle, leaping onto the sidewalk in front of a building Bowen assumed was her home. How interesting that her backyard nearly touched his across the easement. He smiled to himself at his discovery. A coincidence? He didn't think so, but this was something worth investigating with Mr. Stanley tomorrow evening before the old man went home. He watched as Ashlon climbed the short step to her front door and pulled out her keys.

Suddenly, she stopped moving, standing perfectly still. Abruptly, she lifted her head and whirled around, closely examining the length of the street with cautious, narrowed eyes, her breathing labored, but briefly held in check as she scanned up and down its length, and then over the open grassy area of the park on the other side of the street. Never taking her eyes off the street, she carefully reached around and unlocked her door, pushed it open, and backed into the lighted entranceway. The door closed with a slam, and Bowen heard the locks being engaged.

Well, now. That was certainly curious, he thought as he drifted downward to the street, standing behind Ashlon's Jeep and closely watching her doorway. Had she sensed his presence somehow as he'd looked down on her from the protection of the curbside tree's dark, thinning canopy? This certainly confirmed his impressions of this woman's intuitive sense formed by his brief conversation with Mr. Stanley. The old man knew so much about the house because this woman's curiosity had actually driven her to research McAnders House's shrouded history. She had traced as far as 1690 before being stymied by the sudden lack of any further history. Of course, he had seen to that before vanishing from the area back to his home country before the tribunals could find him and put him to the burning stake. He had had to leave on very short notice but had managed to erase all traces of his whereabouts, including anyone who had even scant knowledge of his heritage and to where he was fleeing. But the material loss had been considerable and had taken many years to recoup.

Yes, there was a certain degree of bitterness even after so many years. It had been his own carelessness that had almost been his undoing. But, he was much younger then, still learning the ways of the night hunter. Centuries of experience since then had seasoned him for this eventual return to reclaim what was rightfully his.

There was a bonus this time, he acknowledged to himself with a brief smile. She was here. The woman whose image haunted his daylight sleep and had been so elusive until now, the one whom he had hunted for each night since first seeing her in a sort of dream that had repeated itself until he could remember every line of her face, the color of her eyes, the tone of her voice. Now, he had to win her by all the powers he possessed. However, according to Mr. Stanley, that would not be so easy. Something about her being 'gun-shy'? A past marriage that had left a bad taste in her mouth for all men, Mr. Stanley had explained when he'd noticed Bowen's puzzled expression at this strange colloquialism.

He pulled his duster-length coat close about him and walked back the short distance to his house. No, he decided he did not feel like hunting tonight; one of the dubious perks of his longevity being he needed only a little every few nights to sustain him. Not like in the beginning! A kill or two a night. No wonder he had been detected so easily back then, new to this existence and with a voracious, uncaring hunger that nearly cost him everything. This time would be different, Bowen decided with an unconscious nod of affirmation.

He moved with the grace and silence of a shadow down the length of the street and vanished around the corner, melting into the velvet darkness of the night as he returned to McAnders House.

Chapter 5

Fall had arrived with its usual multicolored splendor, and the forests surrounding Lloyds Corner were breathtaking with their spectacular array of colors. The harvests had been gathered, and temperate days were contrasted with the chill of lengthening evenings.

The day after talking to Irma, as they'd promised, Ashlon and Janey headed out to Irma's farm once Janey had hurriedly showered and changed out of her scrubs after work. The late afternoon was cool enough for the ragtop, the air crisp and clean with the fragrance of evening's approach. They rode together in Ashlon's Jeep due to Irma's rutted lane off the county road that might cause damage to Janey's old Volvo. It hadn't been regraveled yet for the coming winter. Ashlon found this out when she called Irma just before she and Janey left Janey's apartment building to give Irma a heads-up, and had been gleefully warned about the poor condition of the private lane. Ashlon suspected that crafty old lady planned to hijack her Jeep if she ever got the chance!

It was a very bumpy, hazardous drive up to Irma's farm. After parking in front of the large two-story farmhouse, Ashlon breathed a ragged sigh of relief and shakily exited the vehicle, her knuckles still white and aching from her death grip on the steering wheel as she'd fought it to control their access to the house. She was also sure she had several new bruises where her knees impacted the steering column or dashboard with each bone-jarring bounce as she'd navigated the ruts and pits of the lane.

Janey bent over briefly and grimaced in pain. "I think my rear is permanently damaged," she moaned as she rubbed her knuckles across the painful throbbing of her back, and then slowly straightened. She carefully reached inside and grabbed Ashlon's laptop and accordion folder off the floor behind her seat.

"I'll call Grady about it," Ashlon said as they climbed the steps to the wide front porch. She knocked on the door with the brass knocker that looked to be a recent addition. "He usually takes care of these things for his mom. That lane is an absolute disaster area."

The heavy wooden door swung open wide, and Irma smiled out at them. "Well! Come on in, nursey!" she exclaimed. "Glad that old road didn't kill ya!" Ashlon and Janey glanced dubiously at each other as they entered and were ushered into the living room to the left of a short inside hallway. Irma motioned for them to sit on a wide, faded floral sofa set in front of the curtained window. A low, dark wood coffee table sat in front of the sofa. It was nicked and scratched, and had what looked to be small teeth marks on the two front corners. According to Irma, Grady had cut his baby teeth on that old table. Hours upon hours of children's projects and homework had worn the patina off the surface until no amount of furniture polish could ever revive it. Irma refused to get it refinished in spite of her daughter's pleading because it was, as Irma would always fondly admonish, a testament to the life that had existed within that old house, and an heirloom that Grady had flat out stated was the only thing he wanted when his mom eventually passed on.

The room was glowing with soft light filtering through the filmy curtains on the front window. Delicious aromas of cinnamon and honey drifted in from the kitchen, mingled with the fragrance of fresh coffee brewing in an unseen urn. Ashlon felt so at peace here, her heart and mind content and easy in this room with it's carefully placed antique pieces, worn furnishings, and comforting homey fragrances. She was smiling as she set up her laptop on the coffee table. Janey handed the accordion folder over to Ashlon, and she passed it to Irma who had seated herself into an overstuffed recliner set off to one side near Ashlon.

"What's all this?" Irma asked as she slid off the elastic band and opened the folder.

"Handwritten notes from my research," Ashlon replied as she tapped on the keys of her laptop and opened several windows on the screen. "I have it all in here, but since you don't have a computer, you can read my notes when you have time. Come on over here. I want to show you something."

Irma left the accordion folder on the chair and sidled in next to Ashlon. Looking down at the laptop's monitor, her eyes grew wide as an old oil portrait of a startlingly handsome man with pale skin, long dark brown hair, and violet eyes appeared with a script at the bottom of the screen. "Is that …?" she said and looked up wide-eyed at Ashlon.

Ashlon nodded slowly and touched the screen. "Yep. The first recorded owner of McAnders House, Alton McAnders, youngest son of a Highland baron named Angus Lee McAnders. Departed from Scotland to get away from his grandfather. He was forced by his family to leave branded as a traitor to the Scottish crown. His activities while in England were funded by Queen Elizabeth I and her security minister, Walsingham. I suspect he might have been a spy of some sort, and this was Elizabeth's way of retaining Alton for her services. Of course, we all know what happened anyway once the extent of Queen Mary's treachery became obvious. Alton's status as a traitor became a moot point."

Janey whistled softly. "You could get lost in those eyes," she said, looking over at Ashlon. "And that jaw looks like it's made of granite. But why is he so pale in that picture?"

Ashlon shook her head. "Don't really know. Might be just the quality of the paints the artist used, or fading with time. I found it when I did a search of the original clans of Scotland and just happened to stumble onto this portrait in a directory listing of the clans and their origins. It's only partly restored, but you can see the face is still very striking."

Irma shook her head vigorously and pointed to a date on the picture. "That says 1594," she said, looking at Ashlon with a puzzled expression. "But the house was built later than that. Your record there states the cornerstone was first laid in the late 1600s."

Ashlon tapped a few keys on her computer and brought up two timelines: one was historical data correlating to the settlement of the colonies, and the other a timeline of the McAnders House.

"Therein lays a mystery, Irma," Ashlon said pointing to the large gap between 1594 and 1690. "I figure the land must have been staked out and something built on it by Alton McAnders. Then, our boy's name and any descendents disappear during this gap, reappearing briefly in 1690 when a McAnders had built and was living in the house as it is now. But, then, he abruptly vacates it to return to Scotland. I found a few clerical documents out of Salem referring to the tribunals that were in progress at that time, and who was being investigated in addition to the witch hunts. It seems they were targeting anyone who seemed to be non-conforming to their narrow interpretation of normal, and had targeted a certain gentleman who had done business in the area through English port agents. They had letters in their possession permitting them to act as proxies in all business transactions, but they'd actually never seen for whom they were acting. They were paid in English currency, too. And, the signature on those papers was a McAnders. I can only assume he must be a grand something or other relative of Alton McAnders, who came to New England to live when the frontier was opening up."

Irma sniffed and sat back against one of the sofa's plump cushions. "Why would a landed nobleman suddenly leave a cushy situation in England and travel all the way here to build in such an isolated area?" she said, pursing her lips.

"Maybe he was bored or looking for a new business venture. Maybe he was protecting investments and overseeing their administration. And we really don't know how long a McAnders was actually in residence there before he left it," Ashlon said. "But what is known is that he left in a big hurry. The shipping manifests from his company tell us that. He took no furniture or other household cargo, only one small jeweled box and one large shipping crate claimed as personal belongings."

"This just gets better and better!" Janey exclaimed with a chuckle. "More of a mystery!"

"The whole thing's wrapped in a mystery," Ashlon wistfully said as she turned off her laptop and sat back, rubbing her eyes. "And now we have another heir living in the house, and no one knows why this one decided to claim the estate."

"Have you met him yet?" Irma asked with a mischievous smile, wrinkling her eyes.

Ashlon and Janey both shook their heads.

Irma smugly elbowed Ashlon. "Seen him one evening before his furnishings came, and the interior repairs had just been completed. I was talking with Mr. Stanley outside the fence below the front entrance. He was just leaving for the evening, and I stopped to say hello. Stanley's so pleased he was kept on as caretaker and couldn't say enough good stuff about the man. I spotted him up on the widow's walk, just after the sun had gone down behind the hills. There was just enough light to get a good look at him. By heaven, that's one big Scotsman! And he's the spitting image of that picture you have there, too. He waved down at us and then disappeared inside again." She elbowed Ashlon again with a mischievous expression, and then rose to answer a timer bell that had gone off in the kitchen. "You two would do well to make his acquaintance," she called resolutely over her shoulder as she hurried out of the living room. "According to Mr. Stanley, he' unattached!"

She chuckled heartily as she disappeared through the kitchen doorway on the other side of the dining room.

"Just great," Ashlon moaned, rubbing her eyes and shaking her head. "Now she's a matchmaker?"

Janey wrapped an arm around Ashlon's shoulders and patted her arm sympathetically. "Show me an old lady who isn't," she said with a grin.

Ashlon frowned at Janey. "That's what got me into trouble the last time. My grandmother introduced me to Wyatt the Worm."

"At least you got something out of it," Janey said ruefully. "The only thing I got from my ex was beaten up and my savings cleaned out."

"So we just aren't lucky, huh?"

"Only the first time around, Ash. I'm still in the market and hoping the goods appeal to someone before my bones begin to creak and my hair grows into a color I can't hide."

"I hear that," Ashlon affirmed as she folded Janey's hands in hers. She laid her head back against the sofa cushion and closed her eyes with a deep sigh. "Right now, I'm too tired to make the effort."

Janey hugged her firmly. "Don't sound so defeated. It won't last forever, you know," she said. "And you've got all the time in the world."

Irma called them to the dining table just then. "Come on, you two! Take a seat and dig in!" She motioned to them as they wandered into the dining room.

The two women joined Irma at the table, staring incredulously at what was supposed to be only a dessert and coffee gathering, but absolutely delighted by their hostess's efforts. She had prepared a full dinner, they happily discovered. Irma steered them to their seats at the light oak dining table that seemed to groan under the weight of its succulent offerings. And, it was so beautiful with a decorated autumn leaf runner down its length and an ornamental cluster of small seasonal gourds with a tiny carved pumpkin perched at its center on the top. Above their heads, the wagon wheel lighting fixture was hung with garlands of large brilliantly hued leaves and small pinecones twined around the rungs and lamps and scented with the fragrances of cinnamon, clove, and burnt orange. Their mingled essences floated over the delighted diners like remembrances of congenial warmth, comfort, and established hominess.

Janey joyously clapped her hands together as she was handed a loaded plate by Irma, whose face positively glowed in the soft light from the lamps.

"That's it!" Janey declared resolutely as she dug into her plate. "I'm never leaving here because I have died and gone to heaven."

Ashlon lifted her glass filled with an excellent sherry and laughed heartily with her. She couldn't have agreed more.

Wined and dined, satisfied in both appetite and spirit, the two guests helped Irma wash up afterward and then took their coffees out to the front porch to sit and sip and bid the waning day good night. The evening had cooled considerably as the stars began to peek one by one from a deep purple sky unsullied by the artificial lights of street lamps or the fluorescence of store fronts. This was nightfall as it was meant to be experienced.

Ashlon took a deep breath of the loamy-scented breezes drifting up from the woods surrounding Irma's house and happily confirmed she hadn't felt this peaceful in a long time. She smiled to herself as the night surrounded them with the sounds of swaying trees, the movement of unseen things in the depths of the stillness around them, and the soft bleating of sheep Irma kept in her small barn as they settled in to sleep. The faint gurgling and bubbling of a small creek that ran below a gently sloping hill behind the house was clearly audible through the evening stillness. Grady had mowed this side of the clearing earlier in the month. A wide field spread on the other of the creek and had been recently harvested of its feed corn crop, leaving broken stalks for the animals to graze when lean winter fell later on. A cool, mowed grass scent blew across it around the house on a northwesterly wind that brought with it the chilly scent of snow.

Ashlon was brought back from her reveries by a touch on her arm. She turned to see Irma smiling gently at her. "Penny for your thoughts, deary?"

Ashlon nodded. "It gets easier, doesn't it?" she said. "It seems to be."

"Oh yes, it does," Irma sagely assured her. "You have your hard days—a sound, a voice, a fragrance, somewhere you shared together. But it all eventually recedes into loving memory. The pain goes away, but the love remains, and the memories don't hurt anymore." She squeezed Ashlon's shoulder and sat back in her chair, taking a sip from her coffee cup.

Ashlon wiped her eyes in the darkness. Irma was right. The pain was slowly receding, and she could sometimes see Emma's image in a random memory without falling to pieces. She smiled as Irma took her hand in her strong, gnarled fingers, squeezing it firmly.

"I'd say you're doing your recovery work just fine," the old woman gently assured her.

Abruptly, a mercury light fixed to the top of a high post planted at the entrance to the lane suddenly spat and buzzed to life, casting its harsh glare over the parking area and the front porch. The women covered their eyes and groaned aloud at this sudden intrusion on their peace and quiet.

"Oh, hell in a hand basket!" Irma swore, grimacing. "It must be getting on seven o'clock!" She stood up and stretched, then motioned to Ashlon and Janey as she descended the porch steps to the parking area and Ashlon's Jeep. "You two better get on before Minnie comes home. That lane will let only one of you pass, and I don't cotton to put up with a sourpuss if she's the one who has to back out to the road, especially after having such a lovely evening with you two." She hugged the women fondly in turn as they rose and prepared to leave.

"Thanks again, Irma," Janey yawned. "I wouldn't have missed this for the world." She reluctantly descended the porch steps to Ashlon's Jeep, groaning as she climbed in the passenger side and buckled up her seat belt.

Ashlon had quickly retrieved her laptop and their bags from the house, stowing them on the floor behind the driver's seat. She climbed in and started up the engine, then waved around Janey to Irma. "Let me know what you get from those notes!" she called out as she secured her seat belt for the hazardous ride back to the county road.

"I'll call you, dear!" Irma said, waving as the Jeep headed down to the lane and was soon swallowed by the darkness outside the mercury lamp's bright light.

Chapter 6

By the time they reached the county road, Janey had her own white knuckle grip around the sissy handles on the dashboard and above her head on the frame. Ashlon was laughing riotously as they seemed to hit every bump and hole in the poorly maintained dirt lane, and at one point, she had abruptly veered away from a 3-foot drop-off on her side that would have rolled even her Jeep. And, Janey's head had hit the roll bar above her once too often. "Jesus, woman, my boobs are falling off!" she yelled painfully at Ashlon.

Ashlon only grinned over at her and yelled back, "Arncha glad I put on the doors? I would've lost you back there!" Janey shot a middle finger at her before resuming her death grip on the safety handles.

They finally reached the county road. Ashlon, breathing a shaky sigh of relief, floored the accelerator heading back toward town. Janey rolled down her window and took a deep, relieved breath of fresh evening air. The scent of freshly mowed pasture mingled with the remnant of rich honeysuckle growing wild on the roadside as a crescent moon rose from behind the distant mountains' dim silhouettes.

"I'm really going to yell at Grady about his lane," Ashlon assured her friend as they whizzed down the road. However, before heading to town, she took a turnoff and slowed as she pulled into the front entrance of the town cemetery. Janey glanced questioningly at her, but said nothing as they drove through the open gateway. The old caretaker waved them on without looking up from his raking around the high iron fence.

Slowly winding up the narrow paved road, weaving above the silent stones and climbing a gentle hill to its top, Ashlon finally reached a landmark oak tree she always parked under when visiting this part of the park. An old-style incandescent street lamp cast its eerie pale light from the other side of the tree creating wavering, dancing shadows across the road and the hood of the Jeep. Janey frowned nervously as she rolled up her window.

"Don't you think it's a little late?" she said, sounding worried, and maybe just a little scared. After all, a cemetery near sundown…

"I just want a sprig of lavender from Emma's gravesite," Ashlon replied, patting her friend's arm reassuringly. "It took really well, and I want a cutting. It's best to get it at sundown. You wait here where it's warm. I'll keep the engine running and won't be long." She popped the clutch into neutral and set the brake, then quickly got out and disappeared over the hill outside the street lamp's weak glow.

Ashlon had no difficulty picking her way between the grave stones in the fading evening glow, and descended the gentle slope past the black stone crypt near the hilltop, and which overlooked her destination like a dark sentry.

As she had on past visits, she brushed her hand over the stone and the ivy covering its surface as she slowed her walk, running her fingers along the length of the wall, noting its texture, marveling at how different it felt at night than in the day. It felt almost alive and wanting her fingers close against it, caressing it. She imagined the surface even trembled a little under her touch. Sometimes the ivy would snare her fingers and hold onto them for only a moment, and then release them reluctantly as she gently pulled free of their entanglement. As she left it and continued her descent down the hill, she whispered "thank you" and gave the stone a last caress before leaving it. Too bad most relationships couldn't be as accepting and unquestioning, she thought as she moved on down the hill.

Ashlon reached the stone bench set above Emma's resting place. Moving around it, she knelt by the headstone and brushed her hand over the abundant baby lavender blooms that flourished over the child's resting place, its heady fragrance rising under her hand into the cool night breeze. She inhaled deeply and rested her cheek briefly on the headstone, its cool surface soothing as she rubbed her forehead over it, voicing a barely audible prayer only the descending night could hear.

Grasping a slim woody stalk of the lavender, she snapped its stem with her fingernail. Then, with a silent amen, she stood and moved up to the bench, sitting there briefly, listening to the wind and the gentle rustling of the trees as their dying leaves rattled their last songs before dropping to the ground to be covered by the coming snows. She quietly sang one of Emma's favorite lullabies as she fingered the lavender sprig. A change in direction of the winds made her pause her singing. Where was that other music coming from?

It had to be the Presbyterian Church on the other side of town, favored by the direction of the wind blowing her direction over the silent headstones and monuments around her. Rising and falling, entrancing and beckoning at once, their harmonies were exquisite and strangely ethereal as they surrounded her on the tendrils of the night. They rose and fell with the winds as they surrounded her like a ghostly, beguiling siren song.

Nope, definitely not from the church. There was an unearthly beauty to the music no human voice could possibly create. Ashlon closed her eyes, wrapping her arms around herself as she turned her face, bathing in the solace of these entrancing melodies. She unconsciously swayed as the winds caressed the bench and the tiny grave at its head.

She had no idea how long the phantom voices sang. They gradually faded into the night air as the winds fell, the night becoming still once again. Ashlon opened her eyes.

Approaching movement from below the gravesite instantly alerted her. It was formless, silent, and headed straight for her. Run, her sense of approaching danger frantically urged!

Ashlon leapt off the bench and took off at a dead run back up the hill, her legs pumping an evasive path between the gravestones, her heart pounding wildly as she quickly gained the black crypt and veered around it. She fell once but was instantly up again and scrambling with concentrated effort toward the street lamp's glow, now visible at the top of the hill. Behind her, she could hear the heavy footfall of her pursuer swiftly closing in, which only urged her on as her lungs and throat burned furiously with her effort. She had almost reached the crest of the hill when her foot caught a small raised memorial stone and sent her sprawling toward the ground, her temple glancing off the edge of an adjacent stone with a sickening thunk. She sprawled on the ground face down and lay stunned for a few precious seconds, lights spinning in front of her. Pulling herself up to her hands and knees and frantically shaking her head to clear it, she tried but failed to gain her feet. Abruptly, two large, strong arms wrapped around her body and lifted her off the ground, her legs dangling and kicking wildly as her captor crushed her against him.

Ashlon screamed, thrashing wildly against the embrace that now carried her back toward the black crypt. A large hand suddenly clamped over her mouth, and an amazingly deep voice spoke softly into her ear, "Do not fight me."

Ashlon's breathing was ragged against the muffling hand, but she immediately stopped her struggling against this incredibly strong force—she couldn't help it—as he smoothly moved away from the light up above, her back held against a broad chest, full lips pressed below her one ear without any sound of labored breathing coming from them. She couldn't have moved if she wanted to. Ashlon's head ached and swam as she dangled helplessly against her captor. He moved her effortlessly toward the front of the crypt, which was enveloped by the canopy of the tall ancient pine tree engulfing it in absolute shadowless darkness, sending a chill of terror coursing through her. It broke through the paralysis, and she struggled even harder now. However, her captor's grip tightened around her, squeezing her like a boa constrictor and making it almost impossible to breathe. She moaned involuntarily, her head falling forward against the restraining hand. Her eyes closed, and her body went completely limp in that suffocating embrace.

The old opossum trick had worked before, and she fervently prayed it would again.

"No!" Her attacker's voice cried out. Quickly, he knelt under the tree at the edge of its canopy and loosened his grip enough to turn her face up toward him. What he failed to notice, however, was the slow, purposeful movement of Ashlon's dangling hand as it carefully scooped up some dirt and dead pine needles and held it carefully under her until her captor bent lower to look at her face. Her hand whipped up suddenly and threw its contents into where she knew his face should be.

He reared back, snarling with pain and surprise, dumping Ashlon onto the ground as he frantically backed away.

Ashlon pushed herself into a crouch and savagely lashed out a foot that caught her captor's legs at the knees and sent him sprawling onto his back, a deep grunt issuing from the goliath as he hit the ground with a solid thud. Ashlon turned and stumbled out to open ground, swallowing hard—her throat was so dry she couldn't spit. Back up the hill, she scrambled into the light of the street lamp, staggering toward the Jeep, finally reaching it and yanking the driver's side door open. Janey yelped in surprise as Ashlon tumbled into her seat and slammed the door, jammed the gearshift into first, and tore off down the road.

"Good grief!" Janey exclaimed, horrified as she reached out with a handful of tissues she'd dug from her bag to blot at the wound on Ashlon's head. "What happened?"

Ashlon only shook her head. She was panting hard and fighting to focus on the road ahead as she sped out of the cemetery toward town. Swallowing hard again, she managed to utter one word, "Attacked!", before she was finally forced to pull off the road just as they reached the first buildings inside town, where there were lights all around. "Drive," she rasped as she got out and stumbled her way around the front of the Jeep to the passenger side. Janey slipped over the console into the driver's seat as she followed Ashlon's course toward the passenger side door. As she yanked open the door, her eyes rolled back and she slid down the open doorway, passing out cold on the road next to the Jeep.

"Wonderful," Janey growled as she quickly squelched the panic threatening to overwhelm her critical assessment of the situation. Instead, she whipped out her cell phone and speed dialed. The other end rang several times before a male voice heavy with sleep picked up.

"Bueno," it coughed into the receiver. "This better be good."

"Jorge, get your ass to South Oakland and View right now! I've got a big problem here!" Janey tersely said. "Just bring your bag and don't ask any questions until you get here." She snapped the phone shut and immediately left the driver's seat, ran around the front of the

Jeep, and knelt next to her friend. Janey automatically did a head-to-toe assessment, assuring herself that Ashlon's breathing and that she wasn't bleeding much. But one finding sent a small frisson through her as she gently straightened Ashlon's neck and pushed her rolled scarf under her friend's head—there were two small puncture marks just under one ear. What the hell was going on, Janey wondered as she gingerly touched the wounds. Who, or what, had Ashlon been running from out there?

With a shiver, she hugged the side of the Jeep and prayed that Jorge had taken her seriously and was on his way.

Jorge, being Jorge Villarreal, MD, arrived no more than 10 minutes after Janey's frantic call had disrupted his sound sleep. Of course, he would have come anyway after a call like that, but being the town doctor's current love interest didn't hurt either. Ashlon had introduced them after helping Jorge settle into his new office on the main street circle after his move to Lloyd's Corner. She'd been his sponsor upon his arrival and had even hosted him at her home for a week until he found his own place to live. He'd been a physician for a number of years somewhere in the southwest, had a successful practice, and a prestigious position at the University where he taught part-time. But, like many others before, they had taken up rural practice. Jorge had burned out by the competition and the backstabbing of a larger practice, the 'publish or perish' grind, and the headaches of increasingly complicated managed care limitations. One day, he realized that the dull pain in his chest he had ignored for so long, also would not go away.

He finally had to acknowledge it and the other warning signs, and eventually underwent a procedure that saved his heart. However, he also knew what he had to do to prevent a recurrence, and that was to get out of the pressure cooker. An online search found him this spot in New England that seemed to fit what he was looking for. Of course, finding Janey had been a bonus.

He navigated his pickup to within a few inches of the Jeep, which was parked on the side of the road where Janey had said she'd be. Shielding her eyes, she stood and ran to him, frantically yanking open the driver's side door and forcefully grabbing Jorge's arm. "Thank heaven you're here! C'mon!"

"Wait a minute, meja!" Jorge grabbed his bag with his free hand and then allowed himself to be pulled along to the Jeep's passenger side door, which stood partway open, blocking his view of someone lying on the road in a supine position. And she was regaining consciousness.

Ashlon groaned as she tried to pull herself into a semi-reclining position, but fell back when the pain in her head pounded against the back of her eyes like two knives trying to dig them out of their sockets.

"Uh uh!" Janey growled as she gently pressed her hands on Ashlon's shoulders to keep her head back on the make-shift pillow. "You don't need to be moving just yet."

Ashlon's eyes flickered open, looking around until they lit on Janey's face. They didn't seem to recognize her at first, or so Janey thought. The blow to her head looked nasty and could have given her a concussion. Knowing Ashlon, though, Janey wasn't about to suggest they take her to a hospital.

Jorge was kneeling next to Janey, flashlight in hand, examining Ashlon's pupil response and the laceration to her temple just at the hairline. It was no longer bleeding but was going to need cleaning up and stitches. That much he could
ascertain.

"Hey, Ash," Jorge gently called to her, "Tell me what happened, sweetie." Ashlon wiped her arm across her eyes and sighed deeply. "Where am I?" she said groggily.

"Lying on a road in town," Jorge replied evenly as he began carefully cleaning the laceration with some saline and gauze from his bag. "It's almost eight-thirty. Can you tell me what happened?"

Ashlon looked back at Janey, who was still sitting at her head with her hands on Ashlon's shoulders. "I was running from someone," she mumbled, gathering her thoughts. "I tripped, smacked my head against a stone on the hill. Went down and saw stars."

"I'll just bet you did," Janey said as she held Ashlon's short black hair aside for Jorge to clean the wound edges. "Then what?"

Ashlon licked her dry lips as she struggled to bring everything back into focus. "A man," she said painfully, "a really big man. I heard him and took off up the hill. I fell, and he was on me, hauled me off my feet."

"Off your feet?" Janey said incredulously. Ashlon was an easy 5 foot 10 inches and a lithe, solid 175 pounds, which was an asset on her home visits when she had to move her patients or their equipment.

Ashlon managed a brief nod, then grimaced from the shooting pain that small motion created. At least the fog was clearing, and she could think a little more clearly.

Jorge finished cleaning Ashlon's head wound and put a temporary dressing on it. "You're going to need stitches or dermabond," he stated as he bagged the soiled gauzes and empty saline bullets. "Let's go to my office, and I can finish up there."

Ashlon shook her head slowly. "No," she said flatly. "I want to go home. You can follow me there and sew me up or whatever. I hurt the guy when I got away from him, so I don't think we were followed." She turned onto her side and carefully pushed herself into a sitting position, her head throbbing only a little now. Grabbing the Jeep's open passenger door, she pulled herself to her feet and carefully slid into the passenger seat. Janey circled around to the driver's side.

"You take my truck," Jorge reached for her arm as she was climbing into the driver's seat. "I want to keep an eye on her."

Janey had other ideas. "I can do that. I want to hear the rest of what happened," she said with a shrug as she closed the door behind her. "Especially the part where she hurt him." She started up the vehicle once more, shoved it into gear, carefully pulled around Jorge's SUV, and headed into town.

Jorge returned to his truck and threw his bag onto the passenger seat with frank disgust and got in, slamming the door and folding his arms across the steering wheel, glaring at the Jeep in his side mirror as it disappeared. Those women! They were glued together!

Outside the arc of the street lamps, a cloaked figure watched from the protection of night, his eyes glowing with an unnatural purple light as they followed the disappearing vehicles. In spite of the residual pain to his eyes and knees, he had to smile. Now, he had a measure of what she was capable of and would not make such a grievous mistake again. Best to proceed cautiously and patiently, or risk losing her altogether, not after searching for so long to find her. What better way than to use the very thing that linked them together? Perhaps Mr. Stanley would handle the details.

With this resolution, he vanished into the velvet darkness around him.

Chapter 7

The aroma of freshly brewed coffee woke Janey late the next morning. Bleary-eyed with a mild headache behind her temples, she pushed back the blanket and top sheet and rolled into a sitting position on the edge of the sofa bed, rub- bing her face with her hands.

Ah. She remembered now. Ashlon's house. The curtains had been pulled shut over the front window, but the morning sun was still too bright as it filtered softly through the patterns on three deep blue curtain panels. Nearly soundless footsteps approached from around the front of the studio couch. Then, the hot vapor of a steaming cup of coffee was waved under her nose. Janey inhaled deeply, opened her eyes, and gratefully took the large mug from Ashlon, who crouched in front of her, smiling.

"You look like crap," Ashlon commented with a grin.

Janey stuck out her tongue, then took a careful sip off her coffee mug. She sighed with relief as the fuzziness began to lift from her brain and glanced fondly over at the still sleeping Jorge.

"I hope he's got something on under there," Ashlon quipped as she stood again and handed a well-worn chenille robe to her friend. "Come on out to the kitchen. I picked up some fresh pastries at the store this morning."

Janey nodded approvingly as both women quietly moved out of the living room to the kitchen and were soon savoring fresh cinnamon rolls dripping with butter icing.

"What does Jorge like for breakfast?" Ashlon suddenly asked, slyly looking up from the mornin paper.

Janey made a face at Ashlon as she picked up a second fresh steaming cinnamon roll dripping with glaze and chopped nuts, and inhaled the rich buttery cinnamon fragrance appreciatively. "Believe it or not, we haven't gotten to that point yet, smart ass," she said as she stuffed a piece of the sweet roll into her mouth. "You have only one other unusable bedroom, and we both agreed that we should stay with you to keep away any more bogey men. So, I made up your studio couch. You passed out the minute your head hit your pillow."

"Oh, yeah," Ashlon remembered with a grimace. "I figured you'd pretty much found where everything is and stayed here for the night. Really touching, especially when I saw Jorge spooning around you and drooling into your hair. That's why I naturally assumed you two were... uh, intimately familiar?"

Janey dropped her bun onto the plate and screwed up her face with disgust. "I'm going to take a shower now," she dryly declared as she rose from her chair and headed back into the living room toward the staircase. "We'll continue this later," she growled as Ashlon's muffled laughing followed her up the stairs.

'Later' was about an hour later as Janey descended the stairs, feeling much cleaner and definitely smelling better. She'd borrowed some of Ashlon's underthings and scented body powder, so her improved sense of well-being had put her mood to rights again. A glance at the studio couch also informed her that Jorge was up. She returned to the kitchen and spotted him sitting across from Ashlon, sipping his coffee and listening to her on the phone, talking with the sheriff's department about what she could remember about the previous night's assault. From the livid expression on her face and the angry tone in her voice, Janey guessed they weren't taking her too seriously. Or, more to the point, questioning why she'd been out at the cemetery near sundown in the first place.

Ashlon finally chunked the receiver back on the phone cradle and sat there briefly fuming in silence. Then, glaring up at Janey and Jorge, she said tersely, "If he has time, Matt might go by there and take a look around. I even offered to show him where the blood could be found. Oh, no! If it's there, he'll find it. Medieval bastard."

Matthew Clayborn had been in the position of county sheriff longer than anyone could remember. Not that he was any good at his job. There was so little crime in the district that it seemed a shame to vote him out of a position he'd held for long. He was an overweight, middle-aged, condescending good 'ole boy official who likely as not would meet his end in a very unpleasant way due to the fact he would have no earthly idea what to do if a real crime occurred in his district. However, new blood had moved into the area in the last few years, and two of the new residents had law enforcement backgrounds. Maybe the next election would see the last of 'Bud' Clayborn and his pot-bellied cronies/deputies.

"I called Grady about his mom's minefield road," Ashlon added after taking a sip of her coffee to calm herself. "He's coming down today to stay for a while and do some repairs on the house."

"Wow!" Janey exclaimed. "Do you think the ranger service can spare their prize tower watcher for very long?" She had wrapped an arm around Jorge's neck and was sitting on his lap as she finished her roll and now stone-cold coffee. Ashlon got up and went over to the stove, brought the coffee pot over to the table, and poured herself another steaming cup, and gave Janey a warm-up. "He's taking some time off. As a matter of fact, he's just glad someone besides his sister is keeping an eye on things," Ashlon said as she sat down again. She rubbed her eyes, a mild headache persisting since waking that morning and subsequently downing some ibuprofen. She touched the dressing covering her recently butterflied wound, glanced at Janey with concern. "What I told you guys, you believe me, don't you? I mean, it all sounds so weird when

I go over it, like whoever was there had been waiting for me." Janey reached across the table and took Ashlon's hand. Ashlon shook her head and sighed. "This is just too much to handle so early in the morning. I'mgoing festival hopping today to clear my head. You two wanna come along, or get a room somewhere?"

Janey made another face at Ashlon and returned to snuggling with Jorge, who seemed to be warming to the idea of the room somewhere. Ashlon chuckled as she rose from the table, gathering the dishes and cups and depositing them into the dishwasher. She left her lovebird friends in the kitchen and went upstairs to shower and dress, and slap on some makeup. Half an hour later, she came back down with her jacket and shoulder bag in hand, pausing by the front door. She turned toward the kitchen and watched silently as Jorge and Janey continued their hugging, softly talking with an occasional small sigh or a giggle escaping the conversation. Ashlon sighed again, this time with just a twitch of envy. It had been a long time since she'd gone out with anyone or even had the energy to cultivate a new relationship with any man who'd shown even a little interest in her. But truth be told, she also admitted she was just a little gun-shy as well. Wyatt had certainly done that to her; consequently, any man was kept at a cautious distance. There had also been Emma's illness and the toll that had taken—the long work hours before benefits had kicked in, the nearly overwhelming strain and fatigue of heart-sick worry, and then the heavy pain of loss. What man in his right mind would want to deal with all that? After Wyatt, however, she didn't really care.

Yes, it had been a number of years now, and almost a month now since Emma's passing. Ashlon was wary; she was tired, the emotional toll still wore on her, and she wanted to remain a solo act for a while longer. After that, who knew?

Glancing back to the kitchen, Ashlon loudly cleared her throat. Jorge and Janey both abruptly looked over at her somewhat sheepishly, realizing they'd temporarily forgotten her.

"Janey, you know where I keep my spare key. Stay as long as you like and lock the door if you leave. Pantry's stocked if you get hungry again. I'll be back this evening. If the phone rings, let the answering machine take it," Ashlon instructed with a smile, then opened the front door and hitched her bag higher on her shoulder as she stepped out into the brilliant morning light. As she closed the door behind her and descended the two stone steps to the sidewalk, she heard laughing from inside and the gentle creaking of the studio couch, then silence. It was nice to know they were comfortable in her home, and that love and tenderness existed somewhere in her world. That would suffice for the time being.

"Just a freakin' yente, aren't I?" Ashlon muttered with a smirk as she settled into her Jeep and roared off down the street.

The day was glorious. A cloudless blue sky, leaves blowing across the county roads in the brisk winds of the season, teasing at the one yet to come, warm enough to let the top down, but chilling enough to keep the jacket zipped as she sped along on her quest. Ashlon didn't care about time or place that day. She traveled the roads with only a vague idea of where she was going, sometimes stopping at this or that roadside stand and inspecting what it had to offer. She soaked up the glorious sunshine and filled up on freshly pressed apple cider and freshly baked pies. She sampled aromatic barbeques and large kettle soups kept bubbly warm over open fires, bought a door wreath of autumn-colored leaves and acorns, corn stalks and small hay bales for Halloween decorations, and several fat pumpkins. She found a new Inn where she lunched on a delicious pumpkin soup, apple-seasoned baked chicken hot from the oven, and generous refills on the hot spiced cider. The back of her Jeep filled with several quart bottles of locally squeezed cider, jars of peach, boysenberry, and apple jams, a handmade quilt in autumn colors of gold, orange, deep brown, and sunset red, and a 6-foot-tall, handmade scarecrow with a grinning, malevolent pumpkin head constructed of glistening orange fabric with silver threads woven through it. That had been a real find, one she could use year after year.

Finally, as the sun was beginning its evening descent, Ashlon stopped at a restaurant off a county road a few miles from the interstate. It had only recently opened, styling itself as an inn in the tradition of the English country inns often located on well-traveled roads into villages or larger towns. It even had several rooms to rent for a night or so, or for patrons who had taken too much of the sauce and shouldn't be out driving.

The last light of day was settling over town when she pulled onto her street and parked in front of her house. She didn't get out right away, just sat back resting her head on the seat back and breathing a contented breath of the chill blowing down from the mountains. The day had been perfect, without a plan or destination, and her headache had long since disappeared. As Irma might say, it had been the kind of day to just be. Of course, Emma was always fore- most in her mind and memories, but Ashlon could easily imagine her daughter happily jumping up and down, laughing and swinging her arms as she pointed out her mommy to the angels and gleefully describing everything, she would do with the treasures stacked on the back seat and carefully set on the floor behind the seats of her Jeep.

The image made her smile, her throat catching for just a moment. But she kept it together without too much effort. Ashlon shook her head and sat up. Enough of this, she determined resolutely as she got out of the Jeep and hopped the curb, crossed the sidewalk, and leapt the steps to her front door. She'd just turned her door key in the lock when she heard shuffling footsteps approach from behind her and a well-mannered 'ahem'.

Ashlon warily turned. "Mr. Stanley!" she happily exclaimed and stepped down to the sidewalk, giving the old man a quick, affectionate hug. "How are you, sir?"

Mr. Stanley crossed his arms in front of him and said with mock gruffness, "Quite put out that you haven't come to visit me like you used to."

"Ah, that's because of the new owner," Ashlon said. "He might not understand our special association." She pursed her lips puckishly and grinned knowingly at the old man.

Mr. Stanley's face lit up with an amused smile, deepening the myriad wrinkles around his eyes and mouth. "Indeed," he said, touching Ashlon's hand and taking it in his. "However, without our special association, I might not still be gainfully
employed."

Ashlon laughed aloud, patting his gnarled hand affectionately. "Come on in and share some cider with me. Tell me about the new house master." She turned again, unlocking her front door, then ran to her Jeep, lowering the top to rummage through her treasures for one of the cider bottles on the floor.

Mr. Stanley caught her arm and gently turned her to face him. "Oh no, Miss Ashlon, I must be getting home to Eleanor," he said, gently shaking his head. "She would worry if I'm not at home at my usual time, Lord love her."

However, Ashlon pulled a quart-sized, sweaty glass bottle of rich brown cider from her Jeep and pressed it into his hands. "Then take this with you and enjoy it with her." She turned and rummaged around on the back seat, locating a small decorated tin. This she also gave to Mr. Stanley. "It's a butter rum cake, just the right size for you and Mrs. Stanley. Please take it."

The old man laughed and nodded, settling the bottle and tin into the crook of one arm. "I have something for you, too, my dear," he said, reaching into his coat pocket with his free hand, pulling out an envelope, and handing it to Ashlon. "Laird McAnders is having a house warming Monday evening and has invited notables of the town. I've been making phone calls all day and having these delivered. But I promised him I would personally deliver yours since you're just around the corner on my way home. He was curiously pleased when I said that, and I think he most wants to meet you, my dear. Not that I would fault him for that."

Ashlon's eyes narrowed as she frowned. "Oh, he does, does he? Have you been feeding him information about me?" She fixed him with an accusing stare.

"You can't discourage an old man from trying," Mr. Stanley said good-naturedly. "Besides, he wants to meet the other person besides myself who kept his family home from being completely desecrated. I told him of our efforts, clear up to the state level, and he was most grateful. Give him that at least."

Ashlon fingered the envelope thoughtfully. "Well, I guess so," she replied. "Besides, I'm curious about what Irma described to me the last time you two talked. She saw him up on thewidow's walk and was very impressed."

"She was somewhat less talkative at that point," Mr. Stanley said with obvious humor. "He is quite impressive looking, and his manner is courtly. At least to me. But, I truly think you'd like him too, Miss Ashlon, especially with what he's done with the house. I would think you're curious enough about that."

"You know me too well, old man," Ashlon said puckishly. "Okay, I'll be there. But only for your sake and my curiosity."

Mr. Stanley tipped his hat to Ashlon and turned, closely hugging his gifts as he shuffled on down the sidewalk, waving his free hand in farewell. Ashlon watched until he disappeared around the next corner. At the same moment, the street lamp buzzed to life as Ashlon fingered the invitation and glanced down at it briefly. Finally, she stuffed it into her jacket pocket and began unloading the back of her Jeep, pushing a strange feeling down as far as she could until she had a chance to think about it later and why it had started in the first place.

Chapter 8

Sunday was a busy one dedicated to designing and carving Jack o' Lanterns. By evening, she was fairly sick of looking at all of them grinning, leering, or frowning at her from newspapers on her kitchen floor, awaiting delivery to their new owners. She resolutely decided this would be the last time she'd do a project for the Senior Club of Lloyds Corner unless someone else lent a hand. Several of the pumpkins would go for fundraising at the Harvest Dance this coming Saturday, and the remaining few would go to her neighbors who'd requested ones for their own.

With aching hands and heavy-lidded eyes, she retired to her bed just a little after midnight. Janey called just before Ashlon turned out her light to remind her of the open house the following evening.

"So, what are you going to wear to this soiree?" she said with a mock English accent. "What's de rigueur for meeting the lord of the manor?"

Apparently, Janey had been watching late-night PBS again, but Ashlon was too tired to laugh. She yawned noisily into the receiver. "Haven't thought too much about it," she replied in an exhausted monotone. "I've been mutilating large orange gourds all day, and I'm about to drop. My hands are stiff as boards, and I've burned out my favorite electric carver. Call me tomorrow when I might give a flying fart."

Without waiting for a response, she dropped the handset back on the base and clicked off the light, rolling into her blankets with a long, satisfied sigh. She was asleep only moments after closing her eyes.

Another weird dream. They were coming more frequently these last few months, although they'd started after she'd moved to Lloyds She'd Corner. been a servant girl, a queen's privy chamber lady, an indentured laborer, an apple seller in a large city, and many others.

But they were becoming more detailed, more intimate, and always with the same man whom she'd loved in various guises through the ages in which these dreams took place. The rub of it was she could never remember his face or who he was after she woke from any of them. This time, she was a settler living with her father somewhere outside Philadelphia.

She was barefoot on the grass in front of a cabin surrounded by trees, the river flowing just below a long hilltop on which the cabin stood. The warm, soft night was alive with cricket chirps and frog song coming from the bulrushes on the banks of the slowly flowing waters. A cart was parked beneath one of the trees near the horse shed, and she heard soft whinnying from inside. An elderly man, her papa, sat in a hand-carved rocking chair on the front porch of the cabin, his eyes closed as he puffed on a slim, long-stemmed pipe held in one hand. She stood near where the hill began its descent to the river, looking into the sky and smiling as she pointed out the different constellations to someone close to her, a strong arm wrapped tenderly around her waist, his body pressed against hers as his head turned upward following her moving finger. A hand moved up to her chin, grasping it gently and turning her face to his as his lips moved toward hers, caressing lightly at first, then more firmly as he moved to fully embrace her. He was a full head and shoulders taller, but she melted easily into his arms, willingly surrendering to his passion and returning the kiss with an urgency that matched his. She could feel his desire pressing into her and enflaming her in a way her father would have angrily disapproved of if he could see through the darkness the way this man could.

Oh, yes, she knew the secret of this one who held her so tightly he might be trying to absorb her into his own essence. But her deep sorrow remained unexpressed—he would be leaving later that night on a ship sailing for a shore farther north from which he might not ever return. He had promised he would, but he said he had some business to finish up around Boston that could not wait. She stood on her tiptoes and whispered an endearment into his ear, then parted from him to join her father on the porch, tears running silently down her face. The dark one bid them goodnight and reluctantly headed for the horse shed. She kissed her father lovingly on the cheek and informed him she was headed to her bed as well. The old man smiled lovingly at her and patted her cheek, saying something in a strange language, but which made her smile. The dark one he watched with narrow-eyed suspicion.

A small oil lamp shining on the dresser in front of a water-damaged mirror reflected a distorted image of a young, pale woman as she sat and released her long black hair from the coils which had held it around her head. She picked up a silver-handled brush and slowly, carefully worked out the tangles and loops until her hair gleamed softly with rich blue highlights in the yellow lamp light. She put down the brush and stood, moving over to a wooden stand which held a basin with a pitcher in it. She poured water into the basin and washed her face and neck, then reached blindly for a towel on a rack set next to the stand. Instead, a large hand grasped hers and pulled her into two muscular arms, which embraced her close to a broad, bare chest with dark curly hair covering it and trailing a line below the waist of his buckskin leggings. She gasped and almost cried out, but his lips pressed into hers, expressing a hunger that would not remain unfulfilled this time as he held her tightly and lifted her off her feet, moving them purposely toward the bed across the room. Surprised and worried her father would hear, she spoke to him in urgent hushed tones and tried to push away from that resolute force that was threatening to swallow her up. Never had she experienced his strength as she did then! Her struggling was feeble in his iron embrace as he fell with her into the softness of her blankets. She felt no fear at this intrusion, only the urgency and longing that enflamed hers in a way she'd only imagined in daydreams and fantasies. His long dark hair was fragrant with pine and sweet grass as his kisses burned her lips and face and throat, traveling down her chest to each breast as he ripped away her robe and took each one into his searching mouth, drawing on them so deeply that electric waves rippled again and again down through her belly and between her thighs. Her moans only inflamed him further as he tore at the flap on his rough breaches and freed his ready manhood, a deep guttural growl voicing his pleasure as she reached down and ran her soft fingers along its magnificent tremoring length, caressing it against the moisture awaiting it in her soft folds, wanting him, aching for him with her entire body and soul. She wouldn't deny him this last night together.

Her arms circled his neck, raising herself against him, her lips pressed to his. Then she turned her head to one side, letting his lips slide down her neck as she rubbed it against his open mouth. His back arched as he drove into her beckoning wet invitation, and she gasped raggedly as he filled her, joining them in the ultimate embrace of a love that had grown deeper between them during their weeks together, the love that had joined them in secret places away from her father's probing suspicions, always wrapped in night's embrace.

But, this night would be different in that she would never see him again; her father, a giving, loving man, was also an unwise man who had become indebted to another to save his home and meager living. In exchange, she would be forced to marry another in a month's time. She had kept this secret to herself, praying with desperate hope that her dark warrior might take her with him to Boston.

But no. The way he traveled was hazardous, filled with dangers just in the voyage alone. He promised he would return, making her promise she would wait for him, and she had bitten her lip as she had, her secret knowledge hurting her heart more than he could ever know. However, she had tonight and would take it for all it was worth. She lost herself in her warrior's embrace and felt only a slight sting as his fangs deeply pierced the tender skin on her neck, his lips pressing hungrily to her throat as he thrust harder and faster into her, his moment building, driven by her impassioned gasps and moans as she rose each time to meet him. They blended together toward their mutual ecstatic release, their loving, tender, and wild until he pressed one last time into her and his head reared up, fresh red droplets rolling off his lips, a long low guttural moan welling from the depths of his chest at his shuddering release. She was panting hard as wave upon wave of rapturous pleasure made her body shake and spasm under him, her eyes closed as she savored each shock wave of this ecstasy. He collapsed on top of her, pressing his lips against the ragged marks he'd made on her throat, softly, insistently licking them. She reached up and caressed his brow and face as he looked into her eyes with his fierce love for her, and had given her each night they had together.

"We are truly one, my beloved," he softly spoke as his lips caressed hers, his body seeking hers again.

He departed later that night as she slept.

When just over a month had passed and he did not return, her erstwhile bridegroom appeared. He was a brute of a man who made it clear she was the expected repayment for her father's foolishness. She was the price this man had demanded, and her father had reluctantly agreed to it. Refusal would bringabout her father's ruin, and they'd lose everything. She had meekly submitted, but only to the formalities that would free her father from this man. He would never have her, and her determination was set after papers had been signed and witnessed, and the marriage performed.

On her wedding night, as her father tended to their guests, and while her abhorrent bridegroom drank his courage for their conjugal bed, she calmly walked away from the celebrants, still in her wedding dress, and headed unnoticed down the long hill below the house. She walked onto a wide dock that extended over the waters of the river. It had rained for several days, and the wild waters were roiling, muddy, and swift. As if from far away, she heard a scream from above her on the hilltop, and then another, and then her father frantically calling as he ran toward her with the others behind him. She briefly noted them, then turned and gazed over the seething waters running directly below where she stood, hearing only her warrior's words again. She belonged only to him. Even beyond her end.

She stepped off the edge of the dock, disappearing under the raging river waters.

Ashlon startled out of her dream, trembling and sweating as if the tragic passion she'd dreamt had been her own. But her lover's voice! She swallowed with difficulty as she sat up in her bed, breathing hard as she stared into the darkness of the bedroom, her heart beating so fast she thought it would pound out of her chest. So real, so real! Again, she couldn't see his face, but that voice! It echoed in her memory, matching the one she'd heard only two nights ago in the cemetery when it had commanded her not to fight him! But that was impossible, she told herself. Maybe her mind was just playing tricks, making the dream voice the same one she had heard that night. Yeah, that had to be it. Better be it.

She slipped out of bed and got herself a drink of water from the bathroom, then sat in a chair next to the only window in the bedroom as she sipped from her glass held in shaking hands. That had to be it, she reasoned as she relaxed with the cool water and stared out the window into the night sky. She could just make out the silhouette of the widow's walk on the McAnders House, and as her eyes adjusted, she watched a large shadowy form moving around it. Wow! Irma was right about that guy being big. He cut a hole through the darkness!

She immediately let down the blinds and left her water glass on the bedside table as she crawled back into bed, burrowing under the covers, feeling a little better now. "Geez," she mumbled as she nestled down into her pillows. "Maybe it's time I got out a little more." She fell easily back into exhausted slumber, a half grimace still playing on her lips.

And on the widow's walk, he smiled. She had seen him there, just as he had watched her sitting by her window looking out into the night, the way he watched every night, hoping for a glimpse of her. Tomorrow night, he would finally meet her. He suspected she would feel safer, especially after that disastrous mistake of his in the cemetery. Mr. Stanley had briefed him about her calamitous first marriage and how it had left her with an almost pathological mistrust of men in general. He understood only too well that hidden wounds hurt the most and took longest to heal. Fortunately, he had all the time he'd need to accomplish what he set out to do. And she was well worth the effort.

Chapter 9

The following morning, Janey was at Ashlon's place as they planned their outfits for the housewarming and to help deliver the carved pumpkins to their new owners. They breakfasted on warm from the pan cheese blintzes, baked hash browns, and coffee as they mapped out possible ensembles, weighing in what they both owned and how they could use everything to its best advantage.

Ashlon had finally opened her fancy invitation and noted with some satisfaction that dress casual only was required to meet and greet the new owner of McAnders House. She hadn't bought anything in years, not since before closing the one charge account Wyatt had managed to run over its limit and nearly ruining her credit. She had been forced to cash in several gift bonds from her grandmother to clear up that mess. Since then, she had managed on thrift shop finds that had survived several fashion trends. She and Janey dug through her closet and chest of drawers and found a black velvet below-the-knee length skirt and a soft grey shawl collar sweater Ashlon had forgotten she owned. A pair of black pumps would complete the outfit, dressed with silver earrings and a silver chain necklace with a small intricate Celtic knot held between the two extensions. A perfect emerald drop framed in silver dangled from the knot by a short silver connector. It was the only piece of jewelry Ashlon had inherited from her grandmother. Ashlon wore it only on very special occasions, which meant it hadn't been out of her jewelry box in years.

Janey brought her clothes to Ashlon's place later that afternoon after she'd helped deliver the Jack O'lanterns to the senior committee chairman's house; he wasn't too happy about having to keep a couple of grimacing gourds in his outside store room until Saturday night's raffle, but Ashlon didn't give him a choice since she was going to be of Wednesday evening and Thursday, and would be staying with a nurse friend from the Children's Hospital until Friday morning. The remaining pumpkins went to her neighbors, much to their delight, and they insisted Ashlon take batches of homemade fudge, fresh-baked snickerdoodles, and a pumpkin pie, respectively, as their thanks. Any effort to decline these offerings was met with the most passionate urging and entreaties since the residents had already designated them expressly for her anyway when they'd seen her unloading the pumpkins Saturday evening.

"I'm being sabotaged with kindness," Ashlon said with a resigned grin later on that evening as she and Janey dressed for the housewarming. "And the tragedy of it is these are great desserts."

Janey only chuckled and offered to generously take some of it off her hands. Happily, Ashlon split her take in half, including the pie, and wrapped them securely for Janey to take home with her. Ashlon knew Janey would share with Jorge as well, especially if there wasn't any food at this affair. She gave more than half and didn't let Janey know. The invitation hadn't mentioned any refreshments, so they were ready with these emergency rations if they couldn't affect an early departure.

Finally, as Ashlon's little bedside clock chimed 7:00 PM, the two women stood in front of Ashlon's full-length door mirror, inspecting and straightening until they were satisfied. Janey grabbed a cologne bottle off the top of Ashlon's dressing table, tentatively sniffed the spray head, and then gave herself several strategic spritzes at her neck, décolletage, wrists, and the backs of her knees. She closed her eyes and inhaled appreciatively. "I like this scent," she said as she replaced the purple bottle on the dresser. "What is it?"

Ashlon shrugged. "It was a gift, I think. I've had it for so long, the lettering's worn off. You can have the rest of it if you like it." She picked up an amber bottle and sprayed it lightly all around her. "This one's my favorite. My grandmother had several bottles of this stuff in her belongings when I cleared her house after she died."

Janey took the bottle from her and read the tiny label on the bottom. "'Cotillion,'" she read. "How appropriate." She placed the bottle next to the purple one. "Let's go and make some wives jealous," she declared, linking her arm through Ashlon's, leading them out of the bedroom and down the stairs. Ashlon was laughing as they descended to the living room, picked up Janey's food, their wraps and bags, and headed out into the glowing evening light. Since the McAnders House was so close and the evening was absolutely gorgeous, they decided to walk the short distance after Janey stashed her food in the back seat of her car. Arms linked, they headed down the sidewalk, laughing and talking with their heads pressed together, watched by several sets of appreciative eyes gazing curiously out the front windows of their homes as the women passed by.

They were dazzled as they entered the open front gate of McAnders House. Soft globe luminaires lined a new brick walkway leading up to several short steps and the front door, which had been exposed by the removal of the wrap-around porch, and was now protected by a new arched extension. It was hung with sparkling stringed mini-lights hidden in newly planted ivy climbing over support trellises, so the effect was similar to hidden fairies inviting one to look closer. The heavy entrance door had been replaced by a lighter but no less sturdy set of double doors with tempered etched glass panels set in their centers. That night, the doors stood open, allowing invited guests to enter without having to knock. Standing just inside them, Mr. Stanley greeted each guest as he or she passed by him. When he spotted Ashlon and Janey, his pasted-on smile warmed as he hurried out to meet them when they approached the archway. The sounds of a musical piece floated after him as Ashlon and Janey greeted him with a hug apiece. Ashlon smiled broadly as she listened to the familiar melodic strains filling the night.

"Mozart," she happily commented. "Good choice, Mr. Stanley." Ironically, it was 'Eine Kleine Nachtmusik', A Little Nightmusic.

"Lord McAnders left the choice of musical interludes up to me, thank goodness," the old man said. "Frankly, I didn't think pipes and drums were really appropriate for this evening."

"Pipes and drums?" Janey asked, looking at Ashlon.

"Bagpipes and drums," Ashlon informed her. "You know—cats in heat?"

"Oh," Janey merely said with an understanding nod.

Mr. Stanley chuckled, shaking his head at Ashlon. He knew better than to object as he led the women through the entrance and down the short hallway to the foyer, where he took their wraps and bags, securing them in a hall closet away from those of the other guests. He then led them through the spacious foyer into a large open room just to the right of a wide staircase curving up to a second-floor gallery. The air around them was scented with freshly cut wood, varnish, and paint. Ashlon noted that the stairs had been replaced with treated wood; Mr. Stanley informed them was English oak. The foyer and hallway had been repainted, and new, subtly patterned warm bronze colored marble flooring tiles had been polished to a high gleam. Brilliantly colored tapestries hung on the on the walls flanking two high, thickly glassed windows in the gallery above them that connected the wings of the house.

In the dining room where Mr. Stanley led them, Ashlon looked around with open-mouthed amazement at the new paneling, dish cabinets, and the heavy dark wood banquet table with high-backed chairs that replaced the tatty pieces the historical society ladies had originally placed there. On the wall above a large stone fireplace, which had been scrupulously scrubbed of all soot and grime, a coat of arms was displayed with two magnificent crossed Claymore swords over it. A new mantle piece extended the entire width of the fireplace. It had been carved from a single heavy log, plained smooth and finished, and then bolted into the stone behind it. It was ebony black and perfectly flush with the stone support that held it. The dining table was a similar color and supported two golden three-stemmed candle holders. The candles' flames danced and sparked, mimicking the lively candle flames of wall sconces set at 4-foot intervals around the wall paneling. The original wooden floors had been refinished with a thorough sanding and recoated with a protective natural stain. It gleamed with new life under the rich candlelight.

"The rest of the house has been similarly redone," Mr. Stanley commented with justifiable pride. "Many of our recommendations were incorporated into the renovations by Lord McAnders. I think we did very well, don't you?"

Ashlon couldn't answer. She nodded to Mr. Stanley with a wide grin and laughed as Janey gave her a one-armed hug. Jorge appeared at that same moment and snatched up Janey's free hand, whirling her around to face him. Her face lit up with delight as she gave him an affectionate hug.

"Hey, babe," she gushed. "We just got here."

He gave her a quick peck on the cheek. "I saw you and Ash come in when I was in the other room. You look muy bonita, seniorita," he added as he stepped back and studied Janey with an appreciative smile. His mustache always twitched a little when he was emotional.

Ashlon nudged her friend. "You're blushing like a virgin," she said in a low voice only Janey could hear. "Am not!" Janey hissed back, blushing furiously as she firmly bumped Ashlon's shoulder. "May I get you ladies a cold drink?" Mr. Stanley inquired. "The bar is in the library and I've stocked it with a supply of non-alcoholic beverages." They requested ginger ale, which the old man immediately obtained for them. And, happily, the dining table was set with a variety of finger foods and appetizers supplied by none other than Irma and Mineau Roberts of A Moment in Thyme Catering, Mr. Stanley informed them.

He reluctantly had to leave after serving drinks to tend to the other guests. Later, as the evening deepened into full nightfall, Ashlon, Janey, and Jorge wandered the downstairs through the study, then the music room, and finally, the library. The spinet had been cordoned off to prevent guests from touching it, but Mr. Stanley had set up a stand with a prepared history of the instrument for curious guests. A door connected the music room to the sitting room so that when opened, music could be heard between them. The library, with its wide, tall bookshelves on three walls of the room, was only partially filled, but the books there represented a diversity of interests ranging from engineering to medicine to astronomy. Many of the books were incredibly old and bound in protective covers to preserve their contents. There were even rolls of parchment which were tied with silk cord or cloth ribbon and kept in airtight glass top cases that were securely locked. Another fireplace on a wall without bookshelves crackled and hissed with a lively fire, the scents of cedar and pine permeating the room. Above the mantle hung a large portrait of who, they assumed, was another older McAnders, an ancestor. Janey studied the portrait with a look of recognition.

"Ash, where have we seen that face before?" she asked as she turned and looked questioningly at Ashlon, who smiled knowingly at the picture.

"That small portrait I have in my laptop," she said, moving next to her friend, "only this fellow looks much older. See the grey around the temples and in the eyebrows, the lines in the face? Even the clothes are older. Look at that ruff around his neck and the decorated doublet. There's the artist's insignia and the date in the corner. This picture precedes the one I have by at least 40 or 50 years."

"How 'bout that," Janey said thoughtfully. "The resemblance between them is remarkable, don't you think?"

"A lot of interfamilial marriages will do that," Jorge casually interjected as he joined Janey after perusing several of the volumes on the shelves. "You know—cousin to cousin, in-laws become husbands or wives when suitable marriage stock is unavailable. Isolated clans that didn't want to give up their autonomous way of life would rarely bring in fresh marriage blood to keep physical similarities from occurring in the bloodlines. Not all people are so careful about preventing same-blood marriages."

Janey made a face. "Sounds positively incestuous if you ask me. Now I understand what's behind that weird song about someone being his own grandpa."

Ashlon and Jorge were laughing at Janey's chagrined expression when Mr. Stanley suddenly appeared in the connecting doorway from the sitting room and hurried up to them as fast as his arthritic legs would allow. He eagerly grasped Ashlon's hand. "Please, all of you, come with me to the sitting room. Lord McAnders is here and will be down as soon as he freshens up and changes his clothes," the old man declared with barely contained excitement.

Ashlon patted his hand as he led her away. "Take it easy, Mr. Stanley. You'll frazzle yourself into another heart attack if you're not careful," she gently admonished him. He was not swayed from his determined path into the sitting room, however, where several folding chairs had been set up next to the couch and a wingback chair facing the fireplace. Mrs. Stanley occupied this one, looking very queenly with her hands politely folded in her lap. Ashlon immediately moved toward her, gently freeing her hand from the old man's grip and taking Mrs. Stanley's offered hand instead.

"I'm so pleased to see you, Mrs. Stanley!" Ashlon happily exclaimed, giving the older woman a peck on the cheek. "You look gorgeous this evening."

Mrs. Stanley blushed and smiled delightedly. Ashlon knew coming to this event could be very wearing on her. But she did look wonderful in her soft pink two-piece evening suit. Her snowy white hair was covered with a brocade Juliet cap with an attached matching mesh piece that was folded back over her hair. Ashlon caught the light scent of lilac as she sat next to Mrs. Stanley to quietly talk with her. Jorge and Janey had gravitated to the archway into the foyer, and caught Ashlon's attention, signaling where they would be, then discreetly slipped out to the foyer and headed back to the dining room.

Several other people joined them in the sitting room, finding seating away from her and Mrs. Stanley until sitting next to Ashlon became unavoidable. They included Mayor Tisbee (who had often bowed to the whims of the Ladies Historical Society, which was chaired by his wife, Alice), Alice Tisbee, and two council members.

A former council member who had supported Ashlon's and Mr. Stanley's restoration efforts was also present. She'd resigned after funding had been vetoed for the restoration of McAnders House. Doris Wayland was also the co-owner/operator of the only grocery store in town. She and her husband, Jonathan, her business partner, were kindred transplants to Lloyds Corner and had brought with them a badly needed business to the small community. They also had two small children with asthma that seemed to worsen each year, where they had lived prior to moving into the community. Ashlon and Janey had assisted them to find a doctor in Boston who had taken the kid's problems in hand, and with good nursing support close by had turned them around in less than a season. In return, the Wayland Grocery and Dry Goods Store kept prices reasonable and stocked with a good variety of items, including natural, organic foods and personal use items. Janey and Ashlon never paid full price for their groceries.

Doris came over and knelt in front of Ashlon and Mrs. Stanley, greeting them with a broad smile as she began a rundown of her two boys' latest antics that would have been unimaginable before the move. Time quickly passed, and before they knew it, an hour had elapsed. The three ladies were laughing heartily when Mr. Stanley returned to the sitting room and stood quietly off to his wife's side, listening for aninterjection point. Then, he politely cleared his throat in a way that paused their conversations and sent Doris back to her seat next to Jonathan.

"Would anyone care for coffee or another cold beverage?" he inquired, looking clearly uncomfortable as he spoke.

Mrs. Stanley and Ashlon frowned worriedly to each other. "

Is there a delay, dear?" Mrs. Stanley asked with a concerned look at her husband. "Will Mr. McAnders be joining us soon?"

Mozart had stopped playing some time ago, and an uncomfortable silence filled the room. A soft buzzing of voices floated in from the dining area across the foyer. Ashlon's
stomach suddenly growled noisily.

"Well," she sighed with a grin at Mrs. Stanley. "My stomach won't wait until hizzoner decides to bless us with his presence." She stood up and stretched the kinks from her joints, and brushed the wrinkles from her skirt before turning to Mrs. Stanley. "Have you eaten yet? I'll bring you something from the table if you like."

Mrs. Stanley slowly shook her head, gently smiling at Ashlon. "I've no appetite, dear," she said, her voice sounding tired. Gazing up at her husband, she said, "I will take a glass of tea, James," she warmly said. Mr. Stanley nodded to his wife and shuffled out of the room.

"And, I'll be right back," Ashlon said, gently squeezing Mrs. Stanley's hand.

She looked over at Doris and tipped her head toward the archway. Doris shook her head, waved her on with a smile, and went back to talking with her husband.

Ashlon turned her back to the foyer entrance, straightened her skirt by the light from the fireplace, and pulled down her sweater. She failed to notice Doris' eyes had suddenly widened with surprise as she waved frantically at Ashlon to stop where she was. Ashlon turned and caught Doris' frantic waving a second too late, took two steps, and ran squarely into a wide, solid barrier which had noiselessly sprung up while her back was turned. She lost her balance, clumsily stepping backward toward her chair, and would have tumbled over it except for two large hands which quickly grabbed her arms in a gentle grip and pulled her forward onto her feet again. With a sinking feeling deep in the pit of her stomach, she just knew who it was. Boy, this truly sucked and was no way to make a favorable first impression.

Ashlon's nose was pressed into a suit jacket of dark blue silk at roughly chest level, she estimated with stunned realization as she regained her sense of direction. Swallowing hard, her throat suddenly clutched as she put her hands against that chest and pushed back, slowly looking up at an indigo blue collar-less shirt with a single black pearl stud where the top button would have been. Above the collar was a clean-shaven throat and a face as pale as white marble—squared jaw, full pale lips, prominent high cheeks, and a well-defined straight nose. And then she was looking into the most amazing amethyst eyes she'd ever seen. The shadow of a smile played on those deathly pale lips as he gazed down into Ashlon's face and gently lowered her back into her chair without waiting for any rebuttal.

Ashlon grimaced, blushing furiously as she stared into her lap. Never mind that no one had seen him or heard him enter the room, even though he was an impressive height. Oh, Alice Tisbee would have a field day with this one! Ashlon groaned inwardly, imagining the gossip that spiteful woman would generate with the other town busybodies.

Mayor Tisbee was the first to speak as he stood up, pulling his jacket down over his oversized stomach and approaching Lord McAnders with an outstretched hand.

"Sir, I am Mayor Henry Tisbee. I'd like to officially welcome you to Lloyds Corner," he gushed with a pasted-on smile deepening the skin folds of his chubby face, making him look somewhat like a smiling Buddha, but with a lot less likability.

Lord McAnders stepped back, his hands clasped behind him, his head lowered as he pointedly studied the mayor with an expression of barely concealed distaste, and pointedly not offering his hand in return. After a few tenses, uncomfortable moments, the mayor hesitantly dropped his hand and cleared his throat, backing slowly to his chair and seating his ample rear once again, eyes fixed on the floor as he licked his lips nervously. Ashlon and Mrs. Stanley looked at each other with smug smiles. Talk about your social blunders!

Mr. Stanley, who'd returned to his wife's chair, handed her a tall glass of tea with lemon and ice and stood at her side with a delighted smile as he announced in his most impressive voice, "Ladies and gentlemen, it is my pleasure to introduce Lord Bowen McAnders, our host this evening."

Lord McAnders joined him as Mr. Stanley began introducing the guests, starting with Mrs. Stanley, who blushed like a young woman when Lord McAnders took the hand she raised to him and touched his lips to her fingers, clearly a slap at Mayor Tisbee's earlier gesture. Ashlon merely nodded when she was introduced, her eyes fixed on Lord McAnders' pearl button. He bent slightly, unexpectedly cupping her chin in one large hand, raising her face to his so that their eyes met. She felt herself falling into them, unable to look away from their allembracing gaze, and paralyzed by his cool touch to her face. He returned her nod with that same half smile but remained silent as he studied her face. His probing eyes held her prisoner, drawing her into their depths like plunging into a clear, cool lake, inquiring and incredibly sensuous at the same time. His face was so close to hers she could smell a mingling of his scent with her own. It was … wonderful.

"You are as Mr. Stanley described you, Miss Isaacs," he purred in a deep hypnotic baritone as he released her chin, his fingers sliding down the side of her neck and over the collar of her sweater to her necklace. He lifted it in the palm of one hand, lightly brushing the bare skin at the hollow of her throat. His light touch sent a shiver through her as he looked into her upturned face and added so softly only she could hear, "This gem's green fire matches your eyes." He let the chain slide from his hand and moved on to his next guest.

Mrs. Stanley touched her hand lightly. "Are you alright, dear?" she inquired, sounding worried. "You had the strangest expression on your face when he was speaking to you."

Ashlon shook her head and took a deep breath to clear it. Mr. Stanley was also looking down at her with concern. Her mouth opened and closed several times before she got it together again.

"That was the weirdest feeling I've ever had," Ashlon said, her voice trembling as she spoke. She had been completely helpless and powerless to resist.

"Certainly something a well-mannered gentleman shouldn't do," Mrs. Stan- ley commented, her voice as quiet as Ashlon's. "It looked like he was studying you, dear."

"No, not quite that. It was ... personal, like he knew me." Yes, that was it, Ashlon decided, very disconcerted by this realization. He knew her as intimately and personally as one person can know another. The problem was she was absolutely certain she'd never met the man in her life. She would have remembered someone as distinctive as this Lord McAnders regardless of how much time had passed from an initial meeting. Some association through a friend of a friend of a friend, maybe? It was certainly an avenue that had some credence to it, and helped allay a troubling thought that had begun to gnaw at her as if a hidden memory was trying to surface, but was unable to find any familiar landmarks.

Mr. Stanley lightly touched her hand, bringing her back from her ruminations. She suddenly felt as tired as Mrs. Stanley was looking and just wanted to go home now. However, Mr. Stanley had finished his introductions and was waiting to tell her something important. She mustered a weak smile and looked up at him.

"Yes, Mr. Stanley?" she said, trying to sound lighter than she felt inside. "Lord McAnders has asked me to take you on a tour of the house at your convenience," he said, sounding very pleased even after gamely struggling through the stress of a very long day; his voice was mildly roughened, the shadows were deeper under his eyes, and his characteristic shuffle was definitely more pronounced. Critical evaluation: not a chance in hell this evening.

"How about we do it later on in the week, Mr. Stanley?" Ashlon gently suggested as she helped Mrs. Stanley to her feet. "I've got some things to do tomorrow, and I'll be in Boston Wednesday and won't be back until Friday morning. How about Friday afternoon or Saturday?"

This was a diplomatic approach that would have the Stanleys home before their fatigue became disabling and get Mr. Stanley off the hook.

"But he wanted you to see it this evening," Mr. Stanley persisted as he tried to take her hand to lead her away.

Ashlon deftly moved out of his reach and rested her hand on one of his shoulders, giving it a gentle squeeze with iron resolution in her expression.

"I don't think so," she declared with quiet firmness. "It's been a long evening for all of us. If Lord McAnders wants me to see the house tonight, he can take me around. Otherwise, my tour can wait for later on in the week."

Mr. Stanley knew from experience that arguing was useless. He nodded reluctantly and shuffled over to Lord McAnders, who bent low as the old man briefly spoke to him. Ashlon tucked Mrs. Stanley's hand into her arm and, without waiting for a reply, led her out of the sitting room through the foyer, and down the front hallway to the entrance, where they stopped at the closed double doors to wait for Mr. Stanley.

"Thank you, dear, for being so insistent with that stubborn old man," Mrs. Stanley said, patting Ashlon's arm.

"Just kicking into nurse mode," Ashlon quipped with a sly grin. "But, you have to admire his dedication."

They didn't have long to wait. Mr. Stanley soon joined them with his wife's coat on his arm and helped her into it. He gave Ashlon an affectionate kiss on the cheek, then opened the door and escorted his wife out. Ashlon closed it behind them and returned to the foyer, where she stood listening to sounds of quiet conversation from the sitting room. No, she decided, time to find Janey and Jorge and go get some real food. She turned in the opposite direction and crossed the foyer to the dining room. When she got there, however, she discovered Janey and Jorge were gone. The appetizers and plates and glasses had been cleared, and all but three of the wall sconces and the candleholders on the table had been extinguished, the remaining weak light throwing subdued, eerie dancing lights off the gleaming table surface.

Ashlon shivered and hugged herself. She wanted out of this place now and heading for home. She quickly turned and went back out to the foyer, crossing it again to the sitting room. The fire was banked with only glowing embers deep in the ash. Doris and Jonathan were on their feet, saying good night to Mayor and Mrs. Tisbee. Lord McAnders was nowhere to be seen. Doris came over to Ashlon and gave her a quick hug.

"Where's his highness?" Ashlon sniffed as she looked around the room. Doris smirked. "Seems he had something unexpectedly come up and gave us his apologies."

"Sounds like the classic 'good night and don't let the door hit you on the way out', huh? Give Jon and the kids kisses for me." Ashlon hugged Doris and waved to Jonathan, then left the sitting room and headed back through the foyer to the front hallway. She recovered her wrap and bag from the deacon's bench next to the doorway and was securing her oversized shawl around hershoulders when a large hand gripped her upper arm. Ashlon whipped around with her fist drawn back and poised until she realized it was Lord McAnders holding her arm, his expression amused as he gazed at her. She quickly lowered her fist and took a deep breath, relieved she hadn't actually hit him. That would have been a royal blunder!

"You certainly have a hair trigger, Miss Isaacs," Lord McAnders observed. "I take it you dunna like being surprised." His voice was calm and as deep and rich as rolling thunder in a storm with just a hint of humor. He released his grip on her arm. "It's very late," he observed. "A lady shouldna be out walking alone this time of night."

Ashlon frowned as she fixed her wrap around her shoulders again and reached for the door handle. "Well, then, there's no problem. I've never claimed to be one. Goodnight, Lord McAnders." She turned and had opened the door just enough to see the lights outside when his long arm reached out and pushed it closed once more. Definitely miffed now, Ashlon turned and stood almost toe to toe with the man, glaring belligerently into his placid face, her nostrils flaring as she gritted her teeth to stop herself from hurling something at him she'd have to ask forgiveness for during Yom Kippur services.

"Do we have a problem we should be discussing right now?"

she stiffly inquired as she glared up into that stone white face. She was rewarded by the man stepping away from her and extending his hand toward the door.

"My apologies, Miss Isaacs," Bowen McAnders stiffly said with a slight bow of his head. "I confess I often forget how independent American women are. I meant no disrespect. I will say goodnight with a wish to see you soon when you come to my home again." He turned his back and walked away down the short hall to the foyer.

"Shit!" Ashlon grimaced and swore to herself. He was being disgustingly noble now, and she felt like an absolute jerk for being so insulting to him. "Lord McAnders," she called out, running after him and catching him at the foot of the stairs. She sighed with frustration and stared at the floor, trying to find the right words. Biting her lip, she said, "I apologize for my rudeness. I do have a short fuse, especially when I'm tired. I wanted to say ... well ... uh, thank you for your ... uh, concern."

He did not turn around, remaining in dark silence as she'd spoken to his broad back. After a long, uncomfortable moment, Ashlon shrugged and turned to leave. She'd tried. The ball's in his court, she thought with only a little guilt now as she walked away from his sulking lairdship and retraced her path to the front door with veiled distaste. Big spoiled brat was more like it. Securing her wrap around her shoulders, she stepped out into the cold night without being stopped this time, barely noting her progress down the front walkway and through the gate. She turned onto the sidewalk and headed toward home.

The night was silent as her heels ticked lightly on the concrete, quickly leaving the manor behind her as the darkness outside its lights closed in around her. "Thank heaven that's over with!" she muttered to herself, feeling only intense relief now that she was away from the house.

She hadn't gone halfway down the block when a sudden dusty gust of freezing wind whipped down the street from in front of her with the sound of a soft, deep sigh filling her ears, sending a cold chill coursing through her from head to toe.

"What the...!" she softly exclaimed in surprise as she turned her back to it, and then gasped, suddenly startled. Bowen McAnders was approaching her with that weird, enigmatic smile, and he held her evening bag. Ashlon was speechless. He blended eerily with the night as he moved smoothly toward her with the grace of a stalking feline, his long duster-length coat billowing around him like great dark folded wings in the briskly blowing wind. Ashlon's first panicked instinct was to turn and run like hell, but her feet were frozen where they stood.

"I believe this is yours?" Bowen said evenly as he extended her evening bag to her. She blinked maybe twice as she hesitated at first, then took it from him, tucking it under her arm.

"Thank you," she replied, her voice subdued. Boy, did she feel sheepish now! Noble and considerate! "You didn't have to do that."

"Yes, I did," he replied simply as he offered his arm. Ashlon looked at it unsurely, like it might bite her, then pushed aside her suspicions and gingerly slipped her hand through it. He's only being polite, she kept telling herself as he encased her hand inside his arm. Lord McAnders held it close against him as they moved together in silence down the dark, quiet street.

"How long have you known James Stanley?" Bowen inquired casually as they reached the turn to Ashlon's street. She pursed her lips, contemplating a careful answer. Her grandmother had always said don't reveal too much of anything to any stranger at first. Get to know whom you're dealing with first. Truer words were never spoken in regard to this gentleman!

"A number of years now, I suppose," Ashlon said, measuring her reply very carefully. "Why do you ask?"

Bowen looked down at her and smiled. "Just curious, I suppose. You have a comfortable closeness with him and his wife."

Ashlon nodded. "They're good friends."

"I see. They are indeed fortunate," he said in an offhanded way that she found vaguely condescending. Without thinking, she pulled him up short and made him look at her.

"No, your lordship. I'm the fortunate one to know such fine people," she said with a bite to her words. "You should get to know them better now that you're settled in."

He grimaced, deepening the furrows and shadows around his eyes. "I meant no offense," he said with a slight bow of his head. "In my experience, friendships such as yours with the Stanleys are a liability. I must be constantly on guard for opportunists or enemies who present the guise of friendship, but will turn when the opportunity presents itself."

"Sounds like a very lonely way to live," Ashlon commented with a brief shake of her head. She abruptly released the man's arm and walked away from him, closing the remaining short distance to her house. She'd reached her doorstep and was digging around in her bag for her door key, locating the spiral loop she kept it on and pulling it out. Looking up, she discovered with an unexpected jolt that Bowen was standing in front of her, blocking her porch and front door. Combined with the otherunexpected shocks of the evening, Ashlon had had enough and desperately needed to put some space between her and McAnders. She looked up into his face and then over at her door, hinting she needed to go inside. She was freezing, shivering in the stiff breeze that rustled the nearly bare limbs of the tree on the curbside, and her bare fingers were stiff with the cold.

For a brief moment, he looked like he would comply as he drew his hands from his coat pockets and looked away for a moment. Instead, he reached out and, without a word, pulled her against him and wrapped his arms around her, his coat winding around her with a life of its own. Looking down at her, his smile was gentle, warm, and achingly tender.

"Yes, it is a lonely way to live, and I have grown tired of it. I came here to remedy this and hope not to be disappointed." He held her tightly in his embrace, one hand gently pressing her head to his chest.

Ashlon was dumbfounded! She didn't know whether to be outraged by his effrontery or thankful for the warmth inside his great coat. Moreover, she was curiously comfortable in his arms, aware of an unexplainable feeling she belonged there. But that wasn't possible! She'd only met him for the first time that night! Maybe ... maybe it was only her fatigue and not wanting to be contentious this late in the evening. She knew deep down he wouldn't hurt her, either, when Bowen gazed down at her, his gentle expression calming and reassuring.

The longer she delayed going into her house, the more comfortable she grew in McAnders' protection from the cold and the night. Without realizing it, she had fairly melted into his embrace, her arms slowly circling around his waist. Why in the world did she do that, she wondered? It had been such a natural thing to do, strangely enough, wanting to be closer to him. And did he just shiver inside her arms? Ashlon closed her eyes, breathing in his clean, masculine scent, relaxing little by little as she grew toasty against that solidly built body. His one hand reached up and gently caressed her head, his long fingers running through her hair and down the back of her neck again and again. His touch felt absolutely heavenly! How long had it been since she'd been held and caressed like that?

"So soft," he murmured wonderingly when she sighed under his touch. "So soft." His lips touched her hair with a kiss.

In the distance, the clock in the town circle struck a doleful ten o'clock hour. Ashlon opened her eyes, reluctantly disengaging herself from Lord McAnders' arms and great coat, though he held on momentarily, not wanting to let her go. His gaze followed her as she moved away from him, his expression questioning and hopeful as she climbed the two short steps to her door.

"I really have to go," she said with real regret. "I have an early day tomorrow."

"May I see you tomorrow evening?" he said, moving to the bottom step as if to follow her inside.

"'Fraid not," Ashlon replied with a reluctant shake of her head, pointedly avoiding his eyes as she unlocked her door and backed into the entrance. "I won't be back till late, and then I'm out of town until Friday morning. I told Mr. Stanley I'd call him. Goodnight, Lord McAnders. Thank you for walking with me." She flashed one last genuine smile at him, then quickly closed and locked the door behind her. Too close, she decided, taking a deep, relieved breath. Another second or two and this night might have had a different ending!

Bowen remained there on her doorstep, looking up at the house and wanting her to come out with a ferocity that startled him. Of course, he could will her to come to him since he'd tasted her blood that night in the cemetery, but what good would come of that? He wanted her to come to him of her own free will and out of genuine desire for him, not compulsion. It would be so much sweeter in the end, knowing he had honestly won her for his own. Admittedly, what happened tonight had been just a little compulsion on his part; or rather, a subtle suggestion. He had willed her to stay in his embrace because he needed to hold her, needed to put his arms around her, warming her against the chill of the night.

But, then, she had willingly yielded, embracing the warmth he offered. When she wrapped her arms around him and rested her head on his chest, he had shivered with the absolute pleasure of her touch. Bowen smiled to himself as he walked away down the sidewalk heading to his house, cherishing this first encounter. Soon, he hoped, there would be much, much more.

As Bowen glided down the sidewalk and disappeared around the corner, another stealthily hidden figure concealed by the bushes and trees in the park across the street stirred, peering after him with narrowed golden eyes shining in the waxing light of the moon. Sniffing the air, the figure realized this stranger had no scent whatsoever other than the artificial one he wore, arousing suspicion and caution. The man was dangerous, this one knew instinctively, so extreme caution was needed. Standing erect, the figure moved away across the park as quietly as the shadows playing under the moonlight.

Chapter 10

Ashlon left town early Wednesday morning. As she had informed Mr. Stanley, she was away the rest of the week in Boston, attending the evening temple service at sundown Wednesday and the all-day service on Thursday. She'd basked in the sun's glowing progress through stained glass windows in the sanctuary, immersing herself in the Kol Nidre. She listened with other worshippers as the names of loved ones who had passed the previous year were read during the late afternoon Yizkor liturgy. Of course, Emma's was among them. Ashlon felt protected and comforted in the sanctuary that day. And by the end of the last blessing that evening, exhausted and famished, she was ready to face the world once more.

She also very much wanted to get back to Lloyds Corner and maybe see Bowen McAnders again. She'd only just met him, but by heaven, the man had made a solid impression on her. Ashlon grudgingly admitted his insistence on walking her home, and then warming her against the night chill, had thoroughly redeemed him from his earlier snub. Plus, she just plain liked his scent. She could have gotten lost in it. And this truly amazed her. Usually, she never thought much of any of the stuff out there. Not even Jorge's, which she considered barely tolerable.

She liked Lord McAnders, she decided. Really liked him, right down to his gentle, come-hither smile.

Ashlon broke her fast Thursday evening surrounded by friends. They had a wonderful evening together telling war stories of the worst and best patients they'd ever had, who was seeing whom, and the current status of their own relationships, either established or fresh budding. Naturally, Ashlon was thoroughly grilled about any new men in her life, and with some hemming and hawing, described Lord McAnders to her wide-eyed circle of friends. Of course, the responses ranged from 'You go, girl!' to 'Are

you out of your freakin' mind?' A suggestion was made she should get a police background check on this mystery
man since he was obviously European. Ashlon immediately nixed this due to the time and cost involved. Not to mention the absurdity of it. Besides, he was quite wealthy, as evidenced by the refurbishment of McAnders House. So, what if he'd spread hush money around the law enforcement agencies that could trace him? Wouldn't that kind of make background checks futile?
Talk about the juicy, scandalous gossip that would generate!

The suggestions and comments became more bawdy and wilder as the hour grew later and their drinks disappeared. The jokes and laughter grew louder and raunchier until finally, a little after one am, the women called it a night and decided to just sleep where they were. Spare blankets and pillows were pulled out, and they settled into chairs, a double studio couch, and the plush carpeting for the rest of the night. As Ashlon plopped onto her section of the carpet in the living room, her head spinning and a lovely warmth flowing through her body and limbs as she lay there, one of her older nurse friends fell over her into a pile next to her and lay there laughing hilariously with the others. She finally turned over onto her side and propped herself up on one arm, looking at Ashlon with a goofy, bleary-eyed smile.

"Y'know, Ash," she slurred, ruffling Ashlon's hair like she was a big troll doll. "You owe it to yourself. And if this guy can do it for you, strange as he is, go for it. He's interested, and I think so you are. Never let an op ... oppop... nutity get away." She emphasized her last comment with an upraised index finger before collapsing back onto her pillow, that goofy grin still fixed on her face as she fell immediately to sleep.

Ashlon turned onto her back and stared up at the ceiling fan, mulling over what her friend had said and watching the ceiling fan's slow rotation as the lovely buzz she'd tied on reached her eyes, lulling her into a deep dreamless slumber.

He rose Friday evening just as the sun sank below the horizon behind the mountains in the distance. After making certain no one was watching, he left the confines of the black crypt, securing the entrance doors behind him. He had relocated there due to all the renovations being done to the interior of the house and the risk of accidental discovery. Moving faster than human sight could follow, he was soon at his home, entering the front hallway and heading for the stairway.

Mr. Stanley met him as he was walking across the gallery to the wing where his bedchamber was located.

"Good evening, sir," the old caretaker said cheerfully. "Miss Ashlon called. She just returned this evening. I think she might be a wee hungover. Said she was at 'one blowout of a party' last night, to quote her, and unfortunately overslept this morning. And she says she's still not quite ready to be out in public yet." He shook his head with an amused grin.

Bowen's dark, stern features became a little less so as he fought a sudden urge to immediately run up to the widow's walk and confirm the old man's news. How could he begin to describe the all-too-familiar emptiness he had experienced after he and Ashlon had parted Monday evening, as if a big piece of him had been ripped away, leaving him damaged and bruised. It hadn't become obvious until he had entered his house and found himself wandering aimlessly from room to room, trying to catch a remnant of her presence or a hint of the scent she'd worn that evening. Oh yes, her scent lingered in his clothes and on his fingertips and had driven him almost mad with deep, desperate longing. Clearing his throat and working hard to maintain his composure, he nodded to Mr. Stanley.

"Thank you, Mr. Stanley. Will you please arrange for a time she can tour the house?" he asked with practiced non-interest. However, Mr. Stanley noted the tense grip Lord McAnders had on the gallery railing as he spoke.

"Oh, that won't be a problem, sir," Mr. Stanley said. "My wife and I are going to the town's Harvest Festival tomorrow evening, and she'll be there. She and her friend provide medical coverage like they do every year since they've lived here. And I understand several Jack O'lanterns being used for a fundraiser were carved by Miss Ashlon. I don't think I've ever seen anyone who loves them as much as she does, and her designs are quite good."

Now that was certainly a different aspect Bowen found very interesting. But what exactly was a Jack O'Lantern? "Is that a fact?" he asked, trying to sound only mildly interested.

Mr. Stanley was not fooled, however. Smiling wryly, he continued. "You're most welcome to attend, sir. It's a costume affair. And there are prizes donated by our local businesses for the best man's, woman's, and child's costumes. Do consider coming. It really is a rather enjoyable way to spend the evening if you've no plans, and a very good way to meet just about everyone in town."

And, Ashlon would be there, Bowen silently added. "I'll certainly consider it, Mr. Stanley. Thank you."

Mr. Stanley bowed his head just a little so that his lordship wouldn't see his knowing smile. "Then, I'll say good night, sir. Have a pleasant evening." The old man passed on across the gallery and descended the stairs, heading to the front entrance. He took his coat and hat from the closet and departed. He'll be there, the old man assured himself as he passed through the gate and headed toward home.

Bowen quickly shed his coat in his bedroom and immediately headed for the widow's walk after he heard the front door close behind Mr. Stanley. Looking out over the open grounds, he saw Ashlon's curtains were drawn over her bedroom window, but the lights were on, and he heard music coming from the downstairs area. He also noted with acute disappointment that her friend's car was parked behind the orange Jeep on the street. That immediately annulled his intention to go over to her house. Oh well, no matter. He would see her at the Festival—he would definitely go. If nothing else, he wanted to see how Ashlon disguised herself. Bowen knew exactly what he would wear so that she would know him immediately. He wished mightily that he knew what her costume would be so he might immediately recognize her and whisk her away from the crowd before she became too involved in the proceedings. He desperately wanted her in his arms again, pressed firmly against him as she had been Monday evening. After what they had experienced together so briefly Monday night, he would work harder to keep her there longer—like permanently.

"Goodnight, my own," he whispered into the night sky, willing his words across the distance to be heard by her if she wasn't too distracted by her friend and whatever they were doing.

Justin Bailey's barn out back of the grain and feed store had been the site for the Harvest Dance every year as far back as anyone could remember. It was conveniently located right on the edge of town and had plenty of parking available around the back, where a field had once grown nothing but tall grass and weeds before Justin paved it over to accommodate his customers' large pickups with their wider beds and quad cabs. Justin's son, Merle, was responsible for the everyday business, but his dad took a personal hand in getting the barn ready for one of the town's more popular annual events.

After the daytime activities, which included the craft fair, a farmers' market, cider and pie judging contests, the dance at the barn was just about the social event of the year. It was where newcomers could meet their neighbors in a congenial atmosphere and enjoy the potluck bounty provided by the most talented cooks around. A dance band consisting of the local high school's finest band members was joined by several more experienced resident musicians. They'd been practicing together for weeks to present what they considered a pretty varied repertoire of slow and fast numbers.

Justin would be the MC for the evening, a responsibility he took very seriously. He had a microphone stand placed off to one side of where the band would sit and tested and retested it with his "testing, testing, one, two, three", until he had the volume where he wanted it, and the decoration committee ready to strangle him with some of the party bunting they had on hand. Of course, the true test would come when practically every square foot of the barn floor not covered with seating or burgeoning tables of food would support a multitude of moving bodies trying to make their marks on the dance floor, creating a cacophony of mingling sociable voices trying to be heard above each other.

A squad of volunteers had been helping with the decorating since Friday afternoon, and by Saturday night, as the first stars were twinkling in the early evening sky, they'd created a combination haunted house and peon to the bounty of Lloyds Corner.

Early Friday evening, Janey and Ashlon set up the first aid station just inside the main entrance of the barn, out of the traffic flow when the large sliding doors were propped open for the revelers to freely come and go. They were particularly pleased with the addition of a portable defibrillation device Jorge had managed to procure for them from the county hospital. The previous year's Fall Festival dance had almost proven a calamity when one of the children had fallen off the stage and temporarily stopped breathing; a senior had passed out on the dance floor in a pool of sweat; the mayor's wife got knocked down by a group of adolescents trying to mosh to one of the faster numbers played by last year's band and sprained one of her fat ankles, and Mr. Stanley started having acute chest pains and extreme nausea after eating some particularly spicy homemade sausage. What he thought was simple indigestion turned out to be a full-blown heart attack by the time the ambulance reached County.

An ambulance was only 5 minutes away this year, thanks to county's expansion of its emergency response capability, so Janey and Ashlon were fairly confident that this year they were ready for anything. Add the fact that a doctor would be on hand as well, and both nurses could not have been happier.

Ashlon was sure they'd really outdone themselves with their costumes. Janey decided to match Jorge's plan to come as Zorro by dressing as a Spanish senora, complete with a black lace mantilla and a deep scarlet ruffled satin dress, her long dark brown hair rolled into a netted snood at the back of her head. She had drawn her hair back so tightly her eyebrows arched slightly in a perpetual expression of mild surprise. Ashlon had done her makeup, copying a picture of a flamenco dancer she had found online. The results were absolutely spectacular. Janey usually didn't like using makeup other than a lipstick, but this...!

"You look good enough to eat," Ashlon said with a wide grin as she studied her friend in the long mirror in Janey's room. Then, she stuck a black beauty mark on Janey's cheek. "There!" she said, satisfied with its location. "Done. Jorge's gonna have kittens when he sees you."

Janey grabbed the lace-trimmed train in one hand and swished it around, doing a little dance. Suddenly, she stopped and turned to Ashlon, her expression creased with an unexpressed worry.

"Ash, is it really alright? Do you think he'll like it?" she said, critically eyeing herself in the mirror.

Hmm. This was definitely out of character for Janey, Ashlon thought with some suspicion. Usually, she didn't give a damn what anyone thought of her clothes.

"Okay, spill it. What's going on?" Ashlon said as she took her friend's hand and led her over to the bed to sit. "Jorge's not giving you a hard time, is he?"

Janey's eyes widened. "Oh no, Ash, no!" she exclaimed, waving her hands. "It's just that... well," her eyes dropped looking at the floor, "remember last Saturday when you left us at your place and you day tripped the fall festivals?" Ashlon nodded slowly. "Yeah?" she said, barely suppressing a smile when she thought she knew what Janey was going to tell her.

"I think Jorge's going to ask me to marry him tonight," Janey said, and looked up into Ashlon's face, unsure of what to expect.

Ashlon grabbed Janey in a hug and squeezed hard. "I knew it! I knew it!" She joyously exclaimed, pulling Janey to her feet, dancing her around, and threatening to dismember Janey's costume. "Omygawd, Janey! Omygawd! You two talked that morning, didn't you?! Didn't you?! Oh, this is so wonderful! I had a feeling about you two!" They held each other close for a long moment. Janey's eyes shimmered with tears that rolled down her cheeks, and she released Ashlon and quickly grabbed a tissue from the dresser, carefully dabbing her eyes and face, trying not to smear her makeup.

"I was so worried about what you might think," she said, her voice thick with emotion, "especially after what we've both been through."

Ashlon punched Janey's shoulder good-naturedly. "Shame on you! I'm not anti-marriage, Janey. Just anti-Wyatt." They laughed as Ashlon gave Janey another big hug. Glancing over at the clock on the bedside stand, she yelped and jumped up.

"I better get dressed!" She grabbed a garment bag and disappeared into Janey's bathroom.

Chapter 11

They drove in Janey's car and parked out front of Justin's barn under a huge, sprawling tree now barren of leaves, its skeletal limbs swaying and creaking eerily in a dusky evening breeze. A full moon was peaking out just at the crest of the mountains in a cloudless, deep indigo blue twilight sky. Ashlon could see snow caps gleaming on the distant peaks and knew that it wouldn't be too long before the white stuff showed itself in the lower altitudes.

The band was just climbing the short stairs to the stage, and people were milling around the grounds holding paper plates of delicacies and other usual party fare. Ashlon could also detect the spicy scent of pumpkin ale that was brewed by one of the microbreweries in the area. It made her suddenly very thirsty, promising herself at least one frosty mug before the night was over. "Mmm!" she voiced, smacking her lips.

"Yeah, me too," Janey sighed with closed eyes, echoing her friend's sentiments about this seasonal treat. They reluctantly went on into the barn and pushed their way through friends and many hellos to the first aid station. Jorge was already there waiting for them and stood as they approached, bowing low with his black wide-rimmed hat in hand and his black bandana mask in place. "Buenos noches, señoras," he greeted them as he straightened, reaching out and taking Janey's hand and pressing it to his lips.

"Whoa!" Ashlon exclaimed as she watched her friend's face blush almost as violently red as the fan she was holding. "Jorge, you look positively roguish." Jorge grinned broadly. "Isn't this a great outfit?" he said with obvious pleasure. He eyed Janey up and down with close attention as he drew her close to him and embraced her, giving her a light kiss on her scarlet lips. "Janey, que linda, mi amore. Oh, and you look pretty good too, Ash." However, he had eyes only for the woman he was holding, and Janey began to giggle like a little girl with embarrassment as she hid her face behind her open, fluttering fan.

Just good? Ashlon was mildly miffed as Jorge led Janey away in the direction of the food tables, leaving Ashlon alone at the first aid table. She'd put a lot of work, time, and imagination into her costume, thank you very much, and all he could say was It looked pretty good? She'd dressed as a gypsy with lots of shiny stuff sewn into the below-knee-length purple patterned broomstick skirt with a purple sash wrapped around her hips, and a matching bolero vest. The pullover blouse was off white and tightly gathered just above her waist, allowing her flat midsection to show. Her shoulders were exposed, with loose, billowing sleeves caught at the wrists by tight, wide silver colored metal cuffs. She finished the outfit with large white gold hoop earrings and a folded shiny purple hair wrap tied at the nape of her neck. Her short black hair curled gleaming around the edges of the wrap. Ashlon had borrowed the jewelry items from Janey, who had borrowed the fan and lacey dangling earrings from Ashlon. A pair of purple ankle-laced wedged sandals completed her costume.

Only good?

Oh well. She shrugged with a resigned sigh and continued the equipment checks of the new defibrillator and walkie-talkies. Damn, now she was in a crappy mood as she looked over the aid pack and moved it to a location closer to the table. And why was that, she morosely considered as she finished her checks and then headed over to the food tables. Of course, she knew the answer, but didn't want to admit it to herself because she always felt mean and small when she was in its grip: she was feeling jealous again. Flat out, green-eyed monster jealous of what Jorge and Janey had together. Of course, she also had to acknowledge that her current manless state was her own stupid phobia, too. That's what made these spells so hard to swallow.

She snapped up a paper plate from the stack on the edge of the table and started down its length, feeling even crappier now that she'd admitted it to herself, and very ashamed for begrudging her best friends their happiness even a little bit. Thank heaven they hadn't noticed it, and by the grace of heaven never would.

Full night fell softly, and large electric lanterns set around the barn interior suddenly popped to life, casting their rich light over the barn interior. The plank wooden floor had been meticulously swept and air-hosed down to alleviate as much dust as possible when the dancers were engaged by the music and the rhythms they promised as the band warmed up. The rustle of music sheets and scraping of moving music stands stifled some of the noise coming from the revelers; they hushed each other and waited expectantly for the first number to begin, jostling each other and making sure they all had their partners waiting on their arms or standing close by.

Ashlon looked around and spied Janey and Jorge sitting on a hay bale near the barn entrance, heads pressed together as they fed each other morsels off their plates and talked quietly between them, an occasional soft laugh escaping from one or both of them, or a kiss suddenly stolen by one from the other. Ashlon sighed again and managed to push away those terrible feelings and pull up the good ones for her friends. As Janey had said, they both deserved better than what they'd had before. Janey's 'better' was sitting right there with her, his affection and devotion obvious to anyone who saw them together. And, hadn't Ashlon introduced them to each other almost a year ago in the hope something like this might develop? So, here it was, come to fruition, and better than she or Janey could have ever expected.Ashlon pushed through the crowd to the drink area and found that ale she had promised herself. She raised the large Styrofoam cup in her friends' direction, whispered "To their happiness," and took a deep chug off of it. The icy brew slid easily down her throat, and she licked her lips of the foam, savoring the subtle spicing with closed eyes and a satisfied smack of her lips.

"Ash!" a familiar male voice rumbled from behind her, making her jump and nearly drop her cup. Instead, it only splashed a little onto her hand.

She wiped it on a napkin she held under her cup and quickly turned to see who had startled her.

Just a little taller than Ashlon, with a burly, solid build, a deeply tanned face, auburn hair that curled around his ears and blended into a neatly clipped beard, Grady Roberts was awalking recruiting poster for everything the US Forest Service looked for in their rangers, and his mother's second-born. He had an earthy, rugged, not pretty look about him that reminded Ashlon of the original Brawny paper towel guy. He was deep woods, solidly constructed cabins with stone hearth fireplaces, and Indian blankets on the furniture to keep out the cold.

His buddies had nicknamed him Hound because he could read trails and animal prints like most people read books, and track practically anything or anybody in the thickest woods. Grady was often called in to assist search and rescue operations within the northern New England area; he was that good. Now, he smiled broadly as he approached Ashlon and threw his arms around her, splashing her beer again onto the barn floor as he lifted her off the floor with a solid, friendly hug.

"You look simply incredible," he gushed as he stepped back, holding onto her arms and eyeballing her up and down with a frankness that thoroughly embarrassed her and echoed of his mother's influence on his formative years. "I mean, really incredible. Beautiful!"

Ashlon was flustered but regained her composure enough to croak out, "Hi, Grady," as she shook her wet hand and set her cup back on the table to dry off. "And, thank you for the compliment. Where's your mom?"

Grady's smile was warm and friendly as he handed Ashlon another dry napkin. "Mom couldn't make it tonight. She and Minnie are doing inventory. But she told me to look for you at the first aid booth or over by the food tables with your friend."

Ashlon managed a wan smile. This guy was being nice with a capital 'N'. Congenial attitude, polite, with healthy good looks and an up-front no-nonsense approach and genuine open nature, most women found enormously appealing if they didn't know him. But she hadn't seen him in several years, so maybe things had changed with him. He was certainly trying hard enough, she had to admit. She cleared her throat of the hesitancy that had formed there.

"Well, my friend is otherwise occupied right now with the town doctor. So I guess that means I'm pretty much free for the evening until someone breaks a hip or attempts something they haven't done in years."

Grady's smile broadened as he took Ashlon's hand and led her out to the dance floor, pulling her close for a slow number the band had started, something from the Big Band Era, Ashlon supposed. She wasn't much of a dancer, but the music was nice and she really did want to have a least one turn with someone this evening. Grady moved them around the floor with surprising grace for his size. His movements were fluid and coordinated as he steered them through the music.

Oh, this was so nice. "It's been ages since I've danced," she shyly commented with an appreciative smile.

Grady looked down into her face with a pleased grin. "Then I'll claim the rest of your dances for this evening," he replied, pulling her closer so that his bristly cheek rested against hers, their movements slowing to a sway in time with the final measures of the music.

As far as she was concerned, it could go on forever. However, a random glance over at the first aid table on one of their turns told her it wasn't happening. Ashlon reluctantly pushed away from her dance partner, who looked at her questioningly. She pointed in the direction of the first aid table, where she had spotted someone waiting with one hand clutched protectively against his chest.

"Duty calls," she said regretfully, moving away from Grady with a lot of effort. "This better be good!" Ashlon growled under her breath as she approached a middle-aged man who threw her a nasty look. She moved around behind the table and stood glaring at him, waiting to hear or see the dumb thing he'd done to himself.

"'Bout time," the man who was one of the grain and feed employees grumbled. Ashlon grabbed the first aid pack and hefted it onto the table, then opened a long zipper across it width. A box of gloves on a small side table was moved next to the aid pack, and she grabbed a pair.

"Okay, Mr. Vance, what happened?" she said, putting on her best nurse mode as the man slowly opened his hand to reveal a long bleeding slice running along his palm in one of the many creases—Ashlon darkly hoped it was his lifeline. Not deep, but bleeding profusely and crusted with some kind of weird crumbly matter stuck around its edges. She obtained a small basin from the sterile pack box, a bottle of saline from the aid pack, and a small towel from a large plastic bag under the table, and set them up, put on the gloves, and carefully took Mr. Vance's hand. Holding it over the basin, she slowly poured the solution over the wound, wiping with some gauze as she cleaned the shallow laceration. A familiar aroma reached her nose as she leaned in close to examine it. Glancing up at the man, she said, "Tobacco?", and was shocked to see him suddenly turn scarlet to the ears when she caught him looking down her cleavage as she'd bent over to lavage his wound. Thoroughly disgusted, she quickly wiped his hand dry and applied a gauze bandage with some first aid creme and wrapped it with a long piece of Kerlex gauze.

"Next time, be careful when you slice a chew off your plug," she growled, sounding very unnursey but not really caring. "Have Dr. Villarreal look at that on Monday." She threw the wet gauzes into a trash bag hanging from a nail on one of the barn supports behind the table, picked up the basin of bloody water with shreds of saturated tobacco floating in it, and headed toward the open barn doors without another word to Mr. Vance, who slunk away from the table holding his newly bandaged hand protectively in his other hand.

Ashlon took the basin outside and went around to the dark side of the barn where some tall grass still grew, pitching the soiled water onto the ground. She used an old iron water pump with a handle that raised then pushed to pump the well water. Ashlon rinsed out the basin, shaking out the excess water, then returned to the front of the barn, pausing for a moment to take a deep breath of the cool, fresh air before going back inside. Standing at the open barn door entrance, she watched the crowd as it laughed and danced and ate. She spotted Jorge and Janey again, holding each other on the dance floor. They looked ecstatically happy and totally oblivious to anyone around them.Ashlon sighed and smiled to herself, relieved that she'd shaken off some of her grumpy, nasty attitude on Mr. Vance. She stood there for a while enjoying the night, then went back inside to the first aid table and put the basin in another bag, disposed of her gloves, and used a sanitizer on her hands. It had a lotion base scented with light gardenia and didn't dry out the hands, very skin-friendly. She took a quick glance into a small mirror Janey had hung from another protruding nail and fixed her head wrap, wiped a lipstick smear, and spotted a high schooler from the band approaching the first aid station. She knew him from visits to his house several years ago after his momma had had her second baby. Ashlon greeted the young man when he reached the table. He was—what—sixteen now? This would make his sister 4 or 5 years old.

"Hello, Devon," she greeted him as she put away her brush and lipstick, and then retied her slim bandanna around her hair. The teenager smiled shyly and nodded, leaning on the table as he stared at her. He had only a few blemishes on his forehead at the hairline, and the promise of being a handsome man like his daddy. He must be between girlfriends, Ashlon considered as she watched him fidget where he stood nervously eyeing her.

"What can I do for you?" she prompted him, waiting patiently for him to summon up some adolescent courage to speak to her.

The boy cleared his throat and dropped his gaze to the floor, shuffling a foot across the floorboards, clearly uncomfortable in his silence and Ashlon's inquiring gaze.

"Do you want to dance with me?"

The boy's head jerked up in surprise, his mouth working to say something.

"Did your friends put you up to this?"

He barely nodded as Ashlon glanced around him at a group of young men standing near the stage, sniggering and elbowing between them, watching alertly to hoot at their friend's failure and generally furthering his humiliation when he was turned down.

She rounded the table and took Devon's hand, leading him to the floor in front of the stage as the band began to play. With only a little prompting to get him moving, they began to slowly turn in a waltz. Devon clutched Ashlon's hand in a sweaty palm, his other hand barely touching her bare waist. She led him along very easily, smiling broadly as his shyness gradually dissolved through their movements across the floor. Halfway through the music, she let him take the lead until the end, when he dipped her almost to the floor. She laughed as he lifted her back up and kissed her hand in a final gallant gesture.

"You're an excellent dance partner, Devon," Ashlon declared to his surprised pleasure, giving him a hug and lightly kissing his cheek. "Thank you."

Devon blushed a violent bright red clear up to his ears and returned in a blissful haze to his friends who'd watched with silent awe, now pounding his back as they crowded around him for the blow-by-blow details.

Ashlon shook her head and chuckled. It was time for another drink. She returned to the refreshment table where Janey stood alone sipping off a Coke bottle.

"Damn nice thing you did over there," Janey commented with a grin.

"Yeah, now I'm an adolescent's face saver," Ashlon sourly tossed back at her as she picked up another cup of spiced pumpkin ale from a tray and downed a large swallow. "Mmm," she said, wiping her mouth with her hand. She glanced at Janey. "Where's your arm candy?"

Janey took another sip off her frosty bottle. "Potty break. The beer finally processed through."

Ashlon chuckled. They stood in silence, drinking slowly and watching the crowd. Finally, Ashlon couldn't stand it any longer and looked at her friend. "Did he ask you yet?"

Janey's expression became stony as she tightly clutched her soda bottle, her lips a thin, grimacing line. "Not yet. Nope."

"The evening's still young," Ashlon said, trying to sound hopeful, "He's probably just waiting for the right moment."

Jeez, that sounded so cliché!

Janey shook her head. "Tonight, was right so many times. How many right moments does he need?" Her eyes were angry and becoming misty, and she averted her eyes.

Ashlon put down her beer and wrapped her arms around Janey, trying to absorb the hurt and confusion she felt spilling from her friend. "Don't worry, Janey," she said, gently reassuring her friend. "You know he loves you. After all, it's not just any boyfriend who gets up in the night to answer his girlfriend'scall for help when her crazy friend is in trouble."

Janey sniffled several times, but managed a laugh as she looked up at Ashlon nodded as she blotted her eyes with a napkin. "Yeah, I guess so," she admitted with a deep sigh. She smoothed the wrinkles and folds from her dress as Ashlon tucked a few stray hairs back under the lace mantilla, and spotted the subject of their commiserations approaching them through the crowd.

"Here he comes." Ashlon quickly gave Janey's arm a supportive squeeze, then turned smiling at Zorro as he rejoined his date.

"Hi, Ash," Jorge said as he reached around Janey for a bottle of cola. "Where have you been all evening?" He easily flipped off the cap with one of the church keys on the table, and then took a deep swallow.

"Keeping busy," Ashlon replied and winked at Janey behind Jorge's caped back. She had her cup in hand as she stepped away a few paces and turned her attention back to the party.

And realized something was happening.

The revelry had abruptly become unnaturally quiet with only excited whispered murmurings scattered in the throng. All eyes were turned toward the open barn doors, intense curiosity written in every one of them as well as ... slack-jawed awe?

"Oh. My. G-d!" Janey gasped. She reached around Jorge and grabbed

Ashlon's arm roughly pulling her friend over next to her and directing her attention to the entrance.

Ashlon swallowed hard as her heart skipped a beat. He definitely was someone she hadn't expected to see there. And who had just become the talk of the party.

Chapter 12

Lord Bowen McAnders entered the barn behind Mr. and Mrs. Stanley, casually looking around the interior and pointedly ignoring his immediate electrifying effect on everyone staring at him. He really didn't care, Ashlon marveled, but tonight he had earned every envious glance in the place.

Mr. and Mrs. Stanley proceeded through the barn hand in hand, Bowen easily following along, acknowledging every one the couple introduced to him to with a brief word and a small bow. The Stanleys were costumed as a Victorian gentleman and lady, very stately and in character with their address and introductions.

But Lord Bowen McAnders …! If he didn't take first place in the men's costumes that night, the judges would have to be blind.

Ashlon was absolutely transfixed, unable to tear her eyes away from him as they slowly worked their way through the crowd. Bowen was wrapped in a great kilt with the skirting leveled at his knees. He wore a natural cambric shirt under the plaid shoulder sash, which was fixed with a crest and dagger to a leather baldric. This crossed his partially exposed chest to a wide belt that held a heavy scabbard with a great sword at his side. His long, muscular legs were wrapped in the same plaid as the great kilt and sash. Below-the-knee wide-cuffed brown leather boots completed his ensemble. Bowen's hair hung sweeping his shoulders in lush dark waves as he glided smoothly along with the Stanleys. They had spotted Ashlon and her friends and were heading in their direction.

"Dios mío!" Jorge swore under his breath. "Highlander lives!"

The Stanleys were smiling broadly as they approached the gaping silent threesome. Ashlon quickly chugged her cup of beer, recovering enough to give the elderly couple a quick hug as she tore her gaze from Bowen.

"We're rather late, I'm afraid, dear," Mrs. Stanley said as she looked around the barn interior at the lanterns and all the decorations. "My, my! It looks wonderful. Justin and Merle have certainly outdone themselves this year."

"Indeed, my dear," Mr. Stanley smilingly concurred. "Unfortunately, we were detained because our daughter was late picking up our grandson. She was held up by an accident on that sharp curve into town."

Jorge instantly whipped out his cell phone. Moments later, after a few brief, terse words into it, he clapped it shut. "EMS still hasn't shown up, but a First Responder's there. I should go and see what I can do." He gave Janey a quick kiss, turning to leave. Janey grabbed his hand and said resolutely, "I'm coming too!" She gathered her skirts into one hand, blew a kiss to Ashlon with the other, and hustled out into the night with Jorge.

As Ashlon watched them leave, Bowen McAnders, who had been waiting silently by the tables, approached her, studying her with a fixed intensity she could feel drilling into the back of her head. The music had started again, and the Stanleys happily moved out to the dance floor, leaving Ashlon alone with Bowen. The band was playing another slow number, and the partygoers returned to their normal mingling and conversations, ignoring the newcomer in their midst. Yep, he'd become part of the small town fabric now that he'd shown up at one of the town's annual events. He was now an acknowledged member of the community.

"Looks like I'm solo again," Ashlon said shyly, trying to sound as unaffected as possible as she reluctantly turned to Bowen. "And you're not late. The band hasn't inflicted their vocalist on us yet."

Bowen, however, was transfixed by Ashlon, his eyes hungrily devouring every square inch of her. Silently taking her hand, he led her to an open space on the dance floor, then gently pulled her into his embrace and began to move in time with the music before Ashlon could protest or resist his efforts. Hah! As if she would have, she admitted with frank bewilderment, because this is what she had hoped would happen the moment he'd walked into that barn.

Heaven help her! If Grady had been nice to dance with, this man felt so right against her she was almost ashamed of the ideas that popped into her head. It was a repeat of what had transpired Monday evening after the open house, and he'd walked her home. He felt so right holding her and pressed closely against her that she closed her eyes and relaxed in his arms, moving with Bowen to the rhythm of the music. As they swayed and circled around the floor, she felt his lips brush her ear, sending a thrill coursing through her like electricity down to her toes.

"My beautiful gypsy," he purred seductively, his mouth brushing down her cheek until their lips met. Ashlon turned her head away for only a moment before his hand turned it back to lock eyes with hers. Everything and everybody around them faded away as if into a dream, and she moved against him again, wrapping her arms around his neck and standing on her tiptoes as he pressed her even closer to him. She could feel his arousal under the kilt pressing against her thigh. But that kiss! His lips took hers, and her head began to spin as she fell into its spell, was swallowed by it, possessed by it. Every emotion passing through this man was in that kiss, and it told her one basic fact: he wanted her body and soul, wanted her with an absolute certainty that would not be deterred by any earthly force as he willed her to surrender herself to him.

Realization smacked her like being hit with ice water. Abruptly, she broke the kiss with difficulty and struggled out of his embrace, taking several deep breaths to clear her head as she pushed him away at arm's length.

"Ashlon?" he said, moving toward her and trying to draw her back against him.

"You're moving too fast for me," she gasped between shallow breaths. "I'm sorry, but I'm just not ready for this." She shook free of his restraining grip and frantically pushed away from him into the crowd, putting some distance between them as she ran and stumbled haphazardly away from him, heading for the restroom around the back of the stage.

Ashlon had reached the door and was pushing it open when Mr. Stanley caught up with her, frowning when he noticed Ashlon's distress. "Are you alright?" he said with gentle concern. "Did you and Lord McAnders have some kind of disagreement back there?"

Ashlon rubbed her face with her hands as she shook her head. "No, Mr. Stanley. No words. He's … well, a little overwhelming, if you know what I mean." Her voice was trembling as she spoke. She was also willing to bet she looked like hell.

Mr. Stanley nodded. "I do, indeed." His nostrils flared as he grasped Ashlon's shoulders with a surprisingly firm grip. "And if it happens again, you must tell me and I'll have words with him, nobleman or not."

Ashlon managed a relieved smile, rather gratified by the old man's indignation on her behalf. How could she tell him Lord McAnders hadn't done anything wrong? Plain simple truth, she had panicked and bolted when he'd exposed his raw yearning for her. No one, especially Wyatt, had ever wanted her that way. It had utterly terrified her.

"He'll have to deal with me, too," a deeper, younger, masculine voice growled from behind Mr. Stanley. Grady had seen Ashlon rush off and followed behind Mr. Stanley. He had seen what happened between Ashlon and Lord McAnders, and the hackles had risen on his neck as anger flashed inside him like an unbanked blaze. Grady had danced with her, his crush rekindled like it had been in the beginning. This time, he'd sworn he wouldn't let any opportunity get away from him again. Especially not at this critical time.

This was too much for Ashlon. With a groan, she quickly retreated into the ladies' room and threw the bolt on the door with a resounding click.

How long she'd been hiding in the bathroom was only a guess since she hadn't worn a watch with her costume, but she knew it had been a while. Thank heaven no one had needed to use it while she hid out there and recovered. However, it was only a matter of time before…

Someone was pounding incessantly on the door, and she got up from the stool next to the sink, threw back the bolt, and opened the door just enough to peek out. Janey stood there with her hands on her hips, doing a little impatient dance.

"Oh, thank heaven!" Ashlon cried as she flung the door open, exploded out of the doorway, and threw her arms around her friend's neck.

"Whoa, girl!" laughed Janey as she gave Ashlon a brisk hug before quickly edging around her into the ladies' room and slamming the door behind her. A few minutes later, Janey emerged looking vastly relieved as she took Ashlon's arm. They walked together back through the main party area, keeping to the crowd's periphery as they made their way to the first aid station. Ashlon described to her friend what had happened while she was gone.

"This is exactly what I warned you about!" Janey said with a disapproving frown as she took a seat behind the table and folded her arms over her chest. "You've been out of the loop so long you resist anyone's real attempt to get you back into it."

"Oh, so I should jump into it with any warm body that presents an offer?" Ashlon said with mild reproof. "And believe me, that offer came with more than a one-night guarantee."

"Even better!" Janey impatiently exclaimed, throwing up her hands.

Ashlon moaned as she plunked heavily next to Janey behind the first aid table. "There's something about McAnders I can't put my finger on, Janey," she complained. "This is the second time I've felt like he knows me somehow. He behaves with a familiarity that overwhelms me when I'm near him. It's downright creepy."

"Can't keep his hands off you, huh?" Janey grinned, jabbing Ashlon in the ribs with an elbow.

"Stop it! I'm being serious here." Ashlon peevishly moved her chair away from her friend. "It's like being sucked into a whirlpool. I mean, the guy is gorgeous, make no mistake. But it's like he's trying to get into my head or something."

"There's your problem again, dummy," Janey said as she took out her mirror and examined her face. "An opportunity like this comes along practically biting you in the ass, and you push it away."

"I only met the guy Monday night!"
"So? Here he is looking so fabulous, like something out of Braveheart, and you play Miss Ballbuster."

"Janey!"

"So, what about Grady, then?" Janey persisted. "There's a hunka burnin' love if ever I saw one."

Ashlon smirked as she looked around the dance floor and spotted her target. "You don't know Grady the way I do. Case in point— Cherlyn has her claws in him now as we speak," Ashlon said, wrinkling her nose as she nodded toward the food tables. "And he's scratching back."

Cherlyn Mathis was one of the waitresses over at the Scupper who hadn't been victimized by the still unidentified attacker who'd left his victims slightly drained but definitely smiling and unable to remember what had happened, outside of meeting a tall, dark stranger with glowing eyes. Cherlyn was a little younger than Ashlon and pretty in a blonde sort of way. Tonight, she was wearing a tight, thigh-high bad girl slayer outfit that left little to the imagination. She had no kin in these parts and attended college in Worcester. Ashlon recalled one time when she'd stopped in one evening at the Scupper for a bite to eat after finishing a late, way-out-of-town client visit. She'd been confided to by one of Cherlyn's friends about a 'problem' Cherlyn had picked up from one of her past boyfriends. Ashlon had suggested a clinic out toward county hospital that pro-rated charges on a number of treatments and procedures. Tonight, Cherlyn was all over Grady, and Grady's hands were all over her.

"No accounting for bad taste," Janey said in confirmation. She slid her chair over to Ashlon and abruptly extended her left hand under Ashlon's nose.

"What the hell...!" Ashlon exclaimed, about to push Janey's hand away, but suddenly paused as her friend wiggled her fingers.

Something shiny caught the light from the lanterns and sparkled merrily in front of Ashlon's face. She grabbed Janey's hand, her mouth dropping open as she met Janey's eyes.

"He did it!" she breathed, barely containing her excitement as she eyed the diamond ring on Janey's finger. Janey only nodded her reply, happiness absolutely glowing in her face and making her so beautiful at that moment. Ashlon threw her arms around her friend with a loud squeal, laughing and crying along with Janey and her new joy.

"I guess it was the accident out on the highway," Janey said as they rose to get another cold drink. Ashlon was still smiling broadly as they walked arm in arm over to the refreshments table and found the only drink left was apple cider, which was perfectly acceptable to both of them. According to a handwritten sign propped on the table, Justin and Merle had vacated the party to get more supplies from cold storage and would be back soon.

"Anyway, by the time we got there, EMS was on the scene helping First Responder with an extraction from the driver's side. Some out-of-towner miscalculated that turn onto the county road and rolled his car. They said he was going way too fast to pull out of it. Jorge made me stay in the truck, and he went over to the paramedics. They talked together, and then Jorge headed down into the woods. I saw a couple of rescue guys come out carrying a stretcher with a sheet pulled over it. Jorge was carrying a smaller bundle wrapped in another sheet. They were put into the back of the first responder vehicle, and the guy the paramedics pulled from the wreck was taken to the ambulance. Jorge came back and we drove off. He was awfully quiet and didn't say anything until we parked out front here again. Then he pulls out this jeweler's box from his console and gives me a really big hug. I guess he was a little shook up because he said he'd just assumed we had plenty of time before finally settling down. But, seeing that accident, those dead people in the woods ..."

Janey shook her head and took a big gulp of her cider. "He said he realized that he shouldn't take for granted the love he had. Then he asked me to marry him." Janey became thoughtful as she held up her hand to study her ring again. Looking at Ashlon, she cocked an eyebrow. "Now you know why I'm so hard on
you, fool."

"Death makes you think of blessings when you don't exact-ly notice them right away," Ashlon said with a pensive frown. "Jorge must've realized that."

Janey wrapped an arm around Ashlon's shoulders and hugged her close. "I don't mean to be harsh. I want so much for you to have what Jorge and I have. It took so damn long to find it again, and I don't want you passing up any chance if it's there."

Ashlon smiled and gave her friend a peck on the cheek.

"I know, babe. I know." She looked thoughtful for a moment. "It's just that I have this weird feeling I'm destined for something, you know? I'm being steered in that direction; getting there is part of the adventure. I just can't see the path."

"Sounds just fine to me," Janey affirmed after considering it for a moment. "I like it. And it's so you."

Ashlon managed a brief chuckle without a witty retort. She looked over Janey's shoulder, her eyebrows arching. "Here comes Ro-meo."

Jorge approached the table and picked up a cup of cider, took a sip, and made a face. "Ecch! I need more alcohol!" He spat the mouth-ful back into the cup and chucked it into the waste can behind the table.

Ashlon pushed Janey aside and gave Jorge a big hug. "She'll make an honest man out of ya and all that crap," she said, pounding his back heartily, then slid off to Janey's other side again with a grin.

Jorge's mustache twitched as he took Janey's hand and frowned at her. "Just couldn't wait, could you?"

"Hell no!" Janey exclaimed, giving his mustache a little tug. "Not from my best friend. We're practically inseparable." Her face lit up as an idea occurred to her. The band was taking a break for Justin to bring another microphone stand up on the stage in preparation for their guest vocalist, a local woman with only a better-than-average voice, and who provided it for parties and weddings at the drop of a

hat—any hat. She claimed to be a voice instructor retired from professional life. Jorge once remarked the only thing she taught was dogs how to bay at the moon. Janey grabbed Ashlon by the hand and resolutely yanked
her along through the crowd toward the steps onto the stage.

"What the hell are you doing?" Ashlon protested as Janey tried to push her up the steps to the stage once they reached it.

"Your voice is miles better than Beatrice's," Janey stopped pushing on her to explain. "I want to hear 'The Wedding Song' the way you sang it at Bec's wedding last year."

Bec was a mutual nurse friend in Boston who had married her childhood sweetheart in a very strange Goth ceremony with black, red, and purple decorations, and the couple dressed like Dracula and his bride. Bec had begged Ashlon to sing 'The Wedding Song' after the couple made their vows of fealty to each other and exchanged each other's blood-filled vial necklaces. Ashlon had reluctantly agreed to do it. But, boy oh boy, it was the weirdest experience singing it to the dulcet tones of a harpsichord played by one of the groom's buddies, who looked like Lurch from the Addams family and nicknamed Ogre. "At least, you've got a decent band backing you this time," Janey earnestly said. "It's something I want to hear for this occasion. Just for me. Please?" "Don't beg," Ashlon growled, screwing up her face. "It's demeaning."

She looked into Janey's hopeful expression and sighed as her friend made puppy dog eyes at her and clasped her hands in front of her in pleading supplication. Ashlon knew it was a lost cause, finally relenting as she mumbled sourly, "At least the crowd's liquored up."

Reluctantly, she climbed the steps as Janey gleefully clapped her hands and rejoined Jorge, dancing from foot to foot. Jorge looked at her questioningly, but she only held up one finger and whispered, "Wait!"

Ashlon moved across the stage and spoke in a lowered voice to the band director, who nodded agreeably and said something to the musicians. After much shuffling of music, he nodded to Ashlon, who then sidled up next to Jus- tin when he returned to his MC duty at the microphone. She whispered a few words to him as well, with her one hand over the broadcast unit, then stepped away, waiting expectantly.

Justin moved up to the microphone and hushed the crowd. "I've been informed that before our guest vocalist is introduced, someone wants to make a dedication to her friend who became engaged tonight." Scattered polite clapping and the usual oohs and aahs floated up to the stage.

Ashlon spotted the Stanleys after a brief search and mouthed 'Janey' as she pointed over at the refreshment table. They eagerly looked in the direction she was pointing and began to push through the crowd in Janey's direction. Ashlon gave Lord McAnders only a passing glance when she spotted him at the barn entrance, watching her with a fixed, unblinking gaze, his arms folded over his chest. Never mind that her heart skipped a beat as she nervously licked her lips at that brief sight of him. Ignoring him with a determined effort, Ashlon took Justin's place at the microphone, quietly clearing her voice.

"I've been asked for this song as a special favor by my best friends, who've found their happiness tonight." She looked over at the music director and nodded. The introduction was performed on an acoustic guitar played by one of the older musicians who knew the music, like Paul Stuckey, might have played it for the first-time years ago.

Ashlon stepped up to the mike and began to softly sing, "He is now to be among you at the calling of your hearts ..."

The crowd was silent, totally captivated as the soaring music played. Ashlon's voice lifted, carrying on passionately until the music faded and the final measures were played in the guitar's closing chords.

Ashlon nodded her thanks to Justin and turned to exit the stage as the crowd stood there in silence. Tanked, she thought, looking away as she moved toward the wings. Suddenly, an explosion of applause and shouts for more ripped away the quiet, freezing her in her tracks. The music director took her arm and led her over to his stand for a brief conference as he showed her what he had to offer if she stayed and performed another number for them, practically begging her to do just one more. Ashlon briefly considered just refusing altogether; she was no entertainer by any stretch of the imagination, and Beatrice was fretting in the wings, shooting poisonous barbs at her.

She was too full of herself, Ashlon thought as they stared at each other. And then Beatrice's lips moved silently, mouthing an unmistakable word with a sneer on her painted mouth. Ashlon's eyes widened briefly as her jaw set rigidly. That did it. If it pissed off Beatrice, she'd do it.

Looking at the band director again, she defiantly chose another number. A hearty round of applause rippled through the crowd as she stepped up to the microphone again and nodded once more to the smiling director, who sat behind a piano and began the introduction to 'Desperado.' She allowed her eyes to wander this time as she sang, her voice rising over the silent listeners.

Finally, it was finished, and she stepped away from the microphone, bowing to the audience. She moved away toward the other side of the stage with a nod to the music director as she quickly departed, and then rushed out the back door into the parking lot, the sounds of loud applause ringing in her ears. She promptly threw up in the grass next to the water pump. Coughing and spitting as she gasped for air, she lifted the handle once to fill her hand with some cold water, and rinsed the yuck out of her mouth. A few deep breaths to clear butterflies, and then she headed to the front of the barn.

Janey and Jorge found her sitting on the hood of Jorge's Land Cruiser, blowing her nose and mumbling to herself with frank disgust about letting Beatrice get to her. Janey smacked her arm hard enough to hurt.

"Stop it!" she snapped at Ashlon. "They're still clapping in there! And believe me, that's probably as close to real talent any of those people will ever get. You were great!"

Ashlon sniffled and rubbed her stinging arm where Janey had smacked it. "Ow", she said weakly. "You could've made your point in a less painful way, you know." She managed a laugh. "At least I didn't tank. And I definitely pissed off Beatrice. I haven't sung like that in a long time." Not since before marrying Wyatt, she remembered with residual bitterness, which she quickly pushed away. Did kids' songs count, she wondered? She had sung to Emma practically every day of her daughter's brief life, and Emma had often sung along with her, laughing and often wanting to sing the same thing over and over again. Ashlon had sung one of Emma's favorite lullabies the night she died, holding her daughter's lifeless body in her arms as one of the hospice nurses waited patiently by the bedside until Ashlon allowed her to proceed with what had to be done next.

Jorge sat down next to her and put an arm around her shoulders, hugging her close.

"Does that mean you'll sing at our wedding, Meja?" he said with a grin. "Janey and I want you to."

Ashlon stared at them incredulously. "What? No mariachis?" she quipped seriously, stifling a grin under her hand

"Don't be an ass," Janey commented dryly as she punched her friend on the other arm. "C'mon, we'll talk about this later." She grabbed both Jorge's and Ashlon's hands and pulled both of them with dogged determination back to the party.

Chapter 13

The remainder of the evening was spent fielding well-wishers, compliments, congratulations, and rendering first aid for a skinned knee, evacuating an acute chest pain via EMS, treating an asthma attack, and splinting a possible broken elbow when one of the kids in Devon's group attempted to crowd surf and was dropped. Was his father furious as he hauled the kid out and stuffed him into his car for the ride to the hospital? Ashlon and Janey could still hear the yelling as the car disappeared down the road.

Finally, as midnight struck on the town clock, people started filtering out for their homes, or were in the process of saying their goodbyes. Grady had departed around eleven to pick up his mother and sister, leaving Cherlyn to the graces of the guy she had come to the party with, but who didn't seem to mind her efforts to make up with him when they departed.

As Ashlon and Janey packed up the unused equipment and hauled everything out to Jorge's vehicle, the Stanleys approached as a smaller table was collapsed and folded, and trash was picked up.

After his aborted dance with Ashlon, Bowen McAnders had resumed making social rounds during the evening, listened to Ashlon's performance, and then disappeared for a time. But here he was bigger than life as he accompanied the Stanleys, curiously less pale than he had been earlier in the evening. Ashlon pointedly ignored him as she said good night to the Stanleys.

"I had no idea you were such an excellent vocalist!" Mrs. Stanley exclaimed. "You've been holding out all this time."

Ashlon shifted uncomfortably. When would she learn to accept compliments gracefully? She silently rebuked herself. "Well, I didn't have much to sing about for a while, Mrs. Stanley," she said, looking away from Janey, who only rolled her eyes and made a face at her. "Tonight, was a command performance." She turned and quickly stuck her tongue out at Janey.

Mrs. Stanley took her hands with a gentle smile. "We understand, dear," she said. "But I do hope we'll have the opportunity to hear you again soon."

"Oh, you will," Janey interrupted with a grin. "At my wedding."

"Well, isn't that nice," said Mr. Stanley. "We'll be looking forward to it, won't we, dear?"

"Indeed." Mrs. Stanley squeezed Ashlon's hands one more time and then took her husband's arm, allowing him to lead her outside.

Bowen remained behind, watching Ashlon place soiled instruments into a used wash basin and then bag everything for later cleaning and sanitizing. She looked up at him with an embarrassed grimace, remembering what Janey had been harping at her about all evening. She sighed, reluctantly deciding her erstwhile dance partner deserved at least an apology for her sudden panicked bolt. At least, he was giving her the opportunity to be contrite. Whether he accepted it was another matter.

She moved around the edge of the long table and planted herself on top of it just off to one side of where McAnders steadily observed her every move. Pointedly avoiding his gaze, she took a deep breath.

"I want to apologize for my behavior tonight," she began, licking her lips nervously and looking everywhere except at him.
"It wasn't you, Lord McAnders, believe me. I... um, I have a hard time trusting..."

"Men?" Bowen casually suggested, leaning on the table, one hand lightly brushing Ashlon's leg.

Ashlon slid away from it. "Yes," she hastily said, turning her eyes away from it. "Long story short, I was married to a walking train wreck who abused both me and my daughter. He nearly bankrupted me financially and emotionally before he finally deserted me. I decided I didn't want be involved again for a while after divorcing Wyatt."

"Your former husband?" Bowen gently said with genuine interest. Ashlon was heartened, continuing on in spite of the heat she was experiencing with his closeness.

"Yes." She swallowed hard and squirmed uncomfortably under his unabashedly direct gaze. Her mouth had suddenly gone very dry. "But now, here you are, so unbelievably attentive and interested. Frankly, you scare the hell out of me."

Oh, good grief! Did she actually say those things? Ashlon shrank inside with terrible embarrassment as she reflexively covered her eyes, and opened her mouth again, attempting to say something. Well, there went her vow not to act stupid!

Bowen placed a warm finger over her lips with a gentle smile. Ashlon immediately closed her mouth. She could not have said anything if she tried.

He raised her chin so that their eyes met again. Like before, she was falling deep into those amazing amethyst pools that captured and held her so effortlessly within their depths. His mouth hovered close to hers as he spoke with breath-catching earnestness.

"You are so beautiful, you make my heart ache; you sing like an angel, and I hear your voice with that same heart; when I hold you to me, it is my greatest wish to do so; and when I kiss you as I have tonight, you feel my own deepest desire. I harbor no duplicity, only as honest an intention as I can offer. I ask only that you allow me into your trust, and perhaps honor me with your company tonight." He enclosed Ashlon's hands in his and pressed them to his lips.

She was speechless, awed by the emotion of his tender words, the warmth of his hands wrapped around hers, the soft kiss he placed on them. Something inside her was opening to his persistence, beginning to accept this remarkable man and allow him through her wall of resistance.

"Wow!" Janey said dreamily after a long pause. "I think I'll go kill Jorge." With a deep sigh, she picked up the bag Ashlon had dropped and put a hand on her friend's shoulder, leaning in toward Bowen. "If my friend here doesn't thaw anytime soon, let me know so I can work on her, okay?" She chucked Ashlon on the ear and quickly left the barn.

"Ow again!" Ashlon yelled after her as she rubbed her stinging ear on her shoulder, and heard Jorge's laugh float back from the direction of the Land Cruiser parked off next to Janey's car. Within minutes, however, both vehicles pulled away and sped down to the turnoff, disappearing on the road into town.

Ashlon stared with sheer disbelief as her ride vanished, silently vowing a multitude of heinous, painful punishments on her former best friend when she caught up with her again. When she glanced back at Bowen, he flashed a knowing half-smile and released her hands to extract a set of car keys from a leather pouch hanging at his one side. Grinning sheepishly, Ashlon reached behind her and retrieved her coat and handbag from a folding chair. She pulled on her coat and shouldered her bag, then slipped from the table. Bowen once more took her hand and tucked it into his arm as he had Monday evening, inclining his head toward the barn entrance.

They slowly walked to the parking lot behind the barn, now nearly empty of cars except for the cleanup committee, and, of course, Justin's and Merle's oversized pickups. The brilliant full moon had an orange tint to it that made it look like a giant pumpkin, its ghostly glow lighting their way down the path toward the lot. It was really cold tonight. Ashlon could see her breath as they walked. She shivered and drew her coat closer around her with her free hand, closely hugging Bowen's arm as the chill reached through the thin fabric of her costume. Funny, it didn't seem to bother him even though he was in shirt sleeves, and his hand was still warm as it held hers in the crook of his arm. And she couldn't see his breath. As big as he was, he'd have triple her lung volume. Oh well, maybe he was just cold-tolerant and a shallow breather, she reasoned. They reached the parking lot and his car, a Cadillac Seville that gleamed under the orange moonlight.

"Very nice," Ashlon commented with shivering admiration. Bowen released her arm and pressed a button on his key control. The inside light popped on as the doors unlocked. Bowen opened the front passenger side door and motioned for her to enter. She'd just lowered herself into the seat when she abruptly raised her head, looking around the area. Something was very wrong; the night breeze had shifted, and she'd smelled something strange in it. It prickled at her face and tugged at her as she stood, moving her head from side to side, listening to the night around her and Bowen. There was a general feeling of unrest out there, something out of balance. She circled around the car door, her face turned questioning into the breeze for only a moment. She held up her hand when Bowen looked at her questioningly—he remained silent. Looking around the parking lot she smelled something that made the hair stand up on the back of her neck—a faint metallic odor in the otherwise crystal clean night breeze blowing in her face—sort of coppery, like fresh...

And then, she spotted it across the lot, a car parked facing the Cadillac, and on the passenger side, something, or someone, hanging out of the open passenger door, sprawled on the hard top.

Ashlon moved away from Bowen, running toward it. In the brilliant glow of the orange moon, it was plainly visible, the carnage making her gag and gasp in utter horror: Cherlyn Mathis, or what was left of her, lay sprawled on her back, her neck twisted at an impossible angle after something had attacked her, pulled her from the car, and literally torn her to pieces. Bowen caught her as she lurched away from that ghastly scene, falling into him and burying her face into his shoulder. She must have screamed—she didn't remember—because Justin and Merle suddenly appeared, followed by several of the cleanup crew.

Bowen directed them to the bloody scene, then pulled Ashlon into his arms and rapidly pulled her back to his waiting car. She was shaking badly as he held her protectively, and she was moaning. "No, no, no, no...!", her face buried in his chest, her arms hugging his neck with a surprisingly strong grip, refusing to let go of him as he attempted to lower her into the car.

He looked around to see if anyone was watching them, and then bent to Ashlon, his lips brushing her ear. "Sleep now," he softly whispered.

Ashlon went completely limp against him. He removed her arms from around his neck and tucked her neatly into the passenger seat, the passive action seat belt catching her as he closed the door. In the space of a heartbeat, he was in the driver's seat and speeding away before the police arrived.

He took her to his house, installing her in a guest room. He changed into a more conventional set of clothing, then called Mr. Stanley, informing him that Ashlon would be there in the morning when he came in. Bowen briefly described why she was there so the old man wouldn't assume the worst about her presence or his motives. He judiciously omitted the messier parts of Ashlon's discovery of the victim in the grain and feed parking lot. Mr. Stanley offered to call the doctor, which Bowen decided would be a prudent idea given the shock Ashlon had suffered.

She would sleep until he wakened her. He'd made sure of that. For now, he had to question who or what had killed that young woman and left her such a bloody mess. There were several creatures he could think of that could render a human to such a state, and no doubt the law enforcement people would blame a feral dog or some maniac for the crime. He had darker, more unnatural causes in mind.

Bowen had sensed the 'otherness' as soon as they were outside. But he had ignored it; it was of no consequence to him. Ashlon, however, had utterly surprised him and stumbled onto it. This was a complication he could well do without. So far, he had managed to conceal his own activities quite effectively while pursuing his quest, and he wanted it to stay that way.

Whoever, or whatever, was responsible for this outrage had deliberately chosen that person and that area. But why? Mere target of opportunity? His automobile was parked fairly near to where it happened. A coincidence? He hoped so. But every possibility had to be considered. And he needed to know that his own nature wasn't in jeopardy until he'd gotten what he came for.

The door chimes rang throughout the house. That would be the doctor. Bowen departed the bedroom and quickly descended the stairs, crossed the foyer to the entrance hall, and opened the door. Jorge and Janey were waiting under the archway, and Bowen waved them inside without a word, taking them immediately up to the guestroom were Ashlon lay sleeping on top of the damask bedspread of a heavy four-poster with the curtains drawn back.

Bowen crossed soundlessly to the other side of the bed and sat on the edge next to Ashlon's inert form, lightly stroking her hair. He briefly described what had happened in the parking lot.

"Is she unconscious?" Jorge inquired as he removed a stethoscope, blood pressure cuff, and a small penlight from a black bag he had set on the small bedside table.

"No, doctor, merely sleeping," Bowen replied without taking his eyes off Ashlon. "I have certain... abilities, you might say, to plant a suggestion, allowing her to withdraw from that terrible sight for a while. She was most distraught, and I thought it wise to calm her in this manner."

Jorge's eyebrows arched. "Hypnosis?"

"Something similar to it," Bowen replied evenly, "and easy enough to do even if the subject is in a highly agitated state of mind. Miss Isaacs was near hysteria after what she'd found. Since I did not want the police to question her tonight, I brought her here instead of taking her home. No doubt the police will
want to question her eventually, but not tonight."

"Good move," Janey said, eyeing him steadily. They'd driven by Ashlon's house and been very puzzled by the squad car already parked there with its lights flashing and an officer ringing the doorbell. Then, Jorge's pager service had called him, relaying Mr. Stanley's message.

Jorge performed a quick assessment, satisfying himself that Ashlon would be alright until morning, when Mr. Stanley would be there to give him a progress report on her status. He put away his equipment and nodded to Janey, taking her hand and pulling her with difficulty to the bedroom door. Why was she being so resistant all of a sudden? Bowen reluctantly rose from the bed and escorted them through the gallery and downstairs to the front door.

"By the way," Janey abruptly said, her eyes narrowing as she looked up at Bowen, who was waiting impatiently to close the door, "I'll be here first thing in the morning, too," she curtly said, and then allowed Jorge to lead her back out to his vehicle.

After they reached the SUV, Jorge glared irritably at her. "What was that all about?" he said. "He's got everything under control, and Ash is okay for tonight."

Janey glared back at him. "You don't know her the way I do. No one has ever been able to hypnotize her. She can't even tie on a decent drunk. She's got an iron resistance that's impossible to penetrate. The only way to break it down is to knock her out cold. And this guy says some creepy mumbo jumbo and she's out like a light?" She climbed into the vehicle, slammed the door closed for emphasis, folded her arms crossly over her chest as she slumped down into her seat, and ignored Jorge as he slipped into the driver's side.

He started up the engine and pulled away from the curb, heading back into town. "I thought you said this guy would be good for her," he continued with their discussion. "Aren't you being just a little overprotective?"

Janey shrugged. "I don't know. If you could've heard what he said at the party earlier this evening, you would've thought he really wanted her to like him."

"But now? He takes her to his house for safeguarding after doing—what did you call it? —'creepy mumbo jumbo', and now you've got your panties in a wad. I don't see the problem."

They pulled up to Janey's building as the town clock struck one. She looked over at Jorge and shook her head. "Call it a hunch. Call it woman's intuition. Whatever. I don't like the way it feels."

Disgruntled, she exited the vehicle and rang the buzzer to be let into her building. She was vastly relieved as they were immediately admitted. She quickly closed the door behind them, smiling with satisfaction when she heard the sound of the electronic lock engage again. It helped lessen some of that creepy, jittery feeling Ashlon liked to call 'that Halloween feeling'. It was strong tonight. And it wasn't just because of the full moon, either. Maybe Jorge would help her get rid of it later with his own unique brand of medicine.

Chapter 14

I want to wake up now.
No, my love. You must stay here with me a while longer, where you are safe.

She felt warm and safe, held by a strong, loving presence, trying to lull her into complacency.

Who are you? Where am I?
You know who I am. And we are in a place between waking and sleeping.
Why are you keeping me here?
To watch over you and keep you close. Why?
I took you away from something terrible. I'll deal with it like I always have.
Do not fight me, beloved. What did you say?
Do not fight me.

Ashlon abruptly sat up in the bed, gasping with the effort of waking, shaking out the cobwebs just as Mr. Stanley opened the door and peeked into the room. Why all these weird dreams all of a sudden?

"Where am I?" she said, so groggy she fell back and hit her head soundly on the heavy carved headboard. "Shit!" she spat with a pained grimace, painfully rubbing the back of her head.

Oh yeah, that woke her up!

"Lord McAnders thought you would sleep until he returns. It's just a few minutes before eight am, Miss Ashlon. And you're here at McAnders House.

He brought you here last night after that terrible discovery outside the grain and feed barn. He called me immediately to let me know what had occurred and why he'd brought you here. The doctor's been and gone already, and your friend is downstairs with me in the kitchen. She thought you might need a change of clothes."

Ashlon glanced down at herself, realizing she was still in her gypsy costume, which was now hopelessly rumpled and missing some of the spangles somewhere on the bedspread. She felt grubby, too, desperately in need of a shower.

As if reading her mind, Mr. Stanley showed her where the bathroom was and placed several towels on the rack. He handed her a canvas bag with a change of fresh clothes in it. "Your friend brought these things for you." Mr. Stanley informed her.

"Now you know why she's my best friend," Ashlon said with a weak smile and trying to sound congenial.

"She said you've done the same for her," Mr. Stanley said affably. "We'll see you in the kitchen, my dear." He turned and departed.

However, the smile faded from her lips as she stumbled to the bathroom and locked herself inside. After shedding her costume, she stepped into the shower and hastily washed, skipping her hair. Refreshed and less foggy now, she returned to the bedroom, quickly dressed, and stuffed her rumpled costume into the canvas bag. She departed the bedroom, heading to the kitchen where Janey and Mr. Stanley were talking about the previous night's events. Janey motioned for Mr. Stanley to stay seated and rose to get Ashlon a cup of fresh coffee when she appeared and sat down across from the old man at the small breakfast table.

"What do you think?" Mr. Stanley said, waving a hand to the redone kitchen. "It's simple, but very user-friendly." The kitchen was indeed small and efficient, with stainless and black appliances, and from the looks of most of them, still unused. The breakfast nook was furnished with a small trestle table, a dragonfly Tiffany-style dining lamp suspended over it. The walls were painted winter white, with fawn tiling as a backsplash behind the two-basin sink, and a tiled wall with some kind of fruity/grapey design painted under the glaze gleaming from behind the stove and a suspended exhaust vent. A large stainless-steel refrigerator/freezer sat behind the small, centrally located preparation area, a brushed copper pan rack hanging above it.

Ashlon took the coffee from Janey, knowing her old friend was waiting for her comments. However, it wasn't what he expected. "Mr. Stanley, what do you know of Lord McAnders?" She inquired as she carefully sipped the hot brew. It was really good and helped to clear the remaining fuzziness from her head.

The old man frowned at first, but then became thoughtful. "Not very much, actually. We were introduced one evening by his lawyer when they came to look at the house. He moved in about a week after that and asked me if I was familiar with its history. I showed him our drawings and notes." He looked justifiably pleased as he spoke.

"Do you expect him back soon?"

The old man sighed. "Unfortunately, no, my dear. I never see him until evening when he returns. I've assumed he has business to attend to during the day and leaves before my daily arrival."

Ashlon nodded. "And he returns just before you leave in the evening?"

"Yes, that has been his routine. Why do you ask?"
She shrugged and continued to sip her coffee. "He disappeared from the party for a while last night. Did you know that?"

Mr. Stanley's eyes narrowed as his face took on a troubled expression. "He informed me he'd received a call on his cell that his lawyer needed to speak with him immediately last evening. Something about a filing deadline. Really, Miss Ashlon. I don't see where this is going."

"I have to be honest with you, Mr. Stanley," Ashlon said as she rose and put her coffee cup in the sink, and returned to the table to pick up the canvas bag from under the table. "When the police come by here today, they're going to ask you the same things. If you or Lord McAnders can't produce a verifiably good alibi about his unexpected absence last night, guess what?"

Mr. Stanley gasped with realization. "I can't believe that, Miss Ashlon. Lord McAnders is a nobleman with an old family name to preserve."

She leaned in close to him and put her hand on his shoulder. "He's also the new guy in town," she said as gently as she could muster. "The attacks on those women from the Scupper, and now this. The only thing the cops are going to see is an escalating pattern."

And now that I'm suspicious, too, she thought morosely, I wouldn't blame them one little bit.

"Oh dear, oh dear!" Mr. Stanley worried. "I should inform him of this dis turbing situation when he returns tonight."

Ah, youth and old age; so innocent and so blindsided. Ashlon and Janey both shook their heads vigorously. Janey had been closely following Ashlon's questioning and was horrified that she and Jorge had left Ashlon in this place overnight with McAnders.

"Please don't, Mr. Stanley," Ashlon patiently said. "He's been okay with you so far, but if he is responsible, it might set him off. Why don't you go home and wait for him to contact you? When he does, call the police that he's available for questioning, alright?" She was acutely aware of the old man's distress and con- fusion, because she was experiencing something similar. Just when you think you've found a guy you might like and trust, he turns out to maybe be a whacko. She should've listened to her caution and gotten a ride with someone else. But, oh no! She had to let herself get guilted into associating with someone who might be wanted on two continents! Well, maybe that was stretching things a bit. Leave that one for the cops.

Mr. Stanley closed his eyes, his apprehension apparent. "I shall do what you suggest, although I hope you are wrong."

Ashlon gently squeezed his shoulder. "So do I, Mr. Stanley. Believe me. But better to be safe than sorry until this thing is cleared up. I'll call you later." She kissed the top of his head, motioning to Janey that they were leaving.

Janey followed Ashlon out of the house into the morning light and down to the street. Janey's old Volvo was parked at the curb.

"Wanna lift, Ash?" she asked.

Ashlon lifted her face into the sun, inhaling the cold morning air scented with the remnants of dead leaves and pine. Good grief! She'd spent the night in that place with McAnders! Talk about unnerving! "Yeah, I'll ride with you, Janey. I need your company."

Janey unlocked the passenger door and then circled around to the driver's side. She quickly unlocked and opened her door, sliding into the seat. Without a word, she started her car and did a U-turn, heading toward Ashlon's street.

They rode in silence until they reached Ashlon's house. Janey parked behind Ashlon's Wrangler, but left the motor running. She turned to Ashlon with consternation in her expression.

"Talk to me. I know you had an excellent reason for that line of questioning back there, but I want to know why you did it. That old man is scared."

"He should be," Ashlon said as she turned to her friend. "Something is going on here that's mighty fishy, and it started when his highness moved into this community. Maybe it's just a coincidence. And maybe it was him we saw the day of Emma's funeral, Janey. Remember that shadowy figure up the hill by that crypt?"

Janey nodded slowly. "So what? What's that have to do with anything now?"

Ashlon shook her head. "The attacks on those girls from the Scupper started soon after we spotted him. And then, last night, we found poor Cherlyn. I remember he wanted to get us away from there real fast, but nothing after that. What did he say he did to me?"

"Some kind of hypnosis."

Ashlon licked her lips, her jaw clenched. "The night I was attacked in the cemetery, a guy grabbed me from behind after I'd fallen and hit my head. He hauled me off my feet. Off my feet, Janey, not to them. Someone tall and very strong. He was trying to drag me to the front of that crypt. But when I fought to get free, he said, "Do not fight me." That was all, but suddenly I couldn't move, couldn't scream for help. Nothing! I was like a limp rag dangling from his arms. It was only when I pretended to pass out that he panicked, and I felt his grip relax on me. That's when I disabled him and escaped."

Janey frowned. "I don't see where this is going, Ash."

Ashlon groaned. "I heard those same words when I was struggling to wake up this morning. Somehow, I think he was restraining me with whatever he did. He spoke those same words again, Janey. The same words in the same voice. McAnder's voice." Ashlon sat back in her seat and rubbed her hands over her face, a frustrated groan escaping from her throat.

Janey's mouth dropped open, and she paled with understanding.

Ashlon grimaced. "I'm pretty sure he was the one who attacked me in the cemetery."

Janey's mouth hung open, and her eyes were wide. "You're sure about this?"

Ashlon nodded. "I'm more than sure. That's what gets me, because then I have to wonder what he was going to do. What does he want with me?"

There were no good answers they could come up with. But several things they agreed on: keep the doors locked, and stay as far away from McAnders as humanly possible. Let the police sort it out.

And try not to be out after dark anymore.

Chapter 15

Bowen knew something was wrong when he entered the darkened, silent house that evening. He had quickly gone up to the guest bedroom, finding it empty. How did she break through his hold on her, he wondered uneasily as he went to his own room and used the phone to call Mr. Stanley. The old man sounded glad to hear from him, but Bowen sensed he was withholding something. Repeated questioning was diplomatically diverted until they rang off finally. Only one source of information remained: Ashlon.

He went up to the widow's walk to see if she was home. The night was overcast and rainy, so he was cloaked in total darkness as he looked over the tree line and saw her lights were on. And no other vehicle was parked near hers.

However, as he looked down his own street, he watched a police car approach and park along the curb in front of his house. He'd been expecting this. Moving faster than any human eye could follow, he was ready with the front door opened and the porch lamps on at the front of the house when the policeman came up the walk.

"Good evening, officer," he said cordially, spying the bulge of a shoulder holster under the officer's rumpled overcoat.

The plainclothes officer touched his brow briefly and showed Bowen his badge.

"Bowen McAnders?" he said, his voice distinctly fatigued and his manner clearly at the 'don't need no shit' stage.

"Yes," Bowen replied with equal gravity.
"I'd like to ask you a few questions about last night, sir, if I may." He wouldn't take no for an answer at this point, Bowen could plainly see.

"Of course. Please come in," he said evenly and allowed Anderson to pass through the hallway into the foyer.

Of course, questioning was a waste of time for the officer, much to his consternation. Bowen had an alibi for his absence the previous evening, verified by a call to his lawyer at his home. But it bothered Anderson that this guy was so cool and ready with his pat answers, as if he'd had plenty of practice. But his story jibed with that of that really cute girl he had talked to that afternoon. What was her name? But this guy didn't set well with him, and he made a mental note to do some checking up on McAnders once he was back at the district office. However, for the time being, he had to be satisfied.

When the interview was concluded, Bowen showed him to the door. Ander- son gave him his standard 'don't leave town' speech and departed. Bowen watched until the squad car drove off and then returned to the widow's walk. Time to visit Ashlon, he decided. After talking to that policeman, he needed some answers of his own.

Ashlon, in her pajamas and robe, had just put a mini 4-cheese pizza in the oven and was sipping a glass of wine as she paged through the rest of the Sun- day paper when the doorbell rang. Glancing up at the clock, she frowned with consternation when she saw it was 8:30 in the frickin' pm. Janey and Jorge were in Boston for the night so Janey could get an early start on some shopping she wanted to do before going to work on Tuesday. Mr. Stanley had called her to report that Lord McAnders called him earlier in the evening, and the police had been notified. Other than those two friends, she had no clue whom it could be. The light in the front room was off, however, so she cautiously and quietly sidled up to the bay window and peeked out the edge of the heavy curtains at the front door step. She groaned and considered pretending she wasn't home when she spied McAnders waiting there on her porch getting ready to ring the bell again. He could see her house from the widow's walk, so he knew the lights were on in her room, and her Jeep was parked out front.

Busted, dammit.

Reluctantly, she went to the door and undid the bolt, leaving the sliding chain engaged as she cracked open the door and looked out through the narrow opening. "Yes?" she said, eyeing him suspiciously.

"May I speak with you?" Bowen inquired. His voice was cold and emotionless, sending a frisson up Ashlon's spine. His eyes were deep black, empty pits under his shadowed brow as they stared un-blinking at her.

"Not a good idea," Ashlon nervously said. If those eyes were any indication, she'd be stupid to let him in. But then again, it wouldn't matter if he decided to use his size to just bust in the door like charging through tissue paper. However, the next thing he said blew her away.

"Have I done something to earn your caution? Or insulted you in some way that has lost your regard for me?" he inquired, his voice sounding hurt and very puzzled.

A breeze blew from behind him into the partially open door-way. It caught at his hair and whirled it around his shoulders, making it look alive in the dim porch light, and she could smell his aftershave. His duster billowed around him, making him look like something winged and dangerous, almost unearthly.

He looked like something not of this place or time and would have terrified the bejeezus out of most people. However, nothing much ever really scared her. Even as a kid, she had sought out the hidden and mysterious. And this guy fairly screamed he had a hidden nature. Something inside her stirred, something she had pushed down and re-pressed for far too long—the almost overwhelming need to know, that irritating curiosity which most times got her into so much trouble. Fighting to control it, she looked squarely into that dark face. You're not a kid anymore, she reminded herself. Keep it together.

"Why did you attack me in the cemetery?" she asked directly through gritted teeth, noting his immediate reaction to her question. He had startled, and she thought he might back off. If he did, she'd have the cops on him in a heartbeat. However, he remained where he was, the tension and prolonged silence between them a palpable wall.

Bowen groaned and closed his eyes. "I did not attack you. You saw me in the darkness and took off running. I followed, thinking you might hurt yourself in your panic."

"Well, duh! I never expected to see anyone behind me when I was standing there—in the dark! You suddenly appeared without saying a word, and okay, I took off. You didn't say anything like "excuse me", or, "hey there!" You chased me up the damn hill! Why did you drag me to the crypt after I'd fallen? And what the hell did you do to me so that I couldn't fight you?" She glared with righteous anger at him, her nostrils flaring, her eyes wide and hostile.

Bowen sighed heavily. "I was concerned for you when I saw you out there alone. And then, when you panicked and ran, I went after you and saw you fall and strike your head on the stone. It was bleeding badly. I had some supplies under those pines near my family crypt. I had been doing some maintenance on the edifice and did not finish until late. It had been many years since any repair or cleaning had been done on the door or locks. There was level ground there, better for laying you down to look at that head wound. As to your curious paralysis, I took advantage of several pressure points I knew because of my concern for a serious head injury when you fought me so violently. I would never harm you, Ashlon. You must believe that."

He sounded honestly passionate, and his explanation was so plausible that Ashlon stepped away from the door for a moment to consider her position. Gee, and she'd worked up a good mad on, too. There he stood with those amazing, imploring eyes, everything explained. Her resolve was slipping away, replaced by—what? Remorse? Maybe a little guilt?

The timer bell went off in the kitchen, informing her that her pizza was ready.

Peering out the doorway again, she rapidly said, "I'll be right back," and closed the door. Now she had some space to consider her next move. She took her time getting to the kitchen, removed her pizza from the oven, and placed it on top of the stove, and then took a few more seconds to sort out her feelings in light of this new evidence. Finally, she shook her head with resignation as she ran her fingers through her hair, knowing she'd probably kick herself later for the decision she came to.

Returning to the front door, she undid the slide bolt and the chain, and opened the door, standing aside with a guarded expression as she watched McAnders. Could she kick his ass if he tried anything? Well, she'd find out if it came to it. And if necessary, she had ready access to several fireplace pokers.

Bowen didn't move. He stood there staring expectantly at Ashlon and waiting… for what? A written invitation? She suppressed saying it aloud as she said instead, "Well?"

He tipped his head to one side. "Invite me in, please."

"Oh for the love of …!" she exclaimed irritably. "Please, enter my humble domicile. And wipe your feet." She turned away, soundly closing the door behind Bowen after he entered, then returned to the kitchen.

"I must be out of my fuckin' mind," she grumbled as she plated her pizza, then slid the tray noisily into the sink. She took the plate to the table, set it next to her wine glass, and flopped back into her chair.

Bowen remained in the living room, standing in front of the closed door, his hands folded in front of him as he casually looked around before moving into the kitchen. Ashlon motioned to a chair on the other side of the table because her mouth was stuffed with pizza. Bowen moved around the table and looked down at her with mild distaste, then at the chair, his expression doubtful.

Ashlon swallowed, then took a sip of her wine. "What's the matter?" she said as she wiped her mouth on a paper napkin. "Afraid of cooties? It may be old, but it's clean. I can personally vouch for it."

Bowen lowered himself into the chair and crossed his arms on the table, gazing across it at Ashlon. She involuntarily giggled—the sight of this tall, broad, brooding figure in her vastly smaller domicile was so completely incongruous compared with his normal habitat; she almost felt sorry for him. Almost.

"What is that?" he said, pointing at the remnant of pizza on her plate and wrinkling his nose.

"My supper, thank you very much," she growled back at him. "You caught me in the middle of a meal."

"Could you possibly stop eating for a moment, please? There is something we need to discuss."

Ashlon sat back in her chair as she licked some stringy cheese from her lips. "Why?"

"Because you are still doubtful of my truthfulness and sincerity when I say that what happened in the cemetery was a simple misunderstanding. Because you left my home this morning after what occurred last night and sent the police to see me. Let us start with these."

Ashlon took another sip of her wine. "Look, I told you last night I have trust issues. It's going to take some time for me to work through them. And you're not the only one the police questioned, you know. That detective sat here and grilled me for a good hour before he was satisfied, I didn't know anything about Cherlyn, other than I helped her get medical treatment for a personal problem. He also questioned Grady Roberts and the guy Cherlyn left with last night. So don't feel you're being picked on. He'd have found out about you anyway, even if Mr. Stanley or I hadn't called the cops. You're the new guy in town, so don't get so huffy about having to account for your whereabouts last night."

Bowen relaxed back into his chair and actually managed to muster a half-smile as he watched Ashlon finish her meal, put her plate in the sink, and wash her hands.

She refilled her wine glass and returned to the table. McAnders was placated for the time being, it seemed. Now, she just wanted him to leave. He was a complication she just wasn't ready for at this stage of her life, she silently groused as she stared down at the scratched red table surface for a moment.

She looked up at him, her expression troubled. Then again, it would be nice to have someone weirder than herself to talk to. And, boy, did he qualify!

"You know, I'm not a stranger to death—traumas, old age, disease, suicides. I guess I should thank you for whatever you did to me last night. I couldn't get the look on her face out of my head, like she'd been absolutely stunned by what killed her." Her hands were shaking as she cupped her wine glass between them.

Bowen reached out and placed his hands over hers. He noted with some satisfaction that she didn't pull away, but looked down at the table top again.

"What are you thinking?" he gently asked.

C'mon, 'fess up! She looked up at him and shrugged. "I guess I'm kind of okay you came by tonight. Now, don't go thinking we'd make a cute couple or something. But, ever since the funeral, I have invented reasons to stay away from here. Or, I create projects to keep me busy when I'm not working. Like those Jacks O'lanterns at the festival; those kept me really busy last Sunday. Today, I cleaned every corner of this place and even de-slimed my refrigerator and scrubbed the oven. And if you hadn't stopped by, I was going to try to get thoroughly drunk, which may take a while, and then pass out on the couch since I'm not working tomorrow." She looked up at him with a small, sad smile as she freed one hand, gripped the wine glass, and drained it.

Bowen felt such a deep stab of compassion at that moment it took everything in him to keep from sweeping her into her arms and confessing his heart openly. He wanted so much to make her pain go away, surround her with his presence, and banish the sadness and grief still lingering in her eyes. But he held back. The time wasn't right, and if he moved too quickly, she'd turn and run so fast he'd never be able to catch her again.

"However, since I've welcomed you into my home, the least I can do is stay reasonably sober until you leave." Ashlon stood and freed her other hand, swaying unsteadily for a moment as she shuffled to the sink and deposited the glass next to the plate, and rinsed them both with warm water. Ah yes! Making progress on the drunken part!

After she dried her hands on her robe, she grabbed the nearly empty wine bottle and headed for the living room, flopping onto the couch. She carelessly waved her hand around her head. "Go ahead and take a look if you like. Not much to it, but it's all mine." She took a long slug off the bottle and watched as Bowen got up from the table, straightened his trouser legs, pulled down his long coat, and casually moved into the living room. He looked at her framed pictures and the little knick-knacks on the fireplace mantle, curiously studied an elaborate candelabrum with nine candle holders on it, picked up a small glass pumpkin, and smiled as he turned it in his hand. After placing it back on the mantle, he crossed behind the sofa to the stairs, restraining with a lot of difficulty the urge to touch her hair again. Instead, he briefly noted two tall bookcases set at right angles to each other in the corner next to the fireplace. They were stuffed on every shelf. Adult reading had been placed on the upper shelves, and children's books took up the two lower shelves of each bookcase. Moving on, he glanced at her questioningly when he reached the stairs to the second floor. She waved him on.

He climbed the stairs, ignoring, or simply not seeing, a mirror Ashlon had installed on the gently inclined ceiling portion when Emma was a toddler. It was angled just right to reflect where the top stair met the upstairs hall so that she could see if Emma was at the top of the stairs trying to climb over the security gate. As Bowen passed under it, Ashlon glanced over at it out of habit—and then glanced over at it again, her eyes widening in shock. Bowen had passed directly under it, she was sure. She put the wine bottle on the floor, stood up, and went over to the stairs, climbing to the level of the mirror. She looked directly into it and saw her own reflection just fine. She must be drunker than she thought she was!

"Did you paint this door?" Bowen's deep voice came from the far end of the upstairs hallway, filtering through her confusion.

She licked her lips as she looked up the stairs, her curiosity so piqued now she just knew she was going to get herself into some real trouble. She couldn't help it, though. This was a baffling mystery that, added to the other things that had happened concerning Bowen, was too intriguing not to investigate.

"I designed it with Emma's favorite flowers," she managed to reply, checking the shaking in her voice. She heard the rattle of a door handle and the creak as it was opened. Quickly ascending the stairs, she turned right and crossed the short hallway, stopping outside Emma's room. The clothes and furniture were gone now, but she hadn't repainted yet or taken out the kid carpet. That would come in time, small steps as she reconciled Emma's passing.

Bowen stood for a moment in the middle of the room, looked around him briefly, then crossed to the long closet. He stood before it, raised his head as if sniffing the air, then moved back to the center of floor, kneeling down to inspect the carpet, rubbing his hands on it. When he was satisfied, he nodded to himself and stood again. He moved smoothly from the room up to Ashlon, catching her completely off guard when he wrapped his arms around her and hugged her firmly against him. His lips brushed her hair and settled on her cheek.

"There was love in that room," he said, his deep, gentle voice filled with emotion. "I can feel it in the very fabric of the carpet and the warmth that still remains. Your heart and soul made it a special place for her, didn't it? Even in her last days, the love surrounded her so completely there was never any fear." He brushed his cheek against hers, softly touching his lips to it.

Ashlon couldn't move or say anything. She was melting into his embrace, drawing unexpected comfort from his words and the emotion behind them. It was happening again.

Each time she tried to distance herself from him, he inveigled his way back into her good graces by being so damned insightful and charming and compassionate that he confused her all the more. No man had ever been able to weasel his way in this far. But here he was, this incredible, mysterious stranger who persisted beyond where other men would have thrown up their hands in disgust and bolted. She felt his compassion, reveled in the warmth of his arms, the touch of his lips. Her wall of resistance was crumbling faster and faster.

"Why?" she whispered, very puzzled as she gazed up into his face, captured and held by those eyes that held so many secrets, but expressed so much as well.

Bowen kissed the top of her head and pressed her closer to him.

"Because I see in you a loneliness that mirrors my own," he said so earnestly, she trembled in his arms. "Let me fill that emptiness and give you reason to smile again." He'd spoken with conviction, from the depths of a solitude that had become interminable. Yes, he was now very sure of one immutable fact: he would no longer suffer his lonely existence without her. You are mine, he adamantly declared as his lips caressed her hair, her face.

A clock on the mantle downstairs struck the hour with tinkling, melodic chimes. It had been a gift from Ashlon's grandmother that had survived every move she'd made. Ashlon turned away from Bowen, holding his hand as she led him down the hallway, passing a full-length mirror that had been hidden and unseen by Bowen as he'd made his way to Emma's room. It had been covered by Ashlon after Emma's death, a ritual of her people to hide any signs of vanity during a mourning period. Tonight, she'd finally pulled off the sheet as she'd passed it on her way down the hall to Bowen. He saw it too late as they moved passed the mirror to the stairs, caught in the glare of the hallway light.

Ashlon abruptly stopped, staring into it with mute disbelief, her breathing coming faster. Her eyes darted to Bowen's face and back to the mirror, desperately twisting her hand, trying to pull it from his. Bowen tightened his grip, his face becoming a dark mask as he drew himself up to his full height, his eyes hardening as he stared at her.

"No!" she breathed in wide-eyed terror as she struggled and clawed at his hand. "It all fits! Dear heaven, it all fits!" She shrank away from him, death staring down at her through glowing, narrowed amethyst eyes. Or worse than death.

"Ashlon!" he choked, his voice ragged with new despair. It was no use—he was painfully certain that whatever chance had existed virtually vanished in that one terrible moment of discovery, leaving him only one alternative. "I'm so sorry, my love!" His heart-sick whisper moved around her with the terrifying certainty of what he intended to do next.

Bowen pulled her forcefully into his now deadly embrace, baring his fangs, expecting little resistance. However, he had forgotten Ashlon's iron-willed resistance to any coercion, hypnotic or otherwise, and couldn't possibly know of the old folklore passed on to her over the years by her bubbe, her grandmother. She struggled furiously and managed to twist herself around so that she gazed defiantly into his face.

"In the name of the Holy One, I withdraw your invitation into my house!"She screamed at him as his fangs brushed her warm, pulsating throat.

The effect was electrifying and immediate. Bowen reared back, dropping Ashlon as he was yanked away by some unnatural force across the hall and down the stairs. He struggled, but was unable to stop his jerking progress as he stumbled at the bottom, caught himself, and involuntarily opened the front door, backing out of it and down the steps to the sidewalk.

Ashlon picked herself off the floor and ran down after him, slamming the door and frantically locking it. She stood, bracing her back against it, shaking uncontrollably with a terror more intense than she could ever remember feeling. Her grandmother had told her so many stories about such things, stories told to her by her mother and father, where she'd lived and grown up in an old shtetl in Eastern Europe. Dibbuks and golems, ghosts and imps surrounded her tales of the old country.

And vampires—restive spirits that rose to prey on living souls in defiance of holy law.

But, her grandmother's stories of those dark, ugly creatures had never mentioned anything like the beautiful and terrifying Bowen McAnders. Ashlon slid to the floor and leaned against the wall, her heart feeling like it had been ripped out of her chest again. How could such a cruel joke be played on her like this?

"Is this some kind of sick cosmic joke?" she yelled at the front door and began pounding on it as hard as she could. "What have I done wrong? Who did I piss off? I want some answers, dammit!"

Of course, there weren't any. There was only the silence around her as she exhausted herself with screaming and pummeling the front door until her fists ached.

In the short time she'd known him she'd actually connected with him, someone who genuinely wanted to be with her. Hell, he'd even come to her house and accepted her explanation for the police visiting him, for her reluctance to associate with him. And after what he said after seeing Emma's empty room, she'd have let him stay in a New York minute. And then the ball dropped.

She stood up, bracing one hand on the wall as she wiped her face on the sleeve of her robe. Taking a deep breath, she resolutely turned her back to the door and returned to her sofa, plunking onto the soft cushions. Picking up the nearly empty bottle of wine from the coffee table, she tipped it back and drained it, then dropped it on the floor and stretched out on the couch.

No. It was absurd. She couldn't and wouldn't accept such an absurd notion of a monster in the McAnders House. He was only a pathetic wanna be psycho poser playing the ultimate mind game with her for his own sick amusement. She'd been suckered by his good looks, petted and manipulated by a pro. And she'd nearly bought it. She would bust him big time if he showed his face anywhere in her vicinity ever again.

And then, a troubling random thought crept in through a crack in her determination: What if ...?

No. Not going there again, ever. Fact was fact, and fable was fable. She pulled a throw off the back of the couch, curled in it, and fell into an uneasy sleep.

Chapter 16

The next two weeks passed in a haze as Ashlon buried herself in her work, picking up several new patients and staying away from her house for long hours, sometimes not getting home until late in the evening and collapsing into bed. Fortunately, one of her patients was in hospice and had required almost around-the-clock monitoring since the family was having a hard time dealing with what was to come, requiring her to practically live in until he'd passed peacefully late one night. All the arrangements had already been made in preparation for this eventuality, so Ashlon's role became a supportive one for the family as they went through the difficult tasks of the viewing and internment. She stayed with them every step of the way, passing on to them the empathy she'd developed from her own loss only a few short weeks ago.

Janey was beside herself with frustration at this sudden surge of busyness that prevented her from contacting Ashlon except by cell messages—pleading messages, funny messages, insulting messages expressing her anger with Ashlon's unexplained burst of work. Once, she'd even gone to McAnders House and spoken to Mr. Stanley about anything developing between Bowen and Ashlon she should know about. No, Mr. Stanley had responded with a perplexed frown. If anything, they had done a complete one-eighty. No contact between them whatsoever after the Harvest Dance

Since the police investigation cleared Lord McAnders of any link to Cherlyn's murder, Mr. Stanley had been able to relax and enjoy his responsibilities again. But Lord McAnders had changed. Oh, he was still cordial and polite. But there was a new cautious distance, like he was waiting and watching for something, making him too often curt and impatient. He was clearly unhappy with something that was beyond his power to change. Ashlon had not been back to the house since the night of the murder.

And then another body turned up. This time, it was discovered by a jogger as he ran along the county road that ran out past the cemetery. It was half-concealed in the mud and leaves in a drainage ditch next to the road, a few miles outside of town. The runner had smelled it before he'd found it and had sped away in horror before phoning the police once he'd seen it was human. Though partially gnawed by forest animals and working on an insect population, the corpse was identified as an old woman who lived alone up the road from Irma's place. In addition, the coroner's report indicated the time of death was approximately one to two days after Cherlyn's. Ashlon hacked into the police files on the case while taking some badly needed downtime at Irma's restaurant for coffee, brioche, and a slice of spinach quiche fresh from the oven.

"Girl, you are going to work yourself to death!" Irma admonished her as she took a break from some pecan cinnamon rolls she'd put to proofing. "What kind of life is that for a pretty girl like you? And what's come of that nice McAnders fella you danced with at the party? Grady told me about him and was really upset that he'd gotten only one dance with you."

Ashlon looked up briefly at Irma from the laptop screen and frowned. "McAnders isn't what I expected," she said, licking some quiche off her lower lip, adding, "And Grady was too busy to ask me for another dance." She dropped her eyes back to the screen. Hmm. Interesting.

Irma completely missed the dripping irony with her last statement. "Well, then, sugar!" she exclaimed happily as she patted Ashlon's hand. "How about I tell him to get his butt in gear and ask you out?"

Ashlon's attention was fixed on the coroner's report. She glanced up briefly at Irma again. "Hmm?" This recent victim had been mauled by some type of large animal, she read in the coroner's report. Just like Cherlyn. What the heck was going on in their little community?

"He's been so mopey and grumpy lately, I need to get him out of the house," Irma complained.

Ashlon was confused, not following the flow. "Who?" "Hello there, Earth to Ashlon. I'm talking about Grady!"

"Oh, yeah. Sorry, Irma." Ashlon closed her notebook and took a sip of her coffee to wake up a little more. "I've been so busy lately I haven't had time for anything but eating and sleeping."

"Well, then!" the older woman happily exclaimed. "I'll have him call you." She rose to her feet and toddled back to the kitchen, humming to herself.

Ashlon briefly wondered what she'd just gotten herself into, then re-opened her laptop and immersed herself in the pictures from the crime scene and the police reports until she'd committed them to memory. In the back of her mind, something was itching about the murders that she couldn't quite bring into focus. She yawned widely, then reached for the carafe of coffee and poured a warm-up.

The door to the eatery opened and closed with a jingle of the small bell hanging above it. A shadow passed Ashlon's table, barely catching her notice. However, a firm smack to the back of her head definitely got her attention.

"What the hell!" she swore, glaring up at her assailant, who merely smirked at her and sat down in the chair on the other side of the table. Ashlon rubbed the tender spot where that firm hand had contacted it.

"I am totally pissed at you," Janey groused as she liberated a clean coffee cup and saucer from a neighboring table and helped herself to the coffee carafe.

"Sorry," Ashlon mumbled half-heartedly as she pushed aside the laptop and folded her hands on the table. She couldn't meet Janey's eyes, guiltily focusing on her hands instead as she nervously tapped the table.

"Not good enough!" Janey spats back at her. "We're friends, re-member? Friends tell things and support each other no matter what. Something really awful happened to you, and it's driving you nuts! You're never home; you don't return my messages, even the nasty ones. Nothing! Nada! Zip! C'mon, spill!" She glared at Ashlon, waiting.

Ashlon balled her hands into fists. "I can't."

Janey's face turned livid. "I don't want to sound whiney or anything, Ash, but this sucks donkey balls. What can't you tell me?"

Hoo boy! This was one Latina with a hair-trigger temper! Ashlon turned her face away for a moment, thinking, deciding. Janey was right—friends tell, regardless of how unbelievable or how much of a nutcase it might make one look like. She took a deep breath, looking up again. "Okay. You know how when you're a kid, the world is a great place with adventure and fun, and your parents are always keeping you from doing something stupid or dangerous? And they give you this lecture about the bogeyman if you misbehave? Or, in your case, El Chupacabra or the closet monster."

"Okay, Ash, I know this is going somewhere, but I can't see it," Janey said impatiently.

"Shut up and let me finish." Ashlon rubbed her face, thinking. "And then you get older and they tell you other stories. My grandmother told me so many great scary tales from the old country and all the dark things that roamed it looking for non-righteous people to corrupt or eat or whatever. I used to love them and being scared out of my wits. I loved Halloween because of her stories. I read about the old pagan beliefs surrounding them and came to see that my people weren't so far removed from them as I'd been taught. Only they believed in many spirits or gods, and my people didn't."

"Boring. Interesting, but boring. Get to your point."

"I'm getting to it." Ashlon sighed heavily and gulped down the remainder of her coffee. Janey quickly refilled her cup and shoved the cream pitcher over to her.

"Thanks," Ashlon mumbled as she poured a liberal dose of it into her coffee. "You nailed it right on the head. I haven't been myself lately because something happened. I've been staying away from my house and trying to sort it all out, but it's just not working. Janey, I'm thinking there really are things out there that go bump in the night. But what if they're not the myths and fairytales our folks told us to scare us? What if they're real and all around us and we choose to ignore them until they bite us in the ass and yell 'BOO'?"

"You must have had one hell of a scare, Ash. And, I know that very little scares you, so you better explain this," Janey demanded impatiently, pounding her fist on the table for emphasis, splashing Ashlon's coffee on the snowy white tablecloth. Ashlon motioned for her friend to move her chair over closer to her. Once that had been done, she leaned in close and opened her suspicions to Janey.

Mineau had had enough of the raucous behavior out front, politely asking Ashlon and Janey to please leave. Irma couldn't say anything to change her daughter's mind, but had pressed two separate bags of hot iced pecan cinnamon rolls into their hands, and then stuck her tongue out at Mineau as she returned to the kitchen, grumbling to herself.

Ashlon followed Janey back to her apartment, where they continued their discussion. Much to Ashlon's surprise and relief, Janey believed her. But then, Janey had always supported her friend no matter how grave or strange the situation.

"It makes sense, Ash," Janey continued to expound as they dug into the fresh, hot rolls. "Not to add fuel to the fire, but there's something I didn't tell you about. Remember the night you were attacked in the cemetery?"

Ashlon nodded as she wiped a stray drip off her chin. "Yuh huh."

"After I called Jorge to come out and give a hand, I did a quick ABC and checked for other injuries. When I was looking over your head, I saw blood dribbling down your neck: two small cuts right here." She reached out and touched the spot on Ashlon's neck.

Ashlon choked on her roll and took a quick chug from an open water bottle sitting next to Janey's.

"That bastard actually bit me? And you say he used some kind of mind-altering whatever on me after I found Cherlyn?" Now she was really mad and threw a couch pillow across the room.

Janey's face darkened. "That's not a good thing, is it?"

Ashlon paled a little. "He came to see me after the police questioned him about Cherlyn. That's when he pulled that really good act on me and scared the hell out of me. I was actually almost convinced, he was that good. I'm still trying to figure out how he did that mirror stunt. But he kept it up when I said he wasn't allowed in my house anymore. I can still see his face when he was backing down the stairs toward the front door. It was ... desperate, like he was in real pain. I threw a screaming fit once he was gone because I was so crushed after that doggy-eyed kissy huggy act he'd performed after going through Emma's room. Talk about too good to be true. I knew I shouldn't have let him
into the house in the first place!"

Janey tipped her water bottle back and took a swallow. "Oh, he's miserable, all right," she said with vicious pleasure. "I talked to Mr. Stanley a few days ago and learned his lordship is not a happy camper."

"Oh no!" Ashlon exclaimed, suddenly hugely guilty at this glaring oversight. "Mr. Stanley! I didn't say anything to him! He's in the same house with that head case!'

Janey made a calming gesture and managed to keep Ashlon on the sofa instead of rushing for the door. "Not to worry. He's okay for now, and we don't want him having another heart attack over this. But he told me that McAnders has been very distant since, well, you know. Barely says two words to the old man outside of hello and goodnight. In fact, if anything, Mr. Stanley says his weirdship is acting like a man set adrift without any idea where he is or where he's going."

"Great. Just great," Ashlon groaned, pitching herself back into the sofa, grabbing another pillow, and hugging it close.

"Is there something more you want to tell me, Ash?" Janey said prodding her friend with her bottle.

Ashlon buried her face into the pillow and mumbled something incoherent.

"Stop eating my pillow and say something I can understand,"

Janey said impatiently and grabbed the pillow, trying to pull it away from Ashlon.

"I think he was trying to tell me," Ashlon said, uncovering her face, "he loves me." When she didn't hear an immediate response, Ashlon dropped the pillow onto her lap, noting Janey's shocked expression. "Well?"

Janey took a deep breath, opened her mouth as if to say something, then exhaled and remained silent.

"Do you have any idea what this is like for me? He's the most desirable, charming, passionate man I've ever met. When he held me, I felt safe and wanted and cherished. The night of the Harvest Ball, he kissed me for the first time. Janey, I swear it made me dizzy and my toes curled up! But is that really what he feels for me, or is it just part of his craziness working to get what he wants?"

Janey cleared her throat. "Like your attention?" she suggested.

"Among other things!" Ashlon exclaimed, suggestively raising her eyebrows.

Janey pursed her lips, suppressing an urge to grin. "You mean …?"

"Sweetie, I was going to give him a tour of my bedroom before I saw him in that mirror. Or, rather, didn't see him!" She groaned miserably and flopped back with the pillow over her face again.

"You've got some seriously strong feelings for Mr. Tall, Dark and Delusional. Maybe that explains why you've been acting so weird lately. Well, more than usual." Janey moved from her easy chair to sit closer to Ashlon, who could only nod.

"And," she continued as she wrapped an arm around Ashlon's shoulders and spoke into the pillow, "your Romeo of the night set knows it and it's driving him nuts because he's been in your house and you practically jumped his bones."

Ashlon uncovered her face and looked up at the ceiling. "He

had so many opportunities before that night, Janey. And even after he pulled that fang and mirror bit, he was so—I don't know—absolutely miserable about having to bite me. I mean, he even apologized."

Janey snorted and twisted her mouth thoughtfully. "A contrite lunatic. Well, that's different."

"That's one reason why I believe he didn't commit those murders," she said, looking at her friend. "I mean, he's nuts, but only in a weird role-playing kind of way. If he'd wanted to kill me like Cherlyn, he had the opportunity right then and there. And I remember he was as horrified as I was when we found her. I've looked at all the forensics again and again, especially when and where that second victim was discovered. It doesn't add up. I think he attacked those girls outside the Scupper, you know, like he attacked me, but they're still alive with only a memory of a tall, handsome stranger with a nice smile and a neck fetish."

Janey nodded and picked up her water bottle, draining it. "So, now what?" she said.

Ashlon was thoughtful for a moment. "I think I want to go back to the grain and feed parking lot and check out that area where Cherlyn was killed. Then, I want to go to Maddie Bag's place and look around."

Janey's eyes widened. "That second victim was Maddie?" she gasped. "But it's not in the papers yet."

Maddie Bag was a reclusive old woman they both knew well, someone who lived alone with her cat. A reclusive but friendly septuagenarian, who made ends meet by selling her home-canned vegetables and fruits at the town farmer's market and various festivals throughout the year. She'd made her customary appearance at the Harvest Festival, selling off practically everything she brought with her that day. Maddie knew her stuff was delicious, looked great with its attractive packaging, and was some of the best food at the Festival. Her samples always disappeared quickly. Sometimes, Maddie and Irma would combine efforts to the benefit of anyone who appreciated good down-home cooking. Ashlon and Janey had stocked their winter pantries from Maddie's bounty that day before heading home to change for the costume party.

Ashlon smirked. "I hacked the police computers while I was at the tearoom and found the medical examiner's reports on both victims. Same method, so same killer. But they don't think Maddie was killed where they found her. It looked like her body had been dumped there because of the dirt and leaves they found on the body."

Janey grabbed their empty water bottles and tossed them into her recycle bin container, then zipped into her room and returned with her coat, several pairs of examination gloves, and her ear muffs.

"I'm not working for the next two days, so let's go do some snooping," she eagerly suggested.

Ashlon smiled as she stood and grabbed her flight jacket and driving gloves. "I don't know what we should be looking for exactly. But there's a connection between when these two were killed. I just can't see it. If we can discover that, we'll have at least an idea about who killed them."

Janey rolled her eyes as if the answer should have been obvious.

"Well, duh! Those were the nights when the moon was full, Sherlock! Don't you know that's when a lot of violent crimes are committed?"

Ashlon's eye widened, and then she chuckled. "By George, I think you've got it!" she said as she hugged Janey. "At least now we know it must be a psycho who's surfaced with the full moon."

They trudged out Janey's apartment door and downstairs to the street, piling into Janey's car because, as Ashlon cited, the Volvo may be slower, but it was sturdier and offered more protection against any of those things that go bump in the night.

That included whatever or whoever had done Cherlyn and Maddie—they hoped!

Chapter 17

The parking lot at the Grain and Feed had been scoured pretty thoroughly by the crime lab guys, and Cherlyn's car long since towed to the impoundment lot for further evidence accumulation. Only scant traces of blood remained on the pavement where Cherlyn's body had contacted it. Ashlon and Janey hoped something would turn up in the car for the police.

The sky had started to cloud up with the threat of rain as they drove out of town, headed for Maddie's place. They passed the town cemetery along the way, and Ashlon threw a kiss. She also let her eyes wander to the black stone crypt at the top of the hill, wondering if he was in there sleeping—or whatever! Could he be that involved in his demented role-playing, she wondered with a shudder? She quickly turned her attention back to the road as it unwound before them.

They passed the place where Maddie's body had been found. Looking further up the open field with its dry brown cut corn stalks and hearty rye grass and weeds poking between them, Ashlon discovered that with the trees denuded of their leaves as winter neared, she could see Irma's house set in a recess just behind and around the edge of the thickly wooded area that bor- dered her private lane. Ashlon pointed it out to Janey as they sped past it. Janey merely shrugged and drove on until they passed the entrance to Irma's private lane. Another two miles or so ahead, the solid wall of bare trees suddenly opened up again on the left, revealing a small fenced-in yard with a dirt parking area in front of it directly off the road. A small, neat cottage was nestled back toward the tree line.

Janey parked her car near the gate. Out of long habit, both women waited a few moments to be sure there were no dogs around waiting to greet them, or worse, keep them from getting in the gate. When nothing furry appeared, they exited the car and opened the gate, looking around the neatly trimmed front lawn; well-tended, clipped-back rose bushes lined both sides of the fence adjacent to the gate, and decorative shrubs ran around the fence line, which wound around the back of the house. A muted meowing could be heard from somewhere as they approached the front door, which was almost level with a single step up. Janey tried the door handle. Of course, it was locked. Wordlessly, they walked around one side of the house and tried two windows, finding them locked as well. At the back of the cottage, they climbed several steps to a screened-in porch and found the flimsy screen door unlatched. They looked around the porch briefly with its Wal-Mart lounger, umbrella table (no umbrella), and two lawn chairs set under the table.

"A woman of leisure," Janey quipped as they tried the back door, finding that locked, too.

"Screw this," Ashlon muttered. After pulling on a pair of examining gloves, she reached into her pocket and pulled out a small pen knife. She flipped open a long, slim blade which locked in place, and carefully slipped it into the door jam, working it down and in as she kept turning the doorknob until she heard a click. With a satisfied grin, she pushed open the door. Flipping the blade shut, she pocketed the knife and went inside ahead of Janey. "Love these old locks," she commented over her shoulder.

"Now I know what you do on your off-hours," Janey said as she gloved, too, and followed Ashlon. They stood in a spacious, well-appointed kitchen, looking around. Fortunately, there was still enough daylight to make turning on any inside lights unnecessary as they examined the floor and counters, a tiny pantry, and a small laundry room just to the right of the pantry. They moved to the front room and carefully went over the furnishings, then climbed a short staircase to a single sleeping area set up in an alcove overlooking the living room. Maddie's bed was set under a skylight which had been equipped with an electrically operated flexible window cover, a rolladen; she could close it with the flip of a switch on the wall next to the doorway into a small bathroom. The furnishings were simple: a single bed, neatly made; a small bedside stand with a Tinkerbelle lamp on it (Ashlon smiled. So, she wasn't the only one who'd liked it); and a Lazy Boy lounger set in one corner with a floor lamp behind it. A simple, plush scarlet rug was spread under the bed so bare feet wouldn't contact the cold floor on chilly mornings. In an opposite corner sat a chest of drawers. A simple battery-powered alarm clock ticked on top of it.

Janey and Ashlon nosed around briefly, and then, finding nothing, started toward the stairs back to the living room.

"Wait a minute," Ashlon said as she went over to the wall switch which operated the rolladen. "It's going to rain tonight. It'll get soaked in here if this is left open." She flipped the switch and watched as the cover began to slide shut—then suddenly grind to a stop with the whine of metal on metal when it was less than halfway closed. Ashlon quickly flipped off the switch and moved over to the foot of the bed, looking up at the skylight.

"Janey, come here a second," she said as she slid the bed over to one side and moved directly under the skylight.

Janey climbed the stairs again, joining Ashlon. "What is it?" she said, looking up.

Ashlon pointed at the edges of a heavy screen, which, on closer inspection, appeared skewed from its frame. And a hole had been torn in it. Ashlon looked around for something to stand on. Taking off her shoes, she moved the bed back under the skylight and climbed up on the foot board, balancing shakily as she reached up and tried to pull the rolladen down all the way. After some tugging it began to move.
"It shouldn't be doing that!" she called out, lightly panting from the effort. She continued to pull hard until the flexible metal cover rolled completely shut with the high screech of metal on metal again.

"Ash," Janey said, pointing at the cover. "Look."

Ashlon anxiously licked her dry lips. The flexible metal slats had large dents curving inward, and several of the slats had been bent away from the running chain but not broken from it entirely.

"It looks like something hit it from the outside and then tried to pull it from the track," she observed as she ran a hand over the indentations. "Or someone," she added as an afterthought. Janey grimaced and moved aside as Ashlon jumped down from the footboard and pocketed the soiled, torn gloves.
Janey handed her a new pair before they moved the bed back under

the sky-lighted and straightened the sheets and blanket. They headed back downstairs into the living room, returned through the kitchen, and carefully closed the door behind them as they left the house. A furry calico body met them on the back porch, purring and rubbing their legs.

"Now what?" Janey inquired as she reached down and scratched the cat's chin and ears.

"Let's check the tool shed," Ashlon suggested, pointing at a pre-fab, red barn-shaped structure sitting inside the fence line at the lower edge of the yard abutting the forest.

They left the back porch, closely followed by the cat, and crossed the small back yard heading to the tool shed. It was unlocked. Janey slid open the metal door, which shrieked with a metallic complaint across its track, scaring off the cat. Like the cottage, the shed was organized and neat, every tool in its place on the shed wall, except for one empty slot between the hoe and rake. Maddie had drawn the shapes of the tools on a perf board behind each hook, indicating what belonged where. The missing tool looked to be a small garden trowel. Ashlon and Janey glanced at each other and proceeded to move the few pieces of floor equipment one at a time, looking under each piece. It was a long shot, but maybe the thing was there. Maddie wouldn't have been so careless as to leave something like that where it didn't belong. However, several minutes of fruitless searching turned up nothing except a loose floor board over one of the floor joints.

"Maddie was complaining about this at the Harvest Festival," Janey said as she wrestled the shed door closed again. "But, she could never get the guy who put it up to come back out and fix it."

The cat was waiting for them in a fine misting drizzle that had finally started, dropping the temperature a few degrees. Ashlon was chewing her lip as she considered what to do next.

"I want to take another look around the property," she finally said with a sigh of frustration as she zipped her jacket high on her neck and started back up the yard to the opposite side of the cottage from where they'd first approached the back porch, the same side as the bedroom alcove. Janey only nodded and followed as they trudged through the wet grass to the other side of the cottage.

"I was out here maybe twice about three years ago to check on Maddie after she'd fallen and was hospitalized for a sprained hip. She gave me some peach butter she'd put up, but I don't remember her going into her pantry to get it," Ashlon commented. She started pushing aside the heavy shrubbery that butted up against the house as she worked her way up the side and around the front, continually looking and moving the heavy green foliage until they were back around to the rear again. Nothing.

"What are we looking for?" Janey said as she plunked down onto the steps below the porch and adjusted her earmuffs. "It's getting cold out here."

Ashlon sniffed, wiping her nose on her sleeve. She looked down as the cat came up beside her, meowed once—and disappeared through a hole behind the stairs that had been hidden by the thick woody limbs of the shrubs growing on both sides of the steps. Ashlon got down on her knees, examining the plants and finding broken limbs and crushed leaves pressed against the porch's lattice skirting that kept out forest animals. She found a large hole that opened behind the steps. Pushing through the bushes, she followed the cat into a large open space under the porch. There, directly under where the kitchen was situated, she found a ground level window into the cottage with the glass broken out of it. It was just big enough for a body to squeeze through. Ashlon easily crawled to it, avoiding the broken glass embedded in the dirt, and peered through the frame into inky blackness—a cellar, judging by the smell of it. The scant light that filtered through the porch skirting weakly reflected off several glass jars on a shelf near the window.

"Janey, it's here!" Ashlon called out excitedly as she backed out toward the opening. But, as she moved, she spotted something caught on a large shard of glass still fixed in the window frame. "I found something!" She carefully pulled a large piece of rough fur with some flesh still attached to it from the glass shard. Holding it securely in one hand, she carefully turned and started crawl- ing toward the hole by the steps. Suddenly, her eyes widened in amazement when she spotted something even more important buried in the dirt in front of the lattice. The missing trowel. She picked this up by its handle, then carefully pushed back through the bushes into the daylight and stood, holding up her prizes for Janey to inspect.

"What in the world ...?" Janey said as she took the fur wad from Ashlon and closely examined it. Ashlon shielded the trowel with one hand as she held it up into the dull drizzly daylight. It was crusted with dirt and what looked like dried blood. Several fibers were trapped in the crusting. Ashlon carefully pulled at her glove, stretching it over the trowel to completely encase it.

"I hope they'll be useful," Ashlon said as she brushed the dirt off her wet jeans and jacket. "I found a cellar window broken out under there."

"A cellar? In this tiny place?"

"The only place in these small cottages you could keep a lot of perishables like fresh produce cool enough to keep from spoiling too fast if you don't refrigerate them. Maddie liked to can fruits and vegetables she bought from the local produce stands. She kept everything in the root cellar until she could use
them. She said refrigeration spoiled the freshness. That's why her stuff always tasted so good."

"And gave her murderer a way into her house".

"He tried to get through the skylight, but the metal rolladen wouldn't cooperate. He gained access through the root cellar, but by that time, Maddie was able to get out of the house. She must have had that spade somewhere close and used it on her murderer, or it was used on her. But she wasn't killed in the
house," Ashlon said as she stretched her back. "The wounds and deep scratches on her body would've bled like a mother, leaving lots of evidence. I'm betting that whatever got her killed, her back in the woods, and then dumped the body for someone to find once she started getting ripe. C'mon. We've found everything we can here."

Janey pulled off her one glove to stretch around the fur bit as Ashlon had done with the spade, but fumbled it and dropped it as the cat emerged from under the porch steps. It landed at Janey's feet, but the animal's immediate reaction to it was startling and totally unexpected—it backed away from the fur with loud hissing and spitting, its back arching high as its fur bristled. Suddenly it took off like a shot, vaulted the fence at the side of the house, and disappeared in the woods.

Janey picked up the fur swatch and looked from it to Ashlon as she wrapped it in her glove. "That can't be good," she commented as she stuck the glove in her coat pocket and followed Ashlon back to the parked car.

They drove immediately to the district police station and asked for Detective Anderson. They were shown to his office, where they waited for him to make his appearance, placing the glove-wrapped trowel and fleshy fur scrap on his desk.

It was also apparent by the level of activity outside the office that something critical was going on. Janey and Ashlon listened closely to snippets of talk that drifted in through the partly open door.

"Where was this one found?"

"... same condition as the others."

"This is getting stupid ..."

"... dammit! Why can't someone make some decent fuckin' coffee around here?"

"... just a kid, for Christ's sake!"

Ashlon and Janey looked at each other, frowning at that last comment and hoping fervently that the context of it was in reference to something other than a fatality.

Abruptly, Detective Anderson blew in, slamming his door and seating his ample body into his chair with a deep expiratory huff. After dropping several hand-mangled folders on his desk, he glared over his desk at Ashlon and Janey. "You've got 3 minutes," he impatiently growled as he shuffled his folders and opened one in front of him.

As Janey had observed earlier in the day, nothing much ever

scared Ashlon outside of men supposedly without mirror reflections and a blowout on the expressway. However, even though they'd both faced their fair share of psycho family members, vicious watchdogs on home visits, weapons-waving schizophrenics in emergency rooms, and remarkably bad hospital cafeteria food, Janey still had a big problem with raging authority figures. She physically shrank back into her chair and folded her arms around her, looking everywhere except at Anderson.

Ashlon figured that's why her friend had never dated cops or hospital administrators. She looked at Detective Anderson with her most charming smile and pleasantly said, "Forensic evidence," pushing the gloves at him.

"Oh, goody!" he spat at her without touching them. "What the hell are they?"

"Things your guys missed at Maddie Bag's place."

That made him think, Ashlon mused with a smirk. She carefully unfolded each of the gloves, taking great care not to touch the handle of the trowel, and then proceeded to report how she and Janey had spent their afternoon at Maddie's house. After she was finished, she sat back in her chair and looked at her watch, showing it to Janey, who nodded as she bit her lip to keep from laughing.

"I kept it at 3 minutes, Detective," Ashlon smugly said. "And please don't lecture me about staying away from Maddie's place. There were no police tapes anywhere, and her cat needed feeding."

His expression changed from a sneer to reluctant acceptance as he picked up the phone and dialed a number, requesting the presence of someone from forensics ASAP.

A squat, hairless little man wearing a lab jacket showed up less than a minute later. Anderson showed him the things on the gloves and spoke to him briefly. Moleman carefully picked up the spade and the fur and quickly departed.

Detective Anderson looked first at Ashlon and then at Janey. "What do you two do for a living ordinarily when you're not out playing Nancy Drew?" he asked as he leaned back in his chair and studied them through narrowed eyes.

"We're nurses," Ashlon said as she sat up a little straighter and stared defiantly at the detective, daring him to say something that would garner him an ass chewing.

He thoughtfully chewed the end of a pencil. "My wife's a nurse," he suddenly commented. "She manages the neuro unit up at General. You might know her."

Ashlon and Janey relaxed considerably and nodded. Oh, yes. They both knew Carole Anderson as a competent, razor-edged nurse who was as no-nonsense as her husband and just as passionate about her work. She had to be to put up this guy!

"We'll let you know," he said, waving toward the door.

Ashlon and Janey quickly rose from their chairs and departed without a backward glance. Once they were outside in the parking lot, they stood briefly by Janey's car to take in some fresh air before the drive home—and to consider what they'd heard inside. It was getting dark and still drizzling with a cold penetrating chill behind it.

"Quite a day, Ash, quite a day," Janey commented as she scratched her head and yawned.

Ashlon looked into the darkening sky. "They were talking about a third victim in there?" she said with a shake of her head as she studied the rim of the mountains disappearing beneath a thick rolling mist. "Probably killed the third night of the full moon."

Janey put an arm around Ashlon's shoulders. "It'll be another couple of weeks until the next one, Ash. Let the police handle it. I think we gave them enough to chew on for a while."

Ashlon managed a tired half smile and got into the car, hoping Janey was right.

Chapter 18

The morning paper verified Ashlon's suspicions.

The third victim was a blond male, late teens, early 20s, found stuffed into the trunk of a car that had been hidden on an overgrown logging road up north near the edge of the state game lands. A hunter out for small game, and possibly an illegal deer before the official season opened, had been alerted by his dog's snuffling and whining behind the brush-covered car, and pawing frantically at the locked trunk. Since it was locked, the hunter only looked into the car, finding the keys still in the ignition. However, he nearly lost it with all the blood spattered on the seats, dashboard, and floor, wisely deciding to let the local police open the trunk instead. A frantic call placed from his cell phone, and the place was swarming with investigators less than an hour later.

It hit the papers the day after the discovery was made, with an extensive interview of the hunter getting his 15 minutes of fame in two columns on the front page, carrying over to page 10 of the AM edition. Ashlon picked up from her porch the following morning. She was browsing through it as she sipped her morning tea. The cold nights and a water-tight car trunk had slowed decomposition so that a time of death could be more accurately determined.

"Let me guess," Ashlon said aloud. "He was found within 3 days of the first victim in Lloyds Corner." Reading further, she smiled with grim satisfaction, grabbed a pen, and circled the passage in the paper.

People in the community were scared, staying in at night behind locked doors after the first two victims were found so close to their own homes and businesses. Maybe they'd relax a little now with the lack of proximity of this third one, but Ashlon doubted it.

Boy, was this going to put a crimp in trick or treating.

Ashlon had decorated her front entrance anyway with her scarecrow, two ghoulishly grinning Jack O'lanterns, several tall cornstalks, and small bales of hay. She'd tied a big black raffia bow around the porch lamp stem, and then cut the bottom, eyes, nose, and mouth out of a large plastic Jack O'Lantern, fitting it over the lamp after replacing the bulb with one of lower wattage. It was just the right effect as the plastic pumpkin smiled fiendishly over anyone passing on the sidewalk or driving down the narrow street after dark.

One of her neighbors took pictures of her porch and sent them to the town paper. Ashlon thought it was too funny, but the paper ran them with several others in their special interests section.

As she had hoped, the community managed to relax a little and went ahead with plans for supervised trick or treating and the mayor's masquerade ball that same evening, right after the trick or treat hours.

Ashlon had just finished her breakfast when the doorbell sounded. She wrapped her robe around herself more securely and went to the door, peeking through the spy hole. Mr. Brawny, or rather, Grady Roberts, was standing on her porch examining her Halloween decorations with a broad grin.

Ashlon groaned inwardly, not expecting or wanting company today. Jeez! Irma didn't waste any time, did she? Taking a deep breath, she opened her front door and mustered a weak smile.
"Grady," she said, working to keep the bite out of her voice. "What a surprise." Not.

His smile became brilliant and his expression appreciative. And not just for the decorations on the porch.

"Okay, I guess. Do you have a minute?" he said encouragingly.

"I guess so. Come on in." She reluctantly opened the door, waited as he passed by her into the living room, and then closed the door behind him. He smelled incredible, a totally masculine scent. Ashlon reckoned he was wearing one of those pheromone-based men's aftershaves or colognes. Not too heavy on the scent but with the distinct message of 'I'm what you need.' He was too big for her living room since he stood over 6 feet tall and was built like a Mack truck on two muscular legs straining at a pair of khaki Dockers. With them, he wore a black plaid long-sleeved shirt open at the neck by two buttons and a pair of dark brown loafers. His auburn hair had been neatly cut and looked a lot less wild than it had the night of the Harvest Festival Dance, and his beard and mustache were neatly clipped and combed as usual. The man had definitely cleaned up for this visit, Ashlon figured. In spite of her suspicions, she actually felt a little flattered as she motioned for him to sit on the sofa. She took a seat across from him in her recliner. "So what's up, Grady?" she inquired as she pulled her robe around her knees.

He was looking around her small garden house. "You have a nice place here," he commented with genuine interest. "As long as I've known you, I've never been to your house. You were always busy and gone so much of the time. When Mom told me about what was happening with your daughter, though, it made sense. I can't begin to know what it was like going through what you did. I hope you weren't dealing with it alone."

Saying all the right things and genuine expressions of concern. What's he want? What's he up to, Ashlon wondered?

She shook her head and looked down at her hands. "I wasn't. Thanks for your concern." His empathy caught her off guard and she relaxed just a little as she watched Grady's face light up at her response. He suddenly dropped to his knees in front of her and startled her when he took her hands into his large calloused fingers, looking into her face with an impish grin. She was startled, throwing her just a little off balance.

He was being nice, boyishly appealing. He'd dressed and groomed himself just for this visit. Maybe ... maybe she'd been too hasty in her judgment of him at the dance, Ashlon considered as he warmly smiled at her. Give him a chance and see what happens. Janey would definitely say, "Hell yes!"

"Does this mean you'll spend the day with me if I beg hard enough?" he said hopefully. Even on his knees, he was still a head taller than Ashlon, and she suppressed the urge to lean in a little to catch more of his scent. McAnders had been wearing a really nice scent the night he'd been at her house. It fit him well. She had liked that, liked his attention, his compassionate insights, his arms around her, the touch of his lips ...

Of course, she also severely reminded herself, there had been a damn good reason for tossing him out! The guy was undeniably several pennies short of a roll and had actually tried to bite her—again. But, why had he looked so pathetically regretful he had to hurt her? Had he been intent on doing her like the genuine article? Was he the genuine article, G-d forbid? The way he'd fought leaving that night had utterly terrified her and almost had her convinced he might be what she'd seen—or not—in her hall mirror.

Her attention was forced back to the here and now by Grady's touch on her knees. He was humming the music from Jeopardy's final round competition as he patiently studied Ashlon's face. When he finished he added suggestively, "I'll buy lunch," with a sly grin.

Ashlon twisted her mouth in serious consideration, and then she slowly smiled in spite of herself. She couldn't help it. Here was this big, burly man who was so vibrant and full of life, asking so politely to spend some time with her. And willing to spring for a meal. Maybe it was against her better judgment, but she decided to give him one last chance and hope for the best—at least, for Irma's sake.

"Okay, you've got me for the day," she said with a tentative smile as she stood. Grady pulled himself up with her help and flung his arms around her, pulling her off her feet as he planted a kiss on her cheek.

"Good! Now, unless you plan to thrill half of Boston with those fabulous legs of yours, you better get dressed." He looked down appreciatively at Ashlon's open robe, exposing everything from mid-thigh down.

"Go help yourself to some coffee and pull in your eyeballs," Ashlon gasped as she pushed him away, feeling herself heat up with embarrassment. He was laughing heartily as she quickly closed her robe and dashed up the stairs.

The trip turned out to be a semi-business trip to Boston to obtain some kitchen equipment for Mineau's tearoom: a new counter-refrigerator for the front and a walk-in freezer for the back; new vent hoods for over the cooking area, and a ceramic surfaced prep table which would make rolling dough easier for Irma. After the papers had been signed and delivery dates settled, which took the entire morning, they had lunch down by the harbor and did some window shopping afterward. Mostly, it was just walking around and talking, acting like tourists and giving docent guides a hard time about little inaccuracies in their practiced recitations (The hell with revisionist history!)

The sun was setting as they pulled into Ashlon's street, and Grady parked in front of her Jeep. He stopped Ashlon from opening the door on her side, his expression tender, yearning shining in his hazel eyes as he ran his hand along her cheek.

"I had a great time today," he said with a warm smile. "It's been a while since I've spent time with anyone but my mom or sister. Even the business part of it was less of a drag, and that's saying a lot."

Ashlon stiffened, automatically putting some psychological distance between his intent and her instant caution.

"Oh, I can see how buying kitchen equipment wouldn't exactly be on your list of thrilling, fun-filled activities to do while visiting Boston," she quipped nervously, trying to sound lamely humorous instead of dreading the next moments. Stop it! she silently admonished herself. For once in your pathetic existence, allow a desirable man some access. They're not all abusive pricks!

"Are you alright?" Grady asked as he leaned in closer and cupped her face in one incredibly warm hand, turning it up to his, studying her expression so closely that for a moment she thought he could read her mind.

Ashlon managed to nervously shake her head. "No. Just the same old internal conflicts," she managed weakly. Good lord, she was trembling now, and Grady was moving closer, his arms circling around her.

His lips hovered just above hers now. She could feel the intense heat emanating from them mixed with the seduction in his voice.

"And what might that be?" his deep voice softly rumbled, his lips brushing hers so lightly she felt herself melting away. Without waiting for an answer, he pressed his advantage and kissed her as he wrapped his arms around her and pulled her against him.

Time stood still as she allowed herself to fall under his spell, caught in his all-encompassing embrace and snared by the mother of all kisses. Her head was spinning as she felt his body press her down into the seat, reveling in the feel of him against her as his lips covered her face and neck, then back to her mouth, drawing her breath away again with its intensity.

Ashlon managed to gently push him back and took several deep breaths, shocked that the windows were steamed up. Well, there was a first, and much to her grudging admission, a step in the right direction. Grady's eyes were glazed over as he tried to restart their passionate episode, but found himself gently rebuffed as Ashlon looked out the window.

"Neighbors are watching," she whispered as she pointed out several curious faces in the adjoining buildings peering at them through their windows.

Grady sat up, staring into Ashlon's eyes. "Then invite me in," he gently suggested taking Ashlon's hand and kissing it front and back.

At first, she actually thought that might be a good idea since they'd had such a good time in Boston. And it had been so long since she had enjoyed a man's company, other than platonically.

But then, as she looked up into Grady's face to answer him, she caught a familiar hardness in it, a certain smirking confidence that he had finally prevailed over her steadfast refusal of him. The set of his mouth, the lowered eyelids as he looked at her like a piece of prime property he'd finally acquired—Ashlon took it all in, stark realization slapping her with its chilling clarity. This was the Grady she knew too well, and she'd nearly succumbed to the illusion he'd been weaving. Fortunately for her, he'd never been able to keep it up for very long, the arrogant bastard.

Something inside her went dark and cold, and the hair stood

up on the back of her neck as she started pushing against his chest, her expression grimly determined. "Grady, we had a nice day together, but it's late and I have things to do. So goodnight," she said firmly as she tried to squirm from under him, reaching out for the door handle at the same time. Grady reached out and yanked her hand back, folding it under him.

A wild, almost feral look glossed over his face. "Not this time," he snarled, pinning her to the passenger seat, his mouth taking hers again as she struggled against his suffocating weight, biting him hard on the cheek when he turned his head to avoid having his lips chewed. He lurched back but didn't move off. Instead, he pinioned her arms under one of his as she struggled under him, unable to move.

"Bastard!" she gasped under his weight as his lips covered her face, her neck, and his hands ripped at her jacket. He jammed one of his knees between hers and forced her thighs open, immediately dropping his hips between them and grinding them against hers with fierce determination. She could feel his erection straining against his trousers as he jammed it into her crotch. She managed to work one hand free and clawed at his hands and face, jerking underneath him and biting at his cheeks and neck, his lips as his face brushed hers, fending off his mouth each time he tried to catch skin with them. He's trying to bite me! she suddenly realized with new panic rising inside her like an icy wave, imbuing her with desperate strength as she snarled at him and fought him off with everything she had in her. But it wasn't enough. She was inflicting wounds, but he was much stronger, and she was tiring, and now his hand was working to open her jeans under him as he stared down at her with fixed grim determination. He'd ripped open her zipper and was about to shove his hand down her panties when something hard hit the outside of his truck, rocking the large 4x4 back and forth like a swing in a strong wind.

"What the ...!" Grady swore aloud, lifting his head and angrily looking around. The truck was hit again and shoved forward several inches in spite of the brake being set and the gear in park. "Sonuvabitch!" he cursed again and moved off of Ashlon back to the driver's side, looking frantically out the windows for the source of whatever had hit his truck.

And then, Ashlon spotted them. They suddenly appeared outside the windows and peered in at them with empty eye sockets, flesh ripped from faces, necks, and arms that reached out and pushed at the sides of the vehicle. They'd been torn and mangled almost beyond recognition, blood covered, their mouths opened in soundless screams as they battered the truck and peered inside of it. Ashlon screamed once, and then the passenger side door was ripped open. She was grabbed, yanked from the seat, and thrown to the sidewalk, her bags landing beside her.

Run! A multitude of eerie, gravelly disembodied voices shouted at her, and then their owners turned their attention back to Grady's truck.

Ashlon immediately moved. She scrambled to her feet, grabbed her bags, and bolted for her front door. From behind her, she heard the rumble of the truck's engine mixed with the plaintive crying and moaning of those ghastly figures, Grady's loud cursing, and then the squeal of tires as he tore off down the street away from that hideous grasping throng intent on reaching him.

Ashlon was pressed against her front door, hiding her face in her arms and trembling so hard she couldn't hold onto her door key. It dropped from her fingers and hit the concrete of her doorstep with a soft 'clink'. As she knelt and scooped the key up by its plastic coiled holder, she dared to slowly turn her head and look behind her.

Nothing was there. The night was quiet again as a cool breeze blew through the naked limbs of the curbside tree. She looked up and down the street, trembling and licking her dry lips with utterly bewildered confusion, wondering what the hell had happened.

"They're gone," she finally breathed with intense shaking relief as one of her neighbors, an elderly man leaning heavily on a cane, shuffled up to her and patted her hand gripping the one railing, getting her attention. She looked down at him, still somewhat muddled and only barely acknowledging his presence.

"It's quite alright, dear," he rasped. "Scoundrel was far too cheeky anyway." He winked at her reassuringly and shuffled off down the sidewalk to his wife, who waited for him on their porch. To Ashlon's extreme chagrin, she realized he hadn't seen a blessed thing out there other than her sudden fall onto the sidewalk from Grady's truck and that mad scramble to her front door. None of her neighbors had seen anything.

As she finally unlocked her door, she numbly accounted two very disturbing basic facts: Grady's trying to rape her, and those ghostly shades that had saved her. Ashlon slowly backed into her house and closed the door, standing there for a few moments just staring blankly at the floor, shaking her head with her eyes closed. It was hard to think. Air. She needed to get some air.

After dropping her bags on the couch, she crossed the living room to her kitchen without turning on any lights, and stepped outside to her small backyard, gazing up into the heavens and perfunctorily studying several constellations in the clear night sky.

There was no denying what had happened. She'd seen their faces and the awful thing that had happened to them. Had Grady seen them too? She wanted to know. They'd certainly made their terrifying presence obvious in a very dramatic way, and they'd stopped what Grady was trying to force on her. Another more terrible thought occurred to her. What if he'd succeeded? He'd been wild, like trying to collect his due or claim a prize. She'd trusted him, but had been totally, irrevocably betrayed in one of the worst ways possible.

Something like a bubble popped inside her head, saying 'enough'. Closing her eyes, the tears flowed with unleashed anger at the heavens and the night around her, mimicking the terrible silent outcries she'd heard outside Grady's truck, her own misery sounding from her soul with the same acute heart-wrenching pain. Curse Grady, curse Wyatt, curse death itself and sickrooms and losing her dearest heart to an ugly disease like cancer, curse the unfairness of it all!

A torrent rushed down her face, her mouth open, voicing hoarse cries erupting with all the rage and pain she'd neatly closeted away for too long. It all poured out in a raging tide, doubling her over in such terrible misery and anger she would've torn apart anything within arm's reach. Collapsing into a shivering mass, she curled up and pounded her fists on the hard ground until they were bruised and bleeding. She screamed to the heavens, demanding answers, screaming for answers! How much was a person supposed to tolerate before it finally said 'enough', before it had to beg for some kind of solace, for some tenderness and mercy to relieve it of everything it had to endure? It was checkout time, folks, because 'enough' had finally happened.

A massive shadowed figure materialized out of the darkness and knelt next to Ashlon, gently lifting her off the ground. She blindly flailed and pounded at it, smearing something pale with her blood. Large, powerful arms circled and snared her close, closer, gradually inhibiting her wild movement. A cold set of lips brushed her one ear as she instinctively tried to jerk away, still writhing helplessly against her restraint. Softly, ever so softly, a deep voice filtered through her anguished mind, "You are safe, beloved. You are safe."

Ashlon immediately ceased her struggling and sank into deep, sweet oblivion, held securely by strong supporting arms.

Bowen did not call Mr. Stanley as he had before. He swiftly carried Ashlon's inert form to his own room this time and laid her on the bed. He pulled off her shoes and jacket, and then covered her with a light throw taken from a high-backed chair next to the bed. She was a mess; her makeup had run, mixing with sweat and dirt as it tracked down her face in dark lines and smears. Well, that could be remedied easily enough. Going into the bathroom, he ran a basin of warm soapy water and brought it back to the bedside. He dropped a soft terry washcloth into the steaming water and then wrung it out. He washed the grime from Ashlon's face until it shone with its pale natural beauty again. He also washed her battered hands, wincing at some of the deep gouges she'd inflicted on herself with her fingernails during her manic tirade.

It had all been observed from the widow's walk. Bowen had seen her return with that man, and seethed with silent fury as her companion held her and kissed her with a hunger that drove Bowen wild with deep hatred, barely maintaining enough control to not fly down there and rip the doors off that vehicle to kill both of them. Oh yes, he had wanted to make her feel his agony as acutely as he did, but with a supreme effort had resisted it.

Then, something untoward happened. She'd fallen in a panic from the man's vehicle, clearly trying to get away from him. He wondered why, as he finished wrapping Ashlon's hands with soft gauze and then took the wash basin back to the bathroom to empty into the sink. Through a red, angry haze, he'd watched them kissing and embracing. The man had become more aggressive; then, and only then, had she reacted in that manner. Or had something more happened, something he wasn't aware of?

Bowen had watched with deep-seated contempt as the man drove off, Ashlon's terror and pain more than he could withstand. He'd been greatly relieved when she finally let herself into her house.

However, when he'd decided to go back inside, he heard the back door to her house open, and stayed to watch with curious interest as she walked out to her yard. He'd tensed because she was surrounded by a strange pulsating scarlet aura that was growing brighter and brighter until she erupted with all that pain and sorrow and rage in those few agonized moments before he intervened.

He could not allow it and had flown to her, subduing her before she could further injure herself, casting her into a deep dreamless sleep until he felt it was safe to waken her. If she would allow it, he would help her sort out what had happened.

For the time being, Bowen lit candles for her benefit in a sconce hanging next to the bed, and then changed his own soiled, bloodied shirt for an earth-tone V-neck jersey. Kicking off his shoes, he lay down next to Ashlon and gathered her close to him, easily placing her head in that soft place on his shoulder, wrapping his arms protectively around her. He kissed her cheek and the top of her head, and then placed a light, lingering kiss on her warm lips. "I will protect you tonight," he whispered to her composed face. Would she escape his spell as she had before? He sincerely hoped not, because at this moment he was the happiest he had felt since first seeing Ashlon those long weeks ago. For tonight, she was his alone.

Chapter 19

My love, awaken. It is time.

I don't want to. Not now, not ever!

You must, beloved. There are matters to be discussed between us. No! It's just too hard! I can't deal with it anymore!

I will be with you, and together we will work through it.

A pause.

I'm so very sorry for what I did to you.

No, my precious one. Do not ever apologize for your honesty. You can visit me whenever you want at my house.

I am honored by your trust.

A thoughtful pause.

Am I really your beloved?

Oh, yes, my own. Through all the shades of time through which we have passed.

Many lifetimes?

Yes, beloved.

Ashlon slowly opened her eyes. Her vision was blurred, her head ached, and she blinked several times trying to clear it, but gave up. Must still be dreaming, she considered blearily through the fuzziness, trying to claim her again. She lazily watched the light from two candles scutter in their holders above her on the wall. The wicks needed to be trimmed. She was warm and comfortable, and her limbs and head were heavy, like large weights had been tied to them.

Movement in the room. She tried to follow it but didn't have the energy, and then the bed trembled as someone heavy slid in next to her, effortlessly turning her so that their faces and eyes met. A large, gentle hand caught her head as it lolled back, arranging it on a soft cushion near the source of a scent, comforting and familiar to her, but which she was unable to place at the moment.

"Where?" she said, her voice very tired and barely a whisper.

"With me, my own," a deep masculine voice softly replied. "Have you awakened?"

"No," Ashlon sleepily nestled down into that wide, soft shoulder. She curled up against a hard body that yielded to her with embracing arms holding her against it. One large, heavy leg was thrown over hers, completing the silent statement of ownership. She immediately lost consciousness again, secure in the knowledge that absolutely nothing could hurt her now. He wouldn't allow it.

Morning. The glare of early sunrise in her face woke her. She groaned, holding her head as the pounding inside it slowly subsided to let the duller pain take over. She threw back the covers and rose, shielding her eyes from the light. Groping for the blind louver, she viciously twisted it until the slats closed off and the glare lessened to only a dimmed glow through the narrow gaps. And speaking of gaps— there was a big one in her memory as well.

She could remember going out to the backyard last night and looking up at the stars, but not coming back into the house after her meltdown. And, Grady put the moves on her after their date. She'd been played by a pro, caught unprepared by his ardent behavior and almost capitulating. What a blind- sided fool she'd been!

He'd turned into a real prick when she'd refused him and tried to rape her. What an asshole! So much for the sensitive, caring man image. She should call the cops on him. Or better yet, rat him out to his mother. But what the hell had those things been outside his truck? They'd rocked it like a baby cradle, terrifying her and making him madder than a hornet with a hangover. Whatever it was, it had saved her from him; that much was certain, allowing her to escape. She was willing to bet his truck was pretty dented up, too, judging by the level of activity that hit it.

Or had she only imagined what happened out there? Had Grady slipped something into her drink at dinner that played havoc on her mind? Had he meant to drug her and then rape her? Whatever it was, it had played contrary to him and anything he had planned, thank heaven.

Afterward, she'd crumbled into a screaming wreck in the

backyard and probably scared all the neighbors. She grimaced at this thought as she shucked her dirty clothes in the hamper and headed for the bathroom. Turning the water on as hot as she could stand it, she threw herself into the shower. She scrubbed until she was a solid mass of soapy foam from head to toe, scrubbing every trace of Grady off her. She stood under the spray and allowed the scent of the soap to waft up around her as the water rinsed her and relieved some of the pain in her head and neck. Her hands were tender, marked with several small lacerations on her knuckles and the tops of her fingers.

After drying off and putting on a clean pair of jeans, a soft black t-shirt, and heavy rainbow colored slipper socks (Janey had once commented she must have mugged a Munchkin), she blearily made her way down the hall to the stairs. She glanced once into the hall mirror. Jeez, she looked like something even the cat wouldn't drag home. Holding her aching head, she descended the stairs and shuffled into the kitchen. Order for the hour: strong coffee, breakfast, some headache medication, and a tube of Neosporin for her hands.

As she waited for the coffee to finish brewing, Ashlon noticed the light on her answering machine was blinking, but ignored it as she passed the phone and went out to pick up the morning paper. It was Saturday, and she stood on her doorstep taking several deep breaths of the chilly early morning air. One of her elderly neighbors who lived two doors away waved to her from her doorstep. Mrs. Kincaid carefully descended the two steps to the sidewalk and approached Ashlon with a gentle smile, took her offered hand, and patted it affectionately. "Don't fret about last night, deary," the old woman said with understanding compassion.

Ashlon felt herself sink inside. "Mrs. Kincaid, I ... I'm so sorry. I don't know where that came from."

"Tush!" The old woman shushed her. "I think we all need to do that once in a while. Gets the poison out of our systems." She gave Ashlon's arm a squeeze and waved as she returned to her house.

There had certainly been that, Ashlon breathed with some relief and went back inside to her kitchen, settling in with her paper, coffee, and medication. Mrs. Kincaid had made her morning a whole lot better, bless her.

The phone rang again. And rang. Ashlon glared resentfully at the one in the living room, refusing to get up. Finally, the answering machine clicked on her away message. The caller was someone she had no intention of talking to ever again.

"Ash, it's Grady. I've tried to call you, but I don't blame you for not picking up."

"Duh!" she growled, throwing an obscene gesture into the air. Boy, he sure had his nerve after what he'd tried last night!

"Anyway, I really want to apologize for being such a ..."

Asshole? Reeking snot wad? Jerk off? Lucky she didn't call the cops on his ass?

"Insensitive jerk. Please meet me for lunch today. One o'clock at the tea-room? Anyway, if you don't show, I'll understand. Well, okay. Bye."

Ashlon rattled her newspaper irritably and went back to reading. "I gave you your chance and you blew it, dickweed," she snarled out loud. "No more chances! I should know by now a snake can't change its rattle."

The phone rang again as she finished her first cup of coffee. She groaned out loud. Reaching behind her, she lifted the wall receiver and tucked it under her chin as she rose to pour herself another cup. She snarled into the mouth piece, "Eat shit, Grady! And leave me the hell alone before I tell your mom what you tried last night!"

"And a pleasant good morning to you, buttercup," Janey greeted her in a syrupy sweet voice. "Get up on the wrong side of the coffin this morning?"

Deep sigh of relief. "I was afraid you were Grady calling again."

"Word has it you went ape shit last night. And what's this about Grady?"

Ashlon groaned. "Come on over, I need to talk."

Janey chuckled. "I'll just bet you do. Can I bring Jorge?"

"Sure. The more the merrier," Ashlon dryly said. "Bring something sticky and sweet with you, okay?"

"I'm already bringing Jorge."

"Lame. Exceedingly lame. See you in a bit." Ashlon hung up the phone and carried her coffee up the stairs to her room, crossing it to her vanity to brush her hair, slap on a little makeup—and stopped cold, staring at something she hadn't noticed earlier when her head was aching so badly. Propped against the
round mirror of her vanity table was a single perfect black rose. Under it was a small card with one word written in an ornate script: Beloved.

Chapter 20

"Wow!" Janey breathed when Ashlon showed her the rose and the unsigned card. "Just like one of those spooky romance novels." She'd come alone; Jorge made it very clear he had no taste for girl talk.

Ashlon faithfully reported everything that had transpired up to and including her meltdown the previous evening. However, she was totally unable to account for how she got back into her house, waking up this morning in her own bed. They talked it over for a while as they enjoyed the glazed raisin rolls Janey had picked up earlier at the grocery store bakery, and concluded that Ashlon might have experienced a rare, extremely brief fugue episode brought on by extreme duress. That might account for those terrifying apparitions, too, although the drugging theory wasn't completely ruled out. Anyway, it was the best they could come up with.

"So, what are you going to do about Grady?" Janey tentatively asked as she wiped her fingers on a napkin and reached for her coffee mug.

Ashlon frowned as she took a sip of her third cup of coffee. "Brush him off like a bad odor. You know Bud won't do anything if I file a report. I'm not really convinced his mother or sister will listen, either. The more I think about it, the more upsetting it is." She shook her head and flopped back into the thick padding of her sofa. "Thank heaven the zombies had other ideas!"

Janey was shaking her head. "Sure, it's not post-traumatic stress?"

Ashlon hugged a sofa pillow. "It could be. I felt like an extra in a George

Romero movie." Had it been a drug-fed illusion? It so, what had rocked that truck and pulled her out of it? Not to counter Janey's theories, but frankly, the George Romero scenario was looking better and better.

"So, other than blowing off Grady, what are your plans for today?" Janey said, sitting back in the sofa cushions and studying her fingernails.

"Oh gee, my calendar is really full," Ashlon said with obvious sarcasm. "Pick the gray out of my hair, clean out my Jeep, score some high-grade Valium, buy Halloween candy, go to the bookstore—my usual spine-tingling Saturday routine."

"Good!" Janey exclaimed happily and grabbed Ashlon's arm, pulling her to her feet. "You're going to participate in a little recreational commerce and help me find the perfect wedding dress. Go change. I can't be seen with someone who looks like a refugee."

She wouldn't take no for an answer or tolerate any excuse outside of death or dismemberment, which is what Ashlon imagined she would suffer if she didn't go with Janey. And maybe it would help dispel a vague sense of unrest that was getting stronger with each strange occurrence she encountered since, well, since Lord McAnders moved into the neighborhood. Maybe coincidence, maybe not. It was there just out of reach and sucking her into something she just knew in her bones would be very, very bad. First Lord McAnders, and now that thing with Grady.

Oh, this did not bode well at all!

They were gone the entire day to the mall, hitting every store they knew had a brides' or evening formal section. They found many possibilities, no definitions. But, they had, at least, narrowed down the choices in colors and styles. And, yes, being away from Lloyd's Corner for the day helped Ashlon temporarily forget her concerns for a while as she and Janey shopped and ate and talked, and laughed at the Halloween/Thanksgiving/Christmas decorations everywhere.

The mayor was having his annual Halloween Ball Monday evening, and they'd been invited; so, in conjunction with the wedding attire, they searched for reasonably priced formals befitting the season. Ashlon found a new shop tucked back in a corner across from a coffee shop. It was called, appropriately enough, Night Shades, selling clothes and accessories for 'the dark at heart.' Ashlon zeroed in on a gown she swore had been made for her. It was deep scarlet velvet with a lacey black overlay, a Victorian empire waist, drop shoulders, long fitted sleeves which came down over her hands, and a deeply scooped neckline with tiny black roses embroidered around the edge of the bodice.

Janey decided on a more conventional outfit, a sienna colored satin spaghetti strap column dress, calf-length, with a coordinated shrug jacket in golden brown.

Ashlon was smiling broadly as Janey turned in front of a three-way mirror and critically eyed every angle for any rolls or ridges.

"You look spectacular," Ashlon admiringly observed. "It's your color and style."

"You think so?" Janey said, sounding doubtful as she turned for the umpteenth time, smoothing the back and tugging a little on the front to straighten imagined wrinkles or creases or bumps.

"It fits like a glove, the price is right, and Jorge will love it. Trust me on this. That did it for Janey.

They ate an early dinner at a restaurant in the mall and were back in Lloyds Corner before sundown. Janey had an evening planned with Jorge, so she drove Ashlon directly to her place first.

As they pulled up to her house, Ashlon's face darkened as she spat, "Oh shit!", slumping way down in her seat so that she would not be seen by Grady, whom she'd spied sitting on her doorstep. Janey pressed the accelerator, and her Volvo jumped forward, roaring away down the street. She rounded the corner and didn't stop until she'd reached the McAnders House.

Ashlon breathed a sigh of relief and gave her friend a big hug before getting out of the car. She reached into the back seat and grabbed her bags.

"What are you going to do now, Ash?" Janey said with concern.

"Looks like he crawled back to your front porch to grovel."

Ashlon looked at the big house behind the iron fence and shrugged. "Guess I'll visit Mr. Stanley for a while, I suppose. Maybe Grady'll leave once it gets dark and I don't show up."

"Good luck, girlfriend. I still think you should call the police and report his ass, Bud or no Bud."

"I'll give it all the consideration it deserves," Ashlon said, trying not to smirk. She had no doubts about Bud—he and Grady were cut more or less from the same mold.

Janey sighed as Ashlon closed the car door and pulled away, disappearing around the next block.

It was turning colder with the approaching sunset as Ashlon went up to the gate, opened it, and headed up the brick walk to the front entrance of the McAnders House. The ivy had completely overgrown the support trellises and now engulfed the shell over the entrance. The house's entire stone edifice had also been recently sandblasted of years of grime accumulation. The front shutters had been replaced, too, with treated wood sprayed with a black protective polyurethane coat to protect them from the weather. As a result, the exterior looked almost brand new. Ashlon punched the doorbell and waited.

Mr. Stanley opened the door, squinting a little in the evening glare as he looked out. Ashlon had to look twice at the old man. He'd lost weight, his clothes hanging on him. Dark circles surrounded his sunken eyes, and his cheeks were sharp angles under thin skin. His hands had a more pronounced tremor as well. However, when he recognized Ashlon, he managed a warm smile and extended a thin hand to her. Ashlon grasped it firmly but gently, doing a quick scan from head to toe. What in the name of heaven had happened?

"How are you, Miss Ashlon?" he inquired, his voice sounding worn and thin though pleased.

"I should ask you that, Mr. Stanley," Ashlon said, trying not to sound shocked by his frail appearance. Had it been only a few weeks ago when she last saw him at the Festival dance, looking so healthy and dapper in his costume? Did McAnders have anything to do with this, she wondered suspiciously?

"Please come in, my dear," he said, motioning her to follow him inside. Ashlon followed his slow shuffle down the hall, through the foyer to the sitting room. She set her bags just inside the archway and sat next to him on the sofa. He had set tea in front of the fireplace, which crackled and popped in the hearth, warming the room with its heat and mellow orange glow.

Mr. Stanley poured for them and split a blueberry scone with her. He took a long sip of his tea and then looked at Ashlon. If he noticed her concern, he said nothing about it when he spoke again.

"I'm so glad you came by, Miss Ashlon. I was afraid I wouldn't be able to give you that tour you were promised."

Ashlon frowned, guilt rising again at her conscious decision to stay away from the house, but very concerned as well at Mr. Stanley's frail condition. Was McAnders working Mr. Stanley too hard? It troubled her immensely in light of her determination to keep her distance from the house until she could be sure of certain things which she was still sorting through. She also had something nagging at the back of her mind, something she felt she should remember. Ironically, it leant a measure of comfort she was experiencing as she sat there with Mr. Stanley. But, she hadn't been to the house since Cherlyn's murder, she considered as she sipped her tea. It was very good, warming and soothing.

"Mmm. Chamomile and green tea. Very nice for a cold evening," she said, savoring the flavors as they lingered on her tongue. Very nice after flavor, too.

"My wife made the scones. I believe they have a touch of lavender oil in them," the old man said as Ashlon took another bite of her scone, noting the subtle flavor.

They finished their tea in amicable silence. Then, Mr. Stanley rose and directed Ashlon to follow him into the foyer. It was much cooler out here than the sitting room, Ashlon noted, when a slight shiver coursed through Mr. Stan- ley's thin frame as he slowly climbed the stairs to the gallery, Ashlon following right behind him. It had to be the chill in this house and his responsibilities wearing on him, Ashlon decided. Admittedly, his tasks weren't very strenuous, but after that nasty heart attack he'd had the previous year, he had to be careful of extreme exposures. He was dedicated to a fault, but often neglected himself in the course of performing his duties. A true gentleman's gentleman. Even Eleanor could not sway him once his mind was set. Like she had bemoaned to Ashlon, a really stubborn old coot.

Still, she kept her concerns to herself as he showed her the bedrooms, the new iron stairs up to the widow's walk, the recently acquired furniture in each room, in addition to the pieces brought in by Lord McAnders, the refinished floors, some with new plush carpeting. He explained the origins of the hanging tapestries in the gallery, and then continued to the opposite wing where Ashlon was shown the master bedroom with its huge four poster of Scotch pine set at its center, the ornate dragon wall sconces, and a large bathroom with a sunken tub that looked more like a natural pond than a tub, with a slightly raised flat stone rim and Jacuzzi action water jets. Everything in the bed and bath was big and elegant, not unlike the master of the house, Mr. Stanley added with wry humor.

More like self-glamming poser lord of darkness, Ashlon silently sneered. Maybe he should've sprung for central heating while he was at it! Speaking of darkness—she glanced out one of the high windows as they passed through the gallery again. It was getting dark. If he kept to his usual routine, the lord of the underworld would be home soon, so she needed to leave. She followed Mr. Stanley across the gallery as they talked about all the changes that had been made, and descended the gently curving stairs back to the foyer. As the old man had commented the first time Ashlon had seen the house, their notes, and suggestions for upgrades, so meticulously researched over the years, had been well integrated into almost everything that had been done to the interior.

"Credit Lord McAnders for having the good sense to use what we suggested," Mr. Stanley gently admonished her in conclusion. They returned to the sitting room, and Mr. Stanley sat heavily in front of the fireplace again, extending his tremoring arms toward the warmth it offered.

Ashlon put on her coat. "I've had a wonderful visit," she said as she gave him a hug. Was that a wheeze she heard? She looked down into his face and listened closely.

"Have you been sick, Mr. Stanley?" she gently inquired as she reached down, running her hands around his face and forehead, and became alarmed at the heat she felt under her fingers. The old man grasped them in his hand and gently moved them away from his face. However, Ashlon had seen and felt enough to know her old friend was in serious trouble. She even considered calling Jorge and asking him to come over immediately. But, Mr. Stanley continued to be reassuring.

"Now, now, Miss Ashlon. You sound too much like Eleanor. With all the responsibility entrusted to me, I may have overdone somewhat. I've had a rather nasty cold these past few days, but nothing that keeps me bedbound and away from my duties." He stiffly rose once more and followed Ashlon out to the foyer after she'd very reluctantly grabbed her shopping bags, and shooed her toward the hallway to let her out.

But Eleanor wasn't a nurse, and Ashlon knew what she'd heard. She would call Jorge the second she was outside and then wait for him. However, before Mr. Stanley could follow her through the hallway to the front door, he started coughing. It was a harsh, deep, chesty sound with a lot of moisture behind it. Ashlon was almost out the door when it started, and she stood in the open doorway listening for it to stop. Then, events took a decidedly downward turn.

Chapter 21

She edged back inside and closed the door, quickly heading back to the foyer. She dropped her bags, listening for the cough to dwindle and stop. It didn't. Mr. Stanley was having difficulty catching his breath now, and Ashlon saw panic flare up in his wizened face as the cough persisted. The old man was bent over with his effort now, his hands braced on his upper legs in an effort to breathe. Ashlon quickly moved beside him and put her arms around him, talking to him, desperate to get him to relax enough to breathe again, but his panic was mounting, and Ashlon could feel his chest sink again and again under her hand. His lips were turning blue, and his expression was terrible as he opened his mouth, gasping for air. Suddenly, his eyes rolled back, he went limp, and Ashlon caught him against her as he collapsed, sliding him down one leg as she gently lowered him to the floor.

"Mr. Stanley!" she cried out as she dropped to her knees next to him and shook him. "James!" She rapidly undid her scarf and bunched it under his head, quickly undid his tie and shirt buttons, and checked for any breathing effort. Nothing! She positioned his head and jaw, gave him several quick breaths, and was relieved that his chest rose and fell accordingly. She then checked the pulse at his neck. Again, nothing. Mr. Stanley was in full arrest.

Ashlon ripped open his shirt and was about to start compressions when two strong hands grabbed her by the back of her coat and lifted her off the floor. She flailed against them and managed to slip out of her coat, dropping lightly back to the floor. Furiously, she turned and bounced off Bowen, who still held onto her coat, his expression a mixture of anger and confusion. Ashlon smacked him once on the chest as hard as she could and screamed at him to call an ambulance. Then, she turned without waiting to see if he complied, dropped back down to her knees and started pressing on Mr. Stanley's chest again. There had already been too much time lost to debate this.

Meanwhile, Bowen dropped her jacket and vanished into the sitting room. By the time the ambulance arrived, she'd re-established a weak pulse and shallow respirations. She was also exhausted when she gave a brief report to the paramedics as they took over Mr. Stanley's care.

At last, he was wheeled out the door for transport to County, and she closed it behind the paramedics. With a deep relieved sigh, she returned to the foyer for her handbag, finding it near her jacket. Fishing her cell phone from its depths, she pressed in a speed dial number. Mrs. Stanley picked up on the second ring. Ashlon calmly talked to her, informing her Mr. Stanley had taken ill while she had been visiting and she'd called EMS. He was on his way to County, and Mrs. Stanley could meet the ambulance there.

"No, he's okay for now. Yes, I can understand perfectly about living with such a stubborn old man. My bubbe was the same way. Right. No. NO! Call your daughter—don't you drive tonight! Meet the ambulance at the emergency room. Me too. I'm just glad I was here when it happened. Uh huh. Okay, you take care of yourself and I'll come by as soon as I can. Bye!" She snapped her cell phone shut and dropped it back into her bag as she took a deep breath. She was tired now and just wanted to leave. She had no idea what might happen if she remained any longer after everything that had passed between her and McAnders. For all she knew, her life was in peril just being in the house with him and his fixation. At least, she hoped that's what it was. The alternative was unthinkable.

Bowen had returned to the foyer from the sitting room after the paramedics departed and listened in silence as Ashlon spoke with Mrs. Stanley. Ashlon scooped up her coat off the floor where he'd dropped it as he'd headed for the nearest phone. Damn it all, why did he have to be so handsome, and look so caring and concerned and yummy and ...

"Will he live?" Bowen asked, sounding uncertain as he watched Ashlon pull on her coat, pick up her bags, and eye him with wary caution.

"I don't know," she said with a shrug. "But we gave him a fighting chance." "'We?'" he repeated, looking skeptical.

"You called the ambulance without my having to scream at you twice." Ashlon managed to summon a tired, wary smile and then turned to leave again. "By the way, the tea things he set are still in the sitting room."

Bowen suddenly reached out and snatched the bags from Ashlon's hand. She was shocked by his speed and only stared at him in chagrined surprise.

"He is still out there," Bowen said, watching her as he moved away toward the staircase, shopping bags firmly held in his hands.

Ashlon's eyebrows knitted together as she grimaced. How had he done that? And how could he know about Grady? Not that it was any of his business!

"What are you doing?" she said, thrown off balance by his observation. And what the hell was he doing with her bags? She was unable to snare them from his hand as he backed quickly away out of her reach. His head lowered with such a strange, amused expression it unnerved her.

"Grady's my problem and I'll deal with it," she snapped as she made another lunge for her bags and missed when he moved swiftly to the foot of the stairs. "This isn't funny!" she exclaimed very peeved now, forgetting her caution. What kind of dumb game was he playing?

"He dishonored you," Bowen said evenly, lifting a foot to the first step of the staircase and waiting. "I saw it all."

"So, you're a voyeur now, huh? And don't forget, you threatened to kill me! In my own house!" There went any residual fear of McAnders because she was totally pissed off now.

"Death before dishonor. It has been a clan tradition for centuries," he said with an arrogant edge.

Ashlon rubbed her face with frustration. "So you have lots of honorable dead clansmen! And the cops wouldn't believe me anyway. Dammit, give me my bags!" She made one last lunge at them and missed, lost her balance, and fell backward, bouncing her head off the hard tile floor at his feet.

"Shit! Shit!" erupted from her mouth along with the acute pain bouncing through her head up to her eyeballs.

Bowen immediately dropped her bags on the stairs and knelt beside her as she writhed on the floor rubbing her head and cursing the air blue. Carefully, he helped her to sit up. "Are you alright?" he said anxiously. "I am truly sorry. I meant only to detain you and perhaps listen to my suggestion."

Ashlon glared up at him and batted his hand away as she continued to rub her head. "No, I'm not alright, you idiot!" she snarled trying to push him away. She might as well be pushing on a large boulder. "I'm not the least bit interested in your suggestions!" She stood up with Bowen's assistance and gingerly touched the spot on her head that had impacted the tiles, wincing painfully. "That's gonna leave one hell of a goose egg," she groaned. It would take a lot of ibuprofens to keep that thing manageable tomorrow!

Suddenly Bowen slipped his arms all the way around her middle, roughly pulling her against him. He was looking very amused by her pain, which only aggravated Ashlon's bad mood and made it a whole lot worse.

"Oh no, you don't!" she angrily exclaimed as a rush of fear speared through her, and before he could react, she neatly slid out of her coat again, out of his grip to the floor, and rolled away from him. She stood up and glared at him.

"Now that you've had your grinners at my expense, I'm leaving." Just one last attempt for her bags, and then screw it.

She moved around him toward her shopping bags sitting on the first step behind him, but Bowen stepped in front of them and folded his arms over his broad chest, his head lowered and eyes keenly watching for her next move.

Ashlon grimaced with heated frustration, then threw up her hands and growled through her teeth. "Fine! Keep the damn bags!" she yelled at him. "I'll come back tomorrow when you're asleep—or whatever!—and pick them up. I know where Mr. Stanley keeps his spare house key."

Bowen's instant smile was chilling, positively diabolical. "And I know places within this house where you would never find them again," he said silkily.

Ashlon was halfway down the entrance hall when he spoke, but froze mid-step at his comment, swearing under her breath. She turned, and with an equally evil sneer, she spat, "Screw it. I'm leaving."

New dress or no dress, she was out of there! No one was going to yank her around anymore or make jokes at her expense, least of all this pompous, arrogant, great-smelling, incredibly delusional, overbearing dark lord of the underworld.

Her hand was reaching for the door handle when she was suddenly lifted off her feet from behind, Bowen's arms wrapped around her again in a grip she couldn't slip out of this time as he hauled her back toward the foyer. His long fingers were brushing against the bared skin at her ribs and stomach where her sweater had ridden up, and she suddenly convulsed and giggled involuntarily. Bowen dug in his fingers just a little more, and Ashlon helplessly squirmed again in a fit of uncontrollable laughter, twisting desperately to grab his hands with the horrified realization he'd found her tender tickle spots. How perfectly humiliating!

Bowen proceeded back through the foyer, Ashlon twisting and shrieking at him to stop each time he dug into her soft skin with his fingers, moving her effortlessly into the sitting room. She was gasping for breath, her eyes were tearing, and her face was a deep red as she vainly fought him. Then, in one smooth motion, he spun her around to face him and propelled them forward, falling onto the wide sofa in front of the fireplace, his solid mass squarely on top of her, pinning her to the soft cushions. He gazed directly down into her agonized, laughter-reddened face.

She gasped for breath beneath him. Oh, great G-d in heaven! She was imprisoned under him! Horrified, she could only gasp and squirm helplessly beneath him.

The room was warm and dimly lit by the crackling hearth fire he'd stoked with more wood while waiting for EMS to leave. Its flames danced and sparked, reflecting the blue highlights in Ashlon's hair. Thick wet strands were matted and sticking to her cheeks and her forehead. Bowen ran his hands and fingers over her face and up into her hair as he wiped away the moisture, pinning Ashlon's shoulders with his arms so that she was now effectively immobilized from shoulders to feet.

She was breathing heavily, her struggling attempts hopelessly futile under Bowen's lean mass, a mix of rage and terror still fueling every effort to escape. She was exhausted, and her head was pounding under the lump that had formed when her head smacked the tiles in the foyer. After several useless minutes of trying to move while he gazed down at her with placid interest, she finally gave up against his oppressive weight and closed her eyes, resigned to whatever he was going to do to her. She just hoped it was quick and not too painful.

"You are a stubborn, willful, infuriating woman," Bowen softly growled, his deep voice rumbling in his chest. "But you also possess intelligence, deep compassion, and extraordinary courage. Mr. Stanley owes you his life."

"Thanks for the insights, dork! And, he doesn't owe me a damn thing!" Ashlon said breathlessly as she glared up at him. She renewed her struggle against his hold on her arms, but was forced to stop when Bowen shifted his weight. Something long, thick, and solid pressed into her lower abdomen, dragging a ragged gasp from her when she realized what it was. His face was directly over hers, so close that his scent filled each struggling breath she took. But, it wasn't the same one he'd worn at the housewarming or that disastrous visit to her home several weeks ago. It was absolutely intoxicating, ensnaring her senses and drawing her into it like a warm bath to aching muscles, draining the fight out of her.

"That scent," she half-whispered as she became still again and closed her eyes, fighting to clear it enough to stay on her guard. But, she was falling under its spell, surrendering helplessly beneath Bowen, her head rolling lazily against his one arm.

Bowen brushed his cheek against Ashlon's and kissed her ear as he softly replied, "The attar of rare black roses grown here on the grounds. The scent is both elusive and mysterious and must be extracted carefully to preserve the purity of the oils, the source of its magic. I wore it tonight on a whim, but now I am glad I gave in to it." His lips brushed hers and lingered, tasting on his tongue the tea she had enjoyed earlier in the evening. Her breath caught momentarily as he kissed her face further down her throat. Something sharp brushed against the tender skin just below her ear. A new terror sprang up inside her, but she was helpless to renew any further struggling effort.

Bowen tightened his suffocating embrace on her, kissing her repeatedly, his lips igniting fire against her skin. Looking down at her with passion-filled eyes, he gently smiled, revealing gleaming, sharp fangs to her fearful gaze. His scent had intensified, making Ashlon's head spin and dance, keeping her deliciously helpless. And, his soft, passionate kisses were also having a subtle effect on her. They told her that he had no intention of harming her. There had been so many opportunities out there in the foyer, and now here as his bound prisoner. What kind of game was he playing? If he wasn't going to kill her, what did he want?

And then, he spoke to her again, not as a captor to a prisoner, but as a lover single-mindedly intent on winning her regard.

"I have searched through the mists of time for an elusive face I've seen many so times in my long existence," Bowen said fervently, his deep, rich voice a softly caressing whisper, "a kindred spirit as desperately alone as I have been. I knew you from the moment I saw you when your daughter was laid into the ground. I felt your sorrow and ached for the time I might help make it fade into memory. I found you again the night you sat by her grave alone, singing your lovely sad lullaby, and summoned the night sirens as a gift to your sweet song. I was enraptured when you responded to their melodies flowing around you and how you drew comfort from them. No mortal is capable of hearing their mysterious, sweet song but one whose heart is being sought by another. I knew then that you were the one I've searched for over the ages."

Ashlon opened her eyes and stared up at him, startled by this revelation. Her mind was wandering and must be playing tricks on her, she figured. That damn intoxicating scent, so wonderful and compelling. But why keep up this torment? For cryin' out loud, just get it over with!

Bowen stroked her face and hair in earnest, wiping away more sweat beads before they ran into her eyes, kissing her lips, her cheeks and brow, licking her neck around her ears and allowing his lips to slide slowly, languously down to her throat to resume their impassioned licking and kissing. His persistent tender gestures were gradually breaking her resistance and fear, waking something in her, responding to his long body's slow, supple, rhythmic movements on top of her, his cool searching lips and tongue urging her to submit to him, and his gentle urging. Why wasn't she trying to fight him off like she did Grady the previous evening? Was it the gentleness of his voice, his words? Or the persistent touch of his kisses, their soft, compelling expression slowly worming their way into her resolve?

"I see doubt in your eyes, beloved," he softly spoke into her cheek, his voice rough with desperate passion. "I call you beloved, as you have been from the beginning. You've fought against me and resisted in your fear and suspicion of me, but in your most haunted loneliness, I was the one you continued to seek. I had only to wait until you found a path back to me."

She was utterly overwhelmed, powerless against his gentle persuasion. "You left the rose on my dressing table," she said, licking her dry lips. It was so hard to think, to keep it all sorted. New yearnings stirred by his earnest words and searching lips were growing and responding with a longing she hadn't felt in years. "You were in my yard last night."

Bowen smiled seductively, grinding his hips into hers, and was rewarded by Ashlon's deep, throaty gasp. "Your pain was more than I could tolerate. I would have killed the man if he prevented you from leaving his presence. I folded you into my protection and kept you safe, erasing everything but anger at his treatment of you. That brief interlude has sustained me until tonight." He gazed into her face and caressed it once more, drinking in with deep satisfaction the acceptance he saw dawning there, supplanting the fear and suspicion in those wide green eyes staring up at him.

If she accepted him as a man with a full heart, would she allow herself the vulnerability needed to trust and open herself to the love he offered?

With silent apprehension, he felt he was about to find out.

Chapter 22

Ashlon was absolutely stunned. Shouldn't this be scaring the bejesus out of her, she wondered though a drug-like haze as his warm kisses jangled every objection she tried to muster. He said he was untold ages old, if she heard him right. He had followed a calling from across an ocean, eventually coming to this place he had once called home so long ago. And she'd done nothing more than exist in a loneliness as profound as his, drawing him like a magnet to her. Those dreams she'd been having were the guideposts, and he'd followed them straight to her.

Her rational mind kept resisting all of this with stubborn determination. But her deeper instincts were battering away at it just as doggedly, gaining the advantage in light of everything that had happened in the last 24 hours. Hell, let's be honest—in the past several weeks!

Bowen's frank admission quite honestly took her breath away. Not as much as his dead weight on top of her and that unreal bulge pressing between her legs! He was confessing a vulnerability few ordinary men would have admitted. He had professed his love without condition or reservation. Would a crazy person be this eloquent?

However, inane it seemed at this point, she still needed to know, really know he wasn't some nut job who could talk a good story and make it look and sound completely plausible. In her experience, the pathological liars could make anyone believe in them, and that made them very dangerous. She swallowed hard, forcing herself to meet his steady gaze.

"I want to believe you," she said with effort as Bowen caressed his hand over her neck and down her side, watching her tremble with his touch. "I need you to tell me the G-d honest truth now. You terrified me that night at my house, and for a split second, I honestly believed. But then, I wondered if I'd been had by a first-class con artist trying to take me for a ride. That's why I stayed away."

Bowen looked patiently into her face, his eyes glowing unnervingly in the light cast by the fireplace. "What do you require of me?" he said, touching his mouth to her forehead with soft kisses that worked their way around to her mouth again.

"Mmm..." Ashlon softly moaned as his lips pasted to hers with a long searching kiss. Bowen lifted his head, meeting and holding her eyes.

Ashlon caught her breath again. She could get totally lost in that amethyst richness, fall into the depths of those amazing eyes. "Are you really a... a...?" Bowen gently frowned. "Yes, beloved. I have been one with the night for over 400 years." He frowned even more when Ashlon paled and softly gasped. Something shriveled inside him, fearing the worst—she'd reject him and he would have to turn her to protect himself. But, would he honestly be able to do this now? Could he trust her enough to keep his secret if she rejected him and wanted to leave? Those disturbing thoughts made something hurt deep inside him, something he'd only recently discovered was still very fragile and would shatter if she didn't want him, could not love him.

Ashlon stared into his haunted features, felt the tension along the length of his body holding her prisoner under him. She knew what real evil looked like, what it acted like. And now, here was Bowen—beautiful, terrifying Bowen—admittedly a dark wanderer of the night. He could have ended her life countless times from the moment she'd found him out. Instead, he held her now in the tenderest of snares and had bared his heart to her, risking everything. Maybe it was time to do the same.

"I've dreamt of you," she confessed, looking away into the fire. "Ever since I've lived here, I've dreamt of you—of us. We were always parted by terrible circumstances, moving on to other lives, other places. And then, you appeared again, taking ownership of this house. I knew you the first time I saw you. Knew you when you held me and kissed me. It scared me, the things I felt and theway you made me feel, how much I wanted you." Had she said what he thought she said? Bowen slowly smiled. "You've wanted me?"

"At the Festival dance, I was so sure we'd met before because I knew the touch of your lips and the feel of your arms around me. But your intensity and absolute certainty terrified me. I didn't want to get hurt again, so I pushed you away. I thought I'd done the right thing when I discovered what you are and denied you. Tonight, I was here to see Mr. Stanley and was absolutely determined to be gone before you returned. You know the rest."

Bowen brushed his lips across hers again. He could not get enough of their warmth, their flavor. However, this time Ashlon hesitantly wrapped her arms around his neck and raised her lips to his as if asking a question. Bowen pressed his mouth firmly to hers, answering with a passion he no longer had to hold back.

"I can't stay away anymore, Bowen. And, I don't care what you are," Ashlon whispered, her lips brushing his smooth face. "If we're destined to be together, let's see where it takes us this time."

Bowen slowly smiled and kissed her again, this time as an affirmation that she was his alone, and what remained was the sweetest testament she could possibly give him. His desire had gone beyond any more words, and he took her lips with a force that drew a passion-filled moan from her.

Ashlon drank him in like sweet nectar as Bowen took her to a place she never knew existed, and made her body feel his loving with a force that sucked away any residual doubt. He immersed her in a glorious haze of unbelievable rapture, taking her in ways defying any description of them. She must have passed out at some point during the night because she awakened to find they were in his large, soft bed in the master bedroom with the light of many candles surrounding them.

Bowen pulled her to him and resumed his relentless loving until, in that final hour before dawn, he held her tightly one last time, taking her more passionately than anytime that night, wanting to keep them joined for as long as possible before the dawn parted them. Approaching that last darkest hour before dawn, a prolonged visceral moan of almost unbearable ecstasy blossomed from deep inside her. Bowen's head reared up, his eyes glazed as he ground his hips to hers faster than Ashlon thought possible, and then pressed hard into her with a shudder racking his body as Ashlon held him tightly, immersed in his scent and utter helplessness in the throes of his sublime pleasure. Suddenly, his head lowered and firmly sealed his mouth over the tender skin just under and in front of her one ear. She gasped as he bit into her throat, followed by the utterly delicious pulling of his lips as he kneaded the skin beneath his clinging fingers. Her soft moans urged him on, rocking against her in time to his sweet kiss. She came again with a force that made her cry out like she'd never heard herself voice before. And Bowen's sudden, powerful release was so forceful that he released her throat and pushed back with a deep, trembling roar that echoed off the walls of the room. He collapsed on top of her, utterly spent, physically sated, his mouth finding hers for more passionate kissing before drifting back to her throat.

His eyes closed as he kissed gently, persistently. The taste of her sweetness and Ashlon's warm breath on his shoulder were so intoxicating that he lost himself in her passion and embracing warmth.

Ashlon was totally spent, so tired she could barely move. She was also beginning to feel the effect of Bowen's passionate feeding; she gently tugged on one of his ears. He seemed to awaken from a blissful trance and slowly lapped at the wounds. She drowsed as he vocalized a deep-throated soft moan, alternating brief soft kisses with his warm tongue's licking around her new souvenirs. After what seemed like hours, he finished. She opened her eyes and found him looking down at her, a smile playing on his lips.

"What?" she said in a sleepy half whisper, caressing his face and lips, running her fingers through his hair.

"Now we are truly one, beloved," he could finally acknowledge. She had accepted his kiss that bonded them, proving she trusted him without reservation. Bowen rolled onto his side and pulled her into his arms, her head nestled on his shoulder's soft cushion. He circled her legs with his and nuzzled into her soft hair, closing his eyes with deep satisfaction.

She spoke into his cheek before sleep overtook her. "Ani l'dodi, l'dodi li'. I am my beloved's, and my beloved is mine." She met Bowen's gentle smile with her own, and then settled back into his shoulder, drifting off to sleep.

"Just so," he whispered as his lips touched hers one last time.

He was gone when she woke the following morning, the sun struggling through a high thin layer of light grey clouds drifting in from the north. She stretched lazily and seriously considered not getting up at all until she heard a distant phone ringing. It was the distinct ring tone of her cell phone somewhere downstairs. Hastily rising, she wrapped a blanket around her and ran from the bedroom, her bare feet protesting the icy wooden floors as she scurried along the short hall to the gallery and down the staircase to the foyer. Jeez, that tile was cold! She stopped for a second and looked around for her bag. It wasn't there. Fortunately, her phone kept ringing and ringing, and she followed it to the sitting room where she found her handbag, shopping bags, and her shoes and socks placed together on the floor in front of the sofa. Her clothes had been gathered into a shredded, unwearable pile, where she also found a handwritten note with her name on it next to a very well-rendered drawing of a black rose. She quickly extracted her cell phone from her bag and pulled her feet up under the blanket as she curled up on the couch.

"Hello?" she said breathlessly.

"Damn it, Ashlon Isaacs! You're harder to find than a pair of jeans for my butt!" Janey complained on the other end. "Where the hell are you?"

Ashlon almost laughed out loud but stifled the urge. "Janey, it's so amazing I can't begin to describe it over the phone! You gotta come over to my place, like, in about an hour! Okay?"

"You sound very weird, Ash, "Janey said suspiciously, "like you're excited about something—by the way, just where the hell are you, anyway?"

Ashlon was grinning like an idiot, feeling as if—well, it had for that matter—a whole new world had opened to her. "McAnders House," she half-whispered, not exactly knowing why.

Janey's sudden shriek into the phone temporarily deafened her. When she put the receiver back to her ear, Janey was laughing almost hysterically. Okay, now she knew why she'd whispered.

"Omygawd, Omygawd, Omygawd! You finally got laid! That crazy midnight lover was there when I dropped you off and you got laid! Ash, I am so proud of you! But I need details!"

"You're so crass," Ashlon sighed, closing her eyes. And obviously, she wasn't about to inform Janey that Bowen was the real thing. Everyone knew there were no such things, didn't they? Yeah, best to keep Janey in the dark for the time being until it was no longer an option.

"One hour! Bye!" Janey breathily said, then hung up.

She shook her head in dismay as she closed her phone and deposited it back into her bag. She'd palmed the note she'd found on top of her unwearable clothes, remembering vividly Bowen's black rose attar scent overpowering her resistance. Then his unearthly passionate loving throughout the night. But the clothes...? Hmm.

She opened the note, recognizing his formal swirling script as the same one on the card on her dresser. Well, there was a mystery solved. The note explained the mystery of her shredded clothes, too. She read it with sublime warmth and tenderness:

My dearest Ashlon, I must leave you for the day, but I will see you tonight. I will also escort you to the Mayor's party on Monday evening. Mere words cannot describe what we shared last night, but I promise there will be many more to come. I have moved your things into the sitting room and built the fire for when you waken. However, I must also offer my apology for ruining your clothes. In my impassioned haste, I believed you could not remove them as quickly as I. Please bring me a bill for their replacement. Bowen.

He would be going to the ball! And she knew he would look fabulous. However, as Ashlon sat there on the couch, warmed by the fire and her memory of the previous night, she wondered how she was going to get home without decent clothes against the cold outside. Damnation! She should have told Janey to come get her, but it was too late now. Janey never carried her cell phone on her day off, and today she was off and usually not at home. Oh well, this was problematic at best—at least she had her shoes and warm fuzzy knee socks, a warm blanket, and a back door to her house.

She disposed of the rags formerly her clothes, then wrapped the blanket around her after putting on her shoes and socks. With all her bags in hand, she let herself out the back door.

Chapter 23

After a quick warm shower, Ashlon dressed and then sat at her dressing table to consider how she would hide the bite marks on her neck from Janey. There was deep bruising around them—Bowen's lusty kiss had been vigorous and still sent shivers of delight through her at the memory of it. She decided on a turtle neck under a sweater. However, the mayor's Ball was another matter. That thin velvet choker she'd bought to match her dress for the party would be inadequate for coverage, and she figured Bowen had made those marks to last for a while. Oh well, she'd tackle that one later.

She'd just put on a pot of coffee to brew when the doorbell rang several times—Janey's signal. Ashlon fairly bounced to the front door and flung it open to her friend, who was admiring her front porch decorations.

"You really went all out this year," Janey commented as she gingerly touched the scarecrow and shivered at its pumpkin head's sinister grin. "That's truly disturbing."

She followed Ashlon inside. Pausing momentarily inside as Ashlon closed the door behind her, she raised her nose and sniffed the fresh coffee scent filling the downstairs area. Strangely, she scrunched up her face with disgust, and looked like she turned a little green. Suddenly, she clapped a hand over her mouth and made a beeline for Ashlon's downstairs bathroom. Moments later, Ashlon caught the distinct sounds of deep groaning and violent retching into her toilet (she hoped!) Rapidly crossing the living room to her bathroom, Ashlon met Janey as she stumbled out, supporting her as they moved into the living room.

"No coffee for you, girlfriend," Ashlon declared as Janey plunked heavily onto the couch and lay back, closing her eyes with a groan. Ashlon went back into the kitchen and quickly heated a cup of water in her microwave. She found her green tea with mint, and soon had a strong cup brewed, lightly sweetening it with just a touch of honey. Ashlon returned to her living room and put the cup in Janey's hands. "Drink it. It'll settle your stomach."

Janey sniffed it first, took a tentative sip, then another, her smile weak but grateful.

Ashlon plunked into her recliner as she watched her friend take a few more tentative sips from the mug. "Is it a stomach bug or what?"

Janey blinked at Ashlon, looking a lot like a deer caught in bright lights, tears welling in her eyes, and her expression absolutely crestfallen. "Oh, Ash!" she suddenly sniffed, wiping her eyes on her sleeve.

Ashlon quickly shifted from the chair to the sofa and took Janey in her arms, holding her shaking shoulders. "Tell me what it is, honey! Please! It can't be that bad, can it?" She had a sudden disturbing thought. "Jorge didn't dump you, did he?"

Janey looked at her incredulously through moist eyes. "Jesus, Ash! Of course he didn't!"

"Well, then, what is it? You know I don't play well first thing in the morning."

Janey took a deep, shaky breath. "I'm late," she whispered.

Ashlon didn't say anything at first, letting this sink in. "Okay, did you do a home pregnancy test?"

Janey nodded miserably. "Uh huh. Twice."

Ashlon was excited now. Janey buried her face in her hands and lay down in Ashlon's lap. Ashlon stroked her hair and took her hand, giving it a kiss.

"You're going to be a mommy," she softly said, barely suppressing a surge of joy. Instead, she hugged Janey close when she dissolved into tears again.

Much later, after Janey had pretty much cried herself out, they sat at Ashlon's kitchen table, splitting a couple of butter croissants between them.

Janey's color had improved, but she still looked miserable and very emotionally strung out. What didn't help was Ashlon's wide, happy grin that was making Janey crazy.

"Ash, if you don't wipe that stupid smirk off your face right this minute, I'll tell everyone we know you have a vampire fetish!" she snarled as she stuffed half a croissant into her mouth.

"I can't help it!" Ashlon exclaimed turning away as she got up to pour herself another cup of coffee, blessing it with a splash of creamer from the refrigerator. When she sat back down, she'd succeeded in wiping half her grin off her face. "I'm positively kvelling about it!"

"Well, don't... whatever," Janey said with impatience darkening her face. "Shit, Ash! I'm thirty-six years old! And we both know what the odds are at my age of birth defects and multiples and G-d knows what else!" She plunked her head into her arms, folded on the table, moaning, "I can't deal with this."

"Have you told Jorge, yet?" Ashlon ventured as she took a sip of her coffee. "No, not yet. I did the tests early this morning and haven't decided if I should say anything yet. Or at all. I wanted to talk to you first, but I must have rung here a million times and left messages. I was so upset I forgot you had your cell phone on you. When I was finally able to remember your number, I rang it until you answered."

Ashlon reached across the table and rubbed Janey's head with her fingertips, remembering how a good scalp massage always seemed to relax her. And, boy oh boy, did Janey need to relax now! She sighed and dropped her face back into her arms, gradually responding to Ashlon's talented fingers.

"That's better," Ashlon said as she rose again, circled the small table, and stood behind Janey massaging her neck and shoulders. "You've got yourself so worked up, you're not thinking straight. Now listen to me. First of all, you're engaged to a wonderful man who thinks you make the sun come up in the morning and the stars come out at night. I'm willing to bet that a baby with you would be the icing on his conjugal cake."

Janey snorted but said nothing.

"Second, I know that in your deepest heart of hearts, you've always wanted at least one kid. But like me, you were once married to a bastard who beat the crap out of you and any likelihood of a kid with him."

Janey grudgingly nodded.

"And third, for what it's worth, I've seen you with the kids here in town and your sister's kids. I know how good you were with Emma. When she could talk, she always wanted to see Aunt Gea. You're phenomenal with children, and I know you'll be a fantastic mother. Trust me on this." Ashlon ran her arms around Janey's shoulders and gave her another hug, then returned to her chair and sat down to finish her coffee. She watched with satisfaction as Janey raised her head and stared wonderingly at her.

"How do you do it?" Janey said with a weak smile as she wiped her eyes on her sleeve again.

"Do what?"

"Make me feel like a million dollars and loved and cherished and special even when I feel like shit?"

"Because at heart I'm a psych nurse, you're my dearest friend, and I love you. Now finish your tea. We've got to find your Romeo and take him out for lunch. Is he available today, or do we wait for tomorrow during his regular office hours?"

Janey shook her head. "He's out of town at his mother's until tonight. We can spring it on him tomorrow at lunch." She sighed and took another bite of a croissant as she downed the remainder of her tea. Then, she suddenly brightened. "You know that Zorro costume he wore for the Harvest Dance?" she inquired.

Ashlon frowned, wondering how their conversation jumped

to this other track. "Uh, yeah, I suppose so. What about it?"

Janey put her teacup in the sink and threw away her napkin. She smirked at Ashlon. "He's worn it for me several times since then." She rolled her eyes with an exaggerated sigh as she clasped her hands over her heart.

"Janey, you're truly perverted. You know that, don't you? No wonder you're knocked up," Ashlon laughed as she got up and gave her friend another big hug. This time, Janey managed to laugh with her.

Janey spent the morning with Ashlon, helping her clean her place until it sparkled. Then, they went over to Janey's apartment and repeated their efforts. That evening, Ashlon called over to Bowen's answering service and informed him she couldn't see him that night. She was spending the night with Janey, who didn't want to be left alone while Jorge was out of town.

Of course, she reassured him she would see him at the Ball Monday night, but first she was going to absolutely enjoy herself playing spooky music and sound effects, handing out candy, and scaring little kids at her house. It was Halloween, and she had every intention of doing it up just as she had with Emma.

They slept late the next morning, and Ashlon made sure Janey had some warm tea and lightly buttered toast once she got through purging in the bathroom. At noon, Ashlon drove them into town to Jorge's office located on the circle two doors down from 'A Place in Thyme'. She parked on the curb next to Jorge's office. Janey was visibly nervous and allowed Ashlon to lead her into the waiting room. She sat in a chair near the receptionist's desk as Ashlon asked the clerk to let Dr. Villarreal know his fiancée was here to see him with some important news.

The clerk was a pleasant older woman whom Ashlon had interviewed and hired for the job once Jorge moved into his new office. A crackshot receptionist, she was also adept with insurance claims, Medicaid, and Medicare, and especially good at barter for services with their rural patients.

Now, she greeted Ashlon with a pleasant smile and waved over at Janey. She'd be right back, she assured them as she disappeared through a sliding glass door just to the left and behind her desk. Ashlon sat down next to Janey.

It was comfortable in here with real padded seats on the chairs. The walls were painted with a wrap-around mural created by the local high school advanced art class tasked to create their concept of peace on earth. It was remarkable what they had come with: Maya Angelou's poetry, the Dalai Lama, a lion with the lamb, the Desiderata, the tablets of the Ten Commandments, hands around the world, and the United Nations flag with a peace symbol at its center, among other designs. Just went to show the older generation that the younger one wasn't so screwed up after all. The floor had been retiled with earth-tone twelve-inch ceramic tiles that were treated with a protective coating, making them easily cleaned if any human fluid soiled them accidentally. And, because the office was a remodeled retail business, a large show window fronted the street.

They had been there waiting about ten minutes, and Ashlon was leisurely watching the activity passing by in the street and on the sidewalk while Janey nervously paged through her magazine, her eyes on the sliding glass door. Ashlon suddenly sat up, growling through her teeth when she spotted someone across the circle she absolutely did not want to see.

"Oh shit!" she cursed under her breath. "I forgot all about him!"

Janey followed her line of sight and patted Ashlon's arm sympathetically.

"The guy's completely clueless," she said sympathetically.

Grady Roberts had seen Ashlon's Jeep parked outside Jorge's office and ran across the circle. When he reached the Wrangler, he took a quick look inside, then mounted the sidewalk and peered through the glass into Jorge's waiting area. He spotted only Janey, who looked up and sneered at him, and then went back to her magazine. Grady searched down the sidewalk toward his sister's tearoom and headed in that direction.

Janey slowly counted to ten. When Grady didn't come back, she said, "All clear."

Ashlon rolled out from under the receptionist's desk and stood up. "She's got huge dust bunnies living under there!" she said with disgust as she brushed off her jacket and jeans, then cautiously approached and looked out the window before sitting again next to Janey. Propping her elbows on her knees, she leaned forward and cupped her face in her hands with a deep, dispirited groan. "I feel like such a craven coward."

"You are," Janey readily agreed with her. "But after what happened, I can't really blame you."

Ashlon looked up again, her expression becoming smug. "Lord McAnders was going to kill him if I hadn't had that emotional meltdown after Grady wimped and bolted. So he owes me big time."

Janey gasped. "No! You're really serious, aren't you? He told you that? Wow!"

"I know," Ashlon said, slumping back into her chair. "Doesn't the guy realize if the police haven't come to question him by now, then I haven't filed charges on him yet?"

Janey rubbed Ashlon's back. "Maybe the only way to make him back off is to stop playing escape and evasion and confront the problem head-on. Read him the riot act and then follow through at the district office. Anderson looks like the kind of guy who won't blow it off."

Ashlon nodded and sighed as she chewed her bottom lip. "You're right. But what if something else is going on? He acted kind of desperate when he realized I wasn't going to invite him in and make nice."

"Trying to take what you wouldn't give him because he has an agenda?" Janey said. "Sounds pretty thin."

"But why now? I've known his family since we've lived here, Janey. Went to dinners at their house, visited to Irma, and helping her set up her kitchen, assisting with some of her chores when I wasn't working. Grady was there a lot of the times I was, and barely paid me two nods outside of the marginally tolerant kind. Now, all of a sudden I'm Miss Popularity, and he tries to force himself on me? Something just doesn't add up."

Janey was rubbing her forehead with the beginning of a hunger headache slowly edging over her eyes. "From what you told me about McAnders, sounds like he did pretty near the same thing Grady did. But you stayed with Mr. Dark and Mysterious. So tell me, oh wise one, what makes you think it's any different with him?"

Ashlon faced. "Bowen would have allowed me to leave if I wanted to, even after everything he told me. He was … I don't know how to describe it, Janey." Ashlon covered her mouth with her fingers, stifling a laugh. "He told me he loved me, and that he wouldn't go on in the loneliness he's lived with any longer since finding me. Saturday night was like something unreal. He said he'd been searching for me for a long time, that we were destined to be together. And we made passionate love in ways I never imagined existed. And, we went all—night—long!"

Janey's mouth dropped open. "Are you serious?!" she gasped.

Ashlon laughed as she nodded, becoming warm with the memory. "The last hour before dawn was the best yet. My body is still humming, and my toes are curling just thinking about it." Ashlon raised a questioning eyebrow. "Still think I'm crazy?"

They heard polite throat clearing off to the side. Delia, the receptionist, was standing in the open doorway to the clinic area, rapidly fanning herself with a file folder as she smiled with polite embarrassment. "Miss Isaacs, if I may forward a frank comment: You'd be out of your freaking mind to screw that up."

She returned directly to her desk, sat down heavily, concentrating with effort on something on her computer screen.

Ashlon and Janey looked at each other with amazement. Delia usually wasn't given to being so outspoken.

"I rest my case," Ashlon said with a note of finality and sat back, closing herself off to any more suggestions. However, Janey was not deterred.

"Just one last thing, Ash," Janey turned toward her friend, "and I really want you to think about this. Be sure you love him. Honestly, look inside yourself and say this is the man you would take a bullet for, or support against a raging mob with torches and pitchforks and … well, you get the idea. That he's not just a dodge or buffer to keep Grady away. Like you pointed out to me, we've both been hurt and I don't want it to happen to you again. Look inside and see who's looking back. Right now, it looks to me like you need to think on it a little more." She turned around in her chair and resumed not reading her magazine.

Fortunately, Jorge emerged from the back as an uncomfortable silence surrounded the two friends.

"Hello, ladies," he greeted them warmly. "Sorry, I took so long, but I was doing a procedure and it required more time than figured."

Janey dropped her magazine on Ashlon's lap and rose to give him a passionate kiss. "Hi, sweetie!" she crooned warmly. He held her and murmured something in her ear that made her giggle.

Ashlon couldn't help grinning at them. Their regard and affection for each other was obvious to anyone who watched them. Ashlon's assurances that Janey's surprise would be a welcome enrichment to their relationship had just been given a stamp of confirmation as far as she was concerned. And it also had her thinking a little more seriously about what Janey had said. She'd planted the seeds of doubt and questioning in Ashlon's conscience, and they were growing. Could she love Bowen in spite of what he was, and did he truly love her? Or had he created an elaborate smoke screen to lure her into his bed and nibble on her neck? Why would he go to such extreme measures and say those beautiful things to her if that's all he'd wanted from the beginning? Where was her basis for comparison? Certainly not Wyatt!

"Damn it all," she softly cursed to herself. The seeds of her own doubt had never really been purged, she silently admitted. They'd merely lain dormant until new grounds of consideration had been spread over them.

Thanks a lot, Janey, Ashlon silently groaned. But, now wasn't the time to confront this new conundrum. This was Janey's moment, and she'd swallow the self-doubt study until later when she could examine it more thoroughly.

Chapter 24

At Jorge's suggestion, they went to an inn called The Black Lion on one of the southbound roads out of town. Ashlon followed Jorge in her Jeep, while Janey rode with Jorge in his SUV. The countryside was bleak and barren with low, darkening cloud cover threatening cold rain within the next several hours. Ashlon hoped it would hold off until after the trick-or-treating hours tonight. She'd bought a fortune in candy and didn't relish having a surplus on hand to get rid of.

The inn loomed out of a foggy horizon on the edge of a shopping complex that linked to a town called Ware. It magically appeared out of the trees like a way station for the hungry and displaced, a welcome sight. They parked and quickly went inside to escape the biting cold.

It was a cozy place with tables set on the ground floor and a mezzanine and was fashioned in the colonial style of the late 1700s. Ashlon instantly liked it. A large stone hearth on the main floor burned with the fragrances of cedar and pine diffusing through the dining area as wait staff in breeches, hose, and weskits hustled from table to table. Lighting was provided by hanging lamps over the tables that had candles burning under hurricane chimneys, lending warmth and an intimate ambience to the dining areas.

They were escorted to a hearthside table by a pleasant, heavy-set woman clad in a long colonial-style dress, apron, and goodwife's cap. After seating them and handing out the menus, she took their drink orders and departed. Jorge had started to order a rum punch for Janey, but she quickly nixed it for a cranberry soda instead. He looked at her quizzically, but she only shrugged and stared down at the table surface. Ashlon read her friend was getting cold feet about her news and kicked her under the table, making a face at Janey as if to say 'don't you dare!'.

Their drinks arrived with their server who introduced himself as "good day my name is Richard and I'll be at your service this fine meal", as he placed their drinks in front of them—Janey's cranberry soda, Jorge's Corona with lime, and Ashlon's heated mead (after all, this was a colonial-themed restaurant.) Janey immediately ordered and gave Richard her menu, then excused herself to go to the restroom. Jorge was looking worried when he glanced across the table at Ashlon.

"What's going on here?" He fixed an accusing stare on her. "No rum punch, and she ordered half the menu. Usually, she eats like a mouse."

Ashlon smiled innocently at his twitching mustache and took a deep chug of her mead, finishing it. She caught Richard as he passed their table and requested a refill, then looked back at Jorge and shrugged. "She'll say something when she's ready."

Jorge wasn't convinced, but didn't press the issue as he brooded over his beer.

Richard brought the mead and several hot, crusty whole grain mini-loaves in a basket along with hand-churned butter in a small clay crock, setting them on the table. Janey returned looking very pale and ever so slightly green again. Ashlon knew she'd paid another tribute to the porcelain god while in the restroom. She called the hostess over and stood to speak to her so that Jorge couldn't hear. The hostess nodded with a wide grin appearing on her generous mouth, quickly scurrying off to the kitchen. She returned a few minutes later with a teapot and a honey server on the side, setting it in front of Janey. She took the cranberry soda away immediately, giving Janey a wink as she left. Janey immediately turned her coffee cup on the saucer and picked up the teapot, pouring with a shaking hand.

"Ash, could you give us a moment, sweety?" Janey finally said after a generous sip from her cup.

"Sure thing. It's peppermint with a touch of ginger. You'll feel better." Ashlon rose with her mead in hand, gave Janey a peck on the cheek, rounded the table and gave Jorge a sound clip on the shoulder, and left the table to catch the view from a deck out behind the building. She looked over her shoulder once, catching Janey moving her chair over next to Jorge, and then taking his hands in hers. Ashlon pushed open the door to the outside. They were going to be alright.

She strolled to the edge of the deck and leaned on the rail, sipping her mead and letting her thoughts drift. But, they always went back to Bowen and the things he'd said that amazing Saturday night. Could two people really be destined to find each other regardless of how long it took? Had those dreams of hers really been moments in time she'd once lived in? Or, was she merely a hopeless romantic indulging in a wild fantasy that was going to bite her in the ass when it finally crashed? Bowen had certainly declared himself resolutely and eloquently enough, touching her so deeply she'd stayed the night.

In the end, she was the only one who could decide on the course to take, and hope to heaven she picked the right one. Especially when dealing with the supernatural. She was groping in the dark here, hoping a light would come on somewhere.

"It's nice out here, isn't it?" an alarmingly familiar voice commented from behind her, with the scent of Burberry for Men following it.

Shit. It couldn't be.

Ashlon froze where she stood for a moment, her grip tightening around the tall metal mug of hot mead. He must have seen them leaving, the bastard. She took a deep breath and turned. "I'm warning you, Grady. Stay away from me," she grimly said as she backed away from him, uncertain how to handle his presence there. "I didn't call the police in consideration for your mother, but if you try anything again, the gloves are off."

He moved to the rail and looked out over the forest at the edge of the sloping yard below. She never took her eyes off him, staying out of arm's reach. If he tried anything, there were plenty of people inside to help. She also had a tall hot mug of mead in her hands and wouldn't hesitate to use it.

"I don't blame you one bit for not trusting me," Grady said as he continued to look out over the railing into the distant forest shrouded in a cold rainy mist. "What I did was reprehensible. When I thought about it later on, after pulling my head out of my ass, I had to find you and try to apologize. That is, if you hadn't gotten a restraining order yet."

He wouldn't make eye contact, Ashlon immediately noted. Probably knows I can see he doesn't mean it. Oh no! Not going down that road again, Ashlon's eyes narrowed, knowing what he was doing. Been there, done that too many times with Wyatt—kiss and make nice until the next round of violence. It was when the hitting escalated and threatened Emma that she'd acknowledged it had gone too far and he'd become dangerous. She'd called the police. And then he'd disappeared. When the divorce papers arrived, she'd gladly signed them. But the restraining order stayed active, even to this day.

"Okay, you've apologized and been appropriately if not believably contrite.

Now, go away," Ashlon snapped a him.

"Alright, I'll go." Grady turned and carefully moved around her to the restaurant entrance. "Take care of yourself, Ash," he said with a final shrug as he exited the deck.

She didn't say a word, watching him until he was gone. That's when she discovered she'd been holding her breath until the front entrance to the restaurant closed behind him.

This wasn't the end of it. She could feel it in her bones.

Ashlon took a few deep breaths, then went back inside the restaurant and returned to her table, where Jorge and Janey were waiting patiently for her.

They ate their lunch in silence.

Afterward, Jorge passed the bill over to her, a disapproving expression darkening his face. "What the hell was he doing here?"

"Don't worry about it," Ashlon said as she pulled her wallet from her jeans pocket. She dropped several bills on the table to cover the entire bill, then called Richard over and ordered another mead. When it arrived, she raised a toast to Jorge and Janey.

"You're drunk," Jorge stated flatly.

"Never. Been non-alcoholic the entire time," Ashlon said, chugging the mead and giving her lips a satisfied smack. "C'mon, we gotta get ready for Halloween and the mayor's party. Race you back." She pushed out of her chair and headed for the exit, followed by her bewildered friends. Thank heaven they couldn't know the mess running around her head, wanting the solitary drive back home to sort it all out.

By the appointed hour, the clouds had suddenly dispersed, leaving a cold, clear, star-filled sky bumping the edge of twilight with the promise of ghosts and ghoulies and scary things in the night. Street lights sputtered on all over town, and front porch lamps shined on grinning pumpkins and monster figures. Front yards had become graveyards and moaned with the sounds of the restless souls beneath the cold ground. Delighted shrieks and ringing doorbells filled the air with the mystery and magic that only a child's imagination can create on this very special night.

Ashlon's front room was dark. A light show flashed in her front window resembling a thunder storm, and the sounds of a haunted house issued from her CD player under the stairs. Votive candles were lit on the kitchen table to provide just a little safety for her as she answered each call of "trick or treat" with her black cat bowl full of this year's popular candy, as well as her own caramel apples wrapped in orange and black with her name and address on a label attached to the stick.

It was positively bewitching, and one of Ashlon's favorite times of the year. Of course, an end comes to most events, and much too quickly on those enjoyed the most. The official trick or treat time came to an end, and at the appointed hour, Ashlon turned off her porch light and closed her front door. She drew her curtains and took off the spooky sounds and light show. After blowing out the candles and turning on her living room lights, she went upstairs to dress for the mayor's party. Janey and Jorge would be meeting her there. Hopefully, Bowen would be there, too, but tempered her expectations. What was it her bubbe used to say? 'Don't count your latkes before they're fried.' She'd given up the goods, so to speak, so it was prudent not to build up her hopes too much on a one-night venture, regardless of what was said then. Words spoken in the heat of lust might just cool into convenient forgetfulness!

Thirty minutes later, she stood in front of her mirror examining the décolletage needed for the cut of her dress, making only a few adjustments to her push-up bra. Thanks to the miracle of creative lingerie, she had enough cleav- age now to fill out the neckline and bodice without creating a single wrinkle or crease. A new choker had been located at a drugstore in Wade and was wide enough to cover the neck bruise that looked like a world-class hickey. The puncture marks had vanished.

Her dress was form-fitting, pushed off her shoulders, and she'd found a bonus—those long scarlet sleeves had tiny red roses embroidered at the pointed ends over her wrists. She decided not to wear the gloves after all. A garnet and onyx jeweled ring, and black mini-heels that ribbon-tied around her ankles finished her accesso- ries beautifully. A spritz of cologne, some deep red lipstick, a flick of her hair with some mousse, and she was ready. She grabbed her black beaded clutch and left the bedroom, heading downstairs for the front door. However, after turning on her porch light, Ashlon suddenly real- ized she was going to have a problem getting into her Jeep. Her dress was very form-fitting with only a little stretch to the skirt, so unless she hoisted it up to her knees, this was going to be difficult, not to mention exposing a great deal of leg to the neighbors.

As she stood there wondering if she should call Janey to give her a ride, a sudden movement from the corner of her front room near the kitchen made her gasp and turn as a huge form rose in its shadows, moving faster than she could follow, sweeping her into long arms, pressing a hungry kiss to her lips. A familiar scent drifted around her as warm kisses caressed her mouth, traveling down her cheek.

"I could not wait to see you," Bowen's voice was husky, and he hugged her tightly against him. "You look so beautiful tonight, my love."

"Air!" Ashlon gasped. Bowen's grip immediately loosened, but only a little. She took a deep, relieved breath, resting her forehead on his chest with intense relief. "You scared the life out of me," she said with mock disapproval, but unable to hide how very happy she was to see him. His persistant tender kisses softened her expression as she smiled.

"I apologize for startling you," he said sweetly. "Do you require a conveyance to our engagement? I hardly think your vehicle will accommodate your dress."

How perfectly delightful. "As a matter of fact, I was wondering whether to call my friend for a ride."

"You will travel with me," Bowen declared resolutely as he picked Ashlon's hooded evening cape from the couch, holding it for her. She slipped into it and did up the front closure. Then, she took Bowen's waiting arm, allowing him to lead her from the house to the front curb where his Cadillac was parked in front of her Jeep. As he opened the passenger door for her, Mrs. Kincaid came out to her front door step and leaned on her railing, grinning broadly at them. "Deary, you look like this night should, but so rarely does," she called out with a chuckle.

Ashlon turned and smiled warmly at her neighbor. "Thank you, Mrs. Kincaid. I try."

"No, dear. Others try—you succeed. You take care of her, young man!" The old woman shook a warning finger at Ashlon's tall, dark escort.

After he helped Ashlon arrange her dress and cape, Bowen turned and made a gallant sweeping bow to Mrs. Kincaid.

"My lady, your command is my duty's call. Have no concerns for your lady friend." He bowed again and quickly went around to the driver's side, sliding smoothly into the seat. As they pulled out onto the road Ashlon waved at Mrs. Kincaid as they passed by her. She was smiling blissfully as she gave Ashlon two thumbs up.

Chapter 25

The ball was held at the Mayoral residence just east of town. It was a large rambling colonial that had been restored at little cost to the mayor. Ashlon suspected any renovation funding originally earmarked for McAnders House had been siphoned into the Mayoral residence by one of Alice Tisbee's friends at the state level, but she couldn't prove it unless she demanded an audit. Predictably, the chairman adamantly refused to do one for fear of finding other irregularities. That's when Ashlon and Mr. Stanley had demanded all their research be returned and gave up any further efforts.

This still rankled at Ashlon's sense of justice as Bowen pulled into the circular drive and parked under a covered area in front of the house. A valet opened Ashlon's door and assisted her from the car. He blushed violently when she smiled at him and gave him a warm thank you before taking Bowen's arm and heading up the steps to the open front door. She laughed when she caught a hushed "Wow!" but had to stop Bowen from turning and doing something hurtful to the startled young valet who immediately jumped into the car and drove off with a screech of tires. Bowen watched with narrow-eyed disapproval. Then, and only then, did he allow himself to be led inside.

They entered a large foyer with a table set at its center filled with candy and fall decorations, strolling around it toward the bottom of the main stairs. People were milling around in the living room to the left of the foyer with drinks and chattering amiably, waiting on the start of the festivities that were almost
20 minutes late. Ashlon heard some grousing from one of the guests that the band was late.

Alice's son, who had been ghosting the goody table, recognized Ashlon immediately and jauntily sauntered up to her, appearing extremely uncomfortable in his clothes for the evening. Obviously picked out by Alice, Ashlon thought with a smirk. Knowing Max, he'd have come as a serial killer or Spiderman.

"Hello, Max," Ashlon greeted him pleasantly as she examined his costume. He was dressed as a colonial youth in the typical weskite with white linen shirt, brown wool breeches, and hose with slip-on buckled shoes. His dress coat was the same color as his breeches, with silver buttons down the front and on the sleeves. "Max, you look dashing." Ashlon complimented him.

The boy, undersized for his 11 years, grimaced. "I look like a first-class geek. Mom made me wear this stupid thing. Who's the stud?" He gave Bowen a frank appraising stare and waited for a reply from him.

Bowen stepped around Ashlon and stood toe to toe with the boy, gruffly looking down at him. Max, much to his credit, didn't flinch, standing firm with all the bravado an 11-year-old could muster when faced with someone who could have crushed him like a bug. Bowen bent slightly with an appraising gaze. He was wearing a conventional black tie evening ensemble, and his hair was tied back. He was far and away the best-looking man in that house. Ashlon was able to catch furtive glimpses and hear veiled whispers with envious stares from the men and women passing slowly around them. Again, she thanked the stars above for having the good sense to trust him Saturday night!

"Young man," Bowen's deeply accented baritone floated down to Max, who came up to maybe above his belt line. "I am Laird McAnders, young'un, and ye dunna look like a geek." He finished this statement with a courtly bow and the hint of a smile gracing his otherwise emotionless features.

Max smiled broadly and stepped back away from Bowen, returning the courtesy before running up the wide stairs, yelling, "Mom, mom!" as he disappeared over the head of the staircase.

Ashlon touched Bowen's arm, and he looked down at her, his gruff expression disappearing.

"That was a nice thing you did," she said. "He'll remember that for a long time."

Bowen slipped her arm through his again. "His courage is remarkable for one so young," he commented as they moved around the treat table toward the bottom of the staircase.

The lights flashed twice in the foyer. Max appeared again, running down the stairs and making a beeline to Ashlon and Bowen. He slid to a stop next to Ashlon. "Bout friggin' time they were ready to start," the boy snorted as he took her free hand. "Dad wants you guys to go in first. And wait until you see what we did up there!"

Ashlon laughed with a pleased glance at Bowen, who grimaced darkly but said nothing. Apparently, Mayor Tisbee was still on his persona non grata list. She wrinkled her nose at him and allowed Max to pull her along, Bowen moving reluctantly along only because Ashlon stubbornly hung to his arm. As they started up the wide staircase, Ashlon heard footsteps hustling up behind her with light gasping accompanying their approach. She glanced back over her shoulder. "Janey!" she cried out happily. Jorge was beside her and looked just as disgruntled as Bowen. He hadn't dressed up this time, either.

Janey pulled him along, too, as they ascended the long staircase to a set of high double doors looming directly ahead of them. Ashlon decided to lighten the moment a little bit and maybe make this thing more tolerable to their men. Funny how different they were, but how alike they behaved when forced to do something they objected to. Not even the span of 400 years, give or take, could wipe that out, could it?

"As the new students climbed the great stone stairway that wound to the top, they were met by another instructor who wore a high, pointed hat and long velvet robes, a pair of half-moon glasses perched on her nose. 'Welcome to Hogwarts, first years! I am Professor McGonagall!'" Ashlon recited in her best storytelling voice, generating muffled fits of laughter from Janey and Jorge. They reached the top of the stairs as the two great doors to the party hall were opened by the mayor, dressed as an English lord from the 1700s. Bowen scowled at him with deep disapproval, gripping Ashlon closer to him as they approached him.

"Sorry we couldn't start sooner, folks," Mayor Tisbee said, waving them to enter, but not before hastily greeting Bowen and Ashlon with a polite bow as they issued inside. Obviously, the mayor was out to curry brownie points after the rejection of his overture at the housewarming. Judging by Bowen's chilling expression, he hadn't succeeded.

Janey moved next to Ashlon as they paused inside the entrance for a moment and stared with delight at the decorations in the large hall. Glowing eerily in subdued lighting, a multitude of illuminated grinning papier mache Jack O'lanterns hung from the vaulted ceiling by nylon line so fine that they appeared to be floating in midair, and bats suspended around the perimeter of the room were fluttering as if they were living, breathing creatures. Orange and black streamers wafted in a breeze created by ceiling-level vents set at intervals around the room. Electric wall torches flickering like real flames had been placed at intervals on all four walls. Directly ahead of them, on the far side of the hall, a wide, low band stage had been placed for the musicians. It was the same ensemble that had played at the Harvest Festival party.

"What do you think, Miss Isaacs, Miss Ramirez?" Max asked excitedly as he dramatically waved his hand in a circle around the room. He was dancing from foot to foot as he waited for their response.

"Was this your idea, mejo?" Janey said as she reached out and tousled Max's hair. "There! Now you look more like Harry."

"You've recreated Hogwarts, Max," Ashlon said, squeezing his hand still clinging to hers. "It's brilliant."

Max released her hand and jumped up in the air, shouting, "Yahoo! They like it!" gleefully skipping around the room. Alice Tisbee, who was over by the buffet giving last-minute directions to the serving staff, glanced over at Janey and Ashlon and nodded gratefully to them.

"What was that all about?" Jorge said to Janey and Ashlon. "That young man was just itching for your approval."

"My question as well, doctor," Bowen said, looking down at Ashlon, his expression relaxed again since Mayor Tisbee was no longer in sight. The feeling was also returning to Ashlon's hand after he'd loosened his tense grip on her arm. She figured the mayor must have really ticked off Bowen in some other way to incite such a negative reaction, not just that faux pas at the housewarming.

Probably when he had returned to reclaim his property. It had been in the paper, splashed all over the front page after Janey and Ashlon had first spoken about the history of the house with Irma. Yep, the mayor had definitely screwed with the wrong laird.

"Max has cystic fibrosis," Janey explained. "He was hospitalized last year, and after he came home, Ash and I spent a lot of time initially doing Max's treatments and teaching his parents how to do them correctly. You know how labor-intensive they are. So, we kept Max diverted by reading the Harry Potter books to him. The kid fell in love with them, and they gave him an incentive to be more self-sufficient with his routine. He said he wanted something like this for his birthday or whenever if he stayed well through the year."

Ashlon looked around Janey at Jorge. "And now, we have a faithful recreation of a Halloween celebration at Hogwarts," she concluded with an approving nod.

Jorge was hungrily eyeballing the inviting buffet as he grabbed Janey's hand again. "Well, I don't see any house elves here to serve our food, so unless you want to go hungry, we'd better get in line," he suggested, and dragged Janey off to the buffet tables with her laughing behind him.

Ashlon felt a large hand on her shoulder that turned her and cupped her chin to raise her face toward his. Bowen appeared very puzzled. Frankly, Ashlon was surprised he hadn't just hauled her out of there when Mayor Tis-bee appeared and spirited her back to his house for the evening. She would have willingly let him, too, and worried about explanations later!

"You look like someone with a question," Ashlon said, reaching up with one hand to trace the lines across his furrowed brow and down around his mouth. As her fingers brushed across his lips, he clasped her hand and pressed a kiss to her palm.

"Who is this Harry Potter?" Bowen gently inquired as he rubbed her hand across his cheek and back to his lips. Apparently, there was a lot in popular literature he would have to become familiar with if he intended to keep up with her eclectic reading habits, Ashlon decided.

Just ... not right now.

She hummed with pleasure, enjoying the warm, smooth fullness of his lips when he kissed her palm again. His touch did things to her that were simply indescribable, intensely intimate.

"It's a wonderful series of books about a boy wizard," she said with effort.

"I've read them several times between movie sequels. I have all the books.

Maybe you'd like me to read them to you sometime."

Bowen wrapped his arms around her and held her close. "I would like that very much". As he bent to kiss her, Ashlon's stomach grumbled an empty protest. He looked down at her with a wry smile. "Perhaps you had better eat before it becomes any louder," he said, turning her toward the buffet and reluctantly releasing her.

Ashlon was simply amazed as she moved away from him, softly chuckling just loud enough for only him to hear. "Why Bowen McAnders, you just made a joke," she said with obvious delight as she headed toward the buffet, still shaking her head with pleasant disbelief. Picking up a plate from the warmer, she cruised the choices of hot and cold offerings, plus party cookies, chips, and a variety of dips, and petit fours drizzled in Halloween colors. The beverages included a ghastly colored punch in a large cauldron with a block of dry ice to create a boiling illusion (now that was pretty neat!), tea and coffee service in sparkling silver samovars, and cold sodas and bottled water kept chilled in a plastic-lined coffin filled with ice. A bar had been set up on the opposite side of the party room for those wishing for something of a more alcoholic nature.

The band began its first set as she approached the beverage table and indicated her choice to a young man in a neatly pressed service jacket, white shirt, and tie, and more or less intact blue jeans.

As she waited for the server to fill her cup with coffee (and his eyes with Ashlon), she heard a familiar voice from somewhere behind her and turned just enough to see from the corner of one eye.

Grady was dancing with a familiar-looking blonde lady dressed in fairy wings and a diaphanous costume of pastel multi-colored gauzy material caught at the waist with a thin gold cord. She wore green felt slippers pointed up at the toes. Ashlon turned back to the server, shaking her head with frank disgust as he handed her a filled cup of coffee and a creamer pitcher. He was staring at her with a weird, dreamy expression as she splashed some cream into her coffee.

Ashlon felt around her face and quickly looked down at her dress—nope, nothing she could find.

"Are you alright?" she asked the boy off-handedly as she returned the creamer to the table.

The server's immediate smile was goofy and completely innocent. "Don't need to fret about her, miss," he said with a sigh. "You got it head and shoulders over her if you don't mind my sayin'."

Her mood lifted almost immediately. Ashlon's pleased smile made the server blush crimson up to his ears. "Thank you for the compliment and the coffee," she said, moving back up the table line to where Janey and Jorge stood off to one side. Bowen had remained near the entrance doors and was conversing with the real estate agent who had helped him procure McAnders House while he was still in Scotland. Ashlon sidled up next to Janey, who was sipping off a Styrofoam cup.

"Remember when I made that comment about being an adolescent's wet dream?" she casually inquired.

Janey sputtered her orange juice and glared at Ashlon. "I'm drinking here, for Pete's sake! What brought that up?"

Ashlon raised her chin in the server's direction and caught him staring at her again. He quickly turned away and continued pouring out more cups for the table, his hands visibly shaking.

"He thought I was jealous of Elaine over there with Grady."

"Grady's here?" Janey said, scanning through the crowd. "I knew his sister was catering the party, but she didn't say anything about him being invited."

"Probably weaseled an invitation," Ashlon sneered dryly. "And he's being typical Grady. He's dancing over there with Elaine Hicks, the town manager. Is that what they call 'dirty dancing?" she said with mock innocence as they watched him dipping and grinding against a very obviously impressed Elaine.

Janey pointed them out to Jorge, whose eyes narrowed with unmistakable distaste. "Pindejo!" he spat disapprovingly. "No doubt working on his next mark."

Ashlon sighed wistfully. "That's Grady for you, Jorge. I love his mom to death, and his sister is a very smart woman, knows her business. But Grady... well, he treats women like commodities. I'm still trying to figure out why the a sudden interest in me. Last Friday was a very egregious lapse of judgment on my part." Ashlon grimaced at the memory. "Anyway, he's been warned. No more Miss Suzy Sweet Thing."

Ashlon turned away from her friends, finding Bowen in the crowd, follow- ing his progress as he worked his way around the room with Jonathan Wayland, who was introducing him to several county officials.

"I take it you've done some thinking since this morning," Janey said, pulling on Ashlon's arm.

"I've done a lot of thinking since this morning." Ashlon gave her friend a nudge with a meaningful look behind it. "Ever since I was a kid, I've been waiting for something, looking for something meant only for me. I just kind of buried it when we moved here to the Corner, and I was able to get rid of Wyatt's stain. And then, Bowen appeared. He's secretive and mysterious. But he's also without pretensions or airs. I trust him. You gotta admit, that says a lot about a man."

Jorge promptly wrapped his arms around Janey from the back and planted a noisy kiss on her cheek. She started giggling uncontrollably as she nodded in vigorous agreement.

"Does that mean what we think it means?" Jorge said when he noted Ashlon's glowing expression as she watched Bowen. She turned and looked at them with a warm, acknowledging smile.

Janey gave her a one-armed hug. "It's about time you let someone in, even if it's your dark lord of the underworld. If he's your cup of tea, drink him in for all he's worth."

Ashlon swallowed her laugh. That was what she loved about Janey—her complete and unstinting support no matter what.

The sound of raised angry voices abruptly drew their attention to the band stage. Wes Ottman, the band leader, was having a very vocal row with a lady in a sequined cocktail dress, presumably their vocalist for the night. She was gesturing dramatically and then suddenly turned in an operatic huff, pushing her way through the crowd and storming out the doors. Wes looked absolutely pissed as he watched her leave without trying to get her back. Unfortunately, he found Ashlon the same instant his erstwhile soloist disappeared from the hall. When their eyes met, she immediately suspected what was coming next and tried to hide behind Jorge and Janey, hunching down and making herself as small as possible. They immediately closed ranks, but it was too late, due in part to Ashlon being obviously taller than either of them. Wes bent down and spoke to Max, who was sitting just below the stage on the floor with several other children, and pointed out where Ashlon was. He eagerly jumped to his feet and pushed his way through the revelers to Jorge and Janey.

"Mr. Ottman wants to see Miss Isaacs," he dutifully announced.

"He sent a kid to do his dirty work," Janey said, stifling her grin as she pulled on Ashlon's wrist. "Man has no shame."

Ashlon groaned with exasperation as she straightened and reluctantly followed Max. She looked back once to complain loudly, "This is all your fault!" pointing an accusing finger at Janey as she was swallowed up by the crowd, Janey's hilarity following her.

When she reached Wes, she extended her hand in reluctant greeting. He quickly explained that their paid vocalist was refusing to sing any Halloween songs. Then why in the world had she consented to sing at a Halloween party? Ashlon took a look at the music Wes wanted to perform, and then glanced down at the children sitting in front of the stage, waiting for the evening's entertainment to begin.

Disappoint them? Not a chance.

"Do you want to hear something scary?" she said in a low, ominous voice that made them giggle and squirm excitedly. She nodded to Wes, and he exhaled with relief and turned to speak to several people, the band's stage crew. While he quickly gave his instructions, Ashlon lifted a bottle of water from the iced coffin and opened it, taking several long swallows from it. She capped it again and handed it to a pixie of a little girl in a ladybug costume and sitting just below her on the floor. Ashlon asked her to keep her water bottle safe for her. The child hugged it to her and gave Ashlon an uncertain smile.

The lights dimmed, the noise in the hall diminished. The footlights came up with a dim orange glow, and Ashlon commenced the first number. "Now sit right there while I elucidate, the story of what goes on when it gets late!" beginning the tale of the Headless Horseman. The party goers gathered behind the children who were giggling at Ashlon's stage antics, and then suddenly screaming as a headless horseman, surrounded by eerie green light and mist, suddenly rose up from the darkness at the back of the stage and dramatically gestured through the fog generated by a hidden fog machine. He rode around the crowd holding a grinning pumpkin in one hand as a spotlight followed him around the room. He disappeared as suddenly as he'd appeared, and as the song ended, the children breathed a collective sigh of relief. They eagerly looked up at Ashlon with grinning anticipation.

Bowen had finished his social rounds, joining Jorge and Janey at the back of the room as he observed the goings on up front with thinly veiled distaste until he realized it was Ashlon up there singing to the children, absolutely delighting in their wild shrieks of fright and laughter. Her face was glowing when the song ended, and she bowed to appreciative clapping. He frowned impatiently as she informed everyone the next song was styled from one of her favorite movies of the season. True, he had been charmed when she'd sung her tribute for her friend at the Harvest Party, but she was with him now and should not be displaying herself. It was—unseemly.

Ashlon made a dramatic flourish and swept in toward the children, exclaiming, "It's just a bunch of hocus pocus!" and cackled wickedly. Several nervous twitters could be heard from the floor in front of the stage.

Janey excitedly clapped her hands and poked Jorge hard in the ribs. "I love this song!" she said, laughing excitedly.

Jorge grimaced and rubbed his side. "You could be a little less painful in your exuberance, Meja."

"Shhh! Just watch! I've seen her do this a million times. The kids love it." Bowen glanced down at her, his eyes narrowing. "What do you find so amusing?" he said with frank disapproval. "It is merely simple theatrics passing as entertainment."

"Just watch," Janey said, ignoring him and pointing impatiently at the stage. "Ash is a natural-borne performer. And if kids are involved, there's no holding her back."

Bowen's mouth was a grim line as he folded his arms over his chest and turned his grudging attention back to the stage. For a brief moment, he considered going up there and taking her off that stage. The only thing that stopped him was the glowing delight in Ashlon's expression as she smiled down at the children.

Suddenly, the lighting took on a prism ball effect when Ashlon motioned with her arms as if weaving magic.

"I put a spell on you!" she hissed, pointing down at the children, and then at the people behind them. "And now you're mine." There was another nervous Twitter from one of the children and even a few of the adults now. "I'm very good at what I do, I ain't lyin'. It's been one whole year, right down to the day. Now, this witch is back, and there's the devil to pay!"

Bowen's guarded attitude melted as he watched with growing fascination while Ashlon moved dramatically around the stage with her narrative, the children giggling riotously in front of the stage. He also noted with amazement the nervous laughter of some of the adult partygoers with each sweeping turn and dramatic wave of Ashlon's hands. Did they actually think she was casting some sort of spell over them? He found this utterly fascinating, and Ashlon's performance was captivating. Maybe she was a spellcaster because she'd certainly captured his heart, he warmly considered, surrounding him with her sweet enchantment as binding as her performance for the children.

The lighting effects followed her every movement through the music and lyrics, flashing like lightning through the nonsense spell she intoned until her final flourishes through the last measures. The revelers erupted into uproarious applause. Afterward, she performed one more standard, That Old Black Magic, and then was done. Wes joined her at the front of the stage afterward for a bow, and announced a 10-minute break before beginning the next set. He planted a grateful kiss on Ashlon's cheek, thanking her profusely for helping him. The rest of the repertoire could be performed without a vocalist, he reluctantly informed her, but she was more than welcome to stay.

Ashlon thanked him, but politely declined and retrieved her water from the little ladybug, who gave her a huge leg hug before being claimed by her father. Ashlon watched them walk away, very satisfied that she'd given them all a good, friendly scare. G-d willing, that child would never learn what real terror was.

Chapter 26

She stepped off the stage and slowly worked her way back through the crowd of well-wishers as she headed toward Janey and Jorge waving at her from the back of the room. She was unable to find Bowen as she looked around for him through the crowd. He was probably still suffering through some interminable meet and greet of being a VIP. Oh well. He'd find her or she'd find him eventually once she reached Janey and Jorge. She had spotted him beside Janey at one point through her performance and hoped he didn't mind that she was making a spectacle of herself again. The kids had been worth it.

What she didn't count on was running into the one person she didn't want to see under any circumstances. Grady forcefully shucked Elaine and quickly intercepted Ashlon's path, sweeping her into his arms and whirling her around. The water bottle flew out of her hands, nearly beaning an unfortunate bystander standing within range. When he put her down, he planted an alcohol-soaked kiss on her lips as she fought to push him away. When he finally looked down into Ashlon's disgusted expression, he smiled crookedly as she turned her face from his reeking breath. He tried to turn her face to kiss her again.

Ashlon worked one arm from under his and slapped him so hard she thought she heard his teeth rattle. "Damn it, Grady!" she snarled as loud as she could, struggling to get out of his grip.

"You're drunk! Get your hands off of me!"

"I thought we made up earlier today," he said, slurring his words, sounding wounded, and refusing to let go as he tried to pull her closer. He'd been totally unaffected by Ashlon's hard slap. "C'mon. Don't be such a hard ass," he added as he tried to force a kiss on her again. Thoroughly outraged by his comment and his drunken behavior, she slapped him again, even harder since she couldn't get enough leverage to slug him. Her hand smarted after the contact, and his face reddened this time. A flicker of rage crossed it as he tightened his grip, making her gasp for breath.

"Don't do that again!" he growled in deadly earnest as he pressed his lips to her face. Still struggling, Ashlon nearly gagged. She knew she was in very real trouble, looking around desperately for someone to pull Grady off her. She couldn't find Bowen, and no one else was showing any inclination to help her. At that moment, something inside of her clicked like it did when she was faced with a threat. Something Grady would painfully regret.

Elaine appeared from the crowd and grabbed Grady's arm as she sneered at Ashlon. Stupid move, lady! Ashlon grimly thought, every nerve and muscle tensed and ready to act when the moment was right and her arms were freed.

"C'mon, baby," the town manager urged in the most sickeningly cloying voice Ashlon had ever heard. "Leave Miss Talent Show. She obviously has issues."

Grady reached around, still clutching Ashlon in one large arm, cupped a large hand over Elaine's face, and callously pushed her away, forcing her to release him as she fell backward and was deftly caught by Jorge. When McAn- ders hadn't intervened, he'd immediately launched into the crowd, forcefully pushing his way through until he'd finally reached Grady and Ashlon, just in time to catch Elaine before she hit the floor.

"You sonuvabitch!" Ashlon snarled into Grady's sneering face. But, her arms were free now. Without hesitation, she whacked both his ears with the palms of her hands as hard as she could. The expected effect was immediate.

Grady shrieked and dropped her, and she immediately got to her feet, staggering away a few steps to catch her breath. A trickle of blood was running down under Grady's hand from one ear, and he was writhing in agony as Ashlon recovered her breath, putting a little space between them, her right hand drawn back in a fist as she waited expectantly for his next move. The partygoers were murmuring between them, apparently unable to decide if this was only an act or something requiring intervention. No one moved as Grady glared malevolently at Ashlon and suddenly lunged to grab her again. Her fist flew around with all her weight behind it, meeting Grady's forward momentum. His head snapped sharply to the left, and he staggered backward off his feet, falling hard onto the wooden floor, his head bouncing as he landed with a dull thud on the gleaming wooden floor. He didn't move again.

Ashlon was panting hard as she shook her aching hand, still trembling with rage coursing through her as she cautiously crouched over Grady's unconscious form. Reaching down with both hands, she picked him up by his shirt, shaking him as she scowled into his lax bloodied face.

"Don't ever touch me again!" she snarled. "Don't ever come near me again, you two-faced bastard!" That last comment elicited a snicker from somewhere in the crowd.

Other hands gently grasped her arms after she dropped Grady, pulling her away and directing her out of the crowd that closed around the unconscious hulk on the floor. Someone suggested maybe they should bring him around, to which someone else merely said, "Why? He had it coming."

Ashlon smirked with grim satisfaction. The entire encounter had lasted maybe two minutes tops.

"C'mon, Ash, it's over now," Jorge calmly spoke as he turned her away and guided her back toward Janey, who had her hands cupped over her mouth, her eyes wide and frightened. "The police will handle it now," Jorge added as several uniforms arrived, pushed through the crowd, and found Grady still out cold on the dance floor.

Ashlon was trembling and her hand hurt like hell, but by heavens, she felt pretty darn good. "Is Elaine alright?" she asked Jorge as she shook her sore hand and worked the fingers.

"Just a little shook up," Jorge replied with a soft chuckle. "Could have been worse."

"Yeah, I could've killed the bastard," Ashlon said with a grim smirk.

Janey heard her comment as they met up with her at the buffet. She immediately hugged Jorge, and then quickly looked Ashlon up and down, checking for any cuts or bruises before hugging her tightly. "You handled yourself pretty well out there." Her voice shook. "Gave him a chance to back off, then cold cocked him."

Ashlon only nodded, then suddenly stiffened. Jancy heard a muffled, "Oh shit!" as Ashlon quickly moved to Janey's side. Irma and Mineau Roberts were coming from behind the buffet table, heading in their direction. Ashlon lowered her head and watched guardedly, ready to leave if she had to.

Irma looked shaken and stony-faced; Mineau was totally unreadable. But, they appeared determined to say something, and Ashlon girded for the worst. They stopped in front of Jorge and Janey, who both nodded to them and stood ready to intervene if necessary.

"Deary, I think I owe you a very big apology," Irma said, trying to reach out to Ashlon, then abruptly dropping her hand. Only then did she notice that the older lady's eyes were reddened from crying, her lined face drawn and tense as she spoke.
Ashlon frowned suspiciously. "Come again?"

Mineau held out her hand to her, waiting. Ashlon guardedly moved from behind Janey and cautiously grasped it; Mineau grinned at her.

"That was one impressive can of whoop-ass," she firmly said. "My brother's had that coming for a long time. You're someone he's never been able to screw with, and it was driving him crazy. I mean, the way he treats women is abominable, like the toys he uses and then tosses when they've given him what he wants. And he knows how to get what he wants. But, you always saw right through his bullshit."

"Well, now he's in trouble with the law," Irma said bitterly. "That Elaine better press charges if she's as smart as everyone says she is." She took Ashlon's hand from Mineau and held it in both of hers, her eyes filled with the pain only a mother can experience when faced with the brutal fact that one of her children is beyond her help. "I had hoped that maybe—that someone strong would be able to..."

Her words trailed off as she swallowed hard. "Ever since he's been up north … those others he associates with!" she bitterly complained.

"Mom, stop trying to deflect the fact that Grady's a first-class asshole! He's had all the earmarks, and growing up just made it worse," Mineau said with deep irritation as she led her mother away and returned her to the food tables.

Jorge, Janey, and Ashlon looked at each other incredulously, but were able to breathe again.

Mayor Tisbee was in a sweat as he mounted the stage and hastened up to the microphone. "Ladies and gentlemen, now that that mess has been cleared away, let's get back to dancing and having a good time, shall we? The evening is still young and there's lots of food on the tables." He looked over his guests with a desperate fixed smile, and was relieved to see that his speech had the desired effect as the partiers began to separate and head to the buffet or over to the bar or merely wait for the music to start again. Turning to Wes, Tisbee urged the band leader to continue his program. Soon, the dancers were back on the floor after Grady's blood had been hastily cleaned from where he'd fallen.

Ashlon looked around the hall. What she really wanted to know was why Bowen hadn't immediately stepped in to help her when she needed him. Had he missed what was going on? Had someone drawn his attention from the room, and they were somewhere else in the house?

"Where's Bowen?" she said to Jorge and Janey after making one last visual sweep of the party room. Nope, gone. "The last time I saw him was over here with you guys." They looked around, too, but could only shake their heads. When the excitement had started, they hadn't been able to find him either. Ashlon pursed her lips as something went flat inside her. So much for the loving, trusting, supportive presence when the going hit a rough spot.

Max appeared, pushing his way through the crowd to where they stood, and handed a cold bottle of lemon water to Ashlon, who gratefully took a long drink from it. "Mom thought you might need this. That was a righteous punch, Miss Isaacs," he said, gazing up at her with unabashed admiration.

"Yeah, Max. Thanks for the water. Um ... you didn't happen to see where Lord McAnders went, did you?" Nothing got by this kid, Ashlon was sure.

"Your arm candy?" Max's smile was devilish. "Yeah, I saw him. He left when that other big guy grabbed you and was spinning you around out there. Looked really pissed too. He should've stayed for the fireworks! Boy, talk about your assholes! Well, see you later!" Max sauntered off, disappearing back into the crowd.

Ashlon sighed, her niggling suspicions confirmed. She wasn't even angry. Now why was that so weird, she wondered as she took a deep breath and unconsciously nodded to herself. Deep down inside, she knew why.

"Janey, I'll be right back," she abruptly said as she thrust her water bottle at her friend, and left the hall to find the powder room on this floor.

Everything was crystal clear and focused in her mind as she fixed her hair, splashed a little cold water on her face, wiped off some sweat smears, and refreshed her lipstick. Just little things to stay connected. She washed her hands and then returned to the hall. Janey anxiously met her and put an arm around her shoulders, leading her to two chairs next to the hall doors.

"Jorge's driving over to his house," Janey said, brushing a few stray hairs off of Ashlon's gown. "Set him straight on what happened tonight."

Ashlon managed a resigned shrug. "It doesn't matter," she said with a deep sigh. "I was dumb enough to believe this might be different. All those pretty words didn't mean a pile of crap, did they? First time things get rough, he bails. Oh well, at least I found out early enough before I got too emotionally involved." And serves me right for getting involved with an undead head case!

Janey took her hands and moved closer to her. "You mustn't say that," she said. "I've never seen you look at anyone the way you looked at him tonight. And the way his eyes followed you when you were on that stage singing to those kids—something incredible radiated from him straight in your direction."

Ashlon gazed down at the floor. "So what, Janey? He doesn't trust me. He doesn't trust anybody. I believed everything he said to me, and I shared things with him I've told only you. The guy's already tried, judged, and hung me out to dry." She sat there chewing her lip and silently stewing for a moment as Janey rubbed her back, unable to think of anything more to say.

Ashlon looked up as Wes mounted the stage again to begin his next musical set. She came to a sudden decision, abruptly stood, and waved in his direction. "Wes wanted me to sing this set. Since I'm no longer attached, I think I'm in the right frame of mind now." She straightened her dress and exposed a little more shoulder. "How do I look?"

Janey slumped back into her chair as she frowned at her friend. "Fabulous as usual. At least wait for Jorge to come back. You may be all wrong about this." But her words fell on deaf ears as Ashlon disappeared into the crowd. Once her mind was set, it took a bulldozer to budge it from whatever path it was taking.

They went through Wes's repertoire like they'd been performing together for years, Ashlon never taking a break except for quick sips off her water bottle. And then came the final number for the evening, a love ballad.

The music soared effortlessly as Ashlon moved around the stage, looking over the heads of the listeners at Janey who was now leaning on Jorge. Ashlon smiled through the lyrics when they waved to her. They were her inspiration as she waved back and sang the rest of the song, especially for them, her tribute to their unfailing friendship. At least there were a few reliable constants in her world.

And then, it was over. She stepped back beside Wes and bowed to thundering applause. She kissed him again and thanked him for letting her perform for him. It had had a satisfyingly cathartic effect on her emotions, and a feeling of groundedness was returning. She would move forward again; the rest would resolve in time, as it always did. Served her right for getting mixed up with a supernatural being with issues! But, maybe she couldn't fault him there, she supposed. He'd probably been screwed over so many times in his long existence it was a wonder he still got up each evening. Realistically, they weren't a cute couple by any stretch of the imagination, and sleeping with him once certainly didn't qualify her as an intimate confidant. She was well rid of him at the off, she figured, before things got too intense, too involved. Clean slate and all that garbage.

Wes stopped her before she departed from the stage, happily informing her that a hefty check would be in the mail by the end of the week. He'd see to it, or the mayor could expect some nasty editorials to appear in the town paper for his ingratitude. Ashlon thanked him again and then made her way through the crowd amid so many hugs and well-wishing, it appeared they'd completely forgotten the ass-kicking she'd had to do on Grady. Her only reminder was when she spotted Max, who must have had a front row to the fracas. He was imitating her round-house punch and the way Grady went down like a sack of potatoes. His friends were laughing or awed. She smiled a little as she continued on, reaching Jorge and Janey.

"Okay, Ash?" Jorge inquired, giving her a friendly hug.

"You look like mourners at a funeral. Honest, I'm fine," Ashlon said. She didn't want to deal with this now, on top of the residual disappointment of being summarily dumped.

Jorge squeezed Ashlon's shoulder. "I know he was home because his car was parked out in the garaging area. There were no lights on in the house, but he may just be moping. I stood outside the front door and yelled all sorts of insults at him in Spanish and English. Like the kid said—what an asshole." Jorge grinned, diabolically pleased with what he'd done.

Ashlon managed a weak smile. "I think he was referring to Grady,"

Jorge smirked as he patted Ashlon's cheek. "Works both ways."

Ashlon chuckled as she headed for the exit doors. Janey caught up with her at the head of the staircase. "Where are you going?"

Ashlon shrugged. "I'm going home," she said, starting down the steps.

Janey caught her arm and pulled her up short. "In case you haven't noticed, you don't have a ride. And it's 38 degrees out there right now. Jorge says there's a fog rolling in. Let us give you a ride."

Ashlon thoughtfully pursed her lips. "Hmm. Fog, chill, Halloween. And I'm in a crappy mood. Perfect for a walk."

"It's too far in the dark, Ashlon Isaacs! Be reasonable!"

Ashlon shook her head and gently removed Janey's hand from her arm. She stepped up and gave Janey a kiss on her cheek.

"Now, good night, and maybe I'll be in a better mood tomorrow. Or something close to it." She squeezed Janey's hand one last time and then continued her descent downstairs to the coat check. As Janey watched helplessly from the head of the staircase, Ashlon pulled on her long cape, tucked her bag into a hidden inside pocket, pulled up the great hood, and with the soft swish of velvet and satin disappeared out the door held open by a staring and very appreciative doorman.

Chapter 27

She moved through the fog-shrouded streets past silent buildings as quietly as the shadows surrounding her, passing through the town circle as the clock struck 11 pm. Still one hour left of a day that had gone from good to unbelievably screwed, Ashlon thought despondently as she moved through the cloaking silence, an occasional barking dog to usher her along. She crossed the street across from the city park entrance and turned onto the street fronting McAnders House. A heavy mist hung like a low mantle atop the brown grass, enveloping the playground equipment as it blossomed slowly with the cooling of the air around it. The fog would obscure the entire neighborhood by sunrise.

A familiar tall iron fence rose up to her left, and she lightly ran her fingers over it as she walked on, purposely keeping her head down as she passed the gate, which was locked for the night. She briefly slowed her pace, glancing up the walkway to the front of the house as she passed it. Just as Jorge had said, there were no lights burning, not even in the study.

The thought of him intensified her disappointment that had settled in like a bad case of indigestion. I hope you feel this, she thought, gritting her teeth, because you broke my heart tonight. You and your pretty words were nothing but empty fluff. You can damn well choke on them.

She pushed this down as she hurried her steps to the end of the block and turned left onto her street. She didn't slow her pace until she'd reached her front door step. Standing in the orange glow of her grinning pumpkin porch light, she fished her clutch from the pocket of her cape and found her house key. Unlocking and opening the door, she slipped inside, flipping a light switch that turned on a lamp by the couch, and nearly jumped out of her skin—Bowen stood just beyond the glow in the semi-darkness of the kitchen.

He'd changed into a pair of black Dockers and a Henley shirt, and released his long hair from its tie back. He gazed steadily at Ashlon from his lowered brow, his eyes glowing eerily with an intensity that was almost unnerving. So heart-breakingly handsome, and so pathetically clueless.

"I have been waiting for you," he said with marked concern.

"Do tell. Just leave. You seem to be pretty good at it," Ashlon frowned as she took off her cape and carelessly tossed it on the back of the couch. "I don't want to see you anymore tonight. And maybe never again."

"You walked home?" he said, backing away just a little from her anger as she scowled at him.

"Gee, you think? You weren't there to drive me, remember?" she sneered. "I think the word is 'dumped'? Besides, I needed the time alone, and it's perfect out there. Matches my shitty mood."

She started up the stairs for her room. Stopping just before disappearing from his sight, she looked over the banister at him. "For what it's worth, Grady's going to be charged with two counts of assault and battery and trespass. Seems he didn't have an invitation after all. Just came in with the food. I heard the arresting officer when they hauled his sorry ass away. Took them several minutes to bring him around, so I guess I nailed him pretty good." Ashlon half-smiled with grim satisfaction at this, but it quickly faded. "Oh, that's right. You weren't there to see it, were you? It was a Kodak moment that every-one'll remember for years to come, although it might not've happened if someone I thought cared for me had been there to pull him off." She glared at him with her back pressed against the wall.

Bowen moved silently to the stair railing and looked up at Ashlon, his expression a stone blank.

"You must understand. I have learned through a very long existence that trust is a virtue I can ill afford. I could not act without betraying myself to everyone in that room. It is the reason I have survived the centuries, keeping all but a chosen few distant. When I have been betrayed, it has nearly cost me my existence and everything precious to me."

Ashlon shook her head. "So you left me to be mauled by Grady! Bowen, that's unforgivable! I trusted you in spite of your blatant threat made on my life. I was there in your house, albeit in a roundabout sort of way and not for you specifically, but I believed everything you told me and sealed that trust by staying the night with you. I even willingly gave you blood and would have done it again because it made you happy. You're telling me none of that mattered? Then, by G-d, you just lost yourself a girlfriend, buster! I trusted you enough to open myself to you, more than I thought I could outside of my friends. Well, thanks for a whole lot of nothing."

Her expression was grim as she paused in her rant, shaking her head with her mouth drawn into a tight line, deep pain evident in her angry gaze. "I wanted to tell you something tonight that I'd been thinking about today. But, you blew it big time, buster. I'd be out of my mind to even consider it now."

She moved away from him as she rubbed her face on the back of one hand, fatigued and irritated down to her bones. "We've both had our says for what their worth. Please go away." She started up the stairs again.

Bowen was dumbfounded. He'd practically won her, but then betrayed it through one damaging, thoughtless moment of doubt that, in the end, had jeopardized everything.

"Ashlon!" he desperately called to her. "I love you! You must believe that!" He grasped the banister railing and watched her with growing despair as she paused on the stairs.

She refused to look at him. "I'm not certain I even like you anymore. It's late and I'm tired. Please leave before I withdraw your invitation to my home."

Ashlon reached the head of the stairs and disappeared down the hall. Bowen listened desperately to her receding footsteps, followed by the opening and closing of a door. And then the house was silent.

He reluctantly left as she had requested, immersed in a misery deeper than any he could have imagined.

Ashlon drew the blinds before turning on her light. She undressed, throwing her gown on top of her laundry hamper to take to the cleaners in the morning. She felt soiled after being pawed by Grady. A warm shower with scented soap took care of that and restored her sense of rightness again. As she toweled off, she glanced at the clock on her dresser table. It was 11:40 pm. It was still Halloween. There was something she could do before it vanished. Some good had to come of this evening, she decided as she pulled out a clean set of clothes and then grabbed her backpack from the closet.

She cautiously returned downstairs, looking around to make sure Bowen was gone. Once assured, she went to the kitchen and filled a small thermos with apple cider, grabbed a bag of candy corn and a spiced pumpkin scented votive from her small pantry, and found a lighter in her junk drawer. She stuffed everything into her backpack, then grabbed her jacket and a long purple knit scarf from her closet. Emma's favorite. Shouldering the backpack and grabbing her handbag, she flew out the front door to her Jeep. She hoped Bowen wouldn't be watching after what had happened earlier, and even if he was, she didn't care. He was persona non grata as far as she was concerned.

Several minutes later, Ashlon pulled up to the little cemetery gate and parked near the groundskeeper's cottage. His windows were dark, but Ashlon had no intention of waking him. She took out the little knife she had used to break into Maddie Bag's house and easily jimmied the old latch to the entrance gate by the glare of her head-lights. Once it popped open, she turned off the headlights and quickly let herself onto the grounds.

She dug into one of the pockets on her jacket and withdrew a small maglight, but didn't click it on right away. Instead, she carefully traced along the fence line away from where she'd parked until she was sure she was a safe distance away from the cottage and inadvertent detection. She then turned on the light, keeping it directed in front of her and low to the ground. Continuing along the fence, she scanned over the tops of the headstones until she spotted the black silhouette of the dark crypt on the crest of the hill. Fortunately for her, the mists closer to town hadn't drifted out this way yet. She turned, starting up the gentle slope of the hill, moving carefully between the stones until she reached Emma's resting place.

Ashlon knelt by the small grave, marveling at the riot of lavender overgrowing the mound. She would have to clip it back soon. For now, she had another task to perform.

Holding the small flashlight between her teeth, she pulled out the candy corn, candle, thermos, and lighter. She nestled the candle into the lavender at the base of the teddy stone and lit it. Turning off the maglight, she said, "This flame is a reminder that though we're apart, we're never parted, and that one day we'll be together again."

She opened the bag of candy corn and took out a small handful, placing the kernels on the head of the stone, popping one into her mouth. "I brought your favorite candy, Hugabug. It was a wonderful night with all the costumes, the kids coming to the door, and the air filled with magic around them. I wore this unbelievable dress to a party, and the room looked just like Hogwarts on Halloween. Remember with all the pumpkins and streamers and fluttery bats? Did you hear mommy sing, sugar? It was wonderful how everyone liked it."

Last of all, she opened the thermos and poured a small amount of the cider over and around the grave, then filled the small cup and lifted it to the heavens. "Pure, unfiltered apple cider. No finer drink this time of year, especially tonight." She sat down on the stone bench and lay back on the cool marble with the small cup nestled on her chest. She gazed up at a blanket of stars stretching across the sky as far as the eye could see.

She traced patterns for a while between the brilliant points of light overhead. When she tired of that, she put the cup on the ground under the bench and folded her arms behind her head. Could Emma be listening to her on the one night when, according to ancient myth, the veil separating this world from the next was opened for the departed to visit the mortal plain? Ashlon wanted so much to know her little girl was alright and happy. But she must be; she'd seen angels and talked with bubbe as she slipped away from her earthly home.

The cold night sky was so clear and the stars so close she might touch them. Ashlon yawned as she reached up again and drew more pictures between those distant sparkling points, then dropped her arms after a while and clasped her hands over her chest, closing her eyes.

Mommy, are you asleep?
I think so, baby.
No, you're not! (Giggling)
I'm so happy you're here, Em. Did you want to tell mommy something, sugar?
I really can see you from here.
From where?
Here, silly mommy.
Tell me where. I want to know.
With Bubbe and all the angels. They're so beautiful. So don't worry, Mommy. I heard you sing, and it was so pretty. Like the angels. They liked it too.
Thank you, Emma. You've made mommy very happy. I miss you so much.
I'm giving you a hug, mommy. Oh! He says I have to go now.
Don't go, Emmy!
He says it's time, mommy. But don't be sad. He says the big, dark man is only very lost and very lonely and needs you. Mommy, you must teach him to see your light, and then He says you both won't be lonely anymore.
Who says, Emma?
You know! Bye, mommy, I love you!

Ashlon opened her eyes to the tolling of the midnight hour and sat up as she looked once more to the heavens, happiness and amazement smarting her eyes. She'd once heard it called 'cry for happy', and that's what she did now as she burrowed her face into her folded arms and allowed her tears to flow freely with muffled words of gratitude slipped between them.

After she'd pretty much cried herself out and wiped her eyes and nose on the sleeves of her hoodie, Ashlon finished her cup of cider and recapped the thermos, placing it and the bag of candy back in her backpack. She blew out the candle and dumped the melted wax, then put that away as well. The scattered candy corn was left on the teddy's head for the birds in the morning.

Just one more task to perform. She'd been told by Emma that Bowen very much needed her, and something about teaching him to see her light. Did that mean showing him what real trust meant, perhaps beginning with a sign of forgiveness he'd understand? Truth of it, she was no longer angry with him anyway, reluctantly acknowledging his point about not trusting anyone because of past betrayals. Hadn't she been a little like—no, a lot like that about men in general until she'd met him? Frankly, they had both been screwed over one time or another, and learning to trust someone you barely knew was an extreme leap of faith for both of them. It was time one of them took that leap.

She knelt by Emma's grave once more and pulled off a large woody stem with many large lavender blooms on it in various stages of maturity, then straightened, shouldered her pack, and took out her maglight again. With the bright beam guiding her path, she climbed the hill to the dark crypt.

Chapter 28

Damn phone kept ringing and ringing.

Ashlon woke without wanting to and groggily staggered out of the bedroom, falling on the stairs when her foot slipped on the carpeting. Swearing out loud, she limped down to the bottom and over to the phone by the sofa, blearily looking down at the caller ID as she picked up the receiver, not really seeing who it was in her sleep-clouded brain.

"H'lo?" she croaked, cleared her throat, and said again, "Hello?"

"Miss Isaacs? Detective Anderson, District Investigations."

"Okay," she yawned.

"Did I wake you? You know it's almost 10 am."

"For some of us, it's the middle of the night." And he should know better.

"I apologize," he said in a perfunctory manner. "Is there any way we can get together ASAP?"

"Why?" Silence on the other end. This wasn't a good sign.

It wasn't.

"Grady Roberts posted bail earlier this morning. His buddies put up the bond money and are taking him back up north pending his court date. You need to come in and give us your statement as soon as possible. You know, in case he tries to jump bail and not show up." Which pretty much seemed a sure thing, the detective wasn't saying.

Ashlon groaned inwardly, hoping this wouldn't set the timbre for the day. "I kind of expected this. Anything else?"

"When you get here, Miss Isaacs." He abruptly hung up. Ashlon simply stared at the receiver for a few seconds, wanting to know what barn Anderson had been raised in.

She hung up the phone and climbed back upstairs to wash and dress. A quick pull of the brush through her hair, slap on some makeup, grab her jacket, driving gloves, and scarf, and she was out the door in less than 30 minutes on the road to the district police office. Without breakfast.

He'd better have some coffee waiting in a clean cup, she silently groused with a wide yawn as she drove toward the edge of town. The weather was threatening snow, according to the radio. Scant flurries danced their way across her windshield in the frigid morning air, and the sky was a solid light iron-grey mass.

Ashlon parked in the nearest visitor slot at the district law enforcement office and trudged into the small whitewashed building, stopping in front of the sergeant's desk, with the same sergeant behind it who had escorted her and Janey to the back their first visit there. He looked up once, and then again, noticing Ashlon and putting down his pencil.

"Can I help you, miss?" he inquired with the sweetest smile as he eyed her appreciatively.

This was too totally weird. Before, when she had been there with Janey, he'd only glanced at them before calling Anderson. And this guy had to be in his 40's, a solidly married man as evidenced by the embedded wedding band on his finger and family pictures on one side of the desk. Come to think of it, what about the valet and that server last night? Even Wes Ottman seemed to be a little more attentive than he'd been the night of the Harvest Festival dance. The only similarity between these men was her focused attention when she was near them for even the briefest time.

"Yes, sergeant," Ashlon replied, deciding to test a theory she'd been formulating. She smiled back at him and moved just a little closer to the desk. "Would you let Detective Anderson know Ashlon Isaacs is here to see him? He called me earlier and wanted me to come in."

The man's eyes glazed over as he stood and leaned over the desk with that same goofy grin she'd seen on the server's face the previous evening. "Anything you want, sugar," he crooned dreamily. "Anything you want."

Ashlon raised her eyebrows. "And would you be kind enough to get me a fresh cup of coffee, Sergeant? Two creams, please, no sugar."

"You got it," he replied in that same dreamy tone. He picked up the receiver on his desk phone, pressed a button, and spoke briefly to whoever was on the other end. After he hung up, the sergeant stood and motioned he was leaving, turned, and almost fell over his chair because his attention was still fixed on Ashlon. He grimaced sheepishly as he hastened from the room.

Ashlon shook her head with dismay. The scenario had played out better than she'd expected, but also provided proof to an alarming theory, now solidly confirmed. However, now was not the time to panic since, frankly, there wasn't a damn thing she could do about it anyway. And it might prove useful in the future. Just how she wasn't quite sure, but considering the way things were going lately, she had no doubt something would happen sooner or later.

The sergeant returned with a steaming Styrofoam cup in his hands and motioned for Ashlon to come around his desk. He carefully handed her the cup. Ashlon's fingers brushed his; to her amazement, the sergeant shivered and closed his eyes as if experiencing the greatest thrill of his life. After he regained some of his composure, he lead her through a door next to his desk into the main office area.

Detective Anderson met them halfway to his office. His face was livid and stony as he chewed on a cold cigar stub lodged at the corner of his mouth. He jabbed a long, large finger into the sergeant's chest and proceeded to chew him a new one for not bringing Ashlon back sooner.

Ashlon stood away from the two men as the irate detective

viciously vented his spleen on the poor sergeant, who'd suddenly snapped out of the spell he'd been under and looked around totally bewildered, like he didn't know where he was.

M'i bad! Ashlon smirked, feeling totally smug and only a little bit guilty. Detective Anderson finished his tirade. He ordered the confused sergeant back to his desk and then abruptly turned on Ashlon. "What did you do to him?" he snarled, pointing accusingly at her.

She started to protest, but was cut off by his waving hand. "Can it. Come with me." He motioned toward his office and stalked away ahead of her.

Definitely has authority issues, Ashlon decided with a grimace as she obediently followed him into his corner space. He closed the door behind her and motioned to a chair in front of his desk.

The detective was not in a good mood. Ashlon was picking up on some very hostile feelings combined with fatigue and frustration that seemed to indicate he was having a lot of difficulty figuring out something that was driving him nuts. At least, she wasn't the primary focus of all this, she noted with some relief.

"You wanted to talk to me, Detective?" she said pleasantly, taking a quick sip of her coffee. It was fresh, hot, and had just the right amount of real creamer, bless that sergeant.

Detective Anderson puffed once with irritation and took the cigar stub from his mouth, throwing it into the trash can. Ashlon curled her lip in disgust as he wiped his fingers on his pants, wishing she had a bottle of hand sanitizer with her.

"Yeah, yeah, I don't want to hear it," he growled, sitting back heavily in his creaky chair. "My wife does the same thing. I need to ask you a few more questions about those things you and your friend brought in the other night. Tell me again why you two were nosing around Maddie Bag's place, and then, what happened last night?"

Ashlon unhesitatingly reported—again—everything about Maddie's place, adding the events of the previous evening. After she finished, she took a long drink of her coffee and waited, her hands folded around the cup in her lap, her eyes focused on them.

Detective Anderson rifled a folder from a pile in front of him and opened it. "I have here the lab report on that bloody spade, and that skin and hair sample you and your friend brought in. I also have here a new report made by the guys I sent back out to the Bag cottage to take another look around the property." He pulled out still another folder and opened it, looking up at Ashlon. "This is the forensic report on that kid murdered upstate near the game lands. The one found stuffed into the trunk of his car."

Ashlon frowned. "And you're telling me this, why?"

Detective Anderson sat back in his chair and contemplated her very closely. "You and your friend were right. Miss Bags was killed back in those woods behind the house. We took a dog back there and found a clearing with residual scent traces all over it. Plus, Ms. Bag's shoes and one ear were found buried under the deadfall."

Ashlon grimaced and closed her eyes. Poor Maddie! The terror she must have felt seeing her own death approaching. "What about the house?" she cautiously asked.

"They found that root cellar window and the inside entrance to it. Found some blood traces ground into the dirt floor and on the steps leading upstairs. This brings me to the crux of a conundrum that has my lab people stumped."

Ashlon looked over at the open folders under the detective's drumming fingers.

"What did they find, Detective?" she prompted him with a familiar uneasiness.

He sighed and took off his glasses, wearily rubbing his eyes. "The spade had human blood on it, and we sent it off for DNA profiling. It wasn't Ms Bag's blood. So, whoever she used it on would have had some pretty serious wounds. We checked County first and then farther out, looking for anyone who showed up in an emergency room with wide, deep gouge wounds. We even went statewide. Nothing showed up. Either the sonuvabitch bled to death somewhere or he was being protected and treated in private."

"What about any evidence from the other murder sites? And the skin and hair specimen Janey and I found?" Ashlon felt the hair rising on her neck. Not a good sign at all.

"That's my conundrum. Either somebody, or several persons, are playing an elaborate hoax on us and concocting these samples to throw at us, or we have some very disturbed individuals out there and possible animal abuse issues to address, as well as three murders."

The hackles were definitely up on Ashlon's neck, as well as that familiar sinking sensation in the pit of her stomach. Maybe she needed to stop asking so many questions, because this thing was getting more complicated than she'd anticipated. Oh well, nothing ventured, nothing gained.

Maintaining her composure, she decided to see if her recently discovered binding ability would work on this hard-nosed policeman and help him get to his point. She looked directly into his face.

"I understand how frustrating this must be for you," she said in her best counseling-empathetic voice. "What was found at those murder sites, and what about that skin and hair specimen?"

Detective Anderson's eyes widened and his pupils dilated, his face relaxed, and he sat back in his chair, licking his pudgy lips. He must be more tired than he thought, Ashlon thought with satisfaction. He'd reacted quicker than the sergeant had, or maybe she was just getting better at this. Shouldn't this be more of a concern to her than it was, she wondered? And then, another more disturbing question occurred to her: What had Bowen done to her? Of course, this was his doing, she had to acknowledge. Sooner or later, she'd have to swallow her pride and talk to him about this—that is, if he'd let her after the chew- ing out she'd given him last night.

"The hair samples found at the scenes and your sample are a combination of human and canine," Anderson said, interrupting these ponderous thoughts, "though they couldn't match the canine with any domestic breed. So they sent it for zoological typing and it came back as Canis lupus, wolf, from two different animals. So we have either a couple of sickos working with pet wolves or hybrids, or certifiable nut cases running around in wolf skin suits." Ashlon was more inclined to go with the certifiable nut cases in light of the violent brutality of the murders. However, that didn't make the total picture look any better.

Ashlon dropped her eyes and sat back, picked up her coffee cup, and drained the last warm dregs as she considered what Detective Anderson had said. She was getting sucked further and further into this thing, and could feel it drawing closer, like a spiral turning inward toward the center where she was standing. These murders had a common denominator besides the full moon and a couple of loose screws playing around in canine underwear; she was absolutely sure. But what was it? What would Harry Dresden do now?

Detective Anderson took a few deep breaths, blinked several times, and his brow furrowed as he became aware of Ashlon again. "I must have dozed off there for a moment," he said, rubbing his head sheepishly. Clearing his throat, he leaned forward and glanced down at the open report under his hands. "Any- way, that's the long and short of it, Miss Isaacs," he concluded. "Anything you want to ask me?"

Ashlon thought for a moment. After all, she hadn't really believed in bogey men either until she'd been literally bitten by one.

"The next full moon is in two weeks, detective. What do you plan to do to prevent any more killings?"

He snorted in disgust and glared at Ashlon. "What does this have to do with the full moon besides being a coincidence? Yeah, yeah, I'm familiar with that old crank about more crimes occurring during the full moon and yada yada! And my wife maintains that more violent traumas are seen in the emergency room, too. I think it's only because of better lighting." He dug into his shirt pocket and pulled out a miniature cigar, shoving it between his lips.

Ashlon stood up and leaned over the desk, catching his eyes in hers again. She put her hand on top of his before he could bring his lighter up to the cigar. "Listen to me, detective," she tersely said when his face had slackened and the cigar dangled from his lips. "Keep an open mind and be very cautious. Remember that. Now go home and get some sleep." She broke off contact, picked up her bag, and was gone before the blank stare vanished from the detective's eyes again.

Detective Anderson sat back in his chair again, rubbing his face. Maybe the wife was right, he decided as he rose and grabbed his jacket to leave and go home for some badly needed rest.

Chapter 29

Ashlon considered what her next move should be on the drive back to town. Now that it was all up front in plain site (at least to her, anyway), she had to act to protect the people she cared for most. She turned into town and headed to Jorge's office. It was Delia's day off, and sometimes Janey filled in, just as Ashlon had those first weeks after Jorge first hung his shingle on the circle. Pulling around it to the front of his office, she parked on the curb and ran inside.

Janey was happily tapping away at the computer and looked up when she felt the chilly draft from the open door. Her face lit up as Ashlon came around the desk and gave her a hug.
"What's shakin', girlfriend?" Janey said as she gave Ashlon a peck on the cheek. "Pull up a chair."

"Janey, we have to talk, like right now," Ashlon said with urgency in her voice. "Where's Jorge?"

"In the back finishing a sports physical," Janey said. "Are you okay? After last night, I was expecting you to be all cranky and miserable and not a pleasant person to be around today."

Ashlon sighed. "Believe me, I was, for about two minutes' worth of quality teeth-gnashing. So, I went out to the cemetery last night and visited Emma."

Janey's mouth dropped open. "You didn't. At midnight? Were you out of your mind or what?"

Ashlon's expression gave Janey her answer. She sighed. "I shouldn't be surprised. But how'd you get in? Pick the lock?"
Ashlon nodded. "Yep."

"I've got to get me one of those knives! Anyway, you visited Emma's gravesite ..."

"I stayed for a while. It was so nice out there, Janey. Quiet with just a light wind and the night so clear you could touch the stars. I even dozed off on the bench." She paused with a thoughtful glance to Janey. "Emma talked to me." Ashlon's eyes filled for a moment, and speaking became difficult. But she wanted Janey to know what she had experienced. "She told me she was happy with my grandmother and the angels." She stopped speaking for a moment to grab some tissues and dab at her eyes, and blow her nose. Janey nodded for her to go ahead, her hand squeezing Ashlon's shoulder. Ashlon took a shaky breath. "It was one of the most precious moments of my life, Janey. My baby's okay." Ashlon closed her eyes and wrapped her arms around herself, unable to say anymore.

Janey squeezed her shoulder again and gently smiled. "I believe you," she said comfortingly. With a sigh, she smiled and continued. "No one believed me when I told them my mother spoke to me a few days after she passed, just after I filed for divorce. It was a bad time for me, and my ex was making it hard getting anything settled. I remember I was just drowsing in Mom's room—me my sisters and I were clearing her things because my dad couldn't handle it. I saw her as sure as I'm seeing you right now. She looked so happy and con- tented, like she'd never been sick at all. She said everything would be alright, and that you'd show me to my heart's desire."

Ashlon's eyes widened, glistening and astonished. "You never told me this before."

Janey shrugged, grabbing some tissues for herself. "Well, you don't just go around saying you see dead people! Maybe that kid in the movie—but look at the hard time he had. Anyway, you and I stuck it out together and moved out here, and the rest is history." She patted the small bump on her belly. "Something for which I'll be eternally grateful."

They hugged again for a long moment and didn't hear the sliding door to the treatment area quietly open. Jorge appeared with his coat and keys. "Can I get in on this, too, ladies?" he joked with a broad smile.

Ashlon stood and gave him a quick hug and kiss, his mustache tickling her upper lip. She laughed, backing away as she rapidly rubbed her lip with her finger. "How do you put up with that thing?" she said to Janey.

"Like this, girlfriend," Janey happily said and wrapped her arms around Jorge's neck, kissing him passionately. Ashlon discreetly looked away and waited until Janey patted her on the back.

"Any questions, grasshopper?" she sagely inquired. Grabbing Jorge's hand, Janey pulled him toward the door. Jorge gave Ashlon a grin of benign resignation, and she only shrugged as she followed them. Best the good feelings as they come, Ashlon thought, genuinely afraid for her friends. The bogeyman is knocking at the door again.

They lunched at The Woodland Inn, the small, intimate establishment Ashlon ate dinner at the evening of her Saturday day trip. Their menu had changed to include several seasonal dishes, including real plum pudding and roast goose, available only through the end of December. It was while they were waiting on their desserts that Ashlon informed them of her visit to Detective Anderson.

Jorge's mustache was twitching with his concern by the time she finished. He wrapped his arm around Janey and held her close. "If I hadn't seen what happened last night and the way that pindejo acted when he attacked you and Elaine, I'd probably just pass it off as police caution. And now, he's out on bail with his buddies. I think you're right to be concerned. But I can't just leave my practice right now. My friend won't be here for another week to take my patients."

"They can go to County if they need medical care before he shows up," Ashlon insisted. "Stay in Boston until you two are married Saturday, and then leave on your honeymoon right away. You've got open-ended tickets, so just go. I'll drive up for your nuptials."

"But, what about you, Ash?" Janey said. "You're in this deeper than either of us."

Ashlon leaned forward over the table and said in a lowered voice to Janey, "I think I'll be okay, Janey. I want to show you something." She switched her attention over to Jorge and lightly touched his hand. His brown eyes widened, and his jaw dropped open as Ashlon smiled. Jorge's arm dropped from Janey and hung at his side as a blank expression appeared on his face.

"Ash, what the hell ..." Janey said, but Ashlon put a finger to her lips, effectively silencing her friend.

Ashlon looked back at Jorge. "You need to use the restroom right now, don't you, Jorge?" Her voice was gentle, compelling.

Jorge blinked and slowly nodded. Slipping out of his chair, he turned and headed in the direction of the public restrooms.

Janey watched him leave with frank disbelief, her eyes wide and startled. "What was that?" she anxiously said, looking across the table at Ashlon.

Ashlon shook her head and looked down at the table. "I don't know, Janey," she said. "It started last night—remember the server? And then Wes acting all strange? This morning, I charmed the desk sergeant into bringing me a fresh coffee, and got Detective Anderson to tell me what he had in those reports when he didn't want to."

Ashlon sat back, licking her lips. "Something is changing in me, Janey. Jorge will wake up in the restroom and not remember how he got there at all. He'll feel like he's waking from a dream. I can plant any suggestion I choose. And there's only one reason I can think of: Bowen."

"Bowen McAnders?" Janey exclaimed skeptically. "But how, Ash? I mean, he may be weird and all, and I joke around and call him names. But c'mon now!" "Janey, don't you remember what we talked about after we learned about Maddie's murder?"

"About what, sweety?" Janey said off-handedly as she anxiously watched for Jorge's return.

"Bowen, the fangs, no reflection in the mirror, attacked me in my house?" Ashlon persisted as Janey pursed her lips and looked sympathetically at her. Oh, this was just great, Ashlon thought with rising irritation. Had her friend forgotten, or was Janey determined to remain closed-minded about what they'd spoken of that afternoon? Maybe she couldn't handle the thought of such things actually existing. And then, another possibility occurred to her—maybe Bowen had done something to alter Janey's memory when he'd been standing next to her and Jorge at the party Saturday night. Ashlon recalled seeing them talking when she'd spotted them from the stage. She silently groaned with the realization that Janey must have said something that tipped off Bowen, forcing his hand.

Ashlon angrily gnashed her teeth. He'd taken away her only ally in this thing, leaving her to flounder alone with the uncertainty of everything closing in around her. She looked at Janey across the table while her attention was diverted. Something inside Ashlon gradually calmed as she silently studied Janey. Okay, she may have lost a confidant, but maybe in the scheme of things, it was better this way, she reluctantly admitted. Janey's happiness was more important to her than anything else right now. With Jorge and a baby on the way, Ashlon would do practically anything to preserve it. Starting right now. "I did have a lot to drink that night. Talk about an easy target," she said with a deep sigh.

"You saw whatever he wanted you to see," Janey patiently said. "Maybe he was afraid you'd throw him out before he had his say, so he scared you half out of your wits thinking you'd back down. As to that, whatever that was with Jorge—he's been working pretty hard trying to wrap things up before the wedding. He's just tired, is all."

She could and would accept that, Ashlon decided, gritting her teeth. At least Janey and Jorge believed her about Grady and would act accordingly. And really, that's what really mattered most anyway—her friends' safety.

Jorge appeared back at their table, shaking his head and laughing as he rubbed his fingers through his hair. "Darndest thing that ever happened to me," he said, sounding mildly confounded. "Like I was sleepwalking or something and woke up while I was combing my hair."

Janey glanced over at Ashlon with a sympathetic shake of her head. "He's been working way too hard lately. With everything coming up, it's been too much for him, poor baby." She wrapped her arms around him and planted a kiss on his cheek. Ashlon looked away, covering her broad grin as she grabbed a passing waiter and requested a warm-up on her coffee when dessert arrived. No use trying to talk to her anymore, Ashlon decided as she sipped from her cup. Janey's head was a million miles away.

She only poked around her dessert for a bit, a lovely tiramisu, as Jorge and Janey oohed and aahed over the flavors and encouraging Ash to try it. She pushed it away after eating less than half of it. Funny how she didn't have much of an appetite lately. Janey had ordered practically half the menu and ate like a horse once her morning sickness subsided. Ashlon ordered only a small lunch salad with some rare roast beef on it, and an iced tea. Oh well, maybe it was just nerves, or she was coming down with something. She'd see Jorge for a flu shot before he and Janey took off for Boston, which they decided would be the following evening after all. They'd stay with Jorge's mother and finish up their preparations there. At least that was one worry Ashlon could put to rest.

She'd ridden with them to the inn in pretty good spirits. On the trip back, she was quiet and didn't want to talk. Maybe it was the oppressive sky with its puffy grey clouds trying desperately to open and get rid of its crystalline payload. Or, maybe it was because life seemed to be changing around her way too fast. No, she was changing. When she looked in the mirror, she still looked the same, still smelled the same. It was an indefinable shift in her basic sense of self, restructuring her into something else. Shouldn't that bother her more than it was, she wondered? Or maybe it was just nerves and worry, something she could understand. At this point, any other alternative was unthinkable. Why did it all come back to Bowen?

Last evening with Emma had lifted a reluctance she'd harbored to see him as part of her life or becoming part of his. What that entailed, she couldn't even pretend to understand, but she was pretty sure she was getting a small glimpse of it. However, for now, she, however reluctantly, considered him her only possible ally until Grady was brought to trial and permanently put away. She had offered the olive branch by way of her peace offering placed at his resting place last night. Until he found it and understood its significance, she wouldn't take his presence as a given yet.

Ashlon kissed Janey and Jorge goodbye at his office, heading for County General to visit James Stanley. She was feeling guilty and negligent, she hadn't been to visit him since his collapse Saturday night, but hoped he was well enough now to tolerate visitors. The drive out to the hospital cleared her head immeasurably, and she was actually in better spirits once she was away from Jorge and Janey. Unfortunately, she had also been forced to acknowledge a change between her and Janey. Jorge and their baby were now Janey's entire focus. Of course, that's what should happen. But, their friendship was changing, too, and that was the hardest thing to accept. In the end, Ashlon knew they would still be good friends, but traveling on different paths. It was something she hoped she could eventually accept in spite of the years she and Janey had shared, supporting and encouraging each other through some pretty rough times. Janey had her ever after now. Maybe in time, Ashlon would find hers as well.

County Hospital was moderately sized at 200 beds and included a newborn nursery, a telemetry unit, a well-equipped emergency department, and an inpatient medical-surgical unit which combined adult and pediatric patients in two separate wings on the same floor. Mr. Stanley had been admitted through the emergency room to telemetry because Mrs. Stanley had refused to authorize a transfer to Boston General's MICU—too far away, and she knew no one there she could stay with during her husband's recovery.

Ashlon wheeled into the visitor's parking lot. She went inside to the information desk, obtained Mr. Stanley's room number on the 2nd floor, took the stairs, and was soon standing at the central nurses' station. A busy but friendly ward clerk pointed her in the right direction. Soon, she was peeking into the doorway and spied Frances, the Stanleys' daughter, sitting in an easy chair at the foot of the bed with a wiggling toddler on her lap, wanting to climb down and go play with 'gan gan', his name for his grandfather. It was a private room with a small entertainment center in the far corner. A screened window to the right of the bed was open only enough to allow a hint of the chill outside into the warm room.

The toddler immediately stopped wiggling and watched Ashlon's approach with wide-eyed interest as he sat back quietly in his mother's lap and grasped her hand holding him over his belly. Ah, stranger danger. Ashlon recognized the posture without even thinking about it.

Every child over the age of one showed it at one time or another.

Mr. Stanley was sitting up in bed with a breathing apparatus in his nostrils. Ashlon could just pick up the soft hiss of the flow-through. He was very drawn and pale, but the sparkle was back in his eyes again, his breathing was easy and unlabored, and he smiled broadly when he spotted Ashlon approaching his bedside.

"There's my shining knight!" he exclaimed, reaching out a hand to her. She sat on the edge of the bed and hugged him affectionately. Curiously, however, she felt him sniffing her neck and clothing, and then he sniffed her hands when she sat up again. He smiled wryly with a glance at Frances. "I was right," he firmly stated.

Ashlon was frankly puzzled, looking quizzically at Frances. Frances only shrugged as she switched the toddler to her other knee when he wiggled to be turned where he could keep an eye on the visitor.

Ashlon looked back at Mr. Stanley. "Well, I was going to ask how you're doing, sir. But now, you've piqued my curiosity."

Mr. Stanley chuckled warmly and pointed to his nose. "The nose knows, Miss Ashlon. Lord McAnders' scent is all over you. Even soap and water won't wash it away. And when he visited yesterday evening, just before the end of visiting hours, I could smell your scent on him. And you have a very unique scent, Miss Ashlon. Rest assured."

Frances let her toddler down to wander as she followed him on his exploration. "Dad says he can tell if a couple's right for each other by the way their scents blend together." She looked highly doubtful, but let her remarks remain there for her father's sake.

"Anyway, Miss Ashlon," Mr. Stanley continued, "I'm so glad you're here. Tell me what's going on in town. My wife is not prone to be gossipy, bless her, but I do so love juicy tidbits."

"Dad," Frances clucked disapprovingly. "You know you're not supposed to get worked up."

Ashlon thoughtfully chewed her lip. "Lord McAnders was here last night?" "Oh, yes," Mr. Stanley readily said. "We had a very nice visit. He told me about the party and how you and Janey delighted young Max with your compliments about the decor. He was still trying to understand why you two were so thrilled with it, mimicking something from a children's book. I tried to explain, and I think Master Bowen understands a little better. He was also curious about your rescue of Wes Ottman for the first selections he had picked for the party, and how the children loved the scare you gave them. He had no idea you were such an animated performer. I informed him you've done charity work at the Children's Hospital many times and not to be so surprised that you were ready to do that favor for Wes. He did, however, look put out about something, but wouldn't say what. Did you two have a disagreement?"

"You could say that," Ashlon said, but not willing to discuss it at the moment. "I'm here to cheer you up. So here's what you've missed." She held his gnarled hand as she reported the gossip and news around their little town. He was grinning from ear to ear when she finished with the news that Jorge and Janey had moved up their wedding date to Saturday and would be leaving directly afterward for a cruise to Europe. Frances hung on every word while her toddler took apart Grandpa's bedside table after pushing a chair up to it. Mr. Stanley lifted the boy onto the bed as Frances pulled away the table to put it to rights. The toddler, incensed that his fun had been disrupted, began to fuss and hit at Mr. Stanley and made a grab for the nasal cannula, which the old man gently deflected. Then the child made a lunge for his IV line. Ashlon deftly caught his wrist and gently turned it away as she smiled into his face. He froze in his grandfather's arms as he stared at her with wide, surprised eyes.

"I think it's time for a nap, little man," she said in a low, soothing tone. The tot's big blue eyes fluttered for only a second, then closed as he settled onto Mr. Stanley's chest with his thumb in his mouth and promptly passed out.

"How did you do that?" Frances said with obvious relief as she carefully lifted him from her father and laid him on the guest bed located near the bathroom. "He usually goes down kicking and screaming."

Ashlon winked at Mr. Stanley and said, "It's just a knack, I guess."

Frances indicated she needed to get something to eat and drink, and asked Ashlon, if she'd watch the sleeping baby until she came back. Of course, Ashlon said yes because she wanted to ask Mr. Stanley about this scent thing, and did so only after Frances departed for the cafeteria.

Mr. Stanley patted Ashlon's hand affectionately. "Ah, yes!" he continued when she reminded him of it. "You possess your own unique scent, Miss Ashlon. It's nothing one can describe; only that it exists. I would say the closest comparison would be to English lavender, only richer. And I must say it blended exquisitely with Master Bowen's." He reached up and touched Ashlon's cheek. "Why, I do believe you're blushing!"

Ashlon grimaced with embarrassment as she quickly went into the bathroom and looked into the mirror. "You're right. And it takes a lot to make me blush," she called out to him before returning and sitting on the edge of his bed again. Looking at him thoughtfully, she said, "You know, I see you Mrs. Stanley together, and I'm simply awed. To survive the complexities of married life and still come out of it holding hands is a miracle in itself. I see how happy Janey and Jorge are and the life they're about to start together, and I'm absolutely envious; more so because I introduced them to each other. But, what you have is trust in each other. Bowen hasn't gotten to that point yet. We've known each other for only a short time, but he pointedly told me last night trust is a luxury he can't afford, even with me. That's why I don't know if he's even serious about an 'us'. Is there a limit where you stop trying and just move on, or do you hang in there and wait for some miracle to occur?"

Mr. Stanley was silent for a few minutes as he studied Ashlon. "I take it that was what Master Bowen was disturbed about, or something pertaining to it. Perhaps it's because you have such a tremendous capacity for caring, you know what someone needs even if you've known them for only a brief time. That's why we became such good friends and collaborators on uncovering the mystery of McAnders House. Why else would you stick around an old fart like me?" He touched Ashlon's cheek. "I look at you and see my dear wife, those years ago when we were courting. She had no fears or suspicions or doubts about what she wanted, either, and hung in there in spite of my hesitation and rebelliousness. I like to call it her benign campaign of persuasion. And, of course, I came to trust her regard for me and married her."

He was becoming fatigued, lying back into his pillows with a stifled yawn, but managed a warm, compassionate smile as he patted Ashlon's hand. "You must remain strong and determined and let your intuition guide you. Lord McAnders is like a closed book you must learn how to read. I believe he's suffered from friends' or former lovers' treachery just as you have. And it maybe he will never let himself trust anyone again, including you. You'll know if it comes to that point. But never sacrifice your trust and regard for him. It's what he's most watchful for and will anticipate now that he's admitted you into his circle." The old man closed his eyes, still holding Ashlon's hand.

She sighed. "I don't know if I have the endurance for an extended campaign," she said as much to herself as to her beloved friend who had fallen asleep as soon as his eyes closed. Now that was trust, she silently affirmed, giving him a gentle kiss on the forehead as she carefully drew her hand from his and rose to leave. Frances had quietly appeared behind her, holding a food tray, nodded to Ashlon as she placed it on the bedside table, and wheeled it over to the window. She pulled up a higher chair from under a desk across from the bed, removed a book from her carryall, and sat down to enjoy her lunch in peace.

"You should visit more often, Miss Isaacs. This is the first real break I've had in two days," she whispered happily as she spread her napkin in her lap and picked up her silver.

"I'll do that," Ashlon whispered back. "Your dad knows my cell and home numbers. Let me know if there's anything I can do while he's still here."

"Just leave the name of your agency. He'll want you for his home care convalescent visits, I'm sure. I'll get it pre-approved and set up once we know when he'll be discharged."

Ashlon removed a personal business card from her wallet, wrote down the name and number of the agency on the back, and handed it to Frances. Then she waved and quietly slipped out the door.

Chapter 30

Visiting Mr. Stanley had been so pleasant, and she was relieved he was getting better. However, her optimism was tempered—she'd seen too many cases appear to be resolving, and then all of a sudden go sour and the patient crumple in a relatively short time. She wouldn't be totally satisfied until he'd been discharged home and had his family around him.

She was also very surprised that Bowen had visited his old caretaker last night after dumping her at the Mayor's party. He'd sought his own answers, it seemed. Do him good to get some human insight from a non-biased third party, although she doubted if it would do much good at this point.

The snow was falling steadily now as Ashlon wheeled into town and stopped at the grocery store to buy some things she needed, and to chat with Doris, who was working the front checkout that after-noon. Soon, she was on her way home with her groceries on the front passenger side floor as she maneuvered carefully through the falling snow, reaching her neighborhood just as the street lamps flared on in the park. McAnders House was a dark life less hulk as she drove past it, giving it only a brief glance before rounding the corner onto her street.

The bare-limbed tree by the curb in front of her house was beginning to look positively festive with its new white coat as Ashlon pulled a U-turn and pulled up next to it. It got dark early these days, and full night had fallen by 6:00PM. Fortunately, she had a light sensor on her front porch light so the front was glistening brightly under the new snow. She'd cleared her front porch decorations after coming home from the cemetery last evening as well, thank heaven. She got out and affixed the security sensor to the Jeep's top, then took out her two large grocery bags. Once she muscled them to her porch, she propped one of the bags on the rail against her arm as she palmed her keys, attempting to unlock the door without losing the bag. Her one foot suddenly slipped to the side, and her arm bumped the bag of groceries balanced on the rail. As it began to fall, she made a desperate lunge for it, nearly dropping the bag clutched tightly in her other arm. This was just too dumb for words, Ashlon thought with disgust. At least there was nothing breakable in there!

A huge shadow loomed from behind her into the recessed doorway, and a jacketed arm flashed out, snatching the falling bag before it had cleared the rail. A heady masculine scent wafted around her along with the swirling snow and wind. Someone gently pressed against her back, and she smiled to herself as she unlocked her front door and stepped inside, followed by her tall shadow caster.

Ashlon flipped the light switch and headed for the kitchen, dropping her grocery bag on her small table. She immediately put away its contents. The other bag had mysteriously joined the first when she returned from the pantry. However, when she looked around to say thank you, no one was there. She rushed over to the front door, which still hung open, and looked out onto the front porch and side-walk. There was only the softly falling snow. Ashlon hung onto her open door as profound disappointment gripped her. He had just come and gone. Maybe she was expecting too much after the chewing out she'd given him the previous evening, departing immediately to avoid any further harshness between them.

Ashlon sighed with acute resignation and closed the door, intending to put him out of her mind and return to the kitchen to unload the other grocery bag... and froze in her tracks, holding her breath as she stared in breathless fright at two wide, glowing amethyst eyes staring at her from the darkness near the top of the stairs. A scream stuck in her throat as she backed against the closed door, frantically pawing for the handle with only one thought—run!

A huge shadow swept down from the upstairs hallway and surrounded her in its grip, swallowing her sharp gasp in its embrace, phantom lips muffling her outcry as they engulfed hers in soundless passion's expression. Time stood still as she was absorbed inside two strong arms, the breath drawn out of her by the power of their need to embrace and possess. He was like the wind in the storm as he swept her into the night.

In the space of half a breath, she was in his bed, bound tightly in his arms as his lips burned her face, his body meshed with hers, expressing its breathtaking ravenous need. He coaxed, caressed every inch of her, and filled her with his profound desire to keep them joined and never be parted again. Her passionate cries urged him on, bringing her to trembling fulfillment as his own pounding release wrung a groan from deep in his throat. He embraced her to his heart, covering her lips, her face, her throat with light, tender kisses until he pressed deeply into her again and bit hungrily through the tender skin, sealing his lips against her throat, drawing hard against it and savoring the rich warmth flowing into his mouth.

She softly gasped, holding him close with her hand meshed in his hair. Afterward, he raised his head and kissed her throat, kissed her searching lips, tasted her mouth, and delighted in her gasp when he kissed her breasts as his hands caressed and kneaded them, relishing her soft moans as he suckled each nipple with a force that generated shock waves rippling down to her toes with shuddering delight.

Ashlon lovingly held Bowen as he voiced a low, soft moan of contentment into her cleavage, kissing its softness as he pressed his face into it. She idly ran her fingers down his broad back, across his hips to gently squeeze his lush, firm buttocks, and then slide up his long body and arms to his shoulders. He trembled under her fingers when she repeated her soft caressing, and nestled his head onto her shoulder. His deep, soft growl of contentment was music to her ears.

Presently, he rolled to his side and pulled her against him with her head pillowed on his shoulder, one of his legs thrown over hers. His lips continued to hover near her face and cheek, softly kissing them as if he would go on forever. Ashlon's eyes were closed, a gentle smile gracing her mouth.

"Does this mean you have forgiven me?" Bowen's gentle voice rumbled in his chest, vibrating up and down her side.

Ashlon opened her eyes and softly laughed, kissing his cheek. "I think I made that pretty obvious," she replied, perfectly content to be held once more in those strong, loving arms. "You found my peace offering."

"I did, beloved," Bowen softly whispered. "I kept it with me as I slept today, and came to you as soon as I woke. Your faith and forgiveness does me honor, my lady." He lightly brushed her lips with his again and tasted them, drawing on her tongue until she softly moaned into his mouth. She was panting when his mouth moved down her cheek to her throat again, nuzzling it with his nose and lips, softly licking with his warmed tongue.

"My daughter told me I should be with you so neither of us will be lonely anymore," Ashlon managed to speak when his mouth circled her breast again, nuzzling its softness.

Bowen looked up, propping himself on one elbow, his expression puzzled. "Your daughter? But, she has passed."

Ashlon gently smiled as she kissed his forehead. "I'll tell you later what I did after I kicked you out last night."

Bowen wanted her to stay with him in his bed the remainder of the night, but Ashlon needed to go home and make something to eat, put the rest of her groceries away, and show him some information on her laptop. After they dressed, Bowen returned her home in that same startling way he had taken her from it, intending to remain with her for the evening.

She set up her laptop on the coffee table and then went to the kitchen to prepare oriental ramen with mushrooms and chopped green onions. While it was simmering, she put the remainder of her groceries away. Bowen sat on the couch, net surfing on her laptop as she worked. He glanced over at her briefly as she filled a deep soup bowl with the steaming ramen, sprinkled some toasted rice noodles on top, and grabbed a soup spoon from her silver drawer. She sat at her kitchen table to eat. Bowen frowned and snorted when she quickly said a blessing before digging in.

"What was that for?" she said as she scooped up a large spoonful of hot soup and blew over it to cool it, then put the entire thing in her mouth, chew- ing with satisfaction—hot soup for a cold evening. "I always say grace before I eat," she said after swallowing and licking her lips. "Makes the food taste better."

Bowen rose from the sofa and walked over to the table, his nose curling as he silently watched Ashlon savoring her light repast right down to the last green onion slice at the bottom of the bowl.

"Are you finished?" he said with barely concealed distaste. Ashlon smirked at him as she took her empty bowl to the sink and brought a port wine bottle back with her to the table after liberating it from the refrigerator. Bowen sighed heavily and sat in the other chair across from her, grimacing at her with obvious impatience.

"I enjoy my meals such as they are. And it's not healthy to eat fast," Ashlon sniffed with mild reproof. "You don't hear me complain when you dine." She could see his attitude fairly dripping with disdain, evident in his distant, cool expression.

Running hot and cold again, are we? She rose and moved to the couch, placed her wine glass on a coaster, and then logged herself onto the laptop. She tapped the keys and then looked over at him, motioning him toward the couch. "I need to show you something," she said. When he didn't move right away, she sighed and stood again, ambling over to the brooding giant.

"Bowen, look at me," she gently cajoled. Ashlon stroked his cheeks and then cuffed his square chin in her palms to make him look up at her. "There're things I need to tell you. Disturbing things I learned today." When he continued to be sullen and unmoving, she straddled his lap and wrapped her arms around his neck, stroking his long hair, marveling at its thick softness as she ran her fingers through it. Pulling it to one side, she kissed his neck and throat, breathing in his deep, rich male scent. She rapturously rubbed her face across it, running her nose across the width of his neck with her eyes closed, savoring him like a fine wine. When he growled deep in his throat, she kissed around his ear, down his throat, and up to his mouth, which was open and waiting for her lips. His arms slid around her and cradled her as she kissed him and tasted his mouth with her probing tongue. When their eyes met, she smiled puckishly at the new desire burning in them. No, not now! she hastily reminded herself as she pushed down her own desire to drop everything and jump his bones again. She sat up, his arms still gripping her tightly. "If you're in a better mood now, we need to talk," she gently reminded him as she pried herself away from his grasp and slipped off his lap, but held onto his hands. He was frowning when he looked at her, but rose from his chair, allowing her to lead him back to her couch. He sat heavily beside her, initially refusing to release her hands. However, when she needed them to tap in several things on her laptop, he dropped them and surrounded her shoulders in one long arm instead, his other hand resting on her lap.

Ashlon described her call from and subsequent visit to Detective Anderson. She showed him the police files she'd hacked into with pictures of the three murder scenes taken by the forensics investigators. Copies of the lab reports had been posted. Ashlon located the actual narratives Detective Anderson had in those folders. At one point, Bowen looked at Ashlon and pointedly asked, "How did you become so skilled at this breaking and entering?"

Ashlon grinned. "When the need arises, you find the means. Might not be legal, but it gets the job done. And I needed to know since I'm getting sucked further and further into this whole mishugas."

Bowen's expression was puzzled. "This what?" He didn't receive an immediate reply as Ashlon studied the screen again. Instead, he stood and ambled over to the front bay window, occupying himself watching the gentle falling of the snow and tracing elaborate designs on the heavily steamed window panes. Perhaps he would make a new portrait to replace that stern one of his grandfather—Ashlon and himself at his home in Scotland. He felt safe considering this now, even planning their permanent union as he glanced over his shoulder at her, a contemplative smile working its way across his features.

Ashlon's attention was fixed on several newly posted pictures, which included the heavily wooded site of the third murder where the young man was found in his car trunk on the overgrown logging road. According to the report, the hunter's blue tick hound had alerted to something in the car trunk. The picture of both the hunter and his dog had appeared in the local paper near the scene. Hmm. So, if the dog was with its owner for the picture, what the hell was that large one crouching way behind them on that ledge? It was surrounded by a large rock cluster in which it blended perfectly; it had probably moved its position and was caught digitally. She flipped back to the forensics pictures taken around the car and was able to make out several sets of paw prints pressed into the soft earth. The sizes didn't match. Some of them were definitely larger than the hound's by at least one paw's breadth and length, with deep indentations at each toe—long claws digging into the ground. Canis lupis, Anderson had said. But these paw prints were huge. Did wolves get that big, she wondered?

Ashlon sat back, thinking and watching the snow fall. Bowen heard her sigh and rejoined her, sitting close to her with his arm around her shoulders again. He glanced down at the picture that had kept her attention for so long and uttered a menacing growl, his eyes flashing with sudden, vehement anger. "Where was this taken?" he hissed as he glared at the picture on the screen.

Ashlon looked up. "It's part of a forensics file on that homicide case upstate at the edge of the state game lands." Cautiously, she switched back to the previous picture and pointed out the large canine hidden in the rocks. "Can you make out what this is?" she inquired, her green eyes fixed on Bowen's face. What happened next, however, was utterly unexpected.

Bowen became truly terrifying. He sprang to his feet and lowered his head with a deadly scowl. His face contorted with deep loathing as his hands curled into taloned claws capable of ripping out a throat with one fatal swipe. His fangs were fully extended and bared as his eyes glowed balefully with an unnatural light.

"They have been enemies of my kind for untold ages," he hissed with passionate disdain. "We have co-existed for centuries in my native land with clearly defined territories. To violate those boundaries is certain death for the trespasser."

Ashlon was definitely worried now, not to mention scared enough to slide down the sofa away from him. "So you've got a mad on against wolves?" Her voice was trembling. "Granted, they're not native to New England, but it could've been someone's pet that got loose or something, or escaped from a wildlife preservation area."

Bowen's scowl deepened, and his expression became downright deadly. "Something far worse ended the life of that unfortunate boy and most likely those other two." He abruptly turned away and folded into himself in an attempt to quell the revulsion he felt. But what was Ashlon's part in this? he had to wonder? Why was she getting involved at all?

Ok, this was definitely getting too weird, and Bowen obviously didn't want to talk about it. Something far worse than the wolf in the picture, he'd said. According to Anderson, maybe people are acting like animals. A cult of some kind, or a coven operating out of North State? No, had to be much worse to affect Bowen like this. But he wasn't about to spill his spleen at this point, unfortunately.

She was feeling very frustrated, knowing the answer was right in front of her face, but she wasn't seeing it. She'd be able to put it together later once she had a chance to think about it. G-d! She felt so damn thick tonight! Maybe it was time to change tracks and divert to another path for a while.

She quickly logged out of the website and opened a personal file, scrolling down to a framed picture. Time to make this scene a little less tense, and maybe learn some history concerning Lord Bowen McAnders.

Chapter 31

Bowen stalked back to the front window again and stared unseeing at the snowfall, which was letting up, now only light flurries blowing helter-skelter in the light of the street lamp. If he hadn't seen the evidence in those pictures, he would not have appreciated the gravity of Ashlon's concerns and curiosity concerning those murders last month. Unfortunately, this generated a whole new set of worries he felt utterly helpless to resolve. Grady was out of jail pending his arraignment for assault and trespass last evening. Could he have a connection to what had happened last month?

He'd posted bail and fled to a protected area. That much was certain. Ashlon had done the correct thing in warning her friends to get away since they were closest to her and could be targeted by this maniac.

But what about her personal safety? In the night, he was stronger than any threat to her. But, what of the daylight hours? She was so self-assured, especially since taking down Grady after his unwanted advances the previous night. But then, he had been drunken and impaired. Bowen wasn't certain her confidence would be enough to keep her safe against a repeated effort by this individual.

In regard to the murders, Ashlon reported that Detective Anderson was concerned they were not the work of one person. According to the evidence, there were two distinct fur samples indicating several rogues in the area. Another question arose that troubled Bowen even more: why now? What had happened to instigate an upswing of violent activity in this area? A significant event was most likely in the works that had provided the impetus for this new wave of violence. Perhaps when it was learned, efforts could be directed in halting any further killings.

Bowen's dark musings were interrupted when warm arms slid around him from behind. Ashlon looked around him out the window, her chin resting above his elbow.

"It's beautiful out there tonight," she said with a contemplative smile. "I always look forward to the first snow of the season. Makes me want lots of hot chocolate, and maybe curl up in front of a blazing fire with music playing in the background." She looked up at him with a gentle smile that warmed him as much as her body pressed against his.

Bowen turned, wrapping her protectively in his arms, breathing in the warmth rising from her face, and cherishing the feel of her arms around him. Her face was pressed to his chest, and her hands lightly massaged his back under his shirt.

"I didn't mean to upset you with those pictures," Ashlon said after a long silence. "I needed your insight to help sort out some things because the police don't seem have any idea what's going on."

"My only concern is for you, my love," Bowen fervently said, kissing her hair. "I do not know what I would do if any harm should befall you when I am unable to protect you. You must not become embroiled in these other dark affairs."

"Oh, I don't think that'll be much of a problem, Bowen," Ashlon said reassuringly. "I'll stay as far away from them as humanly possible. Let the police deal with 'em. I've got enough to keep me busy."

Bowen looked down at Ashlon's upturned face, an enigmatic smile lighting her features. "I am sure you will," he said, and then softly kissed her forehead. Whether he believed her, however, was another matter.

Ashlon drew a deep breath and rubbed her face against the fabric of his knit shirt. His scent was different, something she hadn't noticed before. It was undeniably alluring in its subtle attraction. "Are you wearing a different scent tonight?" she said, taking a deep breath, filling her nose with its heady aura.

"No, I am not," he said.

"It's something different. Are you avoiding an answer?" It was more powerful than she'd ever experienced, inflaming her desire for him again, even more than what she'd felt when he'd worn his black rose attar. With a monumental effort, she very reluctantly released him and returned to the sofa, picked up her wine glass, and took a long slug off it. Maybe if she numbed her brain enough on the alcohol, she might be able to get through the rest of the evening. She really couldn't withstand the blood loss of another passionate tussle tonight if he got to her.

Bowen returned to the couch, watching Ashlon closely with a tender knowing expression.

"I must apologize for not explaining myself completely. What you perceive is the charisma my kind utilizes when we are aroused by either passion or blood need. My concern for your safety has likely drawn you to it." He leaned in close to her, studying her closely with a half-smile. "Interesting that you perceive it as a scent that nearly overwhelms you." He would have moved closer, but Ashlon put her hand against his chest and quickly moved away with her glass to refill to the top again.

"If you come any closer than arm's length, I can't be held responsible for what I might do, and then what you'll do because we both enjoy it so much," she warned, chugging down half her refilled glass before sitting down again on the sofa.

"I could do what I did earlier when you were unaware I was in the house," Bowen said smoothly, his expression gentle and appealingly hypnotic.

Ashlon smirked back at him. "And I could throw you out into the snow by rescinding your invitation. Self-preservation, you understand."

Bowen sat back again with a nod. He knew a stalemate when he saw it. Ashlon put her glass back on the coaster and woke her laptop. A portrait appeared on the screen with an inscription in old Gothic script printed under it. It was similar to the smaller one she'd found and showed to Janey and Irma at Irma's house. The fact that this one portrayed who was sitting next to her in her living room was simply mind-boggling.

"I found this in a collection kept by the London Museum. Do you know this handsome fellow?" She turned the screen for Bowen to view.

His eyes widened as he observed the portrait on the screen. "You found this, you say? By my father's beard, I thought it had been lost in my flight from my ancestral home."

Ashlon checked her references again. It was her turn for wide eyes as she looked from the picture to Bowen and back again.

"I knew it. I knew this had to be you. You served Queen Elizabeth I, didn't you?" she said, the awe she was experiencing almost overwhelming her.

Bowen gravely nodded. "I was contracted by Sir Francis Walsingham to her Majesty's service over a 20-year period after the doctrine of the 39 Articles was established, effectively solidifying the Church of England apart from the Pope. It was with my grandfather's blessing that I was there. However, his only motive was for me to pass information back to him through his operatives for his contacts connected with Queen Mary. This I resolutely refused to do. I served only the one true queen. But Her Majesty insisted on my keeping con- tact with my grandfather so that his network could be uncovered and brought to justice."

"You became a double agent, didn't you? That's his portrait in your library, isn't it?"

Bowen hung his head and turned away. "It was painted after he had received his knighthood from Mary's regent while she was imprisoned. It was an empty gesture, though, with Mary's execution a year later."

"Your services helped safeguard Elizabeth's authority through the succession conflicts and religious wars. England hasn't had a monarchy as remarkable as hers since. And, you ensured Scotland's future survival under James as her successor after she died."

Bowen stood and moved stiffly away from her, his arms folded over his chest. "You have certainly researched me in depth, have you not?" he said, sounding oddly defensive.

"Not you specifically. It evolved around the house; historical documents led Mr. Stanley and me back to you when you were still calling yourself by another name," Ashlon said, feeling him withdrawing away from her behind his wall. A very hard, suspicious wall.

Just great. Another touchy mood swing fueled by his trust issues. "Mr. Stan- ley and I had to dig into records that hadn't been touched in ages for the his- tory behind McAnders House. We were determined not to let Alice Tisbee screw with its history."

"So you are saying all your efforts at uncovering me were for the benefit of my home? It had nothing to do with me? I find that difficult to believe," Bowen looked at her, his eyes veiled.

"Don't flatter yourself. Finding your name as the original owner was a major coup, not the primary objective," Ashlon sniffed as she irritably closed her laptop. Grinding her teeth, she snapped, "We saved your house from being leveled or turned into a parody of itself. And then, when we learned a McAnders heir was moving in, we were ecstatic, not to mention vindicated. So you've got only yourself to blame because of that housewarming you hosted. Otherwise, I would have archived that damn picture and forgotten about it."

This was becoming too exasperating as Ashlon puffed with frustration and moved off the couch, stalking to her back door to get away from this temperamental male ego with his mystery man complex.

The clock on her mantle struck 10 pm. Is that all the later it is, she wondered morosely as she peered out her back door at the new pristine snow glistening in her yard, weighing down the limbs of her weeping willow. It was a magical, sparkling, untouched canvas inviting an artist to make something of it.

Suddenly, she felt an overwhelming need to get away from the moodiness hanging over her living room like wet black crepe. Time to get some fresh, clean air into her lungs and perform a time-honored ritual she and Emma had faithfully observed every year without fail in the season's first significant snowfall.

She bolted out the back door.

"Ashlon?" was all she heard as the door slammed shut behind her. She leapt off the small back porch and fell into the deep white powder, creating a snow angel in a spot just below the porch, then hopped to a new area a little further out and flopped into the snow to create another one. The snow had started falling lightly again as she created one angel after another across her yard—a whole chorus of them. Then, she ran under the willow and yanked one of the limbs, laughing riotously as a snow shower fell all over her. Scooping it into her bare hands, she packed it into a tidy ball and looked up at Bowen, who now stood on her porch glaring at her with stern disapproval, his arms still folded over his chest. Ashlon wrinkled her nose at him, shook her head with mock dismay, and called out, "Incoming!"

Bowen realized too late what she meant as she nailed him with her snowball. She was busy making another one when he leapt from the porch and flew toward her. She squealed and managed to hit him again on his chest before eluding him under the willow tree. As he moved swiftly toward her, she backed away and suddenly jumped up, grabbing a limb and pulling hard, bringing a heavy shower of snow down over Bowen, temporarily obscuring his vision.

"Yes!" Ashlon crowed, punching the air. She spun around, taking off at a dead run toward the gate to escape to the front of the house. She could hear his rapidly pursuing footsteps and guessed he thought she might slow to open the gate. Wrong! She reached a mound in front of her gate that always caught her lawnmower during the summer, and with a step-leap sailed over the low gate and rolled nimbly to her feet on the other side, never slowing as she sped down the lee side of the house with a trailing laugh, disappearing around the corner to the front.

Bowen was smiling in spite of himself when he caught up to her. He knew she had had far too much to drink, but her riotous behavior was infectious and had coaxed him out of his dark mood as he had chased after her. He found Ashlon seated on the hood of her Jeep, eating the snow she'd scooped from her windshield.

"That's more like it," she said, flicking snow at him as he approached. "You were such a sourpuss."

He wasn't quite sure what had precipitated this sudden need for rapturous play other than the alcohol, although he suspected it had also been his unexpected guardedness concerning himself and his history. It was something he had not been particularly proud of, but Ashlon had shocked him with her knowledge of him and the era. She had done her homework, positively congratulating his safeguarding of a beloved queen's monarchy and his homeland's political integrity in a single lifetime. However, his grandfather had never forgiven him for his duplicity when it had been discovered. To ensure his safety, his father had banished him from the family home until after his grandfather's death.

Bowen regarded with new understanding this amazing woman sitting in front of him, her face turned up as she caught snowflakes on her tongue. She had a probing intellect and boundless curiosity about everything. She expressed a deep passion and tenderness that simply overwhelmed him in their loving. Bowen was utterly captivated by her shining face with her reddened cheeks and nose, her warm breath blowing large clouds of condensed moisture into the air around her. And, he was simply awed by the life that emanated from her like a brilliant aura on this cold, wintery night. Why then did he continue to probe, to test, to doubt her when she had given him absolutely no reason to do so? He had opened his heart to her, and then turned his back on her when she needed him the most. Yet, here she was, trusting him again only because of a mysterious assurance she had received the previous evening. If that was not love's honest expression, then he had been in the darkness far too long and did not deserve her.

"You're wet all through," he admonished with mock gruffness as he spread his large hands on her knees and felt the wet cold of her jeans.

Ashlon shrugged. "It doesn't bother me. I'll just get into a hot tub and parboil later. However, for right now ..." She scooped up another handful of dry snow and blew it at him, then slipped off the opposite side of her Jeep hood and danced into the quiet street, her arms stretched out to the sky, her face lifted into the falling snow.

"There's so much to be thankful for!" she called out as she danced and skipped around him, nimbly avoiding his attempts to grab her. "The things that you love, keep them close. Like new snow and hot chocolate and good friends and anyone who can love you in spite of how grumpy you get!"

Bowen finally caught her in his arms, and she laughed and put her cold hands on his face, gazing up into his eyes. "Like me," she firmly declared as she stood on tiptoes to kiss him. "Remember that."

He hugged her close to him, his face pressed to hers. "My love, my own," he passionately murmured over and over.

He was once more her loving Bowen, Ashlon breathed with a sigh of relief. And, maybe a few steps closer to the trust he so desperately needed to make it worth staying with him in spite of their vast differences. Only time would tell, and she hoped she had the patience to see it through.

Chapter 32

In one breathless moment of discovery, Bowen's doubts and suspicions had been temporarily put aside by Ashlon's happy frolicking in the first snows of the year. But now, she was shivering as he held her in the middle of the snowy street.

"I th-think I n-need that hot t-tub now!" she stuttered, gripping him close, her arms tightly wrapped around him. Though Bowen wasn't wearing a coat, either, and his shirt was as wet through as her sweater and camisole, he didn't feel the raw cold's grip like she did. However, he could feel her violent trembling and bent down to her one ear, softly kissing it before he spoke.

"Close your eyes," he whispered. She did, burying her face into his shirt. Ashlon felt a sucking sensation in her stomach and a dizzying whirling about her head that stopped almost as soon as it had started.

Bowen scooped her up and carried her swiftly up the stairs of his home to the master bedroom, setting her on his bed. He pulled a fluffy goose down quilt over her, wrapping her in it so that only her face was exposed. Touching her lips with a finger colder than her numbing chilliness, he commented critically, "You're turning blue", and wheeled, rapidly disappearing into his bathroom. Ashlon heard water running and realized he was filling his large sunken tub. The scents of patchouli and lavender oils also reached her runny nose, which she carelessly wiped on the quilt. Bowen returned to the bedroom, now stark naked and deathly white from his hairline down to his toenails. The hair on his head and chest—and another area—looked stark black in contrast to the ghastly pallor of his skin.

Ashlon looked up blearily, feeling a little punchy. He was a huge, lovely white snowman with glowing purple eyes! Darn, she should have built one of those instead of those pathetic snowballs. She wanted to go dancing again and just forget every little worry that had been plaguing her since getting involved with him. Why did she have to fall for tall, dark, and dead?! Why was she so cursed with curiosity that got her into more trouble than she could handle? Maybe that's why she'd loved reading the Curious George stories to Emma. She could readily identify with that cute little monkey. Even her own grandmother had said it so many times as she grew up. Janey always warned it would happen sooner or later, too, and by heaven, here she was in the snowman's kingdom, and why was he taking her blanket?

What's he saying about the cold? Of course, she knew about the effects of hypothermia! She wasn't stupid! Of course, he wouldn't feel it because he's a snowman and dead for hundreds of years, but he's still walking around and—jeez! Now he was pulling her clothes off her! If he wanted her again, why didn't he just come out and say so?

Fortunately, Bowen remembered well the symptoms of acute hypothermia when he saw it, and in spite of her combativeness, managed to quickly pull Ashlon's wet clothes from her. She was feebly trying to push him away and curl up into a ball on the bedspread as he finally pulled off her wet jeans and underclothes. Of course, he could have easily ripped them to shreds, but having already ruined one change of her clothes did not dispose him to be as destructive this time.

Picking her up and cradling her against him, he returned to the bathroom and carefully stepped into the steaming tub, foamy with a thick layer of aromatic bubbles, and gradually lowered them into the water. Bowen knew it would sting her badly and feel twice as hot as it really was at first, and sure enough, she gasped and swore out loud as the water touched her bottom and toes. But, he held on through her struggling protests and completed his slow immersion, settling onto the bottom. He turned Ashlon to lie reclining on top of him, her head on his chest, his legs wrapped around hers, the water up to her neck just under her chin. He lay back against a thick towel spread on the side of the tub and held on until she stopped her feeble wriggling and became still, her eyes fluttering closed. He released her arms from her sides and clasped his large hands over her flat belly.

Ironic that he had imagined what he and Ashlon might do in this tub, but unfreezing her had been the last thing on his mind! For the present, however, he was completely blissfully content holding her on top of him as he settled back and closed his eyes, the aromatic steam rising around them from the circulating steaming water.

Slowly rising through a fog, Ashlon realized she was nice and warm again, could feel her arms and legs, and her thoughts were becoming less muddled. Where was she, anyway? The last coherent memory she had was dancing in the street and then snuggling against an incredibly cold, wet shirt and telling Bowen she needed to warm up. Images of large snowmen with glowing coal eyes kept popping into her head.

She finally realized she was in his incredibly large sunken tub. The water felt marvelous and smelled wonderful, too. Then, she noticed she was stretched out on top of Bowen like a great big lumpy lounge chair. Turning only her head, she looked up at Bowen's face, his head relaxed back on a terry cloth-covered tub pillow, his eyes closed in perfect repose with an expression of absolute contentment soften-ing his features.

Now she understood as she settled back against him again. Admittedly, she'd gone a little crazy in the snow because she couldn't stand his brooding moodiness any more, giving in to an overwhelming desire to immediately separate herself from it and gambol in the new snow. She'd done things like this before, but always made it to her warm bathtub before freezing became an issue. Then, she remembered the large amount of alcohol she'd consumed before diving out the back door into the snow. Gaack! No wonder she'd lost all sense of feeling cold and stayed out too long. But it was Bowen's fault; if he hadn't been acting all cool and hostile in the first place about her revelation of his early history, she would have probably just gotten sick in the bathroom downstairs and then gone to bed to sleep it off. Thank heaven she hadn't told him the other things she'd learned!

Detailed medical journals had been kept by an unnamed physician in service to the Queen, and who maintained records for Walsingham on his operations, including one Bowen Alton McAnders. According to this unidentified physician, a strange plague had hit several of the southern garrisons stationed at Portsmouth and Brighton, emerging undetected from the channel separation from France. Citizens and soldiers alike were dying of it, and desperate measures to isolate its spread were taken, including the burning of bodies and the renewed killing of rats in the affected areas. A few supposed witches were subsequently executed after confessions were extracted from them. The malady would disappear for a few weeks, and then reappear like an apocalyptic wave following the coastline. More deaths, more executions, until the disease reached Dover. It never went inland more than a few miles, but the worry was that once it reached Dover, it would head inland toward London. The queen was advised to move north temporarily, and messages were sent to Dover recalling her agents to travel with her. One of these agents, Alton McAnders had refused to leave; communications from one of his embedded operatives in Calais indicated that an unusual troop of mercenaries had been dispatched several weeks earlier to infiltrate the English coastline and 'soften it up' for a landing by troops loyal to Queen Mary of Scotland, garrisoned on the French coast, waiting for their moving orders. After sending communications back to Walsingham, he stayed behind with the garrison and waited.

The physician went on to write that several weeks later, the plague had abruptly halted at Dover, and that any sign of a French-backed incursion had also been effectively eliminated, but at a terrible cost. The entire garrison had been wiped out. Several unidentified bodies, presumed to be mercenaries, were also found among the dead; or rather, their charred remains were found with only clothing remnants identifying them. Alton McAnders was found barely alive and bleeding from multiple wounds and strange animal bites. He died during transport back to London, and his body was subsequently returned to his family home in Scotland with all the honors due one of Her Majesty's loyal valiant servants.

The sound of running water interrupted Ashlon's thoughts. Hot water was running into the tub, and several jets came on to mix it into the cooler pool until the flow and jets cut off once a pre-set temperature had been reached. Pretty neat, actually. She looked up at Bowen again. He was still in shutdown mode. Once warmed, he had simply withdrawn into himself and appeared to be in a meditative state with his hands locked firmly on Ashlon's stomach.

Looks like I'm not going anywhere for a while, she thought to herself. But, it was pleasant here, and at least the big guy seemed to be out of his slump. Ashlon sighed and lay back again, resting her arms on top of Bowen's. She closed her eyes and actually nodded off. When he stirred, she awakened and tried to sit up. Bowen wouldn't let her.

"I'm getting all pruny!" she complained, trying to open his hands.

Bowen did not budge. "A few more minutes, love. I have questions to ask you." His deep voice resonated along her spine with a note of seriousness that made Ashlon stop her half-hearted efforts at escape and lie back against him again, her face turned up to his, waiting. He gently smiled as his hands caressed her belly and up across her breasts. She hummed with pleasure when he cupped them in his large hands and rubbed his palms over her nipples. But, when she tried to reach down under the water, he stopped her and restrained her hands in his, crossing them over her abdomen and holding them there.

"What is a mishugas?"

Ashlon grinned. "It means a crazy convoluted mess with a touch of chaos." Bowen nodded. "I have never heard an English word like that before."

"It's not," Ashlon said as she freed one hand and traced a path through the foamy bubbles on one of his arms. "It's Yiddish. My grandmother said I was always getting into one when I was a kid. And I was always creating one for her."

Bowen hugged her closer. "A troublemaker, I see.

Ashlon shook her head. "Only for myself. I was usually able to talk my way out of it. Anyway, I never got anyone else into trouble with the things I did."

Bowen loosened his embrace enough to turn her so that she now lay prone on top of him with his arms wrapped around her back, his hands cupping her firm buttocks. "Now, explain what you meant when you said your daughter told you 'He' said it was alright for us to be together, and who 'He' is."

Ashlon rested her chin on Bowen's chest and ran her fingers thoughtfully through the hair around his pectorals and down the firm center line of his abdomen. He caught them before they traveled any lower and placed them back on his chest, holding them there, his eyes narrowing.

"That is far too distracting," he chided her gently. "Are you going to answer my questions?"

Ashlon sighed. She'd understood what her daughter meant, knowing in her heart she wouldn't have continued her association with Bowen if Emma had said otherwise. But, would he accept what she told him? Best just to be up front and honest at this point, and hope he understood.

"'He' is the creator of heaven and earth. The One my Emma's with now," Ashlon said with such conviction it startled Bowen, who'd been expecting a more conventional explanation.

His expression became troubled. "Impossible. My kind has been rejected by the church because we exist in darkness and hunt to feed. A great evil created me, and now I am cursed by the very faith of which you speak. My absolution comes only with my destruction."

Ashlon reached up with her free hand and touched his face. "In case you haven't noticed, Bowen, my beliefs are different, and its teachings are different. Evil deeds make an evil person. It rules every action and thought. But, while you may have been created by evil, you aren't ruled by it. You see, doing evil isn't a given; it's a choice. Yes, you take blood to exist. Yes, you dwell in the night and have powers I have yet to understand. But here I am with you now, soaking in a lovely tub without any fear that I'll be harmed by you. In fact, you probably saved my life tonight. That constitutes a selfless act of mercy.

"Evil doesn't give or sustain anything, it only takes and diminishes the one who uses it to hurt others. It destroys wantonly and with little reason. You've made this house live again as a thing of beauty, and given an old man immeasurable happiness and purpose in your service. In return, his devotion and friendship have been given freely to you. Do you discount that? What about me? I fought you in the beginning because I didn't think I could ever trust or love any man ever again. When you revealed yourself in my house that night, I threw you out because I was afraid; but there I was last Saturday night here in your house, saving someone's life, and then staying the night with you because you convinced me we needed each other. And, now, here I am again with you without reservation or second thoughts, because I don't want to be alone anymore. I think you want the same thing, too. I even risked frostbite to bring you out of your black mood and tell you how much you matter to me. I don't make a fool out of myself for just anyone, you know. There's no evil in you, Bowen. It may have left its mark on you, but you don't bow to it. It's what we hold in here"—she touched over his heart—"and our conduct toward others that makes the difference." She noticed that his grip had loosened on her as he'd listened, but she was unable to devise how he was taking what she had said. If anything, she had to say he was in shock.

Ashlon slipped off of Bowen and moved to the other side of the hot tub, propping her arms on the rim, watching him with uncertainty. Maybe she'd said too much, given him too much to absorb. Slipping out of the tub, she walked around it and picked up a large fluffy towel from a warming bench. She wrapped it around her body and quietly went into the bedroom. A blazing fire was crackling in the large stone fireplace, and a fine mesh screen had been placed in front of it. Ashlon picked up her clothes from the floor and hung them on the screen to dry, then sat cross-legged on the thick carpet in front of it, drying her hair and hoping she hadn't gone overboard in there.

She'd always considered herself a woman of faith in spite of having rejected many of her grandmother's strict tenets in the search for her own expression that didn't smack of the dogma she disliked. Form without faith, is what she used to call it. She sat in front of the fire meditating on these things for a long time. She'd give Bowen his space, she decided as she lay down on the carpet and closed her eyes, drifting into a comfortable sleep in front of the fire.

Maybe an hour later, she awoke. Ashlon got to her feet, crossing the bedroom to the bathroom doorway and looking inside. No one was there. She turned, thinking he was in the bed waiting for her, but again she found no one.

"Shit", she swore through gritted teeth. She walked back to the fireplace screen and checked her clothes. Her jeans and socks were damp dry; and her sweater, camisole and panties were mostly dry. They'd get her home.

Ashlon quickly dressed. She was down the staircase in a flash and quickly checked the study, library, music and sitting rooms, then went through the kitchen and let herself out the back door. Ditched again. She angrily vowed that this was absolutely the last time he'd do this to her.

It had stopped snowing again and the new powder gleamed with a ghostly light reflected from the street lamps in the easement. She quickly crossed the back yard, passed the green house, and was out the gate. The snow had drifted against the fences back here, but Ashlon was able to wade through it to her own gate without too much trouble. She entered and went through her yard to the back door, pausing for a moment. All her snow angels were only faint depressions under the new powder. Smiling, she flopped down again and made a new snow angel, then hopped into a spot next to it and created another one. She rose brushing herself off, and blew a kiss to them, then went inside and locked the back door. The kitchen light was still on, fortunately, and she stamped her sneakers off on the mat by the door before taking them off and hanging them on a clothes rack in the pantry. Then she pulled off her socks, sweater, and jeans and stuck them in the washer to do the following day. She padded back out to the kitchen thinking of a cup of hot chocolate when she caught shadowed movement from her living room and quickly turned in its direction. There sat Bowen on her couch, barely visible in the muted light shining through her front bay window.

Ashlon was confounded at first, then figured he'd fled here to sort out a few things. She turned off the kitchen light and quietly made her way into her darkened living room. Pushing away the coffee table she knelt in front of Bowen, her hands on his knees as she looked up into his troubled expression. "Bowen?" she softly called to him.

His eyes focused on her as if he hadn't heard or seen her enter the house. And she'd made enough noise to rattle the front door when she slammed the back door after entering.

"Ashlon?" he half-whispered. He was definitely in the throes of a dilemma through which she could only watch and hopefully offer a little guidance.

She sighed heavily. "I've confused you. Sometimes I go too far because I'm very passionate about what I believe. I've had to be, with everything I've gone through over the years. Otherwise, I probably wouldn't be here now, on my knees, in my underwear, in front of someone I've been learning to love over these past few weeks as something more than a two-legged leech. But, I never meant to distress you. It's up to you now what to accept or reject. It's a matter of—a matter of faith, I suppose." She pushed herself to her feet using his knees to help her get off the floor. Bending over him, she kissed him on his forehead, gently caressed his face. "Stay as long as you want. I rather like that view from the front window. It's very peaceful no matter the weather or the season."

Ashlon suddenly felt very tired, and the clock on the mantle was about to strike midnight. She had some visits to do in the morning, and then packing for Boston and a wedding. Reluctantly, she went to the front door and made sure the locks were engaged, then wearily climbed the stairs, looking back only once as Bowen rose and moved to the window, clasping his hands behind him, his head lowered in contemplation. She hoped that any decision he made wouldn't end up hurting her too badly. However, she'd survive if it came to it. Of that she was certain, because, as she had pointed out to Bowen, it was simply a matter of faith.

Chapter 33

The following day dawned with a milky sun reflecting off the snow. Ashlon showered and dressed as usual and went downstairs to the kitchen with only a mild headache behind and around her eyes in spite of all the wine she'd had the previous evening. A hot cup of tea and some ibuprofen took care of it as she read her morning paper while munching on a toasted English muffin with butter and grape jam. When she finished, she went into the living room and slid the coffee table back into position. She also noticed several special-interest and non-fiction books from her bookshelves were stacked on it. With a measure of satisfaction, she noted that her couch cushions were still somewhat indented from a long, heavy body lying on them until fairly recently.

Well, now. This was definitely a new twist she hadn't expected, and actually made her feel a little better about last evening. If they eventually parted, it would be on a more enlightened note.

Ashlon left the books on the table and went to her shelves, browsing through several other selections and picking two more for the stack on the coffee table. She felt certain Bowen would benefit from them as well, Torah notwithstanding.

Grabbing her handbag and her home visit bag, she was out the door and driving down the road in the crisp, welcoming morning air.

Late that afternoon, she was packing a kit sack in the living room for her road trip to Boston; she would be staying at a friend's apartment over the weekend. She'd decided to leave a day early because of an almost pathological need to get away from things for a while to figure out a few things without anyone's undue influence clouding the process.

Janey and Jorge's wedding would take place Saturday afternoon at his mother's place, and Ashlon would see them off on their trip late Sunday morning. His mother owned a condominium on Beacon Hill with a breathtaking view of the harbor and knew it would be ideal. Jorge's mother really liked Janey and would stand in as the matron of honor, which Ashlon thought was a really neat thing to do for her. Janey liked her, too. Ashlon could see this marriage getting off on the right foot if your future mother-in-law made such a good impression.

Her phone rang, and Ashlon took a quick glance at the caller ID. 'Unavailable' was calling, so she didn't answer it. No message was left. She went into her laundry room and was checking a dryer load to see if her favorite jeans were dry when the phone rang again. Once more, 'unavailable' displayed on the caller ID. Ashlon stood there waiting for some kind of message, but again, nothing. Oh well, maybe whoever it was dialed the same wrong number, she considered with a shrug. As she folded her jeans and put them in her bag, the phone rang again. Ashlon experienced that peculiar uneasiness that was usually followed by something creepy happening, and every instinct told her not to answer the phone. Instead, she unplugged the cord from the back of the base. Then, she sat on the couch and dialed up Janey on her cell phone. Her friend immediately picked up.

"Hey, Janey. Ash here."

"Hey, Ash!" Janey exclaimed, and then, off to one side, told Jorge who was on the line. "Anything wrong? You sound kind of creeped out."

"I don't think it's anything, Janey, but I just received several calls in a row from 'unavailable'. With Grady on the loose, it didn't feel safe picking up the phone. Just wanted to see if you had called. I pulled the cord off the base."

"Good move. I'd probably let Anderson know, too," her friend advised.

Ashlon moved to her front window and looked outside at the park and along the street. "He's got that pretty well covered with a phone tap. And he's had a surveillance crew in the neighborhood since Grady took off. I gave his tail a roundabout tour of our l'il old town when I visited my patients today."

Janey laughed heartily. "So other than that, whatcha been up to since we last saw you?"

Ashlon briefly described just the usual things, leaving out the hot tub incident and Bowen's crisis of faith. "Anyway, you got the skinny up to this point.

Right now, I'm packing to leave for Boston. Do you remember Dax from the nursing pool at Children's? He owes me one so I'm staying at his place."

Janey groaned out loud into her receiver. "You're going to stay with HIM, Ash!? Goth and nasty, who makes your lord of the underworld look like a ray of sunshine?"

Ashlon grinned as she shook her head. "First of all, he's not my lord of the underworld. And yes, I'm staying at Dax's place. He's overnighting with his current boyfriend for a long weekend and he owes me. I may go clubbing while I'm there. His leather and vinyl wardrobe may come in handy. I'll do some shopping tomorrow for the wedding."

Ashlon could hear Janey sighing. "Yes, mother?" Ashlon quipped.

"Shut up and listen, smart ass. You'll be having dinner with us Friday night at Jorge's mom's place. She really wants to meet you. Oh, word of warning: she's kind of a yenta, so don't be surprised if she tries to fix you up with someone while you're there."

It was Ashlon's turn to groan into her phone. "And, of course, you've been encouraging her, haven't you, you bum?"

"What are friends for? See you Friday." Janey hung up as Ashlon just stared at her phone, shaking her head with amused dismay.

She finished packing and loaded her bag into the back seat of her Jeep, hanging an outfit for the wedding on a hook. She went back into the house and plugged the phone back in long enough to use it. She called Bowen's number, which redirected to his answering service, and left a message she would be out of town until Sunday evening, and he could come to the house if he needed anything while she was gone. Mrs. Kincaid had her spare house key. Don't try to call her in Boston because she wasn't taking any calls while she was out of town with her friends. Another call went to Detective Anderson with a similar message.

With that done, she detached the phone line from the base again and grabbed her keys and jacket. Making one last sweep and ensuring doors and windows were secured, she fairly ran out the front door, slamming it shut behind her to engage the lock, tested it to make sure it did, and slid into the seat of her Jeep, gunning her engine. Time to get the hell out of Dodge for a while.

She popped her favorite road trip CD into her player. Ashlon spun out of her parking space and off through town, headed for the expressway, blasting ZZ Top at max volume.

Ashlon was definitely in better spirits when she reached Dax's apartment building and picked up the door key from the security desk inside. After she'd gotten settled in, she called Janey to let her know she was going to supper and would be back in a while—leave a message on her cell if she needed to get in touch with her. She went to Faneuil Hall and had a light fruit and chicken salad, then got her hair trimmed up a bit at a place with a stylist who actually knew how to give a decent razor cut. She wandered for a while window shopping and just relaxing far away from any more stress of dealing with extremely depressing undead mood swings and homicidal maniacs. Maybe she'd stay in for the evening and catch up on her charting from today's patient calls and turn in early for a change.

She did just that when she returned to the apartment. After a quick shower and changing into a loose-fitting t-shirt and sleep pants, she settled in on the plushy light gray carpeted floor, her back propped against Dax's wide black leather sofa. Ashlon spread out her work on the low glass top coffee table. She had the TV turned on low while she tapped away on her laptop, her notepad propped on several large books next to it. One hot chocolate and a TastyKake Butter Scotch Krimpet later, she finished her charting and closed up her notebook. Amazingly, it was close to midnight, and Ashlon stood to stretch and yawn. She took her empty cup out to the kitchen and rinsed it in the sink.

With the TV still turned on low, she stretched out on the couch with the latest Tony Hillerman mystery. Or rather, she soon was drowsing with the book still open on her chest. The stress of the day slipped off her into restful oblivion as she nestled into the soft leather with a large couch pillow under her head.

She'd been asleep for maybe an hour when she was abruptly jarred awake. Dax and his current boyfriend, Jareth, burst into the apartment with a rush of cold air entering behind them as they quickly slammed and locked the door behind them. Both men were clad in vinyl and mesh, which did a lot of positive things to accentuate their splendid contours, Dax having just a little better definition. They looked like male models for any fashionable S and M magazine. And right now, they were both absolutely terrified.

Ashlon sat up and was immediately spotted by Dax. He instantly dove onto the couch and grabbed her arm, yanking her away down the hall to the back of the apartment with Jareth close behind them. She was scrambled to the farthest bedroom, and Dax practically threw her through the doorway, Jareth slamming the door and locking it. The two men huddled together on the bed as Dax put a shaking finger to his lips when Ashlon opened her mouth to say something. She made a large gesture with her arms and soundlessly moved her lips, asking, 'What?'

She immediately found out. Something like to an explosion shook the walls. Both men shrieked in wide-eyed terror, immediately scrambled to the bathroom, slamming and locking the door behind them. Ashlon scratched her head with absolute puzzlement until she suddenly sensed it—a menacing, unnatural presence, incredibly strong, and in hunting mode. It had been to this building before, had entered without invitation, and it knew what it was looking for, tracking the fear to this apartment. She was curiously calm as she culled all this from the intruder, and probably should have been more concerned, she calmly supposed. However, after that, all conscious awareness abruptly shifted, becoming purely instinctual, territorial, and lethally dangerous.

Something moved over her brain like a violent purple haze, and her face twisted with indignant outrage. She softly snarled as she left the bedroom, her hands curled in clawed menace as she slowly moved up the hall toward the front room. Her head was lowered, alert and watchful, listening closely as she searched through the semi-darkness with shadowed, glowing, malice-filled green eyes. Her quarry hadn't moved from the front doorway. He was searching, too.

She reached the front, watching from the shadows. There he was, standing in front of the open doorway surrounded by a preternatural mist, tall, blond, beautiful, and terrifying, absolutely ravenous for the two pretty boys he'd gotten friendly with and tried to pick up at the Dungeon. She could smell his blood lust become enraged frustration when she appeared like a pale vengeful wraith from the darkened hallway, her loathing for this thing invading her haven, dripping off her like poison. He was young, this one, arrogant in his presumed superiority, and he'd made the error of tracking his prey to their home lair. Her present lair.

They faced off in the living room, Ashlon blocking the hallway. Her smile was both breathtaking and absolutely lethal as she hissed menacingly at the stranger. "How dare you!" she spat in a low, deadly whisper, the ring of ages past human reckoning echoing in her challenge.

The young one's face went blank with confusion and the first thrill of the danger this woman presented. She had not made the passage, but here she was as deadly as any ancient. He could sense as much, reluctantly acknowledging he was in deep, deep trouble when he spotted the barely visible marks still prominent under the bruising on Ashlon's neck. Even worse, he could smell the distinct scent of an ancient exuding from every pore of the woman's body. He knew with growing uneasy certainty that what he did in the next few minutes would mean either his continuance or his ultimate destruction, because she was consort to one of the oldest of them, and possessed all the strength and power he'd passed to her through their intimacies and his kiss so obvious for him to see. Immediately dropping to one knee, he lowered his face and bowed before her as she glided up to him, standing almost on top of him.

"Lady, I humbly beg your forgiveness," he pleaded for his very existence. "My blood lust clouded my reason. I could not know those two were under your protection." He chanced looking up and was surprised with a savage slap across his face that knocked him backward, sprawling in front of the open hall doorway.

Ashlon instantly stood over him, her eyes glowing malevolently as she picked him up by the front of his shirt. "You are an obscenity," she spat at him. "You hunt for sport, not for need. You kill for pleasure, instead of taking only what you will use. You hunt in the open, instead of with stealth and concealment. If I hear of one human fatality with your markings, or you are seen feeding in the open, I will hunt you down myself." She threw him on the floor and turned her back to him, moving over to the couch and picking her book off the floor. Turning, she glared at him and pointed at the open doorway.

The stranger hastily scrambled to his feet and, in half a breath's span had vanished.

Dax and Jareth hesitantly, fearfully emerged approximately 15 minutes later and cautiously inched their way to the front of the apartment. The only sounds they heard were the soft blare of the TV and Ashlon's soft snoring as she slept stretched out on the couch, her book open on her chest. The door was closed and locked again. Both men looked at each other incredulously and then down at Ashlon, not quite sure what had happened, only that somehow, she'd saved them from what they were sure was certain terrible death, and firmly implanted in both of them an added resolve to stay far away from the Dungeon!

Chapter 34

Ashlon woke late Thursday morning and stretched out lazily. Nothing to do—she felt a little guilty about taking the time off. However, she was also grateful for it since it gave her a chance to just settle back and think about what she would do if Bowen decided he couldn't deal with his emotional vapor lock. She reluctantly concluded that staying in the Corners would be impossible given their intense, albeit short relationship. It would kill her to know he was so close, yet so very far away. Maybe it would be healthier to look for a new environment with the possibility of meeting someone not of the supernatural persuasion. She wondered if Rabbi Summerson was in today, and if he could see her briefly for a counseling session.

No, that wasn't it. What she needed was to just sit in the sanctuary at the temple and do some quiet meditating about her next course of action and hope she'd receive some kind of guidance. Just sit there for a little while in the dark and quiet.

Ashlon skipped breakfast and drove to Temple Israel on Longwood. She managed to slip unseen through the administration area, and then discreetly entered through the side entrance to the main sanctuary. It was warm and dark inside except for the dimly lit bimha and the eternal light, the Ner Tamid, hanging over the cabinet holding the Torah scrolls.

She sat on the end off the center aisle, about halfway up through the main sanctuary's large seating area. Looking around, she remembered the absolute peace she always experienced here on Yom Kippur, wanting very much to recapture that feeling in light of everything that had happened in such a relatively short time. She rested her forehead on her hands folded on the pew in front of her. But, how could she be at peace when the one she cared about most was suffering such torment? How could he have existed so long with the weight of it all pressing on him as it had? And how was she supposed to show him the light, like her, Emma had said? What if he refused the possibility, rejecting it and her?

So many questions; too few answers.

She softly whispered her appeal with an edge of sadness to it. "I don't think I can do this anymore. It's just too hard alone, and I need your counsel. Please help me to find a way around all this. That's all I ask. Show me the way for both our sakes, wherever it takes us." The silence closed in around her as she rocked back and forth in earnest, voiceless prayer.

Presently, a hand touched her shoulder, interrupting her reverie. Must be the Rabbi. She slowly looked up, her troubled thoughts still foremost in her mind. No, not the rabbi, she realized. It was an older man she recognized as the caretaker of the temple. His lined features warmed with a gentle smile as he gazed down at Ashlon. "Why do you task yourself, child?" he said.

Ashlon stared at him, uncertain whether she should answer. But, he looked so caring, and his hand on her shoulder was warm and strangely comforting. Without further hesitation, she opened her heart to him. "I want so much for someone I care about to understand that he isn't alone. That he's never been alone." Her plaintive voice was a whisper through the stillness. "But I think I may have driven him away, and I have no idea how to approach him again without chasing him off permanently."

The old man shook his head. "You can't blame yourself. You're the first person in his present existence who's ever dealt honestly with him, and sees him as far better than he sees himself. You've shown him a new understanding and pointed his way toward learning more about it, and you as well. The rest is up to him now. He'll be helped along the way from those you've touched with your caring and your love. Just be there when he turns to you. Whether he decides to seek out these truths himself or desires a guide in his quest, he will, in the end, turn to you."

The old man gave her shoulder a firm squeeze and a reassuring smile. He shuffled off up the aisle, disappearing into the darkness surrounding the exit doors to the main lobby.

How had he known? Ashlon wondered as she stood and shouldered her bag, leaving the sanctuary. His words had been wise and insightful, and they'd helped a lot; she figured he must have heard her talking to herself and surmised the problem enough to offer his sage advice. But what was his name?

Ashlon went straight to the office and asked to see the administrative director. She was directed to an individual several doors down from the secretary's. The placard on his desk read simply, Jon Schoenberg. He looked up at Ashlon when she knocked on the open door and smiled at her, motioning to a chair in front of his desk. She quickly dropped her eyes and cleared her throat as she sat.

"What can I do for you, Miss Isaacs?" he said as he distractedly shuffled some papers in front of him.

"There was a man in the sanctuary. I believe he's the caretaker. I want to let the Rabbi know that he helped me work through some problems, and I'd like to know his name," Ashlon said with a hopeful smile.

Jon Schoenberg's brow line furrowed, and his expression became vaguely nervous. "We have no caretaker, Miss Isaacs," he said brusquely and nervously leafed through some papers again.

"But, I recognize him from when I was here for my daughter's funeral," Ashlon persisted. "He even placed a pink rose on my daughter's coffin after the funeral service."

"As I've said, we have no caretaker!" Jon said emphatically. "Mr. Goldman was our regular caretaker, but he died of a heart attack last month. We're still interviewing for his replacement."

Ashlon fell silent as she took this in. Mr. Goldman had passed last month? Then who was the man in the sanctuary? A frisson ran up and down her spine as she forced herself to look up at the administrator. "Do you have a picture of him?" she ventured.

Jon grimaced as he dug through one of his drawers and pulled out an old employment record and proceeded to thumb through it. Presently, he found what he was looking for: a picture taken of a

Temple employee of the Month glued to a release for the temple's monthly newsletter. Jon handed it to Ashlon, and watched as she studied it.

"You saw him, didn't you?" Jon nervously said after a long moment of silence.

Ashlon glanced up at him. "Have you?" she said cautiously.

Jon looked down at his hands in his lap. "I thought I did. But …" He shrugged.

"I know I did, Mr. Schoenberg," Ashlon said resolutely, "as sure as I'm seeing you now."

Jon shook his head wearily and sat back in his chair. "Just great!" he exclaimed, rubbing his face with exasperation. "And I know we're both not crazy. So how do I tell the Rabbi his sanctuary's haunted by the ghost of our old caretaker?"

Ashlon stifled a knowing smirk as she stood and returned the picture to him. "Sooner or later, that's how. And then, you might want to call The Atlantic Paranormal Society to look into it, but I understand they're pretty busy this time of year. Get on their waiting list. They go by 'TAPS' on their website."

She grabbed her bag and departed, heading for her Jeep. Although problems still existed, she was relieved. At least she could acknowledge that there was, at the end, some kind of resolution that wouldn't hurt so badly. Now, it was time for some therapeutic shopping, and then chill for the rest of the day.

It was Friday, and she'd slept on that comfortable couch again instead of in the guest room. Dax gently shook her awake, handing her cell phone to her after she blinked at him and muttered, "What?" It had been ringing incessantly in her bag.

Dax and Jareth had decided to stay in her proximity after that terrible night and were sharing Dax's room. One of them was always smiling at her when she'd catch him, and frankly, she was getting a little tired of it since she had absolutely no idea what was going on with either of them.

When she finally answered her phone, Janey was blathering on the other end in a near panic. The fabrics for the hangings had arrived at the same time as the flowers, and everything was in chaos. Ashlon managed to calm her down enough to be coherent and learned that Janey's future mother-in-law had forwarded some conflicting decorating ideas that were alarming Janey to no end. Her requests were being completely ignored by Jorge's mother, and she angrily whispered into the phone. If Ash didn't get there pronto, there would be one dead ex-mother-in-law doing the dead man's float in the harbor!

Ashlon promised several times she would be there in less than half an hour. Just have some breakfast on hand for her when she got there. Oh yes, blueberry scones and tea were perfect. She clicked off and put her phone on the coffee table as she stood, stretched languorously, and yawned.

"Great couch, Dax," she commented through another yawn as she shambled into the kitchen and poured a cup of coffee from the urn on the counter. She ignored the adoring, reverent stares Dax and Jareth were beaming at her as she departed the kitchen, taking her coffee with her, and picked up her cell on the way to the guest room to wash and dress. Janey called twice more.

When she came back out, she deposited her mug in the sink. Much to her extreme chagrin, Jareth was holding her jacket for her, Dax her keys and purse, and both men were brilliantly smiling. Ashlon eyed them suspiciously as she slipped into her jacket and took her things from Dax, wondering what kind of game they were playing.

"Thanks, boys," she said just a little creeped out by their courtesies. Jareth quickly opened the door for her as she gave him one last puzzled glance, briefly noting the small bandage on his upper throat as she headed down the hall to the elevator and the parking garage.

Chapter 35

Less than an hour after Janey's last panicked call, Ashlon had managed to charm Jorge's mother, Ana, and together they planned and executed the decorations using Janey's chosen colors of rich sienna and lustery cream. They offset the combined yellows, oranges, greens, and soft reds of the flower sprays and altar baskets that would flank a wooden arch where the priest would stand to conduct the couple through their vows. Ashlon had discreetly incorporated most of Janey's ideas disguised as her own (she would have done the same things anyway since they thought so much alike!)

By the end of a very productive day, the flowers were ready for a final misting and a 'done' stamp was given to the combined living and sitting areas' new appearance.

Janey was ecstatic, and Jorge was duly impressed by what had seemed to him a monumental task. All that remained was setting up of seating in the morning, and staying out of the way of the caterer when he arrived early the following afternoon to begin arranging the evening reception. Janey gave both Ashlon and Ana big hugs and kisses as they moved into the dining room for dinner that night.

"It's what I've always pictured my wedding would look like," she said, her face glowing and so happy that Ashlon felt her eyes sting just a bit.

Dinner was delicious: roast Cornish hens in rose sauce, re-stuffed sweet potatoes with sweet cinnamon butter, and stir-fried herbed pea pods. An excellent wine rounded out the meal with the promise of a torte and brandy for dessert later. They moved to the family room for coffee and talk in the meantime. "Oh, by the way, I've invited a friend to drop over and join us for dessert," Ana said off-handedly, with a glance at Ashlon. "I think you might remember him, Jorge. He's a chief resident at the General As of last week." A timer went off in the kitchen, and Ana excused herself to tend to it.

Jorge rolled his eyes with an expression of extreme discomfort. "Ash, I'm sorry," he said. "My mother has these fantasies I've been trying to break her of for years."

"So who's the Romeo she's talking about?" Janey said as she sipped her iced tea and folded her legs under her after slipping out of her shoes. She nestled against Jorge when he wrapped an arm around her shoulders.

"His name is Shawn Connelly, and he graduated a year ahead of me. He's a good doctor, but has a reputation as a player. Has a string of broken hearts several miles long behind him. I think he's looking for someone with money, actually, because he's in debt up to his styled hairline."

Ashlon grinned wryly as she sipped her coffee. "That's leaves me out, then. The only money I have is the house I own. Bubbe's lawyer thought she had some investments somewhere, but she never told him about them. He said if anything ever surfaced, he'd let me know. Well, it's been several years since she died and nothing's surfaced."

"You always have us, honey," Janey said reassuringly.

"That's right," Jorge added. Then, on a more serious note, he said, "By the way—how's it going with McAnders?"

Ashlon grunted sourly. "I don't know. Just when I think we're okay, he pushes me away. I get the distinct impression he doesn't know what he wants, but doesn't want to cut me loose."

"Gee, I'm really sorry," Jorge said with sincerity. "I hadn't realized ... especially after the Halloween Ball. You guys made up?"

"Yeah, we kissed and made nice the following night. And then, once more, he goes all crisis and withdrawn when I tell him I'm Jewish. I think I've been through enough male angst for one lifetime and know when it's time to bail, especially on an issue like this." Ashlon finished the remainder of her coffee and slumped in her chair, staring into her lap.

Ana re-entered the room as Ashlon finished speaking. Someone was with her. "Janey, Ashlon, I'd like you to meet Dr. Shawn Connelly. Jorge, you already know, Shawn."

Jorge stood and extended his hand to Ana's guest. "How are you, Shawn?" He said affably. "It's been a while."

Shawn Conner's smile was dazzling as he flashed the result of about a zillion dollars' worth of orthodontic correction. His hair was as black as Ashlon's with the same blue highlights playing in its short, styled waviness. With healthy, better than average good looks, a swimmer's build, and exuding self-assurance, he presented the appearance of a man who knew his place in the world and how to play it to his best advantage. Ashlon had to agree with Jorge's evaluation: definitely on the prowl.

"It sure has, Jorge," Shawn said. "You've taken up a rural practice, haven't you?"

Jorge managed a polite smile. "Not exactly rural, Shawn, but I like it, and my patients are good people. Shawn, this lovely lady next to me is Janey Ramirez, my fiancée."

Shawn turned his dazzling smile on Janey and took her offered hand, kissing it. "My congratulations, Miss Ramirez. I hope Jorge knows what a prize he's getting." He released her hand and started around the sofa toward Ashlon.

Oh brother! Ashlon thought with disgust. She was watching as Janey blushed up to her ear lobes and giggled with embarrassed delight. He's smooth. Gotta hand it to him. She noted his approach without any real interest until he was standing off to one side of her chair. Wearing neatly creased dark blue serge trousers with a V-neck gray long-sleeved knit pullover and a slim gold chain around his neck, he smiled down at her, extending his hand. And now his eyes grew a little wider as he studied her with marked interest.

Jorge was next to him in a heartbeat. "And this lovely lady is Ashlon Isaacs, Janey's best friend. She introduced us a year ago when I started my new practice."

Ashlon reluctantly extended her hand and managed a weak smile and a short nod in Shawn's direction. He encased her hand in his and pressed a much longer kiss on it than he had on Janey's.

"Then I'm the fortunate one tonight," he said warmly, "and may have her company if she'll allow it."

Ashlon felt like gagging, but held it in.

"Of course, she will!" Ana exclaimed happily. "Dessert is ready, everyone. Let's all go and enjoy it!"

Ashlon flashed a 'help me' glance at Jorge. He only shrugged and helped Janey to her feet. They went on ahead as Shawn offered Ashlon his arm, which she reluctantly took as she rose from her seat and made a face at Janey when she grinned back at her. Shawn tucked her arm securely in his and gallantly led her into the dining room. Once at the table, he pulled Ashlon's chair out for her, and she sat down across from Janey. Jorge helped his mother with the torte, slicing thin, rich servings and plating them to pass around the table.

Ashlon passed one to Shawn, who touched her fingers as he took his dessert plate.

"Thank you, Miss Isaacs," he said with another brilliant smile that lit up his baby blues.

Ashlon only nodded and took a brandy offered by Ana. She took two quick gulps from it and then focused her attention on her dessert. Janey was grinning like an idiot at her from across the table, and Ana was making small talk with Jorge and Shawn. Ashlon concentrated on dessert, tuning out the conversation around her.

Shawn placed his arm around the back of her chair as he was being informed by Ana that Ashlon was going to sing at the wedding tomorrow. That got her attention! She swore if she'd had a gun, she'd have shot Ana right on the spot! Instead, she made humble and nice, protested kindly to Ana, and fixed that practiced strained smile to her mouth, telling herself the evening would be over soon. Shawn was polite, expressing how nice of Ashlon to do it for her friends. He was disgustingly condescending, like a man who'd heard his share of so-so vocalists and was duly unimpressed. Good. Ashlon breathed a silent sigh of relief.

But, oh no, Janey wouldn't let his comment sit there! She insisted that since Shawn wouldn't be at the wedding (something about being on call), Ashlon should sing something for them now. Ana could play the piano in the sitting room, and they would show Shawn what she and Ashlon had done.

Ashlon so desperately wanted that gun now. She gritted her 'make nice' smile until her face ached and flashed her 'I'm gonna hurt you later!' grimace at Janey. Shawn once more took her arm as they followed Ana into the sitting room. Ana turned on the track lights to a rousing "ta da!"

It was even more beautiful surrounded by different lighting, and Janey hugged Ashlon so hard she knocked the breath out of her.

"Oh, Ash, thank you! Thank you. It's so beautiful!" Janey cried as she squeezed Ashlon tightly. Ashlon glanced over at Ana, who appeared as stunned as she did.

"I guess the misting made a difference, Ana. Maybe we could use this lighting for the ceremony once everyone is seated," she hastily suggested, unable to stifle a smug grin as she looked around at the decorations. Can I cook or can I? she happily kvelled.

Shawn turned to look directly at Ashlon. "You and Ana did all this?"

Ugh. She'd almost put him out of notice. However, she politely nodded. "It took us all day, and it looked wonderful in the sunlight. But under these track lights, it's spectacular."

Shawn smiled his most dazzling smile yet. "Beautiful and talented—both of you!" he hastily added as he turned and gave Ana a quick kiss on the cheek. "Now, how about that song?"

So much for the reprieve. Ashlon handed Janey over to Jorge and followed Ana to the piano set under a floral arch. Ashlon and Jorge had moved the piano there earlier that day. It was actually a Clavinova, an electric piano with programmable voices on it for practically every instrument in a symphony orchestra. Ana programmed a grand piano and pulled some music from a small file hidden next to the Clavinova. She showed Ashlon what she had, and Ashlon nodded at one of the numbers. Ana began to play, and Ashlon sang. It was a blessedly short number.

When she finished, she smiled down at Janey with deep satisfaction as Jorge gave his fiancée a loving hug and kiss. It had been the song they'd heard on their first date.

Shawn surprised Ashlon by taking her hands in his. He looked genuinely moved as he gazed at her. "That was amazing," he said with unfeigned pleasure. "I feel like a dunce now for what I was thinking."

Ashlon shrugged as she glanced at Jorge and Janey with a sly grin. "Like Beatrice?"

Jorge groaned. Ashlon and Janey laughed, nodding in agreement as Ana rose from her piano and drew down the keyboard cover. She paused there for a moment, shaking her head again in wonder at what she and Ashlon had accomplished. Not what she had envisioned, but Ana grudgingly admitted that working with Ashlon had been a good idea. Funny, though, how Ashlon had gently directed the fabric placements and arrangements of the flowers and materials, and Ana had gone right along with her ideas with only a few suggestions of her own. Not at all like the strong-willed woman who had taken over the decorating before Janey had summoned her friend. It was puzzling to Ana as she followed the others back to the dining room after turning off the lights behind her. Not at all like her to allow such interference in what was basically a family affair.

However, Janey and Jorge were ecstatically happy with the results, and that's what really mattered.

Still...

Ashlon headed for the door after saying goodnight to Ana, Jorge, and Janey. She'd be back the following afternoon to help Janey dress and tend to any last-minute details before the ceremony started at five. Shawn offered to walk her down to her Jeep parked in the garage of Ana's building. She accepted, even though he'd acted so smarmy during the evening; maybe she was warming up to him a little bit, she grudgingly acknowledged.

They left Ana's apartment and rode the elevator in comfortable silence down to the garage. As they walked toward the visitors' slots, Shawn took Ashlon's hand. Okay, she'd go with that. It was warm and comforting on such a cold night, surrounded by concrete and dim lights. She showed him where her Jeep was parked near the exit, and he stood close by as she dug out her keys. After she'd thrown her bag on the floor in the back, she turned to say good night.

Suddenly, Shawn grabbed her in a firm grip and slammed her against her Jeep, pressing a hard kiss to her lips as he crushed his body against hers, using his knee to force her thighs apart as he ground his hips into hers. He'd knocked the wind out of her, but she managed to grab his hair in both hands and yank his head back so hard he uttered a strangled gasp. Ashlon stared down at him for only a second and then head butted him hard enough to drop him against the car next to hers.

With an enraged snarl, she grabbed him by the coat lapels and flung him several feet beyond the back of her Jeep. He landed in a stunned heap in the middle of the drive. Advancing on him as swiftly as the wind, she picked him up with both hands and glared with loathing into the terror in his face. She grabbed his chin, forcing him to meet her eyes. When his face went slack and expressionless, she pulled him close, nearly touching his face to hers.

"You are without a doubt a vile predator, twisting trust with your filthy hands into something shameful and dirty for your own selfish pleasures. And you've had much practice at it. You won't remember what I did to you out here tonight, but you'll never again force your craven will on any innocent who trusts you. Consider yourself fortunate that you've learned a valuable lesson tonight. Do I make myself clear?" Shawn nodded slowly as if drugged. "Good!" Ashlon spat. "Now go home." She dropped him like so much rubbish and stepped over him, returning to her Jeep. She turned and watched as he painfully got to his feet and stumbled over to his Mercedes.

Ashlon climbed into her Jeep and drove off without a backward glance.

Chapter 36

Saturday dawned brilliantly sunny with slightly warmer temperatures predicted. Ashlon slept in as she did most Saturdays and refused to budge until almost 11 am. She shuffled out to the kitchen, noting with relief that Dax and Jareth were gone, and brewed a strong cup of hot tea. She was perusing the morning paper when her cell phone rang. She carried her tea into the living room and folded her legs under her on the sofa. Fishing her cell out of her bag, she scanned the number on the caller ID. It was Bowen's answering service. Ashlon considered whether she should take the call. Finally, not wanting to be called repeatedly, she flipped open her cell. "Hello?"

"Miss Isaacs?" A male voice said on the other end. A young, pimply faced voice from the sound of his crackling pipes.

"I hope so."

"Miss Ashlon Isaacs?"

"I thought we already established that, junior. What do you want?"

There was a brief pause, like pimple boy was making up his mind. Ashlon almost hung up.

"Lord McAnders has been trying to reach you since Thursday evening and would like you to call him as soon as possible. Says it's important."

"You can tell Lord McAnders ..." Go take a flying leap? "Tell Lord McAnders we'll talk when I'm back in town, as I stated in my original message Wednesday afternoon. I'm turning off my cell phone now. Do you think you can tell him that, or do I have to spell it out in Morse code?"

"Uh, okay, Ms. Isaacs."

"Good boy." Ashlon clicked off in a huff and finished her breakfast, indecently pleased with herself.

At five o'clock sharp, right on schedule, the wedding commenced and was picture-perfect. The bride was beautiful and radiant; the groom was proud and handsome. The flowers were vividly alive and aromatic, especially the yellow roses with their orange edged petals diffusing their sweet, heady fragrance over the ceremony. As planned, Ashlon sang for her friends when they kissed for the first time as husband and wife. Then, it was over.

A reception fit for royalty had been set up on tables lining three walls in the dining room, the wedding cake and two samovars set on Ana's dining table. After the first cutting by the newlyweds, Ana and Ashlon were given the first pieces of the rich buttery crème cake with white royal frosting decorated with tinted frosting flowers that looked exactly like the ones gracing the ceremony. It wasn't too sweet, and oh so delicious, a hint of almond flavor with each bite. As a surprise, Ashlon sang a song she'd been practicing for the newlyweds since Janey had first shown her Jorge's engagement ring. It was Unforgettable. Janey was in tears again, and the guests applauded heartily when Ashlon bowed and was subsequently surrounded by well-wishers.

Ana drew Ashlon from their midst, giving her an affectionate hug. "You've helped so much to make this day happen," she said with genuine warmth. "It's no wonder Jorge and Janey think so fondly of you. I hope you find as much happiness as you've brought them, my dear."

"There was never any doubt in Jorge's mind that they belonged together," Ashlon said as she watched the newlyweds dancing together to a slow number played by the quartet set up in the seating area after some of the chairs had been cleared.

"Jorge tells me you've been seeing a man on and off since October," Ana ventured.

"More off than on, I'm afraid," Ashlon said wistfully, unwilling to say anything more.

Ana wrapped her arm around Ashlon's shoulders. "Do you love him?" Ashlon looked at the floor, pondering just how to answer this question.

He'd won her heart in spite of her stubborn resistance to his persistent efforts. She'd danced in the snow to convince him of it. But, how do you change old prejudices and suspicions nurtured over hundreds of years? You don't, that's what. Now she also faced rejection for professing a faith she was convinced had brought them together. Maybe she should be running in the opposite direction, given what Bowen was and the era he had come from. Ashlon finally looked at Ana, an ironic sadness in her expression. "Yes I do, but I'll just have to get over it sooner or later. Put it on my 'to do' list."

Ashlon gave Ana's hand a friendly squeeze and then moved to the bar for another drink.

She resolutely refused to catch the bouquet later on that evening.

Late Sunday afternoon, Ashlon saw Jorge and Janey off at the airport, asking Janey to write her as soon as she could. Oh, and send lots of postcards!

And that was it. She'd packed her things earlier that morning, straightened Dax's apartment, and left a note to thank him for letting her stay there. She left her key at the security desk on her way out and drove on to Ana's apartment to say goodbye to her and to thank her for a great weekend. She then took her friends to the airport, lots of tearful hugs and goodbyes, and then she headed toward home.

Ashlon arrived back at Lloyds Corner just after nightfall, thought twice about it, and decided to stay at Janey's place for the night. She just didn't have the strength to face Bowen that evening. He would know she was home again before the engine on her Jeep had started cooling.

The security guard at Janey's building knew her and readily let her in, asking about Janey. Ashlon gave him a quick update, much to his pleasure. He was looking forward to her return after her honeymoon and giving them a gift he was saving for them.

After settling in and relaxing with a cup of tea, Ashlon called Detective Anderson's office to leave a message she was back in town, and let his guys know they could resume their spook activities. She also listened to her voice mail from her agency. Mr. Stanley had been discharged from the hospital on Saturday evening, and was now home. He was asking for Ashlon as his post-discharge nurse, and could she start on Monday or Tuesday? Ashlon was smiling when she called the Stanley residence, gratified to hear Mr. Stanley answer the phone. They scheduled his first visit for Monday afternoon, and she reminded him of the paperwork drill they'd have just like before. He sounded tired but happy to hear from her, asking her probing questions about Janey's wedding and where Ashlon had stayed over the weekend. He was demonstrating a good healthy curiosity, and his questions were intelligent and insightful. Well, that was one evaluation Ashlon could happily chalk off her intake list: cognitive functioning. She filled him in on the details with descriptions of everything, especially of the happy bride and groom. And, yes, she was to receive copies of all the pictures from their wedding and their subsequent honeymoon trip.

Ashlon was about to ring off when Mr. Stanley stunned her with what he said next. "I thought you might like to know, Miss Ashlon. Mr. Bowen asked me what I thought about your becoming his betrothed." She swore she could hear a laugh in his voice.

Ashlon could barely speak again. "He said what?" She couldn't have heard that right!

"Oh dear, I may arouse his ire because of it, but I just couldn't keep this to myself any longer. I suppose I'm the closest person he considers a friend and confidant. I do believe he intends to make his intentions clear sometime soon. I must confess that I took him to task for being so—equivocal when he visited me Friday night, my dear."

No, no, no, no! Ashlon moaned, utterly bewildered. "Mr. Stanley, I know you meant well, but—Lord McAnders and I don't seem to be meshing. I'm not even sure where I stand with him, to tell you the G-d honest truth." She really wanted to scream now. Her frustration level was nearing the breaking point, and yet—and yet, what if ...?

Is this what the old man at the temple was talking about?

Ashlon shook her head, angry at herself. Get a hold of yourself, idiot! He might be testing the waters, trying to reel you back into his little passive-aggressive game!

Mr. Stanley was clicking his tongue disapprovingly. "I sincerely believe you are mistaken, my dear," he gently chided. "When we talked, he was rather upset you hadn't called him while you were away, and wasn't very happy with your curt message to his answering service."

Too fuckin' bad! "There were some problems," Ashlon said stiffly.

"So he mentioned as well," Mr. Stanley said. "However, he readily admitted some of it was his doing, but he also expressed some frustration in dealing with such a stubbornly resolute woman. He confessed he'd been thrown off-balance by something you'd said to him the day before you left for Boston. He didn't give me any specifics, but the gist of it was something you said regarding the nature of your beliefs. I informed him that you've always been a strong woman like my dear wife. You both have strength of faith and the ability to endure even the most severe adversity because of it, and that you are cut from the same mold."

Ashlon was quiet, positively blown away by this. "Mr. Stanley, you've honored me more than I can say, especially when you put me in the same league as Eleanor."

"Ah, but has that altered your acceptance of Lord McAnders?"

Ashlon sighed again, unable to sort her own feelings now in regard to Bowen, but definitely seeing him in a new light, demanding to be examined. "We'll see, Mr. Stanley. We'll see. That's all I can promise. However, I'll see you tomorrow. Be ready to do some work for me."

"Goodnight, dear. Get some rest. And don't worry. These things have a way of working out. You'll see."

"If you say so, Mr. Stanley. Good night, sir."

Ashlon hung up the phone and sat back on the couch, hugging a cushion, her thoughts so confused she felt like a traveler searching through thick fog for a signpost. It was just as the old man at the temple had advised her. Bowen had taken a turn, and now it was all so mixed up that Ashlon was unable to make any sense of it. A betrothal? Unthinkable! What could that mean to someone like him? Maybe Bowen was just measuring the response he'd get from someone he respected.

A clock in the kitchen struck ten, and Ashlon decided to put it all aside for the night. She was tired and knew Bowen couldn't come here to disturb her. That was a comfort, at least, for one night. Tomorrow, who knew?

Bowen paced the widow's walk anxiously, watching Ashlon's house, keeping a lookout for her Jeep to drive up to the curb and park. She would jump out and grab her bag, toss it over her shoulder, and head into her house. He'd watched these routines countless evenings since first learning where she lived.

There were so many things he needed to tell her. He'd taken her invitation to heart and had gone to her home each night of her absence, reading through many of the books she possessed, including the ones she'd pulled and left with his original stack on the coffee table.

He'd also found her CD collection, to his amused bewilderment. Ashlon had a taste for alternative works as well as her ambient music: Midnight Syndicate figured prominently, as well as a number of works by Corvus Corax, Dead Can Dance, VNV Nation, and London After Midnight. He wondered about them, figuring they represented a natural inclination for those secret shadow places nurtured from her childhood activities and interests, so removed from what was considered ordinary. She'd once mentioned she'd gone ghost hunting. Had she ever found any? No doubt she also did gravestone rubbings when she was younger.

Out of curiosity, he'd inspected every square inch of her small home, including her closet and clothing drawers. He'd found several T-shirts with gravestone epitaphs imprinted on them. One was an Edgar Allan Poe quote; another, a Shakespearean quote. That one made him smile—he'd known William quite well and had financially backed several of his performances at both the Globe and Rose Theatres. He had even considered being a player himself, perhaps doing minor roles just for the experience of being in front of an audience. However, his duties prevented this—Sir William Percy, who answered only to Walsingham, stressed a high degree of anonymity during his missions. However, he'd managed to attend performances when he was in town. He was partial to many of Will's sonnets and even created several of his own for a young lady he had been courting before that disaster at Dover.

Ashlon's library had been the real treasure, though. He'd stretched out on her large couch each solitary night and poured through histories, commentaries, and philosophies, and began to understand. Ashlon's deep abiding belief in this unseen creator was the common bond her people laughed about, revered, and celebrated. Indeed, it was the source of all their practices. And, oh, the richness and variety of these practices! Apparently, interpretation of these laws by their greatest minds only encouraged more questioning and subsequent creation of an astounding variety of rituals and thoughts. But the basics, the foundations, remained the bedrock in spite of them. Or maybe, because of them.

In addition, as incredible as it was to Bowen, none of these varied practices and thoughts were wrong, only different expressions of the basic precepts. How very different from the rigid dogmas that had been drilled into him over a lifetime, and the painful consequences of questioning or disobedience.

Even with the relaxed practices of the new church, many of the original concepts remained basically unchanged, only more liberal in interpretation. However, his father and grandfather had said he was damned for turning away from the true faith. Bowen could still remember the rage he had felt, and the resulting estrangement from his family. The guilt and recriminations lessened only a little after Queen Mary had been imprisoned. His grandfather died a year after he had been knighted by the regent.

Six months later, he was notified to return home after the sudden deaths of his older brother and father from smallpox. His mother hadn't cared about all this warring over who worshipped in what way. Ashlon reminded him a little of her. His mother just wanted him home. But first, there was the defense of the Dover coast and the unseen horror that followed in its wake.

That French bastard had taken a perverse liking to the beau grand homme who had been mortally wounded on the field of battle at the White Cliffs, making him a creature of the night. He'd even had the temerity to accompany Bowen's body back to Scotland after his death, and watched him rise upon their arrival three days later as his newest initiate to the realm of the night walker. Bowen had eventually killed this perversity when it threatened his mother, but the stain of his curse eventually resulted in his fleeing his beloved home and eventually England.

The night he needed to exist invaded him like a black pall, separating him from everything he had known and loved, watching it all become dust in the course of passing time. His mother, his fiancée, his Queen—all passed into memory. Even his newly built home in the colonies had to be vacated when his existence was threatened by the very agents he had trusted with his business affairs. He'd destroyed them and fled back to his family home, once more taking the memory of sad green eyes and thwarted love with him.

Through the centuries, he had learned to accept his fate, occasionally disappearing to take on a new identity, listening for and following the calling of a love that always eluded him because of discovery, and the women who loved him taken away from him by death or some other equally despicable circumstance.

He had found love again in this exceptional woman who saw only the best in him, and to whom he had been called again. She had touched his heart as no one else could.

Why in creation's name had he turned away from her? Or, maybe he should be asking if she had had enough, turning away from him, and that's why she hadn't taken his call while she was in Boston?

No, he resolutely declared. That was unthinkable. He would make it right for them somehow, starting this night. His love for her demanded it.

He wanted to believe—had to believe because she did—that he had been purposely guided to her kindred spirit calling out to him through his loneliness and self-recriminations, leading him back to this place and closing the circle. To his Ashlon.

Where was she? He paced impatiently around the widow's walk. Come home to me, my own. His passionate appeal carried across the broad expanse of quiet night, searching.

My love, come home to me!

Chapter 37

Ashlon abruptly woke from a sound sleep and stared at the clock in the kitchen. She'd been asleep several hours when something woke her. She'd suddenly opened her eyes and knew deep in her innermost soul she had to get home now, this very moment!

Fortunately, she hadn't unpacked any of her clothes since she'd fallen asleep on Janey's couch in the ones she'd worn that day. She threw her toiletry bag into her kit sack, pulled on her jacket, and grabbed her handbag and keys. Out the door she rushed, making sure it locked behind her, and nearly fell down the stairs, hurrying to the front entrance. Breathing a sigh of intense relief that she hadn't actually killed herself, she stuck Janey's key in her jacket pocket and quickly exited the building to her Jeep. She tossed her kit sack into the back and hopped into the driver's seat. Gunning the engine, she took off in a hail of flying snow and road debris.

Less than ten minutes later, she pulled up at the curb in front of her house, wondering what in the world had made her do this in the middle of the freakin' night! Oh well, she concluded with a shrug, she'd done weirder things on impulse, and this certainly didn't rank up there as one of them. She jumped out of the vehicle and grabbed her kit from the back, tossed it onto her shoulder and headed for her front door. Maybe a cup of hot chocolate would help her figure this out, she decided as she palmed her keys and unlocked the front door, reached around the door jam, and felt around for the light switch to turn on the living room lights.

She never got the chance.

A swirl of cold air suddenly circled around her, and a soft, deep sigh filled the night. Her kit was yanked from her hand and thrown to the floor inside the doorway as she was pulled outside to the porch. An enveloping presence closed in, turning into strong, embracing arms and a pair of glowing amethyst eyes that gazed down at her with such joy and tenderness her heart skipped a beat. Warm lips found hers and kissed them with passion all too evident in its intensity. Ashlon's head was spinning as Bowen pressed his face to hers, a low, deep moan escaping from him. "I thought you would never return!"

"I'm so sorry," Ashlon said earnestly, her arms around him and holding him close, burying her face into his wide neck and deeply inhaling the scent of his skin. "I didn't know what to expect until I talked to Mr. Stanley this evening. But I heard you, Bowen. I was over at Janey's place, sound asleep, and I heard you. I had to come home."

"Home to me, beloved. I need you like the night to exist." Bowen lifted her face to his and kissed her more tenderly this time. "You are shivering, my own. Let us go inside so we may talk." He reached around her and pushed open the door. Refusing to release Ashlon, he picked her up and cradled her against him as he moved inside and closed the door with his foot, reaching behind him to flip the light switch on the wall. In that same moment, he heard Ashlon's deep, choked gasp.

"Oh my G-d!" she breathed. He looked at her questioningly as he released her, and then saw what made even his blood run cold.

The inside of the house looked like it had been hit by a raging hurricane, apparently someone's calling card.

Bookcases were overturned, and books were scattered everywhere. Furniture had been flipped over and dismembered or ripped open as if with knives or some other sharp instruments. Pictures had been shredded. The carpeting was torn up in large chunks, and her sound system had been dismembered, lying in pieces in front of the fireplace. A low wooden cabinet holding her CDs was, strangely enough, untouched except for several deep gouges on the top and sides.

All her knick-knacks had been shattered into unrecognizable pieces, and her grandmother's clock lay in pieces under the over-turned fireplace screen. Ashlon's small enamel top kitchen table and three chairs had been torn apart, and wood splinters lay scattered everywhere. Her stove and refrigerator were deeply scratched and dented, and the doors had been pulled off. Everything in her pantry had been torn off the shelves. Ashlon turned and ran up the stairs to her room. Careful not to touch the door handle, she noted that the door gapped a little, but couldn't be pushed open, as if something was jammed against it and preventing it from opening.

"Bowen," Ashlon called from the hallway, "Help me open this door."

He was beside her immediately, gently moving her aside. Putting his shoulder to the door, he pushed effortlessly and opened the door. The sound of a large piece of sliding furniture accompanied his effort. Ashlon ducked around him and entered the room. All her linens were shredded, and her mattress and box spring had been ripped apart. At least the bed frame was still intact. The chest of drawers lay on its side, and most of her clothes had been ripped into little shreds. Long claw marks ran the length of all the walls and her large round vanity table mirror had been shattered. The closet was in similar condition with almost everything ripped and torn beyond use.

"I was here only two nights ago," Bowen grimly said, his hands gripping Ashlon's shoulders. "This must have been done when I was tending to business affairs last evening."

"We'd better not touch anything," Ashlon's warned. "I'm calling the police." She turned away, staring at the floor as she grasped Bowen's hand, her head bowed as they left the room and headed downstairs. She felt like she was weighed down by an unbearably heavy load, moving slowly in utter helpless silence. Since her table and wall phones had been dismembered, she grabbed her bag and went back out to her front porch to use her cell phone. Bowen joined her, standing behind her as he scanned the area around them with narrowed-eyed intensity.

Minutes after her call, the police arrived. Detective Anderson accompanied them. Ashlon watched them, her expression as grim as death as he got out of the front squad car and shuffled up to her.

"What have we got?" he asked brusquely. He didn't bother acknowledging Bowen.

"I thought your spooks were supposed to be watching my

house," Ashlon tersely said, her eyes narrowed and angry.

"You know perfectly well they were, Ms Isaacs," the detective irritably retorted. "I don't like your implication, it was dropped while you were out of town." He moved toward Ashlon with his hand raised.

Bowen's face darkened ominously as he stepped in front of her, folding his arms over his broad chest, and glowering down at Detective Anderson.

Several uniforms got out of their squad cars to keep an eye on the long-haired giant who looked like he could dismember any of them and not break a sweat. His silence was more threatening than anything he could have said to them.

"Who's this? Your bodyguard?" Detective Anderson sneered sarcastically as he cautiously backed away from Bowen.

"Just as good, Detective," Ashlon replied, holding on to one of Bowen's arms. "You remember Lord McAnders, don't you? He owns that big house just around the corner on the next street."

Detective Anderson barely nodded at Bowen, his tone changing, becoming somewhat less threatening. "What's the nature of your complaint, Ms Isaacs?" he cautiously said, avoiding Bowen's fixed glare.

Ashlon opened her door and made a sweeping motion with her hand. "Go take a look."

Bowen didn't move as Detective Anderson and a uniform gingerly squeezed past him and proceeded into Ashlon's house.

"Mother Pus Bucket!" the detective softly swore. He turned and looked at Ashlon with new understanding. "I take it you found it like this?"

Ashlon was feeling the impact of finding her home so destructively violated and took a deep breath, fighting back the urge to run like hell. "Yes. I just got back into town, and Lord McAnders met me here. When I unlocked the door, we went inside and found it like

... like that."

Detective Anderson stepped outside and motioned for the evidence team to get started. Soon, several white shirts were in her house, dusting surfaces, combing the floors, and turning the furniture. Two of the team members went upstairs to scour the bedrooms.

"This is going to take a while, Ms. Isaacs. In the meantime, do you have a place to stay?" Anderson realized too late what a stupid question that was when Bowen reached into the doorway, picked up Ashlon's kit sack, and then moved off the porch, extending his hand to her. Anderson moved back inside the doorway as Bowen tried to lead Ashlon away. He had to gently pull her along, her gaze fixed to her house with every step he got her to take. Why was she delaying, he wondered? He desperately wanted her away from this place under his protection. He smelled what had destroyed her home and remembered what they had spoken of that night she had shown him those crime scene pictures. Someone—something—hadn't liked the fact she was out of town.

Anderson stood on the small porch mulling over what he'd seen inside, shaking his head and scratching his face in thought. Abruptly, one of the evidence team members appeared in the doorway, a grim expression darkening his face.

Ashlon knew that look. It meant only one thing—merely bad to unbelievably worse, that's what.

"Anderson, come have a look at this," the uniform said, motioning toward Ashlon's living room. The policeman glanced quickly at Ashlon, then disappeared inside. She looked at Bowen with a puzzled frown, shrugging and shaking her head. A moment later, Ashlon heard a softly uttered "Aw shit". She forcefully shook off Bowen's hand and ran back into the house.

When her sofa had been turned right side up, something had been discovered on the floor beneath it—the body of a blond-haired naked man lay curled on his side, a distinctive tattoo visible on one wrist. And, he was someone Ashlon knew too well.

She choked, her face turning absolutely white as she looked up at Anderson in utter shocked dismay, unable to speak. Bowen was beside her in an instant, pulling her into his arms, trying to turn her face away from the grisly sight. She hid her face in Bowen's shirt, gripping it as if her life depended on it. He wrapped his long coat around her, intending to whisk her away as soon as they were finished here, and flashed a warning glare at Detective Anderson.

"Do you know who he is, Ms. Isaacs?" Anderson gently inquired, nodding toward the dead man.

Ashlon looked up at the policeman, strained dark circles under her eyes. "Wyatt Jacobsen, my ex-husband," she said, her voice choking as she spoke. "We've been divorced for several years. But I haven't seen him since before the divorce. He just up and left me and my daughter one day and never came back."

One of the female investigators standing by the fireplace was shaking her head and gave Ashlon a quick, knowing, sympathetic glance before turning back to her evidence gathering. This small supportive gesture helped gird her enough to hang in there a little longer. But only just.

Detective Anderson was tired, and now he had a homicide to contend with along with everything else in this place. He flipped out his phone and dialed a number. Looking at Ashlon and making a pointed effort not to make eye contact with Bowen, he said, "I know where you'll be, Miss Isaacs. We'll contact you if we need any more information."

Ashlon was too tired and heartsick now to object. "May I get a few things from my room, please, detective?" she asked, barely able to get the words out and trying to keep from looking at Wyatt's body. Detective Anderson waved his answer as he spoke on the phone, turning his back to Ashlon. She looked up at Bowen, who was frowning disapprovingly, but said nothing. Ashlon quickly ran upstairs to her room and found her cell charger, a few intact pieces of clothing, some toiletries, and her home visit bag in which she threw the other things.

She returned downstairs, and after one last glance around the destroyed rooms and Wyatt's now covered body, walked outside where Bowen was waiting.

Chapter 38

She moved mechanically to her Jeep and threw her bags in the back seat as Bowen climbed in, placing her kit sack with the other things. She drove off to Bowen's house and pulled up to the curb, but Bowen directed her around the corner to the driveway and his large, lit garage area.

She pulled into the garage next to Bowen's Cadillac, shut down, and sat there for a moment with her head laid back on the headrest, closing her eyes to get her bearings. Bowen touched her cheek before getting out of the Jeep, motioning her to follow.

Ashlon sighed, automatically reaching into the back for her bags. Bowen was faster, removing them. He led Ashlon from the garage and through an ivy-covered archway, down a snow-covered walkway to the front door.

A weird numbness had set in, like every frayed nerve she'd developed that evening had suddenly lost all enervation, and she was moving under sheer impulse power. Her mind had simply shut down after that terrible discovery, and now her movements were merely reflexive, enough to keep her from collapsing into a huddled mess.

Bowen could feel it. She was teetering on a very thin edge after the shocks of this night, especially after the discovery of that body. Bowen had little doubt of the man's fate. He had been killed for disobeying a directive and had paid with his life. Bowen had seen it many times through the centuries, when conscience made victims of weaker group members. They were ruthlessly culled permanently from the others. For now, however, his immediate concern was Ashlon, who remained silent, her veiled eyes fixed on the floor in front of her boots.

She followed him through the entrance hallway and foyer, then up the stairs and across the gallery to his bedroom—their bedroom now. A fire was burning brightly in the hearth, providing the only light in the room.

Bowen set Ashlon's bags on the floor in front of the bed, and then cautiously watched her while she slowly, distractedly shed her jacket and threw it on a chair next to the fireplace. Her back was toward him as she bent and pulled off her shoes and socks, and then stood again, pulling at her grey sweatshirt. Bowen moved up behind her and worked his hands under both her camisole and top, lifting them off of her in one even move. Then, he reached around her and unbuttoned her jeans as he lowered his head to kiss the back of her neck.

"Don't." Ashlon's quiet rebuke was flat, emotionless. She moved away from him and reached for her kit sack, hoisting it onto the chair. She pulled out a t-shirt and a pair of sleep pants, then disappeared into his bathroom, locking the door behind her.

This was not good, Bowen darkly considered as he turned down the counterpane on the bed and drew the curtains back on both sides. He also lit the sconces on either side of the bed, providing a little more illumination. He removed his own clothes and hung them neatly on his metal valet for morning, pulling on a plush robe as he rounded the bed and stood at the bathroom door, listening closely. There was water running in the shower, and for a moment, he thought of going in there with her, but then pushed it away. When she was ready, she would come to him; he trusted this now. And, it would happen if he was patient enough. In the meantime, he crossed the room and went out to the gallery, moving down the stairs to the kitchen.

There were several important things there he'd brought in after Ashlon's misadventure in the snow. He quickly assembled her favorite cold-weather drink in a large mug and returned to the bedroom, once more listening outside the bathroom door after checking to see if Ashlon was in bed yet. To his amazement, she was chanting/singing something in a strange language.

Bowen set the steaming mug on a stand near the door and listened intently as this chant progressed to its end. He had heard these same words spoken at Ashlon's daughter's graveside many weeks ago; they were obviously meant to comfort the mourners, he reasoned. But, she was now saying them for Wyatt!

Bowen moved away from the door, confused and wondering about what he had heard. Was this another expression of who she was, praying for the well-being of someone who had hurt her so badly? Had his apparently violent death so moved her? An unseen power that listened to even one earnest voice lifted in behalf of another? It was inconceivable.

Such compassion had been lacking in him when he had mouthed all the platitudes required for an appropriate response as his father and brother were laid into the ground. He'd felt little at the time. only peripherally acknowledging his mother's softly cried grief. His survival was a vindication, he'd coldly convinced himself. Now, in retrospect, he was deeply appalled by his arrogance and utter disregard of what she must have been suffering. Not so curiously, he could hear his mother's voice in the softly uttered prayers on the other side of the bathroom door.

Had Ashlon also lifted prayers in his own behalf as his mother did, he wondered? How many times had he questioned the circumstances that had led him to her, but thanked them every night when he woke and she was still there? He had doubted her, sorely testing her with his mistrust and suspicions. Her tenacity had prevailed, however, and he was finally convinced of her constancy and discretion in his existence. If this was the result of Ashlon's deeply held convictions, then Bowen understood why she said those things to him that night before she left for Boston. He still had difficulty accepting these ideas because of old, ingrained prejudices still hounding him. But, he was beginning to understand a little better the light that guided her. Maybe in time he would come to see it, too. He also realized there was only silence in the bathroom now.

Ashlon opened the door and ran smack into him as he'd moved in a little closer to listen. Bowen caught her and folded her against him; this time, she didn't push him away, circling her arms around him and resting her head against his chest, hugging him close.

"Thank you for giving me some space," she sighed, her eyes closed as she rubbed her face against his soft robe, inhaling its scent with a contented expression. Then she detected another sweeter scent and lifted her head to look around. She spied the steaming mug on the stand and looked up questioningly at Bowen. "Chocolate?" she said with smiling disbelief.

Bowen reached around her and picked up the mug. He led her over to a chair on the other side of the bed and made her sit, then handed her the mug.

"I believe it is your beverage of choice when you are distressed," he wryly commented as he propped himself on the edge of the bed. Ashlon was scrubbed pink from the hot water in her shower, and the scent of lavender surrounded her, a scent he would always associate with her loving presence.

Ashlon stared at him, her eyes wide. "You made hot chocolate?" she said incredulously as she sniffed the rich aroma steaming from the mug.

Bowen rolled his eyes, then suddenly looked down, finally noticing the pajama pants she was wearing. His eyebrows lifted with a silent question as he gazed at Ashlon. She took a few tentative sips from her mug and breathed a deep sigh, looking up at him gratefully and noticing the direction of his gaze.

"What?" she said between sips.

Bowen shook his head as an amused expression crossed his face. "Those pants are ... unusual," he commented, sitting on the floor in front of her and folding his arms atop her legs as he watched her savor the hot chocolate in appreciative silence.

Ashlon carefully swirled the chocolate that had settled on the bottom of the mug into the remaining milk and drank it down. Bowen reached up and wiped a brown mustache off her upper lip with his thumb. After placing the mug on his bedside stand, she leaned forward with her arms over his, her expression becoming serious.

"Thank you. That really did help," she said, running her hands along his folded arms. "I'm going to have to cancel my appointment with Mr. Stanley tomorrow, and call my insurance company to come out and assess the damage when the police are finished," contemplating what had to be done. "I've got to call Wyatt's folks, too." She sat back in the chair and rubbed her face with a deep groan. "This isn't going to be pleasant. They never liked me. Even blamed me when he vanished."

"I truly wish I could be there with you through this," Bowen earnestly said. "But I will help when I am able."

Ashlon thoughtfully stroked his face with a finger, suddenly very tired as she let herself get lost in his eyes. There was something different about him, as if he'd come to some deeply satisfying resolution. "Did you glean anything from my library?" she tentatively inquired. "Or merely enjoy putting a permanentdent in my sofa cushions?"

Bowen studied Ashlon's face as he cupped it in his hands. A brief look of sadness passed over it, and then was gone just as quickly. "I understand you much better," he softly replied. "Why do you wake each morning and go about your day putting so much passion into everything you do, but still give me that same measure when we are together? Why do you give so much to your friends, expecting nothing in return? And now, why you can mourn for someone you have not seen in a very long time? I believe what Mr. Stanley told me. I could never conceive of such unquestioning trust before meeting you, beloved, and yet have benefited from it from the very beginning when you first walked into this house."

A gentle, self-effacing smile replaced the darkness in Ashlon's face. Bowen stood, pulling her into his arms and holding her close. "I will not pretend I understand it all. But maybe that will come in time as long as you stay with me and love me."

Ashlon felt her throat tighten. "Loving you was never the issue," she said. "I was waiting for you to trust me." She wrapped her arms around his neck and raised her lips to his. Bowen kissed her with everything he felt inside, gripping her close to him as if trying to meld himself to her, to fill her with the devotion he had never been able to fulfill in all the long, dark, lonely centuries of his existence.

Bowen lifted her into his arms and carried her onto the bed, his kiss never leaving her lips as he settled next to her, still holding her tightly against him. His lips traveled to her ear with soft, light kisses. "Take them off," he whispered so softly she shivered as his lips continued their soft path over her neck and throat, and his hand crept under the loose elastic of her sleep pants.

Ashlon, however, was thoroughly wiped both physically and emotionally. She wrapped a handful of his long hair around her hand and gently pulled back, bringing his surprised face close to hers. "I'm utterly exhausted, and what the heck is wrong with my pajamas?"

Bowen knew better than to argue and withdrew his hand from her warm belly. "I will give you a reprieve for tonight, my love," he said puckishly, settling into the sheets and offering his broad shoulder for a pillow. She settled into it and sighed with deep contentment as he folded her against him once more.

"And the problem with your pajamas is that you're wearing them," Bowen purred into her ear as he nuzzled it, and ran his large hand down her leg, studying the pattern of tiny white Jolly Rogers on the black fabric. Again, he considered this just another expression of Ashlon's strange sense of humor and her taste for the unique. But, tonight wasn't the time to address this or any other issue—Ashlon had fallen almost immediately into deep, exhausted sleep. He softly kissed her lips and slid his mouth to her throat as he moved her up just a little, lightly kissing until his lips felt a soft pulsing under them. He looked into her sleeping face, hesitating for only a moment. If nothing else, she would not keep him from this. His lips parted, and he bit deeply into her soft, yielding skin, needing to taste her warm sweetness filling his mouth again with an intensity he'd never felt so strongly before tonight. She sighed, relaxing even more in his embrace as he moved one leg on top of hers in affirmation of his claim over her. Gently, ever so gently, so as not to wake her, he sealed his lips on her throat and firmly pulled against it, his mouth filling again and again with her sweet warmth as he caressed her face with unimaginable bliss and contentment. Would she eventually allow him to turn her? Why not now so that she would wake with him tomorrow evening and every evening thereafter?

Reluctantly, Bowen answered his own question: because it had to be her choice. Without that freedom to choose, she would reject him as surely as night followed day. No, he would content himself having her next to him now and filling himself with her sweet life's essence so willingly given. It had been almost a week since he'd tasted of it, and he drank it in like a parched desert suddenly renewed by the seasonal rains. And making passionate love in this manner bound her to him ever closer, ever more intimately, until one night, when he would complete the circle. For now—enough to satisfy him, but not weaken her. Reluctantly, he lifted his lips and licked a few crimson drops from them, then settled in to lick and kiss her throat of what little still oozed from the bite marks and heal them. As before, his soft, deep purring filled her ears, and he watched her smile in her sleep.

"One night, beloved," he softly whispered, his lips touching hers, "I will bring you to me and show you rich twilight's descent and the sparkling jewels as they appear in the sky. Until then, I will keep you close with desire such as you've never known before. One night."

All too soon, Bowen could feel daybreak approaching. He rose from the bed, pulling the sheet and duvet over her, bending to give her one last kiss on her open lips. She stirred a little, but didn't waken. He quickly dressed. As an afterthought, he drew the curtains around the bed so that dawn's light wouldn't waken her too soon. He slipped quietly from the room after casting one last loving glance at the bed.

"Until tonight, my own," he said as he closed the door without a sound. Snuggling into the warmth of the blankets and sheets, Ashlon smiled in her sleep and mumbled, "Kay, Bowen."

Chapter 39

Ashlon settled into her temporary home. Significant evidence turned up on the ones who'd trashed her place—hair samples, a few fingerprints, and some blood spots on the carpet that didn't belong to the late Wyatt Jacobsen. The coroner's report stated Wyatt's neck had been broken neatly and efficiently, resulting in sudden death. His head had been practically yanked clean from its axis. Only someone who was unusually strong or skilled could have done such a thing.

Where Wyatt had been hiding all those years after deserting Ashlon was anyone's guess. He'd dropped off the face of the planet. Even his parents had no idea where he'd been, as Ashlon found out when she called them after the police let her know it was okay to do so. They had already talked to Mr. and Mrs. Jacobsen, so when Ashlon called them, they were actually glad to hear from her. They'd asked polite, safe questions; yes, they knew Emma had passed at the end of summer, expressing their regrets appropriately. And that had been it. The last link with her former life was severed and sealed forever.

Ashlon was able to keep her appointment with Mr. Stanley, but didn't tell him right away where she was staying until he made mention about her terrible ordeal—he'd read of the break-in and murder in the town newspaper—asking where she was staying while the mess with the police was cleared up and repairs were done on her home. Ashlon very prudently informed him that Lord McAnders was putting her up for as long as she needed, and laughed with relief when he approved of the arrangement. He even commented that she could temporarily assume his duties while he was convalescing. Ashlon emphatically assured him that she could never replace him even temporarily.

Mr. Stanley was very gratified by this, assuming his treatments and exercise regimen with new vigor and purpose from that very first visit.

Detective Anderson took his sweet time and finally gave his okay to call the insurance company late the following day. He'd questioned her closely about where she'd been and what Bowen was doing at her house the entire time she was gone. This piece of information he'd gleaned from Mrs. Kincaid, who had watched Bowen coming and going each evening that week Ashlon was gone. She absolutely adored him because he would sometimes stop to chat with her in the evenings after picking up Ashlon's spare house key. And he always made sure she was there to receive the key when he departed in the mornings. Mrs. Kincaid was an early riser, always there to receive the key again.

Smart move! Ashlon was sure Bowen had done this intentionally so that his movements would not be suspect should anyone question his presence there. He'd told Mrs. Kincaid he was doing some research while Ashlon was out of town, and had been given permission to use some of her books as long as they didn't leave the house. When Ashlon was questioned about this, she readily confirmed what Mrs. Kincaid had told Detective Anderson. And yes, she trusted the Scottish nobleman implicitly.

Detective Anderson condescended to a smarmy remark about not wasting any time getting tight with Bowen after Grady's disgrace. Ashlon immediately fired back at him with utter disdain, flatly informing him there had never been anything between her and Grady to begin with, and that Bowen's intentions had always been completely honorable. Besides, it wasn't any of Anderson's business anyway.

Anderson had grudgingly apologized, his attitude not defensive so much as it was challenging, and maybe just a little jealous when he'd glared at Ashlon as they sat across from each other in the kitchen at McAnders House during Anderson's questioning. She wasn't sure, but she thought he was acting a little protective, judging from the nature of his questions, which centered on the physical safety of the house, who was with her in the evenings besides McAnders, her comings and goings during the daylight hours, and so on.

Her opinion of him softened after that, and she apologized to him for being so testy and rude. He was only doing his job and yada yada, promising him both hers and Lord McAnder's cooperation. That settled him down a little and actually made him less adversarial toward her, thankfully.

She set an appointment with the insurance adjuster to come out and inspect her house for the data he'd need to formulate some estimates and put out feelers for a contractor. Mr. Stanley was coming along nicely with his post-hospitalization regimen, and Bowen was as happy as she'd ever seen him. She was thrilled he wasn't so damn moody anymore.

However, the difference in his mood was due in no small part to a deeply personal reason—the house itself was very different to him because of Ashlon's continued presence.

She had settled comfortably into McAnders House, making it comfortable for her by molding it into someplace habitable for her. Fires were constantly burning in the bedroom and sitting room, and she'd brought a space heater into the dining room. She'd bought a rather nice portable stereo system with removable speakers, and put it in the sitting room in a spot next to the fireplace, mounting the tiny but powerful speakers on opposite sides of the mantle. She found the phone plug-in as well and hooked up her laptop through it so that she could transmit all her correspondence and reports to her agency. And she'd leave the computer out for Bowen to use when she was sleeping at night.

Once she was allowed back into her house, she moved all her undamaged books, CDs, and movies over to his house, setting them up in one of the empty bookshelves in the library. She left the heavy cabinet in her house with a sturdy plastic tarp thrown over it to protect it until it could be moved into Bowen's storeroom at the back of the house. Ashlon also bought in some groceries and stocked his kitchen so that she wouldn't have to eat out. She bought in a small microwave, essential new cookware, dishware, and stainless table- ware. Nothing like a little home cooking to make a house more of a home, even one as big as McAnders House.

Her first evening as its newest occupant, Bowen had entered the house and found her lying on the plush area carpet in the sitting room, her legs crossed on the couch with her laptop propped on them, the keyboard on her lower belly as she tapped away her notes on her home visits that day. Low volume music filled the room, and a fire roared in the fireplace. A personal-sized bag of popcorn was open on the floor next to her. She was pink from a hot soak in that incredible bathtub of his, and she was wearing an oversized blue t-shirt, a fuzzy pair of riotously colored socks, and sleep pants sporting multi-colored cartoon puppies romping all over them on a white background with the word 'woof' all over them. Ashlon hadn't heard anyone come in and was humming along with the music as she tapped away, occasionally dipping into the popcorn bag for several fluffy white kernels and dropping them into her mouth. Bowen silently watched as he leaned against the archway, taking in this scene with quiet pleasure. He was gratified she'd settled in so comfortably. Those pajamas were somewhat better than the ones she had worn the previous evening. However, he had other plans for her that did not include clothing.

He'd slipped away to their bedroom and quickly showered, pulling on his robe when he was done. He turned down the bed, and then plainly heard the click of her laptop as she closed it. Smiling to himself, he listened to Ashlon softly humming and the rhythmic padding of her slipper socks on the tiled floor as she crossed the foyer. She'd gone into the kitchen. He heard the water running and the clink of a glass as she got herself a drink of water. Then she was skipping, doing a hopscotch on the tiles, back to the sitting room. The music eventually finished, and he heard her move the screen in front of the fireplace, cross the foyer to the front hall, and click the switch on for the outside lights. Bowen was genuinely surprised by how much he anticipated each and every noise and motion she made downstairs.

The house had felt so different when he'd entered it that evening—warmer, inviting, as if it welcoming back someone who had been away for a long time. How had she accomplished this in a single day, he wondered? How moved he had been! So much so, that after he had built up the fire in the bedroom hearth he could no longer wait, vanished down the steps, and, in the blink of an eye had her in his arms and in their bed, loving her with all the strength he possessed, folding around her and filling her up again and again, her passionate cries urging him on, and feeling her heart quicken with each ecstatic moment. He could not get enough of kissing her and touching her, making her tremble with such exquisite pleasure he wanted more of her, until she fell asleep in utter satisfied exhaustion.

Ashlon slept later than usual the next day. What in the world had gotten into Bowen? She just couldn't understand. His love had been overwhelming and absolutely breathtaking. Not that she was complaining, however!

Once she was up, she stayed clear of the professional cleaning people who came in that day to do the house. It was while they were cleaning the downstairs windows that an idea occurred to her how to make the house more livable for Bowen, and get him out of that cold distant crypt. Occupying the house and not being seen leaving it during the early morning hours would also lessen his chances of having his whereabouts questioned by the police now that Ashlon was staying there.

The idea came to her as she studied the large uncurtained windows of the music room, the study, the dining room, and the bedrooms. Ashlon recalled a television show from some years ago about a police detective, also an ancient vampire, who worked the night shift in a major metropolitan area. He owned the upper level of a warehouse converted into his home. One wall of the large living area had several long high windows on which he had installed total sun-blocking shades, which he lowered with a remote control. A light sensor would detect when the sun was setting and would automatically raise the shades. Ingenious idea, actually.

After an online search, Ashlon found a company that could install exactly the same thing, no questions asked. She had the distinct impression they had installed a number of these for exceptionally light-sensitive people before. Maybe even like Bowen. She took measurements of the windows upstairs and down that day, and contacted the company via e-mail about an attractive house they might like to use as a model to display their product as it was installed, since she hadn't seen anything like this on any other site. And they could show how the aesthetics of the house would be undisturbed and perhaps even enhanced by the addition of these shades.

They bought it! A representative was sent out and an estimate obtained. Ashlon promised to be back in contact within 48 hours since she was acting for the present owner and needed his okay.

The insurance adjustor visited Ashlon's home late Tuesday afternoon and produced his estimates minus her deductible, and promised to have Ashlon back in her home before close of business the following Tuesday. A contractor would start Thursday, clearing the wreckage and begin needed repairs. He gave Ashlon the names of flooring people, furniture stores, and appliance dealers his company worked with as well.

Ashlon said nothing to Bowen about her house or moving out the following Tuesday. He hadn't mentioned anything about her staying any longer than was necessary. Monday evening, she would remind him, but for now, she remained silent about any of it, and he never asked about it. Ashlon forced herself to concentrate on what was here and now.

Bowen readily approved the idea of the shading for the windows and gave Ashlon the go-ahead and a credit card for installation. Work commenced in the master bedroom and then progressed to the downstairs windows. Bowen subsequently moved his primary resting place into a secret room behind his massive armoire in the master bedroom. By Friday evening, all the windows were finished. They had sensors for closing at first light of dawn as well as opening at dusk. This feature absolutely delighted Bowen. Now, he could stay until the lethargy of dawn began to creep over him, not hurrying off to the crypt before it incapacitated him.

Bowen would leave e-mail messages for Ashlon describing how he spent his time while she was sleeping, pointedly expressing his wish she could be there with him, covertly suggesting his solution with some of the most stunning poetry Ashlon had ever read. Bowen wrote in the style of Shakespeare's sonnets. They were beautiful, reading that touched her deeply, crafted to enchant and sway her from the ambivalence keeping her from allowing him to finish what his kisses had started.

How could she even consider it, she wondered again and again through that week? What about the things Emma had told her? Help him to know your light, Emma had said. That couldn't happen surrounded by eternal darkness, could it? No, she had to trust what she'd been told and continue on this path with Bowen, however long it took.

Meanwhile, by the end of the week, Ashlon's house was coming together like a well-thought-out puzzle, with all new carpeting and flooring installed upstairs and down after the painting had been done; new furnishings and appliances were brought in and installed between Friday afternoon and Saturday afternoon.

This was one of the advantages of owning a smaller house, Ashlon was pleased to discover: faster cleanup and expedient repairs. The furnishings would be delivered Monday morning, and then she could go home. Home?

She returned to McAnders House Saturday afternoon, immediately after her bed frame and headboard had been delivered from storage and set up in her bedroom, thinking about what home meant and how much weight it held for her at this point in time. Bowen still hadn't broached the subject of her staying with him. He knew she loved his house and seemed assured of her love for him, trusting her implicitly with every aspect of his existence.

Maybe she was expecting too much after living there such a short time. Perhaps his trust issues were still hanging in there somewhere like a gray cloud refusing to evaporate. Because, let's face facts—he'd had several centuries to nurture them, she reasoned. So, one week of living with her and getting laid regularly certainly wouldn't make all that go away now, would it?

Ashlon kept her silence and continued as if nothing had changed, and in a few more days, she would be out of there and back in her own surroundings, however unfamiliar they might be since the renovation.

She went into town Saturday after washing up, rather than sitting around and mulling over these matters, deciding to have a late lunch at Irma's tea-room. She still liked Irma, wanting to see her again and let her know she didn't hold Grady's behavior against her. Hell, Ashlon had known about Grady's playing around ever since she lived in Lloyds Corner, especially after she had had his mother as a client. What was puzzling to her was his sudden increased interest in her that involved a level of violence she'd never seen in him before. Could he possibly have anything to do with the murders, she wondered, but decided to keep that ugly surmise to herself only because she wasn't ready to believe such a thing. She knew Detective Anderson was pointedly leaning in that direction, even if he was unable to make any definitive connections from the evidence. But, he suspected something was in the air, possibly with the next full moon. Ashlon didn't want to know what it was and preferred to keep it that way.

Lunch hour was winding down as she closed the door behind her at the tea-room and was shown to her favorite table by the window. The waitress was new but self-assured, efficiently taking her order. Ashlon asked her to let Irma know she was there when her order was taken to the kitchen. The waitress only nodded, asked what she wanted to drink, and disappeared to the kitchen.

Ashlon sat back in her chair, watching the kitchen entrance door as it swung shut behind her server. After a few minutes, Irma hesitantly swung it open and looked through the doorway, then shuffled through it and entered the dining area. Ashlon stood as the old woman tentatively approached her table.

"How are you, Irma?" Ashlon gently said as she hugged the very surprised older woman. She could feel Irma relax and even chuckle, a mirthless hollow sound.

"I've been better, deary," Irma said wearily, her face drawn and older looking, her eyes sad and searching. "I'm glad you're here, nurse. I've missed you and your friend, and was afraid you might not want to come 'round anymore. Not that I'd blame ya any."

Ashlon shook her head, a comforting arm around Irma's shoulders. "I'd never blame you or Mineau for what Grady did. He's never taken anyone seriously."

Irma mustered up a relieved, upcurving of her lips in the semblance of a faint smile. "You don't know how good that makes me feel, sweetie, after what pert near everyone in town witnessed at the mayor's house."

"No one that mattered, Irma," Ashlon tried to sound reassuring. "Your real friends won't ever desert you."

Irma only nodded. "I hope so," she listlessly replied. "Our business dropped off only a little these past few days. We still see our regulars, fortunately."

Ashlon smiled as she pulled up a chair near hers and had Irma sit in it. She told the older woman all the latest about her house, Janey, and about Bowen and McAnders House. Irma nodded and looked please that Ashlon had fulfilled one of her requests about her finally finding someone.

"I had a feeling about you two from the beginning, you know," Irma said with something of that familiar sparkle in her eyes. "Told Grady so, too, and that if he wanted any chance with you, he better stop messing around and do something about it. But Grady never listened, even as a kid. Said you'd come around when he was ready. Can you imagine that? Warned him, I did! And look what happened!" Irma was genuinely angry now, her hands rolled into fists on her lap as her nostrils flared.

Ashlon sympathetically took the woman's hands in hers. "We can't control how a person lives his life any more than we can control the weather, Irma. We can only steer it in a direction that minimizes the damage."

"I hear you there, deary," Irma said with a small nod. Then she leaned in toward Ashlon, and Ashlon lowered her head, sensing the older woman didn't want anyone else to hear what she said next. "I kicked him out the day his buddies posted his bail. But, before he left, I overheard them talking about some kinda secret about something coming up next Tuesday night, and Grady better get something lined up or he was going to have to forfeit something big. They didn't know I was listening, and then I went back into the kitchen. Honey, it scared the bejesus out of me the way they said it!"

"You should go to the police with this, Irma," Ashlon said earnestly, the hackles rising on the back of her neck, and boy, was she getting tired of it!

"I did. That Detective Anderson made a report."

Ashlon breathed a sigh of relief. "You did good, Irma. Sometimes doing what's right is the hardest thing in the world. You may have saved someone from getting hurt, too." She rubbed Irma's arm, then looked over her shoulder and laughed. "Mineau's shooting darts in this direction."

"Piffles! Let her," Irma said and stood to hug Ashlon before returning to the kitchen. "You take care of yourself, nursey. And your big Scotsman."

"Always, Irma," Ashlon replied as her lunch and a hot tea pitcher arrived.

Chapter 40

Ashlon was sitting Indian style on the floor propped on the couch front in the sitting room that evening when Bowen quietly descended the stairs in his dressing gown and slippers. He noticed she was concentrating on her laptop, studying something on its screen. A bright fire burned in the hearth again, the screen placed in front of it since her feet were so near the warming flames. Bowen also noticed she was occasionally scribbling on a small pad lying next to her leg as she tapped away on her keyboard.

Bowen silently entered and stretched out on the sofa in back of her, looking over Ashlon's shoulder. He saw that she had accessed a directory of the state game lands and had hacked into employee records, assignments, transfers, and dismissals. He glanced down at the notes she had scribbled on her pad, reading several names she had written. A few were crossed out, but 3 or 4 names appeared consistently. One of the names was Grady Roberts. No surprise there. The real surprise was that one of the other names was Wyatt Jacobsen. Apparently, he had joined the forest service shortly after leaving Ashlon. She put down her pencil and lay her head back on the sofa cushion as she rubbed her tired, achy eyes.

Bowen touched her forehead with a cool hand and stretched it over her eyes. Ashlon sighed deeply at the relief it offered. "That feels good," she said with a deep, tired sigh. "What time is it?"

"It is nearly six o'clock, love," Bowen softly answered, kissing her forehead. "I've been at this for several hours," Ashlon wearily said as she put the laptop to one side and turned onto her knees. She climbed onto the couch and stretched out in front of Bowen. He wrapped his arms around her, nesting her against him.

"What are you laboring over?" Bowen asked, looking down again at the scribbles on the notepad.

"Only a hunch," Ashlon replied snuggling back against him. He was warm against her back, and she idly slow-traced patterns up and down his arm with one finger as she silently stared into the fire.

Bowen gently caressed her face and hair. She relaxed against his length, her eyes half-closed. The fire's flames dancing and flickering drew her into them, her thoughts mulling over everything she'd learned that afternoon. The connection was something Irma had said at the Mayor's costume ball and had stuck in the back of her mind until she'd talked with Irma again that afternoon. It was making some sense now. The records she had found indicated Grady had been transferred from the Berkshires to his new location within the last few years, a ranger post in the state's protected, densely wooded game lands. Why move from such a rich area and a higher wage than what he was earning now, she wondered? Something had drawn him back to this area within the last few years. But what? And why had Wyatt joined him? Grady had kept this fact from her all this time, the bastard. As far as she knew, Wyatt had simply disappeared from the face of the earth. That's why Ashlon had never tried to collect child support from him. But then, she had wanted nothing from him anyway, hoping he would never surface again.

She was half-sleep, drawn into an all-encompassing darkness toward a far-away glimmer of light. As she drew near to it, she emerged onto a clearing surrounded by thick forest, a small cabin set in the depths of ancient trees reaching skyward. Tall pines and bared skeletal fingers waved in the cold wind. A huge bonfire was blazing in the center of the clearing, its flames leaping and dancing toward the night sky with a full moon overhead, its brilliance blotting out the stars around it. Deep night lay beyond its glow in the depths of the forest.

Movement around the tree line caught her attention. A number of large animals prowled silently as shadows in and out of the trees, avoiding the clearing. They were agitated, and their tension was palpable as they paced and whined with lowered heads, crouching nervously in their prowling. Abruptly, all movement stopped, and they silenced, glowing yellow eyes turning on two faceless men who walked from the cabin toward the bonfire. They were both powerfully built and naked in the flickering light, circling the fire as they squared off opposite each other as combatants, non-human guttural snarls and growling issuing from deep within their chests. Their heads were lowered as the timbre of their challenges increased menacingly. At the edge of the woods, the animals watched and waited, whimpering and keening with excited expectation.

Suddenly, both men exploded into full attack mode, but not as men—they had rapidly become large wolves, one red and one black, slamming into each other in a fury of slashing claws and deadly fangs, ripping huge chunks of fur and flesh from each other.

She couldn't scream, couldn't run as the battle raged in front of her. Not men pretending to be animals! Men becoming animals! Dear heavens, that's what Bowen had meant that last night at her house when he said something far worse than a mere wolf had killed that unfortunate boy in the north woods! These were lycanthropes—werewolves!

She heard deep growling from behind her. With sinking terror, she turned. A large grey wolf crouched before her, ready to spring, its yellow eyes wide and fixed on her as it snapped and snarled its threat. Ashlon was suddenly grabbed from behind and hauled, kicking and screaming, to the cabin. She was swallowed by darkness as a large furred body surrounded her, and white fangs lunged toward her throat.

Ashlon's eyes flew open wide, rolling wildly and unseeing. Her breath came in rasping gasps as she fought, but was unable to get away from the dream still holding her in its grip.

Bowen turned her to get a better grip on her and shook her gently. When she didn't respond, he shook her harder and more urgently. "Ashlon! Ashlon! You must waken! What is wrong? Waken now!" he said forcefully as he gripped her close and rocked her, his face pressed to hers. He continued to talk quietly and rock her gently until finally, after too many uncertain moments, she began to relax and her breathing became less strident, more even in rhythm. Her eyes fluttered tightly closed, and a low moan issued from her throat as Bowen held onto her. He could feel her body relaxing against him, but her trembling per- sisted. Then, her lips began to move, trying to form words as Bowen tensely watched her efforts. He lowered his face until their lips were almost touching.

"What is it, love? What are you trying to say?" he asked, listening closely as he turned his head and put an ear close to Ashlon's lips. Ashlon took one long, deep breath, and as she exhaled, she uttered, "Challenge. Pack challenge," in a hoarse whisper. She settled back into Bowen's arms and was finally still.

Challenge? Bowen gripped Ashlon protectively close. Now, he understood what had escaped him, why that first murder last month had alarmed him. Somehow, Ashlon had seen it and brought it back to him. Bowen was certain: a challenge for pack leadership in the area, and it had spilled into their community. The victims' connection to it was still unclear, but would eventually emerge after it was all over, he was sure. However, he had no concern for any of this at the moment. Ashlon was beginning to stir.

Bowen lay back, sliding Ashlon against him, holding her to his heart, wanting her to awaken and describe what she'd seen. He didn't have long to wait.

Ashlon groaned and stretched against him, and Bowen loosened his hold on her, resting his hand lightly on her side. She rolled suddenly and disappeared off the edge of the sofa. Bowen heard a soft thump as she landed on the thick carpet, and then, curiously, muffled laughing. He peered over the edge of the cushions as Ashlon covered her eyes with her arm, still chuckling to herself.

"That was dumb," she said, wiping her eyes on her sleeve. "I fell asleep." She was shaking her head, her humor short-lived as she remembered those terrible, vivid images. "That dream was awful."

"Do you remember any of it?" Bowen asked tentatively as he reached over the edge of the sofa to touch her face. Her skin was warm under his fingers.

Ashlon nodded, rolling to a sitting position, her expression grim as she hugged her knees. She told him everything she could remember, and then was suddenly thoughtful. "I was doing research into the state game lands and their administration, their rangers, especially the ones in Grady's circle. I wondered if the murder victims had something in common with them.

"What did you find?" Bowen said as he sat up.

"They were all connected in some way to people living and working with the state game and parks service in Grady's service region. I also looked into crime statistics for the past few months, and there were three other unsolved homicides up and down the New England wooded areas, like those three in October. They all had some kind of connection to the staff up north. I emailed everything I've found to Detective Anderson to get his take on it. He'll see the connection, too, I hope."

Ashlon was unconsciously rocking with her arms wrapped around her knees as she spoke, then abruptly stopped, her expression changing to something Bowen couldn't quite read.

"The next full moon is Tuesday night." Ashlon abruptly stood and began pacing nervously between the sofa and the fireplace. "I've got to get the last of my stuff moved back to my house after the furniture delivery Monday morning," she said with a worried expression. "I cleared my calendar just so I could move my stuff from here before Tuesday night."

Bowen fairly exploded off the couch. He grabbed Ashlon's shoulders and roughly turned her toward him, glaring hard at her. "What do you mean 'moving'?" he angrily exclaimed, his eyes blazing down at her.

Ashlon had never seen him this way before and was genuinely frightened. "Bowen, you're hurting me," she said, working to remain calm as her temper flared.

He relaxed his grip only a little, his expression melting with genuine pain and confusion as he looked incredulously into Ashlon's grim expression.

"You can not possibly be serious about returning to your house," he said, his voice thick and pleading as he pulled her closer to him so that he was gazing directly down into her livid face. "It is not safe for you to go back there."

"So? The deal was I stay here until my house was repaired and livable again. I have nowhere else to go. That was the deal, right?" Ashlon's eyes were beginning to smart and burn as she fought back angry tears. "Well, wasn't it? And I have police protection."

"Perhaps that was the agreement at first, but it ... you cannot possibly think of leaving now!"

"Why not?" Ashlon tersely said. "Make your point, Bowen."

He wrapped his arms around her and pressed her head against his chest. Ashlon could feel the tension coursing through him, but remained silent and didn't move to hold him, not just yet. He kissed her hair and ran his hands up and down her back as he spoke in earnest. "How can you question what we have shared this week, my own? This house was a mere shell, lifeless and cold, until you came here and made it a home, made us a home. Your every sound, every movement, your unique quirks, your daily routine, the way you fill a room with your presence, even those strange sleeping clothes you wear, have become so much a part of me, of this house. I am completely content with each moment you are here and we are together. My existence would become lifeless and empty again if you removed the light of your presence from this place. You must remain here with me and make this your permanent home. Please, beloved."

Only then did Ashlon dare to breathe again, relaxing against him as she wrapped her arms around his neck. "No matter how much I love you, if you hadn't asked me to stay, I'd have been out of here when the time came," she informed him. "I'm not prideful, but I'm no beggar, either."

"You have not answered me," Bowen said impatiently.

She was silent for a brief moment, surrounded by his presence like a protective cloak against the uncertainty in the darkness. She would need every ounce of his strength to get through what was closing in on them like some malignant shade. He would provide that and more as long as she kept him close.

"I will, Bowen. I'll stay here with you." She smiled as he deeply sighed with profound relief. It vibrated against the side of her head pressed to his bare chest, a heartfelt sound that sent a thrill through her. Even an eternity with him wouldn't be long enough, she decided, but it would have to do.

"Come with me," Bowen said gently, urgently, as he released her and took her hand, leading her out of the sitting room to the foyer and up the stairs to the master bedroom. He led her across the room to his wardrobe and opened one of the large doors to reveal several drawers inside. Releasing her hand, he opened a drawer near the bottom and removed a carved wooden chest with jewels inlayed on the lid, silver leaf vines curled around the jewels and down around the latch. Bowen tripped the latch, opening the box. Inside it were velvet-lined drawers holding silver and gold hair combs, cuff links with jeweled inserts, necklaces of diamonds and pearls, and rings of silver and gold. There were the black pearl buttons he'd worn the night she'd first met him, and the diamond stick pin he'd worn on his tie for the mayor's party. Bowen removed a black velvet drawstring pouch. He opened it and turned it onto his hand. A silver ring set with tiny solitaire-cut rubies set flush around the ring's circumference fell into his palm. Each ruby was flanked by a seed pearl and caught the candlelight, reflecting it like tiny crimson sparks, making them seem alive. He held it up for Ashlon to see.

"It's beautiful!" she breathed, looking from the ring to Bowen's pleased expression.

He dropped the pouch back into the chest and reached down, grasping and lifting Ashlon's left hand. He slipped the ring onto her ring finger and then kissed it. "It was my mother's," he said, looking meaningfully into her eyes. "She gave it to me before she died and made me promise to be true to my nature and allow it to find love in its own time and place. Please accept it as a testament of my love for you and your promise to stay with me."

Ashlon stared wide-eyed at the ring, and then into Bowen's face. His eyes were huge and glowing their deep, rich amethyst color, a gentle smile playing on the corners of his full mouth.

She swallowed hard, catching her breath. "I'm honored, Bowen, truly honored," Ashlon said, overwhelmed as she held her hand up and gazed in wonder at the ring now gracing her finger.

Bowen pulled her into his arms, kissing her passionately. "I think she would have loved you as much as I do," he said, picking her up, moving her to the bed as the candle suddenly lowered their brilliant flames allowing the fireplace dominates the lighting in the large room. Bowen tore away Ashlon's robe and possessed her body with an urgent intensity surpassing any other time he'd loved her, wanting her as he had never wanted anything before. He could finally acknowledge their union as complete and irrevocable, and heaven help anyone who came between them.

Much later, Ashlon was awakened from a light sleep by warm and searching lips kissing her, tasting her mouth with renewed passion, needing to be satisfied once more. Bowen's arms circled around her, lovingly holding her as his eyes caressed her in their depths and held her captive, his fangs now fully extended. He played his lips down her neck, reveling in her anticipation as he kissed a pulsating point on her throat and nuzzled it. Ashlon softly moaned, her lips brushing his cheek.

"Let me complete your passage, my love," he softly whispered. "There is nothing to fear as you sleep, and then awaken to our love with all the treasures of the night before you."

Ashlon gazed at him as she ran her fingers through his hair and lightly caressed his upturned face. She realized with considerable surprise, she wanted to say yes to him. Was it because she was absolutely certain now he would be there to guide her through the darkness? Or was it the thought of a new journey and momentous changes to herself and the way she perceived the world? Some of both, perhaps, but something held her back—there was still a crucial task ahead of her that demanded she wait until it was completed, because once that final step was taken, there would be no going back.

She wasn't afraid anymore, either, only curious now. Did you truly die when you became like Bowen, or merely transition into another state of being by whatever power created someone like him? She could already feel the changes in her through their previous intimacies and his taking her blood. Ashlon suspected she had done something during times she had blanked out while in Boston. She hadn't hurt anyone, she supposed. Dax and Jareth had been positively grateful for what had happened after that loud noise at the front of the apartment had terrified all three of them. But, how had she changed, she wondered with some concern? And why couldn't she remember what had happened?

Bowen could always tell when she was deep in thought. He moved over her, gazing down into her face. "Tell me what you're thinking," he softly whispered, caressing his face over hers.

"Hmm," she breathed, taking pleasure at the contact as she carefully replied. "It's not the right time yet, Bowen. I have to close out my home visits, sell my house. And something else I can't put my finger on yet. It's just a feeling right now, but I have to trust it. Heaven knows it's gotten me out of some nasty situations in the past. My poor grandmother! What she put up with. I gave away all my dresses once. And I spent nights investigating supposedly haunted places. You know, come to think of it, I actually met someone like you when I was a senior in high school."

Bowen's eyebrows rose and his eyes widened in surprise. "Really?"

Ashlon thoughtfully stroked the furrows of his brow. "Funny, I should remember it now. I had to take a summer class that year if I wanted to graduate. It was a night course in chemistry which I detested, but needed for the credits. The prof looked like an okay sort, but everyone said he was a little strange because his eyes never looked at you while he was instructing. He was an excellent teacher. I aced all the tests and the final. He called me to his desk on our last evening after most everyone had gone, and I was talking with a few friends outside the classroom. We were going to meet later at a pub close by, so they went on ahead. Professor Benjamin Warner—that was his name. He said he enjoyed seeing how serious I was about learning the material and wished all his students were as dedicated. What could I say? I thanked him for having a great class. And I told him I gave him all fives on his end-of-term eval.

"Then, he got the strangest look. He asked me if I knew. What could I say? I couldn't lie to him, because he deserved better. I told him, yes, but it didn't matter. It was no one's business but his own, and his secret was safe with me. I even gave him a hug before I left, gave him a chance to do whatever if he didn't trust my discretion. And that was that. You're the only one I've ever told about it. Didn't even tell my bubbe, my grandmother. I was afraid she'd sic the cops on him, or accuse me of making up stories and ground me."

Bowen was certain now that Ashlon had been destined to meet him, understand him, teach him to understand her, and eventually love him as he loved her. Had loved her from the first moment he saw her in that cemetery. Her life had been a wealth of unique experiences, leading her back to this place, whether she recognized it as such, and back to him when he found her. And this time, he vowed to get it right and protect her from whatever fate might try to separate them again. Forces were in motion even now that threatened them, so measures had to be taken as soon as possible.

Bowen resolved to put an important decision into action. After she had moved into McAnders House, and he was assured of her love for him, he started arrangements to take her back to his home in Scotland and introduce her to his tenants, his groundskeepers, and his household staff as his future Lady McAnders. Since she had accepted his ring, he intended to take her there as soon as possible. This issue of turning her was important to him, but could be delayed until they returned to Scotland if she so desired. However, he had no intention of becoming a widower. They would have to confront it eventually. For now, however, Bowen's heart's desire was satisfied as long as Ashlon was with him. As soon as he could finalize the arrangements through his lawyer, he would surprise her on Monday after she returned from her home visits and attending to her house.

He felt a gentle tugging on his ear and looked down into Ashlon's amused green eyes.

"What are you thinking?" she said, smiling as she pulled him down to kiss him with a tenderness that sent a wave of intense pleasure coursing through him. She sighed with deep contentment, closing her eyes and licking her lips at the deliciously close touch of his skin against hers. His mouth caressed hers with soft light kisses that made their way once more across her throat, this time biting deeply through the tender flesh. She softly gasped as her hands ran through his hair, pressing the back of his head ever so gently as he held tightly to her, sealing his lips to her skin and softly kissing, drawing her sweet offering to him, his body moving once more into her inviting warmth.

She was moaning softly at first, and then he heard her gasp and cry out, her body jerking and spasming in its final mind-numbing release. He gripped her hard as his own orgasmic force ripped his mouth from her throat with a soul-searing groan, rippling through him like a burning wave of fire. He collapsed on top of her, immediately sealed his lips to her throat again, rolling to one side and locking her in his embrace, drinking in her life essence, losing himself in its warmth and Ashlon's breath against his face. Her hands were twined in his hair, holding him to her. Voicing a deep-throated groan, he accepted.

Ashlon knew she was going to feel this later. But, now, she wanted him to take from her, her hands entwined in his hair as she held his head to her throat, his fervent, gentle kiss caressing again and again against her skin. Sublime undulating waves of pleasure coursed through her each time Bowen drew against her throat. Time stood still in those velvet minutes, absorbed by Bowen's all-encompassing hunger.

A familiar cushioning lassitude had settled in by the time Bowen sighed deeply with sated satisfaction, his warm tongue now licking the wounds. His deep-throated soft purring was even more hypnotic this evening. Ashlon sighed, contentedly closing her eyes and drifting off to sleep with Bowen's arms around her. He would always be close and there for her, she knew, no matter what happened.

Chapter 41

Ashlon woke a few hours later, her stomach very empty and her mouth as dry as cotton balls. A warm nose on the back of her neck told her Bowen had shut down. When she turned to him, she noted he looked a great deal pinker and healthier than he had earlier. She'd been pushing fluids and vitamins, and iron-rich foods all week, especially the fortified grains, dark leafy green vegetables, and lean meats. She had also been taking midday naps. Bowen's lusty appetites in both respects could really wear a person down if she didn't take care of her- self. Oh, she wasn't complaining. But for someone who had several hundred years of loneliness to make up for, it wasn't easy staying healthy enough to enjoy him and the vigor he expressed each time he took her to their bed! And now, his healthy color and contented, peaceful expression expressed volumes.

Ashlon kissed him lightly on the forehead and then carefully got out of bed so as not to disturb him. She pulled on his warm robe and her own slippers and left the room, quietly closing the door behind her. She felt a little lightheaded, but outside of that, just fine as she crossed the freezing gallery and descended the stairs to the sitting room. She picked up her laptop and notepad, moving to the kitchen where she turned on the oven and opened its door to chase away the chill. She then turned on the hanging lamp over the trestle table and set up her laptop and notepad, noticing a message about new mail to look at. It could wait—food first!

She broiled a thick meaty lamb chop, and warmed up some pre-cooked herbed asparagus and small red potatoes she'd bought from Doris' deli section. She also drank two glasses of cool water before sitting down to her late evening meal with a glass of milk. Funny, Ashlon reflected with a grin, how nurses were notorious for pushing clear fluids on their patients, but failed to do the same for themselves, especially on busy shifts.

Well, being with Bowen had certainly cured her of that. She'd also cut way back on her caffeine intake and had only one or two cups of coffee during the day and maybe one small latte the entire week! Ah, the days when she could have mainlined the full-strength stuff and still not have enough to keep her going. How gradually she had made these lifestyle changes since knowing Bowen. Ashlon laughed when she remembered how she'd once referred to the brooding giant as a bogeyman! And now, she couldn't see herself without him. She wished she could talk to Janey about it all and compare notes about their experiences, although she'd have to hedge certain facts about Bowen just to keep the conversation on an equal basis!

Oh well, Janey and Jorge wouldn't be back for another week, so she might as well be patient and keep her journal updated until then.

Ashlon opened her e-mail and deleted just about all of it until she came to a message line that made her squeal with unabashed delight. She opened the message from Janey, who was now in sunny Spain, settled into a beautiful villa by the Mediterranean Sea, soaking up the sun and surf and seeing the sights with Jorge. There was a computer in their villa and Janey had sent her a message as soon as she'd been able. Ashlon grinned broadly as she read her friend's lengthy message.

Janey could feel the baby moving. Jorge was as happy as she'd ever seen him and had contacted some relatives on his mother's side in Madrid, so they'd be going to see them in another day or so. Janey also discreetly inquired about Bowen and if Ashlon had any new prospects. She highly recommended married life, promising she'd help Ashlon find the right man like Ashlon had helped her. Janey closed her letter with her love and more news to come later.

Hoo boy! Ashlon was gratified that Janey was so happy. But how to tell her all the news without alarming her? She cleaned it up a bit, starting with her return from Boston up to Bowen's giving her his mother's ring. She prudently left out finding Wyatt's body, but everything else was reported, including Mr. Stanley's successful recovery and Ashlon's eventual discharge of his case that coming Monday. How wonderful to talk to her friend again! As long as there was a computer link between them, they would always be in contact. Ashlon happily pushed the 'send' button, closed up her laptop, and settled down to finish her dinner.

Janey sent another e-mail on Sunday and demanded all the details of how she was back with Bowen, and what the hell she was thinking when she said yes!

And had the police turned up any suspects in the trashing of the house? They both agreed that there was no doubt in either of their minds that Grady had something to do with it. However, Ashlon was also very sure he'd murdered Wyatt, too. She had expressed this when she'd gone down to the district office to talk with Detective Anderson the past week after he'd called her that he needed to see her on an urgent matter. He concurred and had asked her to do something for him to ensure her safety while at the McAnders House. She agreed.

Ashlon took her laptop and her dirty clothes over to her house to use the washer and dryer, spending most of the morning there amid her new surroundings, trying to summon up even a small feeling of home. It wasn't there anymore. She reluctantly acknowledged that everything that had made this house hers was gone now. Even Emma's old room had been redone and was devoid of anything remotely close to the personal warmth it had once possessed. She was moving on now, making a new home at McAnders House. Her old life was drawing to a close, and a new one had opened with her presence in the old house. She felt as if she had always lived there. Maybe she had, when she came down to it. The house had always beckoned to her in some way, knowing its owner's spirit would keep her coming back until he returned to claim both her and the house. She told all of this to Janey, knowing she would understand.

Later that day, after returning to McAnders House, Ashlon put away her nice warm clean laundry in the wardrobe she now shared with Bowen, and stripped the sheets off the bed, putting them with Bowen's things to be done later in the week by his laundry service. She'd remade the bed with a set of deep red Egyptian cotton linens she'd found in the linen closet off the hallway, and hung the robes in his wardrobe. Ashlon also called Mr. Stanley to confirm their appointment for Monday afternoon for her exit visit with him.

And, she made a special trip to Boston to see Ana, Jorge's mother. Ana had left a voice mail on Ashlon's cell phone, a request for her to come for tea that afternoon, and Ashlon had happily called her and told her she would be there. They met at a small tearoom not far from Ana's building and had a wonderful time talking and enjoying each other's company as they had during the wed- ding preparations and afterward.

Yes, she assured Ana. She was back with Bowen and showed her his ring. Ana was very impressed and commented that Ashlon looked far happier than she had a week ago, although a little paler than she remembered.

Ana had also heard from Jorge and Janey, giving Jorge directions to her relatives in Madrid. Ana just loved the idea of being a grandmother and informed Ashlon she had some things for the baby when Jorge and Janey got back from their honeymoon. They would be living in Jorge's house in Lloyds Corner, and Janey would sublet her apartment until her lease expired.

And so, their visit ended as Ana gave Ashlon a warm hug and kiss before they parted, wishing her every happiness.

The day was cold but sunny as Ashlon drove back to Lloyds Corner, stopping at the grocery store for a few things. She chatted with Doris briefly as she checked out, then went to Janey's apartment and gave her key back to the security man, thanking him for letting her in that night she'd returned from Janey's wedding, but wouldn't need the key anymore. Ashlon also gave him an update on how Janey and her new husband were doing, then said goodbye to him and turned home. Her final stop was the post office to pick up her mail from a rented post box. It had been a day of goodbyes, she realized, as she pulled into Bowen's garage and grabbed her groceries and mail from the Jeep, heading around the back to let herself into the kitchen. Taking care of loose ends or arranging to tie them up, it seemed. Tomorrow she would contact a real estate agency to start the process of selling her house, and her lawyer to give power- of-attorney to Janey and Jorge. As she unloaded her groceries, she smiled to herself and wondered what was in store for her once it was all said and done. Was this something set into motion the night she accepted Bowen's ring, making arrangements that would eventually close out her old life in preparation for the one to come with him? No, there was something else, something still unfinished, but for the life of her, she couldn't see it yet.

Still a little time before sundown, she noted as she glanced at the clock she'd bought for the kitchen and hung on the wall behind the trestle table. It was round with gothic numbers painted around its face and stacks of books painted on the lower third of the parchment-like surface. In swirling script was written, So many books, so little time! Ashlon made a big mug of hot chocolate and carried it into the sitting room, intending to pop a movie into her laptop and settle into the sofa to watch it.

As she waited for it to start playing, she sorted through her mail and discovered a large manila envelope with her grandmother's lawyer's name on it. Mar- tin Soloman had taken care of all her bub-be's legal dealings up to and after her death, but Ashlon hadn't heard from him in years. She was very curious as she carefully opened the large envelope, suddenly gasping and turning paler than she already was as several bank checks spilled out of the envelope along with legal papers Marty had sent for her to sign. She found his letter informing her he had dissolved several of the smaller accounts in her bubbe's be-half, and checks were issued to the survivor listed on the accounts, i.e., Ashlon, minus his legal fee. He also needed her to sign power-of-attor-ney documents which would allow him to secure the larger holdings he had located in two out-of- state banking and investment business-es! All told, with the interest they had accumulated minus his legal fees, Marty estimated the total net worth of all these hidden accounts at maybe half a million, give or take. Her signature would have to be notarized, but he wanted the papers back as soon as possible to begin work on the other claims.

Ashlon was absolutely stunned as she picked up the checks, softly gasping again at the amounts on them. The smallest one was $7500 from a bank close to where she had lived with her grandmother near Concord. The largest one was from a major investment firm in Cambridge for a jaw-dropping $25,000! All told, she probably held close to $75,000 in her hands, which were now shaking so badly she had to put down the checks and lean forward, taking deep breaths to keep from passing out.

Pushing to her feet from the sofa, she slowly walked from the sitting room and crossed the foyer, climbed the steps, and crossed the gallery to a shuttered door. Ashlon opened it and climbed the steps to the widow's walk, where she stood in the biting chill for a long time with her hands clenching the rail. She watched the sun finish its descent on the far horizon as hot, angry tears traced down her cheeks.

Bowen rose when the evening sky held only a soft red glow and went searching for Ashlon. Wonderful not having to delay until total darkness now that he was in his home! It gave him so much more time with her.

He heard the movie playing on her laptop, but didn't find her there in the sitting room. When he spotted the papers on the couch, he picked them up and leafed through them. Then, he noticed Ashlon's full mug of chocolate. It was cold. This was not a good sign, he considered worriedly as he dropped the papers on the end table and went in earnest search of her, finally climbing the stairs to the widow's walk. However, she wasn't there, either. Now, he was very concerned, wondering where she might have disappeared to since her friend was still out of town, but he could think of no one she might visit this time of evening other than Mr. Stanley. Bowen took out his cell phone and pushed in the quick dial number, speaking briefly to the old man. No, she wasn't there, but Mr.

Stanley requested that Bowen please let him know if there was a problem.

Bowen rang off and looked over the rooftops to her house, which was silent and dark across the easement. His unease growing, he considered talking to the plainclothes policemen who patrolled the neighborhood. And then, he heard something familiar far off in the park across the road—the faint sounds of hard labored breathing and the steady pace of a runner on the track that ran around a man-made fish pond at the center of the park. The town facilities department had cleared the snow and ice from the track after the last accumulation, and defrosted the fountain at the center of the fish pond before the pipes could freeze and rupture. If they did, the track would be useless, too hazardous to use in this weather.

What in the name of heaven was that head-strong woman doing out after dark running in this cold weather, Bowen wondered? He needed to get her inside before the police found her and reported it to Detective Anderson. He might come out to the house as a consequence and Bowen had no desire to see him again. He'd wait several more minutes before fetching her home since he had not spotted the patrol in the neighborhood yet. There were other, more pleasurable ways to work through whatever had sent her out there in such weather, and he had every intention of being the agent of her comfort. He turned his attention back to the park area and watched as the lamps suddenly flickered to life along the streets below and further on in the depths of the park.

Her pace was slowing, and he noted that she changed directions, heading back toward the house. Night fell softly around him as he waited for her to come into view. Thin wispy mists were rising over the cooling scant snows as he listened to Ashlon's approaching steps, her panting breath easing and becoming less labored; she would be back on this side of the pond and heading up a gentle slope, its crest within sight of the house. He peered impatiently through the darkness and waited.

Abruptly, out of the cloaking silence, he heard a terrified scream—her scream! Her slow pace had suddenly become rapid and pounding. Bowen also heard the soft padding of pursuers rapidly closing in on her.

Enraged, he spread his arms to the night and flung himself over the edge of the widow's walk, landing on the other side of the street. He moved faster than human eyes could follow to rapidly intercept the frantic, running footsteps headed directly toward him. He spied Ashlon scrambling up the hill from the pond. Rapidly closing the gap between them loped two huge gray animals with glowing yellow eyes and open slavering maws.

Bowen knew instantly these were not ordinary animals, and apparently, so did Ashlon. She was nearly at the crest of the hill when one of the animals lunged forward and leapt high to knock her down. Ashlon immediately stopped and dropped into a tight crouch. The animal sailed over her and landed off to one side in a flurry of flailing legs, rolling part of the way back down the snowy hill. The other animal wasn't as haphazard and timed its leap to land directly in front of her, blocking her path. It stood there snarling and snapping as Ashlon uncurled, but kept her crouch almost at the same level as the wolf's threatening fangs.

However, when she raised her head, Bowen saw why the animal hadn't immediately attacked. Ashlon's eyes were glowing green with a raging malevolence directed at her attacker as she opened claw-like fingers, her own snarling threat rumbling from deep in her throat. She remained stone still, but Bowen could feel her quivering anticipation like a tangible aura. The wolf suddenly attacked. Ashlon rolled off to one side and caught it smoothly by the neck, giving it a vicious twist. Bowen heard a sickening crunch as its neck gave away, and watched Ashlon drop it at her feet before glaring down the hill at the other wolf. It appeared to have second thoughts and ran off, slipping and sliding back down the hill with its tail tucked between its legs. Bowen easily caught up with it and dispatched it in the same manner as its companion. Let the police sort this one out.

Ashlon picked up a handful of snow and used it to clean the blood and spittle off her hands, then turned to climb the hill to the top, Bowen joining her at its crest. He marveled as he beheld this beautiful and deadly woman, calming now and more controlled as she stared into his face. Horrified realization abruptly replaced the green rage in her eyes. She immediately turned and took off across the flat, moving rapidly toward the house. Bowen caught up with her, grabbed her arm, and forcefully turned her, studying her face with probing eyes. "Do you remember what happened?" he said, urgently searching her stricken expression with concerned apprehension.

Ashlon closed her eyes with a soul-wrenching pained groan. "Yes, this time I do," she said sorrowfully. "Heaven help me."

"What are you doing out here when you know it is not safe to be alone after dark?" Bowen angrily said as he tightened his grip on her arms, roughly shaking her.

"What am I? A prisoner?" Ashlon spat at him as she tried to pry off his restraining grip.

"No, but neither are you free to roam about at night as your willful nature is wont to do. As long as Roberts is still at large, you are not safe."

"Well, the problem is pretty much handled at this point, isn't it?" Ashlon snarled at him as she clawed at his hands, trying to get free. "Dammit, leggo! I've had enough for one night!" Her green eyes were beyond angry as she desperately pried and pulled at his hands to release her.

Understanding dawned as Bowen held fast to her. She was utterly terrified by what had just happened. She had wielded a power that literally snuffed out a life, and it upset her more than she could handle. He spun her around with her back to him and wrapped his arms tightly around her, pinning her arms by her sides, letting her storm and rage and struggle until she finally wore herself out, dissolving into a misery of silent tears as she drooped against him. Only then did Bowen quickly move them through the park and back to the house.

He had never seen her so angry, but suspected the real source of it had not been the animals' attack. That had merely made it worse. Something else had sent her out in the evening to the park track to run herself to exhaustion. However, she'd also make herself sick after the gift she had given Bowen the previous evening, and that he would not allow.

Once they reached the house, Bowen guided Ashlon back inside to the sitting room and pushed her down onto the couch as he knelt in front of it, removing her soaking wet snow runners and socks. Ashlon stared morosely into the hearth fire, totally closed off and refusing to look at him.

"Put your feet up," he directed as he grabbed a knit throw from a side chair and spread it over her lower legs, tucking it around and under her feet. He then picked up the cold mug of chocolate and took it to the kitchen to reheat it. When he came back, he set the hot mug on the side table near her arm, noting she hadn't moved at all while he was in the kitchen. He moved over to the hearth and stacked more wood onto the grating, watching as the hungry flames leapt and crackled to new life. He leaned an arm on the mantle and looked into the flames. There was something he needed to say to her, but he hesitated at first, looking from Ashlon folded in on herself, back into the flames licking voraciously at the new wood he had placed in them. Times like this, he wished he could just heave a heavy sigh as he summoned up what he needed to say.

"I owe you an explanation about what you experienced out

there tonight," he said, staring into the fire. Maybe this would prompt her to reveal what the real source of her anger was as well, he reckoned.

Ashlon remained silent, her face turning away from him, pressing into the soft fabric of the sofa back.

"You have moved further along the passage to joining me. You have attained new insight and skills that are at your disposal whenever you are threatened or in danger, and now you have a new awareness of what you are becoming. But, it has taken form in a way I have never seen before. Purposeful, directed, not indiscriminate like the newly risen."

"Oh, goody," Ashlon sneered with quiet disgust. "As if I'm not enough of a freak already."

"Do not treat this lightly!" Bowen emphatically rebuked her. "You have allowed me the greatest intimacy I can possibly imagine when I hold you and love you and taste the life you share with me. In exchange, I believe you have developed the means to protect yourself against the predators out there waiting for you. It has not totally changed you yet; it is comprised of your strengths, augmenting and directing them in new ways; your senses have opened to new sights and sounds; you perceive things differently. Treat it as the gift it is meant to be."

Had he just been condescending with her? "Is that how you felt when you found you'd been changed?" Her voice rose angrily as she impatiently threw off the blanket and stood up, recovering her shoes and socks. "According to certain diaries, I don't think so. You weren't any more prepared for it than I am now. And to be perfectly honest, this isn't what I expected to happen. So don't go lecturing me about changes and acceptance and rolling with the punches or what the hell ever. Yes, I'm terrified of what I'm becoming, because I'm just me—Ashlon Isaacs. I felt things out there tonight and did things that are totally against of my nature. I'm not a violent person, Bowen, and G-d knows I've never killed anyone, even if they desperately deserved it!" She paused for a second, rubbing her face with frustration. "And the reason I was out there tonight at all was because I was angry enough to chew nails and needed to figure out a few things. I learned this evening that my dear bubbe had a fortune hidden away. She kept her secret through her lawyer until anyone who might contest her will or file a claim against her estate had all passed away. And here's little 'ole me thinking she lost track of only a few hundred dollars because she was old and had to raise me alone. Only her lawyer was aware of this little secret; so, I get a big envelope with several fat checks tucked in it and documents saying, 'Oh, by the way, there's more!' I sure as hell could have used that money when Emmy got sick and I was living out of my car when she was in the hospital those first few years. That sonuvabitch lawyer lied to me the whole time, so I'm really mad as hell at him, and I'm mad at my bubbe for lying to me even on her deathbed, and now I'm just plain pissed off with your sanctimonious revelations, so just don't say anything more."

She stormed out of the sitting room, running up the staircase two steps at a time. He listened to her retreating footsteps on the wooden gallery floor, and then the hard slam of a heavy door.

Bowen hung his head and stared into the fire, deeply troubled and at a complete loss. Of course, she had been correct when she tossed that tidbit back at him about finding he had been changed. Only after he had destroyed that offensive little obscenity was Bowen free to adjust his acceptance of his new persona, bringing it more in line with his true self. His mother thought that was just fine; she said it made him better able to appreciate and tolerate the people and the world around him. He had certainly become a better man than his father or grandfather because he had known true suffering, his mother had said. Someone she could now truly like as a person (such as he was!), as well as love as her son. Strange how he could remember this now in light of Ashlon's angry retort; he felt almost ashamed that he had forgotten such an important thing. Ashlon possessed an almost visceral understanding of such things. But what was this about her late grandmother and a hidden fortune?

Bowen moved to the sofa and sat down, picking up the thick packet of papers from the end table and leafing through them, then looked at the checks, amazed at the amounts written on them. Ashlon's net worth had definitely increased, but she wasn't happy about it at all, apparently viewing it as some kind of grotesque joke. Perhaps he could suggest she contact his financial manager and let him handle this after reviewing everything with her lawyer. It would be a start, at least; an olive branch he could offer.

That is, if she would ever listen to him again. He was uncomfortably reminded of her reaction when she learned what he really was, and wondered if she would be as reactionary as she'd been then. He girded himself for the worst, and by heaven, she brought it on.

Chapter 42

Several minutes later, he heard booted footsteps descending the stairs into the foyer, heading into the kitchen. And then, much to his heated chagrin, he heard the back door open and slam shut. Bowen quickly went out the front door after grabbing his long coat and listened for where she he was headed. He heard the sound of the side garage door being opened and instantly reached it before Ashlon could turn the key in the Jeep ignition. He yanked open the passenger side door, meeting her angry glare.

"Where are you going?" he calmly asked. "Movies!" she spat back at him. "In or out?"

Bowen spent half a second deciphering what she meant. Then, he folded his coat around him and climbed into the passenger seat, buckling in. Ashlon backed out to the street and took off down the road, heading out of town.

Bowen disliked this small vehicle and considered it beneath his betrothed to be seen in it, but wisely said nothing since Ashlon possessed such a fondness for it. Bowen decided he would tolerate it for this night, if only to keep a loving eye on Ashlon while she was immersed in her present dark mood. Besides, he had not been to a movie for quite some time, considering most of them offensive mental tripe and not worth the shillings to see them. The last one he had ventured out to see was Casablanca. He knew Ashlon's tastes because of her DVD collection, which contained several classics as well as more tasteful current films, so he was hopeful for tonight.

The nearest theatre was located next to the mall off the interstate, several miles from Lloyds Corner. Once Ashlon reached the interstate, she floored it and sped down the road. She reached into her visor CD holder and selected a disc, slipping it into the player. The vocalist was a tenor Bowen didn't recognize, but the music certainly surprised him when he remembered what he'd seen in Ashlon's collection the previous week. This was almost operatic and absolutely splendid.

"Who is this?" he casually inquired.

"Andre Bocelli," Ashlon answered shortly, her eyes fixed on the road.

Bowen relaxed in his seat as the road unrolled before them. After a while, he heard Ashlon softly humming with the music as if she was intimately familiar with it. Bowen happily suspected her anger must be receding; she sang only if she was at ease or occupied by something, another one of those pleasant things he had learned about her during their time together in his home. He wondered if she was even aware she was doing it. He smiled inwardly with this intimate insight that made him love her all the more, and which bound him ever closer to her.

The theatre rose up brilliantly out of the darkness, with the large mall behind it. Ashlon expertly swung into the large parking lot and parked near the back. Since it was Sunday evening with several new releases to choose from, it was also packed. Ashlon jumped with practiced ease from her seat and set off up the aisle without waiting for Bowen. He carefully exited and straightened his trousers and coat before easily catching up to her as she was crossing the drive to the ticket windows. She refused to let him hold her arm as she got in line, taking the lead as they approached the window, and shook him off again as she pulled out her wallet to pay for the tickets with a curt, "I've got it."

Bowen did not object, staying close as they progressed toward the window.

It was a busy evening at the theatre, but fortunately, the lines moved rapidly along. Soon, they were at the ticket window. Bowen watched silently as Ashlon bought their tickets. He hadn't heard what they were seeing, keeping his alert eyes on everyone around them. One of them was also here, he knew. Just where, however, was another matter. But, he has his suspicions as he stares hard at someone moving in the line next to them.

A tall man with the build of a professional wrestler, long dark blonde hair waving around his shoulders, neatly clipped beard, and black t-shirt, jeans, and a denim jacket with a biker logo on the back, was eyeing Ashlon intently from the line left of theirs. When Ashlon finished at the window, he reached across the short space between them and tapped her elbow. She turned and looked as he winked at her. With great satisfaction, Bowen noted her expression turn dark as a thunderstorm

"Hey, sugar, shake the stiff and I'll take you in," he suggested with a brilliant smile.

Ashlon immediately stepped around Bowen before he could react, facing the biker. "Buzz off, Bozo," she snarled with a chill that could have frozen water, "he's with me." She brushed by him without a backward glance as she palmed their tickets. She entered the theater, closely followed by a scowling Bowen, narrowly eyeing the blond man.

The stranger lifted his hands in a conciliatory manner as he backed off from them. He was the one Bowen had detected. Now, he was truly grateful he had opted to accompany Ashlon tonight and very pleased by her overt negative putdown of the man. Obviously, she had a lot of practice using this type of rebuff.

After Ashlon had procured a drink and her favorite movie snack, blue corn nachos with lots of hot melted cheese and sliced jalapenos, they proceeded down a hallway and entered a door to a dark hallway into their movie. The lights were very low, but Ashlon easily found the seats she and Janey always favored—first two from the end about halfway up the rows. She made Bowen sit on the end since his legs were far longer than hers. Ashlon settled into her seat, making sure to lower the armrest between them.

"What are we to see tonight?" Bowen turned to Ashlon, his deep voice resonant even at low volume.

"Pride and Prejudice," Ashlon said as she stuffed a jalapeno and cheese-coated blue corn chip in her mouth with blissful relish.

Bowen's lip curled. "That is truly disgusting," he observed with a sniff. Ashlon slowly looked over at him with quiet disdain. "Coming from the guy on a warm liquid protein diet."

A woman sitting on Ashlon's other side leaned in close to her and clicked her tongue sympathetically. "Athlete?" she asked.

"Yeah, sort of," Ashlon growled, slumping into her seat as the lights went down completely and the movie started. She knew the story by heart. It was also one of her favorite books. She had owned a well-worn copy in her library before it was destroyed. Ashlon reveled in the story all over again as she finished her nachos and dug a wet nap from her bag to wipe her fingers and mouth, stuffing it into her empty drink cup afterward. She was also feeling much better since eating something. Her anger had pretty much dissolved by the time the movie reached the mid-point, and she rose from her seat to go to the restroom. Bowen brushed her legs with his as she squeezed past him, and he wouldn't move, wryly gazing up at her as she reached the aisle and headed for the exit door.

When she returned, she had to maneuver around his legs again as he nonchalantly looked around her at the movie screen. She nearly fell into his lap. When she finally reached her seat, she immediately noticed he'd raised the armrest between their seats. However, she didn't lower it again once she was in her seat.

The movie had reached the part where Darcy first confesses his love for Elizabeth and she refuses him.

Bowen leaned over and asked in a low voice, his lips touching Ashlon's ear. "That makes no sense. Why did she refuse him when she had everything to gain by marrying him?"

Ashlon turned and brushed back Bowen's hair as she leaned back toward him. "Because he's arrogant and condescending, referred to her inferiority and his struggle to overlook it to propose marriage, blatantly insulted her family, and at this point in the story, he doesn't deserve a person of Elizabeth's caliber."

Bowen nodded and looked into Ashlon's face, smiling gently. She grudgingly half-grinned and sat back in her seat. Bowen's arm settled around Ashlon's shoulders, and she laid her head on his shoulder when he drew her closer to him.

Then, the letter to Elizabeth from her sister, that Lydia had run off with Wickham and Darcy's subsequent search for them in London, redeeming himself to Elizabeth by an unselfish deed that won her over. And then, the movie was over and the house lights came up again. She and the lady next to her were positively gushy about it, talking like old friends until they were able to get out to the aisle to leave. Remembering the man at the ticket windows, Bowen immediately took Ashlon's arm to keep her close to him so they wouldn't get separated in the crowd exiting the theatre. Once outside, they headed through the lot to Ashlon's Jeep.

"How are you feeling now?" he casually said as they neared the rear of the parking lot.

"Hungry. I'll pick up something on the way," Ashlon said. She was hunting for her keys like always, locating them deep in her bag. When they reached her Jeep and she had unlocked the passenger door, and she was stopped in her tracks and pinned to the side of the Jeep when Bowen caught her in his arms.

"How are you feeling, my love?" he slowly repeated, gazing earnestly into her face, holding her firmly and drawing her into the depths of his eyes, ensnaring any will to move or protest.

"I'm alright, Bowen," Ashlon reassured him as his lips touched her forehead. The coat flaps of his open duster arched around her, alive and surrounding them like great black wings.

"Good," he said, but didn't release her. "Now give me your keys. I am driving home."

"Uh uh," Ashlon protested, clutching her key D-clip resolutely. "No one drives my Jeep but me. HEY!" Bowen had grabbed her hand.

"I am not asking," Bowen easily opened her fist and extracted the keys, then opened the passenger door for Ashlon. However, she didn't move. She was staring around Bowen's restraining arm with narrowed-eyed intensity at something behind them as she warned in a lowered voice, "We're being watched."

Bowen turned, keeping his back to Ashlon. There stood the

tall blonde stranger who had tried to talk to her earlier that evening, his stance canted casually to one side with his thumbs hooked in his jeans' pockets. His expression was enigmatic as he watched them.

Bowen's lips curled in a snarl, but he held back as Ashlon stepped to his side, his arm outstretched to restrain her from going any farther.

"What do you want?" she curtly said. "I told you to buzz off."

The tall man smiled and held up his hands to show he wasn't armed. "Easy, sugar," his deep voice laughed. "Put a rein on the boyfriend, okay? We need to talk."

"Why? I don't know you."

"There's a bad moon rising, if you catch my drift, sweet thing. Ditch the dead guy, so we can talk."

Ashlon thought she understood his meaning, but could barely restrain Bowen from a full-frontal attack. Looking back at the stranger, who appeared very amused by this show, she said, "You can speak in front of him," nodding at Bowen.

The stranger shrugged and approached them, stopping just outside of Bowen's deadly reach. "I represent certain concerned individuals who want to safeguard their identities in this area. On Tuesday evening, a contest for the right to lead this group is taking place in the north woods."

"Stop veiling your words. I know what you're talking about," Ashlon said impatiently, waving her hand. "Unfortunately, I'm in this up to my armpits."

"Of course," the stranger smiled. "It's our way, and I meant no insult. The favored contender has a mate who's expecting very soon. But his challenger rounded up a group of renegades who've taken out several of our key members over the last several months, including my younger brother, who carried the older adolescents."

Ashlon nodded. The young man was found in his car on that

old logging road. "I'm truly sorry."

The stranger shrugged and carelessly waved with one hand. "He shouldn't have been out there alone. Anyway, the more recent ones were eliminated for similar reasons."

Well, there was the answer she wanted. "What's this got to do with me?" Ashlon said, wishing fervently he'd make his point a little faster—Bowen was getting itchy under her restraint.

The stranger smiled again, a brilliant gesture. "You hurt Grady, sugar. Badly. Severely dented his chances at becoming the pack leader. Damaged him physically, which affected his support among his rogues. Subsequently, you now hold an honored place within the pack. It also puts you in very real danger from Grady and his remaining supporters."

Grady? Grady was one of them? Was that the red wolf in her dream? Oh boy. Now she felt really thick for not seeing it in the first place—his unusual interest, his aggressive behavior, the rape attempt. This kept getting better and better, Ashlon thought with bewildered frustration. What next? A zombie war?!

Ashlon slowly shook her head. "No shit, Sherlock," she said disdainfully, which made the stranger chuckle. "Werewolves. Until a few weeks ago, I'd have said you were all nuts. By the way, I was attacked in the park tonight. They must have been two of Grady's supporters." The stranger's humor faded instantly. "This evening? Where?"

"City Park at Lloyds Corner. I jog the track there in the winter. Faster track than the street with better footing." Ashlon made a face at Bowen, which the stranger could not see.

"I'm hip, sugar," the stranger said with an understanding expression. "My kind appreciates similar conditions for trailing and hunting. But what of the two who attacked you?"

"They were dispatched," Bowen said, his deep voice a thin rumbling growl.

"Two less feeders to worry about, I suppose. But now the others'll know you're protected," the tall stranger said, thoughtfully eyeing Bowen. "An ancient blood, no less. You keep high company."

Ashlon nodded shortly to the stranger. "Thanks for the 411," she said as she urged Bowen through the open passenger doorway, quickly snatching her keys out of his hand. There were some perks to being an almost nightwalker, she considered.

Thoroughly disgruntled and still watching the stranger with overt suspicion, Bowen swung his legs inside and closed the Jeep door. Ashlon sighed. She was very tired now and just wanted to pick up something substantial to eat, go home, soak in a hot bath until she got good and pruny, and then go to bed. Her surprise meter was definitely pegged for one evening, and she desperately needed some downtime to mull it all over. As she walked around the back of her Jeep, the blond stranger suddenly caught her arm in one large hand, turning her to stare down at her with glowing golden eyes. His frown was gentled by a guileless smile playing on the corners of his lips.

"Mmm," he softly growled. "Too bad I didn't find you first, sweet thing. I had no idea someone like you lived in these parts."

Ashlon pulled her arm away from him and scowled, righteously irritated. "I've lived in 'these parts' for several years, and now you have the nerve to say such a thing? Up until recently, someone like you wouldn't have looked twice at me or given me the time of day. Suddenly, I'm Miss Popularity. And, the fact that I was almost killed tonight and Bowen was there to rescue my ass only makes me appreciate him more." Ashlon took a deep breath. "Thanks for the briefing, Conan. How about from now on, you keep an eye on things from your end? I've got mine covered."

She turned away and stomped to the driver's side door, yanked it open, and climbed in. When she looked in her rear-view mirror, the stranger was gone. Viciously jamming her key into the ignition, she started the engine, kicked the Jeep into gear, and tore out of the parking lot.

"I believe we could use more Andre Bocelli," Bowen sagely observed as he turned on the disc player again.

"What a shmuck," Ashlon grumbled as she gripped the steering wheel and headed her vehicle back out to the interstate.

Bowen was smiling warmly as he massaged Ashlon's neck with one hand. "I heard what you said out there."

Ashlon relaxed under his gentle fingers. Glancing at Bowen, she said, "It's only the truth, you know."

"What if he had found you first?" Bowen ventured, closely watching Ashlon's expression.

She twisted her mouth as she thought about this for a moment. He was certainly one incredible looking piece of manhood, especially the part straining in his jeans. "Nah," she decided, shaking her head. "Don't really care for blonds. I prefer the dark, brooding types." She grinned over at him, biting her lip thoughtfully.

Bowen nodded, very satisfied, and sat back in his seat to enjoy the rest of the ride home.

Chapter 43

"That is really quite distasteful, Ashlon," Bowen again protested as they sat together in the kitchen later that evening, Ashlon devouring her mushroom Swiss grilled chicken burger on a toasted sesame roll with a side of onion rings she'd picked up on the way home. She'd poured some sweetened iced tea with lemon into a big tumbler and was now thoroughly happy as she rapturously chewed each juicy morsel. After a particularly large swallow, she shook her head and curled her nose at Bowen.

"I didn't ask you to sit there and criticize my eating habits. You feed your way, I'll feed mine, so I can feed you," she flatly declared as she dangled a large onion ring and caught it in her mouth. "You know, there's something I can't figure out," she said after swallowing, wiping her hands, and taking a sip of her tea.

"The fact that you are dripping grease all over your pants?" Bowen casually observed as he handed her a damp cloth.

"Damn!" Ashlon swore as she frantically wiped at what hadn't already soaked into the fabric. "Oh well, I have a good pre-wash. And don't think you're so smart! Only two individuals saw me on the way out to the track this evening, the two cops who were patrolling the street. They wanted to know where I was heading, so naturally, I told them. They were the only ones who knew I was out there. And it's the first time this season I've used that track."

"When I was looking for you from the widow's walk, there was no patrol car to be seen anywhere," Bowen remarked. He and Ashlon surmised the same thing, and it wasn't good.

Ashlon was nodding as if she had heard him thinking, her expression troubled. "I think I'd better call Detective Anderson."

She disposed of the remains of her meal, washed her hands, and left the kitchen for the sitting room. Bowen followed her and stirred the hearth fire to life, adding more wood. He sat down next to Ashlon, who had plopped onto the sofa and held the table phone in her lap as she punched in a number written on a business card she'd dug out of her bag. She'd folded her legs under her and leaned against Bowen, his arm around her shoulders.

"Hello, Andersons," a woman's brusque voice answered on the other end of the line.

"Hey, Avi? Ashlon Isaacs."

"Hey, Ash! How you doin', babe? How come you haven't come to see us lately? And where's your bud been hanging out?" Avi exclaimed. Avi was the nurse manager on General's neuro unit and the grumpy Detective Anderson's better half.

"I'm between assignments right now, and Janey's on her honeymoon."

"Shut up, no way!" Avi exclaimed. Ashlon grimaced at the temporary increase in volume. "Well, when you see her, tell her I'm just glad she found someone who can handle her. Anyway, you need to talk Gil? He's kind of kept me up on what's been going on. Hey, sorry about the ex, too. Sincerely."

"Water under the bridge. Unfortunately, I need to tell him about something that happened this evening. He around?"

"'Fraid not, sweety. He got called out earlier when a couple of transients found two bodies in the woods near their shelter outside of town, near the cemetery. They were buried under some deadfall and looked pretty fresh. You know how that goes."

"No problem, Avi," Ashlon said, biting her lip as she glanced at Bowen. "I'll go down to the station tomorrow after he's had a chance to calm down a little."

"Honey, that man doesn't know the meaning of calm. He's one raw nerve away from a major MI as it is now," Avi sighed with exasperation.

"I hear you. Maybe that'll slow him down a bit."

"Not unless I do him first. Take care, honey. I think one of the kids just damaged herself."

Ashlon heard a child screaming in the background. The 'I'm not really hurt but I need attention,' kind of scream.

"You take care, Avi. Bye." Ashlon said as she hung up the phone and put it back on the side table. She looked over at Bowen, who seemed amused at what he'd heard. "What?"

"There is a kinship between you and others of your profession," he said, drawing her closer to him. "Yet you and Janey and the detective's wife perform widely differing functions in dissimilar areas. Explain this to me."

"I think it's because we're all made from the same mold. We have more or less the same reasons for being what we are, no matter where or how we practice. Does that explain it for you?"

"Most succinctly," Bowen said, running his fingers through Ashlon's tousled curly black hair. "I also heard what your friend said. Roberts or his associates must have found the bodies in the park and disposed of them."

"It also means I can't trust the police anymore," Ashlon said. "So, unless I sequester myself in this house for the next 2 days, I've got a big problem. Unless Blondie out there has sentries posted to keep an eye on things."

"You cannot leave this house," Bowen said. "Even they canna be everywhere."

"I don't have a choice, Bowen," Ashlon said, looking up at him. "I'm dis- charging my patients next week and putting my house on the market after the furniture's delivered. I've got to have those papers looked at by my lawyer and get them signed and notarized. And, I've got to deposit those checks. As a matter of fact, that's going to be the very first thing I do in the morning. Then, I can pay off my bills. I can't put my life on hold because a couple of hairballs are out there somewhere. You've given me something I can use to protect myself, and Blondie's got his watchdogs—or whatever. I'll just have to trust that for now."

There was something else she had available, too. There was a weapon hidden in the cabinet in his back storage room, one that could easily be hidden in a pocket or her backpack/purse. It had been Wyatt's and came with very special bullets Wyatt had specially made when he first bought the thing many years ago, perhaps afraid even then of what he'd gotten himself into. Ashlon had passed it off as just in keeping with his increasingly bizarre and violent behavior. After he'd disappeared, she'd kept it cleaned and oiled and fully loaded for general purposes, she convinced herself then. But now, especially now, she might have to put it to good use. In the morning, she'd recover it after Bowen had retired to his resting place.

Ashlon stood and stretched, fatigued to the bones. She looked down at Bowen; his face was unreadable.

"C'mon", she said, holding out her hand to him. When he didn't take it right away, but continued to sit and darkly glower into the fire, she shrugged and began to walk away. "Okay," she sighed with an exaggerated rolling of her eyes and clicking her tongue. "Guess I'll just have to scrub my own back." She casually walked off toward the staircase without a backward glance.

Bowen immediately launched himself off the couch, set the screen in front of the hearth, and swept Ashlon off her feet before she'd reached the bottom of the staircase.

She was up early the next morning, just after Bowen retired. He was still mildly piqued due to Ashlon's insistence on going out to perform her daily routines in spite of the threat hanging over her head, as well as her obstinate insistence on wearing her Sponge Bob sleep pants and faded yellow crop top to bed after what had turned into a very pleasant bathing experience with low lights, scented water, and soft music. Ashlon also showed Bowen how creative she was. He had been delightfully amazed how long she could hold her breath as her kisses trailed down the length of his abdomen and continued below the water line. She'd caught him completely off guard in a way he'd never experi- enced before. And then he'd returned the favor.

Ashlon promised she would be even more accommodating the following evening, but she needed to rest for her day's work. Bowen had reluctantly agreed, and once they were together in bed, he held her as they quietly talked until she dropped to sleep. Ashlon liked the idea of his consulting his financial manager, and would be awaiting a call from him, asking Bowen to give him her cell number. She would make it an evening appointment so Bowen could go with her.

It was snowing the following morning when Ashlon left the house and drove around the corner to her house, parking at the curb in her usual spot. Had it been only one whole week since her life had changed? She was amazed how events had progressed since her return from Boston, as if a plan was unfolding with her at its center. She was reasonably okay with it, although the changes she'd undergone during this time were still very unsettling to her. And that revelation about Grady had completely blown her away. In retrospect, however, she shouldn't have been surprised, especially in light of his recent Jekyll/Hyde behavior. She'd tossed him off merely as a street variety psycho. Her grandmother would be laughing off her support stockings by now if she was alive! What an image that made!

She'd been praying a lot lately, especially now that a chapter was closing on this part of her life and another one was about to open, its pages still blank. Her prayers more often ended with a plea to be shown again the way she needed to go, and the wisdom to recognize it. She often recited her favorite Psalm, emphasizing the part about walking through the shadow of psalm, emphasizing the part about walking through the shadow of death and fearing no evil.

However, no road had jumped out at her with signposts pointing out any direction. That didn't mean it didn't exist. There was probably just another side trip or two she had to make in order to find it, and she was game enough to look for it, as she had many others up to this point. Ashlon had faith enough to know she wouldn't be misguided.

"Well, look who's here!" a familiar, friendly voice exclaimed from next door as Ashlon unlocked her front door. Mrs. Kincaid, an early riser like herself, trundled out to meet her on the sidewalk in front of Ashlon's doorstep and gave her a big hug, beaming up into Ashlon's happy expression.

"Been staying with that big guy of yours?" the older woman said with a knowing grin.

Ashlon nodded. "Sure have, Mrs. Kincaid. Wanted to keep an eye on my house while it was being repaired."

Mrs. Kincaid shook her head as she lifted Ashlon's left hand and eyed the ring on her finger. "'Bout time you decided to move on with him, deary." And then, Mrs. Kincaid winked at her and said in a hushed voice, "Even if he is a lit- tle strange keeping those night hours."

Ashlon almost laughed out loud. "He is that, but in a nice way," she said as she led Mrs. Kincaid into her house. It was warm inside and smelled of a frank newness that was extremely unsettling, reinforcing her resolution never to live there again. She and Mrs. Kincaid sat in the kitchen at the new table while Ashlon made them some tea on her new stove. She'd brought in a few items in case—well, just in case. The tea kettle whistled, and soon she was sitting at the table and enjoying Mrs. Kincaid's company.

"Of course, I kept an eye on him, deary," Mrs. Kincaid said above her steaming teacup. "While you were in Boston with your friend, he came by each evening and we'd talk very friendly, like. I could tell he missed you something fierce, he did. Like a lost soul coming over just to sit in your space and drink it in like water to a thirsty man. Asked a lot of questions about you and us, and the neighborhood. Told him what you did for us when you first moved in with that sweet baby of yours. He didn't understand at first. Well, he soon did, I can tell you." Mrs. Kincaid winked at Ashlon as she added, "He sort of got this weird look like he was getting mad, and when he opened his mouth like he was going to say something mean, I cut him short. I says to him, 'Hon, if that's something you can't understand, then you don't know our Ashlon at all, and you'll never win her until you do. She'll see right through you like clear glass and drop you no matter how much it might hurt her. So you go and do your readin' and thinkin', and you might learn somethin' that'll help you keep her.' He never said another word."

Ashlon was shaking her head, smiling broadly. "Mrs. Kincaid, you've been one of my truest friends. And you're right. I was ready to just move on down the road that night I got back from Boston. A lot changed after that. I think our week apart made a difference, helped us both see things a lot clearer." She took the old woman's hands in hers and squeezed them affectionately. "You've been a good neighbor, Mrs. Kincaid."

"Tush, deary!" She stood and stretched, holding onto Ashlon's arm as they went back outside and walked easily down the sidewalk back to the older woman's doorstep. Mrs. Kincaid turned and looked at her with a sparkle in her eyes. "You've always given so much of yourself, deary. It's your love and sense of what's right that keeps you strong, no matter what you do. We've benefited by it. And now, that man of yours will, too. Well, I'd better get back inside before Mr. Kincaid misses me. He can't pick out a pair of socks without my help." Ashlon kissed her on the cheek. Mrs. Kincaid carefully climbed up the short steps and went back inside her house.

It was close to 8 am. Ashlon decided to lock up and go to the bank, then come back and wait for the furniture delivery. After she'd made her deposits, she stopped at the tea room and bought a couple of blueberry scones and a take-out coffee from Mineau. No, her mom hadn't come in this morning, which wasn't unusual on a Monday. Mineau expected her later on in the day when they opened for lunch.

Ashlon picked up the morning paper from Doris' grocery, and then went back to her house. An hour later, a large truck arrived in light snowfall, which promised to get heavier later in the day. Ashlon directed the placement of a new studio couch, two side chairs, several bookcases and two side tables, and a chest of drawers upstairs. A new mirror had been found to replace the one that had been broken on her vintage dressing table.

Much to her consternation, their supervisor was the tall blonde biker guy from the movies the previous evening. He winked at her as the other men gave her papers to sign acknowledging the delivery, and then climbed into the truck cab with him. As they were pulling away, he leaned out the window and touched one eye, then pointed at her. She could hear his deep laugh when he pulled his head back in the window as the truck disappeared around the street corner. Ashlon only shook her head with consternation as she went back inside. With a deep sigh, she pulled on her jacket, shouldered her bag, took one last long look around, and then departed. After locking her front door, she glanced down the street as she headed for her Jeep. Maybe she should have let Bowen at him after all, feeling smugly justified even considering it.

The remainder of the morning and part of the afternoon dissolved in the routine of her nursing rounds as she discharged two of her patients to other nurses who would be visiting after Thanksgiving, and totally discharged another who was ready to go back to work. Her last visit was in the mid-afternoon with Mr. Stanley.

Chapter 44

She happily pulled into his driveway and waved to him when she spied him looking out the front window of his living room as she went up to the door. It was immediately opened by Frances, who smiled and motioned her inside, taking her jacket and placing it on the deacon's bench inside the door.

"Dad's been waiting for you since after lunch," Frances said with easy familiarity. "He's been feeling really good. I swear he thinks you're magic."

"He's a hard worker," Ashlon said with an easy smile. "If all my clients were like him, I'd be out of a job." They laughed easily as they strolled into the living room. All of the Stanley's knickknacks and collectibles were neatly arranged above the reach of little fingers, or displayed in two large étagères. The carpeting had recently been replaced in the downstairs as well.

Ashlon greeted Mr. Stanley, proceeding with his vital signs and then starting into his therapy routine. After they'd finished, Ashlon helped him back to his chair in the living room. She rested her hand on his shoulder. "I hereby pronounce you practically convalesced," she announced in her best official voice.

"I heard that, dear!" Mrs. Stanley called from the dining room with a pleasant chuckle. "Come have a cup of tea with us."

"We're summoned," Ashlon wryly said to Mr. Stanley. "I've also got something to tell both of you."

He was puzzled as he accompanied Ashlon to the dining room and took his usual seat next to Eleanor, while Ashlon sat next to Frances, who poured the tea and served a lovely light almond cake drizzled with glaze.

"Now, my dear, what's the big mystery?" Mr. Stanley eagerly inquired.

Ashlon extended her left hand and placed it on the table in front of him. Mr. Stanley's eyes widened with surprise as Mrs. Stanley began to laugh happily and picked up Ashlon's hand.

"Wow!" exclaimed Frances. "That's quite a ring!"

"It's his ring, isn't it, dear?" Mrs. Stanley said, her expression gleaming.

Ashlon nodded, and the old couple laughed as Frances hugged her and congratulated her. They wanted details, so Ashlon told them as much as she dared, how he had finally asked her when she had said she was going to be moving back into her house after the new furniture arrived today. How he had been almost frantic for her not to leave after being in his house for over a week and making it her home with him. And, most of all, how he'd grown to appreciate and anticipate all her little quirks and habits, even putting up with her strange taste in nightwear. He had finally professed his love, and she accepted his mother's ring.

"What will you do with your house now?" Frances inquired, her expression becoming hopeful.

Ashlon knew what she wanted to hear: it would be something she could afford. Thinking on it a bit more, Ashlon remembered herself as a single mother with an infant only a few years ago, finding her perfect home priced just right and far away from her old life. She'd slowly fixed it up through the years into a place she loved. Now, she could no longer call it her home, but maybe someone like her could. It was a no-brainer.

"Frances, tell you what. I'd rather sell it to someone who'll take the time to meet the neighbors and make the place her own. I'm selling it intact with everything in it except my dressing table and bed. I'm sure we can settle on something you can afford. How's that sound?"

Frances was simply too surprised for words. Her parents were aglow with the prospect of their daughter living closer to them. They even offered to help her with the purchase.

"I'm going over to my lawyer's office after I finish here to give him some papers, and I'm going to give power of attorney to my friends Janey and Jorge to act as my agents when Bowen and I are away. My lawyer can start on the paperwork once I tell him I have a buyer ready and waiting."

That suited Frances just fine. With that settled, the afternoon passed agreeably as the conversation flowed and the small cake disappeared.

A grandfather's clock in the upstairs hallway bonged the four o'clock hour. Ashlon glanced at her watch and reluctantly informed them she really had to get going before her lawyer left for the day, thinking she hadn't remembered her appointment with him.

Mr. Stanley walked her to the door as Frances got her jacket and bag for her. Standing outside on the covered porch and giving Mr. Stanley an affectionate kiss on the cheek, Ashlon told him how much she appreciated everything he'd done for her—and for Bowen. If not for the old man, she might not have sustained her interest in the McAnders House as long as she had. Only that link, kept alive through their friendship over the years, had enabled her to eventually find what was missing in her life. So rarely did one find a companion and a kindred spirit in one package.

"And quite a package he is, eh, Miss Ashlon?" Mr. Stanley said with a wry smile and a wink.

"You're so bad, Mr. Stanley! I meant you!" Ashlon exclaimed, blushing so violently it drew a warm laugh from the old man. "I'll keep you and Mrs. Stan- ley posted as things progress. My lawyer will have everything drawn up, hopefully by the end of the week. Frances should be able to move in before Thanksgiving." She gave his hand one last affectionate squeeze, then jumped off the steps to the front walk and headed for the driveway. After throwing her things into the back seat, she rounded to the other side and was soon firing up, gearing down, and pulling out of the driveway. Mr. Stanley had gone back inside, and as Ashlon backed onto the street, she spied him peeking out the curtains again, watching her departure.

As she carefully started down the snowy street toward town, two large white panel vans appeared from the opposite direction. Suddenly, the front van veered in front of her and abruptly stopped, blocking the road. Ashlon took only seconds to assess the situation, rapidly geared into reverse, and spun her tires as she wheeled backward away from the roadblock. She was immediately cut off by the second van as it sped past her and slid to a stop in back of her. Instead of slowing down, Ashlon floored the accelerator and nailed the back van directly in the driver's side panel, pushing it back several feet into Mr. Stanley's front yard fence. Quickly gearing into first again, Ashlon floored the accelerator and sped directly toward the van in front of her, intending to veer around it in a desperate dash for Anderson's office. One of the passengers jumped out, pulled what looked like a weapon, and pointed it directly at the oncoming Jeep. Ashlon reacted instantly, ducking way down behind the steering wheel, her Jeep still careening toward the van. She heard shots fired; a bullet sliced into the impact-resistant windshield glass. Without slowing down, she headed right for the gunman, who prudently decided to leap to one side as the Jeep slammed into the passenger side panel and sent the van skidding into a snow bank on the other side of the road.

The Jeep stalled. Ashlon desperately twisted the key in the ignition with her foot on the clutch to restart it. But it was too late. As soon as the engine fired back to life, her door was ripped open and two meaty hands grabbed her, viciously yanking her from the cab. Kicking and screaming, she fought the ski masked attacker and had almost freed herself before a large fist flew out of nowhere and hit her hard on one side of her face, knocking her cold. The attacker holding her dropped her inert form on the road and cursed the damage she'd done to his face and hands with her nails, viciously kicking her hard in the ribs as he painfully rubbed several long, deep gouges she'd clawed into one of his cheeks and neck. His companion angrily pushed him away and roughly picked her up off the road, throwing her over one shoulder and carrying her to the front-most van. He tossed her through the open panel into the interior cargo area, then forcefully pulled the badly dented door shut. One of the other attackers from the second van climbed into Ashlon's Jeep and started it up again as the other men returned to their vehicles, maneuvering them back onto the road and slowly moving in the direction out of town.

With shocked, angry tears running down his face, Mr. Stanley had quickly grabbed the phone off the side table next to where he sat and frantically phoned the police to report the attack while it was still in progress. Mrs. Stanley saw the horrified expression on his face and immediately joined her husband as he rapidly reported what he had just witnessed. As soon as he hung up the phone, it occurred to him to make one more call. Picking up the receiver once again, he dialed Bowen McAnder's answering service.

The police response led by Detective Anderson arrived within minutes of Mr. Stanley's phone call. He found a very distraught old man watching for their arrival. He quickly opened the front door to step out onto the porch and meet the detective. Anderson obtained what he could from him, directing the uniforms out to the street to look for anything that might have been dropped or left behind. The only evidence they found was some shattered glass and plastic, apparently from where Ashlon's Jeep had damaged both vans, several sets of tire tracks, and blood staining in the snow on the road. This hurt the old man most of all as he described the vicious punch and then a ruthless kick her captor had inflicted on Ashlon as she lay unconscious on the road.

No, the vans were unmarked, and the men all wore ski masks and black one-piece work coveralls. Detective Anderson then inquired if Mr. Stanley had called anyone else, and was informed almost defiantly that Lord McAnders' answering service was called immediately after the police were notified.

Detective Anderson silently groaned and rubbed his eyes. This meant he would have to see that dark, brooding giant face-to-face again and explain to him why he should not be going out on his own to look for his girlfriend.

Not that that would stop him, he admitted to himself, but it might squirrel weeks of undercover work. Plus, he wasn't too worried about finding Ms. Isaacs. First, they'd taken her alive, so obviously her captors needed her for something or someone. And second, he had placed tracers in Ashlon's shoulder bag and her Jeep with her approval, in the event something like this should happen. He also had a sneaking suspicion that if there was any way to escape from whatever situation she'd been dragged into, Ashlon would immediately take it—if she wasn't too badly hurt. For some weird reason, that made him feel somewhat better about this whole mess. She was like his wife—crafty and intelligent. A very effective combination that seemed peculiar to the nurses of his acquaintance.

Heaving a sigh of resignation, he climbed into a squad car and directed the uniform behind the wheel to head to McAnders House.

The house felt strangely empty that evening when Bowen left the master bedroom and headed into the gallery. It was dark downstairs, not even a light in the entrance hallway, only one lamp with a light sensor in the sitting room that had automatically come on with the failing light of day. He descended the staircase and immediately checked there and the kitchen. Both areas were life- less and chilly, like a unique warmth had been sucked from them and cried out to be re-ignited again. His suspicions aroused, he immediately headed back through the kitchen and out the back door into the heavy snowfall, fairly running down the walkway to the garage. Her Jeep was gone, the exiting tracks long since covered in fresh new snow.

Bowen looked up into the leaden clouds still weakly lit by the remaining glow of the setting sun. Extending his arms, he leaped skyward and lighted on the widow's walk. Shadowed eyes searched the surrounding streets and out toward the park, listening for any little sound that might shed a clue to Ashlon's whereabouts. But, her house was dark, and the park was silent under its gathering white mantle as the street and park lamps flickered to life. Move- ment on the street caught his attention; he observed a lone police car pull up and park at the curb outside his gate. This was definitely not a good sign.

In the blink of an eye, he was back inside the house and quickly moving through the entrance hallway. He turned on the exterior lights and opened the door, catching Detective Anderson halfway up the front walk heading toward the house. Every instinct told him the Detective did not have good news for him. He was silent as the policeman approached and stopped just under the archway. Bowen pointedly stared at both him and the uniformed policeman fidgeting nervously behind him.

"Lord McAnders," Detective Anderson said with a short nod. "May we come in, sir? I need to speak with you on an urgent matter."

Bowen stepped back inside the entrance way and motioned for the police- men to enter. Once inside, he led them to the sitting room where he turned on the other lamp flanking the sofa, and motioned for the men to sit. Ashlon had found matching table lamps at a flea market when she was coming back from Boston after visiting Jorge's mother, and bought them because the room needed more lighting and they would look fabulous in there. She'd wired one with a light sensor. Bowen grimaced with this remembrance as he stood by the cold hearth. Of course, she had been right.

Detective Anderson felt the hackles on his neck rise at Bowen's penetrating gaze and stony silence. However, he'd willingly stepped into the dragon's lair, so he proceeded.

"I apologize for disturbing you, Lord McAnders. But something has happened to Miss Isaacs that I needed to tell you personally." He paused momentarily, letting this sink in.

"Go on," Bowen said, his deep voice veiled and neutral.

"At approximately 4:15 this afternoon, Miss Isaacs was leaving the home of a Mr. James Stanley after a visit with him. She was attacked and subsequently taken by several men who surrounded her vehicle and rendered her unconscious. Mr. Stanley witnessed the attack, including two of the suspects' assaulting Miss Isaacs, rendering her unconscious." He watched as Bowen's expression took on a dark, frightening expression that bespoke a power he just didn't want to know about.

"Lord McAnders, you need to know my department has had an investigation going on for several weeks, aided in part by Miss Isaacs and evidence she and her friend helped gather. And because she seemed to be of interest to certain individuals, she also consented to have her vehicle and her personal bag marked with tracers so we can find her anywhere with our GPS equipment. I'm asking you, sir, not to interfere with our investigation at this critical juncture and possibly endanger her life. I have units on standby and they'll be dispatched as soon as we track and lock in her location." That took balls, he congratulated himself as he stood and pulled his coat closed around him. Especially since Bowen now looked like he could, likely as not, snuff both him and the uniform without a second thought.

"As you wish, Detective," Bowen simply stated in a quietly deadly tone as he escorted the policemen to the front door and let them out. He watched until the squad car pulled away from the curb and drove off down the street before closing the door, pressing his forehead against its cool surface as he closed his eyes, summoning all his supernatural strength and stretching it into the darkness around him.

Their blood bond was still strong; Bowen could feel Ashlon around him. He knew she was alive as long as he could feel still feel that. There was time tonight to find her.

He locked the door and quickly removed his duster from the closet, pulled it on loosely around him. Then, he went back up to the widow's walk and turned his face to the black, embracing night sky, listening, searching with veiled glowing eyes. Extending his arms to the embracing darkness, he surrounded himself with the rich black iron of night and vanished into it.

Chapter 45

Soft, low keening gradually penetrated Ashlon's throbbing head as conscious- ness returned. Her one side ached like a bad tooth, and when she moved, a sharp stabbing pain flashed from her chest to her toes. She inhaled sharply at its intensity, groaning as she rolled with difficulty onto her back. Why couldn't she move her arms or legs? She opened her eyes and tried to focus on something moving off to one side, a slow rocking back and forth.

Ashlon lay still for a moment as the agonizing pounding in her head subsided to a bearable level and she was able to focus a little better. It was chilly, and the smell of wood smoke permeated the air. She could hear the crackling of a small fire and see it dimly flickering on the walls. As her vision cleared, she was able to make out the form of a shaggy-headed girl hugging her knees, voicing that strange mournful keening, her expression utterly hopeless as she rocked. Her long dark hair was a tangled mat, exposed skin areas were dirty and caked with dried blood, and a large ragged cloth was wrapped around her, barely hiding her torn dress but not the fact that she was very pregnant.

As Ashlon's awareness steadily improved, she discovered her hands had been bound and secured to an iron ring on the wall in back of her. Her feet had been bound separately and were tied to similar rings on the floor below a thin bare mattress pressed against a wall of what appeared to be a small cottage or cabin.

Cabin?

Ashlon took several frantic breaths, fighting down a sudden panic as she realized with bewildering certainty that this was the same cabin she had seen in her dream. But why was she here? She looked over at the girl and swallowed hard.

"Who are you?" she asked in a hoarse whisper that hurt her throat.

The girl stopped rocking and her eyes opened wide. She looked like she'd been roughed up a little, too, judging by the dried blood on her swollen lip. "I'm Misha. I thought for sure you were dead," she said with a woman-child's high frightened voice. How old was she? Sixteen? Seventeen?

Ashlon managed a weak smile—it hurt her jaw and she could taste blood in her mouth. "Takes more than a mugging to do me in," she said, and then swallowed again. Yep, blood. "Why are we here?"
"I was taken from my home while my mate was out preparing the battleground. You were brought here several hours ago. You were unconscious for so long, I feared you were dead. I'm glad you're not. I've been so scared."

Ashlon suspected, however, she was badly hurt, worse than the girl could see. Her side only ached if she was still; if she moved, a shock of stabbing penetrating pain crushed the breath out of her. Ashlon figured she had several injured ribs. Thank heavens for her heavy leather bomber jacket!

"Can you move?" she asked breathlessly, and gritted her teeth against the blinding pounding in her head, especially the side on which she'd been slugged by that freight train-sized fist she had seen coming at her just a little too late. She probably had a fractured cheek and eye orbit where that bastard had con- nected with her face.

"I cannot," Misha moaned. "They've bound me hand and foot as well, and I think one ankle is broken."

Ashlon managed a mirthless chuckle, which made her cough. The resulting agony racked her badly, and she could taste fresh blood in her mouth again. Definitely not a good sign! She gasped with a pain-filled grimace. "We're in a fine spot, aren't we?"

"I think you are injured worse than I," Misha observed, her smudged face pained and her eyes filling with tears as she tried to reach out and touch Ashlon.

"Yeah," Ashlon softly whispered through the haze as it settled over her again. She slipped into unconsciousness once more. How long she was out this time, she didn't know. What brought her around again was a sudden rush of frigidly cold air sweeping into the cabin interior when the door across from them was opened. It was fresh and clean smelling, filled with the night scents of pine and early winter. A veil of whirling snow followed two men as they entered the cabin and unhurriedly closed the door behind them. Ashlon managed to focus on the two large forms as one stayed by the door and the other approached the mattress on which she lay shivering from the sudden cold blast. She kept her eyes narrowed as the man got down on all fours and brought his face close to hers, sniffing around her eyes and cheeks. With a shock of recognition, she realized it was Grady. She tried to move away from him, but started to cough again, and a splatter of blood hit him in the face. Grady reared back with a snarl and quickly wiped his hand across his face, then delivered a vicious back-handed blow to Ashlon's face. She groaned with the agony that shot through her head and neck in one searing wave of pain. But, she gritted her teeth and refused to give him the satisfaction of a scream.

"Do you see, Aaron? Even when she's absolutely helpless, she still fights. Can anyone dispute my choice of this woman now?" Grady said actually sounding pleased with her lack of response.

"She looks like shit, man," the other man stated simply with what Ashlon took as a note of concern. "Those guys of yours really messed her up."

"That's why they're dead, now, isn't it?" Grady sneered. "And that's why I brought you here to tend to her and make sure she lives until tomorrow night. Once she's turned, her wounds will heal fast enough. And, when I'm declared the leader, I'll mate her in front of the assembled pack. She's ripe for the taking. Then we'll get rid of the pregnant bitch."

Both men were startled to hear a mirthless rattling laugh rise from the dirty mattress. "You're such a clueless shit," Ashlon breathlessly snarled at Grady with absolute revulsion. Mate with him? She'd rather be dead.

He immediately grabbed her by her jacket collar, yanking her upward and shaking her as he glared down at her face. "How dare you speak to me like that?" he snarled, his eyes wild and angry.

"You've probably heard this before, asshole," Ashlon angrily whispered through gritted teeth before her head reminded her of the insult it had taken, "Eat shit and die." She closed her eyes, letting her head fall back onto the mattress.

"Grady! Man, take it easy! She's just baiting you, and you're not making my job any easier!" the other man complained, trying to pull Grady off of Ashlon's limp body.

Grady held her for a moment longer, then dropped her back onto the mattress and stood, glaring down at her with malice-filled eyes. "Just clean her up, Aaron. Keep her alive until tomorrow night." He wheeled around and stalked from the cabin, slamming the door behind him in a flurry of wind and snow.

The other man knelt by Ashlon and gingerly touched her face. "Man alive!"

He softly breathed. "What did you do to that guy to make him so mad?" Ashlon forced her eyes to open when she heard him pull something across the floor, and saw it was a large wooden bucket filled with water as he reached into it and pulled out a rag, ringing it out and gently dabbing Ashlon's face with it.

"This should take the sting out of those cuts. But I don't know about those ribs of yours," he mumbled to himself as he lifted Ashlon's sweater and lightly touched a deep bruise covering a large area on the side of her chest.

"Why are you helping him?" Ashlon rasped hoarsely, focusing with effort on the man's face.

"Lady, to tell you the truth, I just don't know anymore," Aaron said with disgust as he dropped the rag into the bucket. "He's like someone I don't know anymore. Used to be my friend, but now ..." His words trailed off as he rose and moved the bucket back next to the fireplace. Was that regret she'd seen in his expression?

Ashlon coughed hard, grimacing as she spit more blood onto the filthy mattress. "He killed Wyatt," she gasped between breaths, her eyes welling with both the pain in her chest and the memory of Wyatt's contorted, lifeless body on her living room floor.

Aaron drew near to her again, his expression stricken as if he'd been hit with a blunt object. "What?! I don't believe you!"

Ashlon managed a short nod. "Saw a picture ... you ... and Wyatt. Group Forest Service," Ashlon swallowed hard and struggled to breathe. "Killed last weekend." She closed her eyes, working to stay lucid.

Aaron moved in closer and slipped a hand under Ashlon's head, gently lifting it as he peered down at her face. Suddenly, her eyes opened wide, and she caught his gaze as he searched her face. Captured him in her deep green eyes and held him fast, binding him completely. Aaron's expression relaxed, and his mouth went slack.

"So green," he softly mumbled.

"Put me down, Aaron," Ashlon whispered, pushing back the pain to speak. He gently lowered her back onto the mattress. She managed a trembling breath as she focused on him.

"Untie my hands and feet."

Aaron moved immediately, undoing the ropes holding Ashlon prisoner to the iron rings, then sat back on his heels passively watching her as she struggled into a sitting position. Her arms had gone almost completely numb and were about as useless as lead weights hanging off her shoulders. However, she was able to breathe a little better now with her arms freed.

"Go untie Misha while I work some feeling back into my legs and arms." Ashlon directed as she slowly flexed her fingers and hands, bending her joints as she watched him move over to Misha and undo her bonds. Misha was staring at Ashlon with wide, amazed golden brown eyes.

"How did you do such a thing?" she said. "Is he completely subject to your will?"

Ashlon managed a small nod. Now that she was sitting up, the pain at her side was more tolerable, but moving had made her head start to pound again.

"We need medical attention," she said as she rolled to her knees and then pulled herself upright using Aaron as a support. He stared passively at Ashlon when she touched her hand lightly on his cheek. He shuddered and moaned with the utter pleasure of her touch, reaching up and taking her hand to press it to his cheek.

"Where's my Jeep?" Ashlon said, holding onto him as she tested her legs, finding them sound enough to walk.

"In the parking area, down over the hill on the other side of the woods," he murmured as if drugged.

"And who has my keys?" "They're still in the vehicle."

Well, in spite of the disaster this evening had turned into, there was a bright spot after all. Granted it was no bigger than a pinpoint, but it was better than being totally in the dark.

"Pick up Misha and take us to my Jeep. We should avoid being seen."

A gentle smile crossed Aaron's face as he released Ashlon's hand and bent down, gently lifting a very surprised and impressed Misha. Turning, he headed for the door. Bracing her chest with her arm, Ashlon followed and opened the door to allow Aaron to exit first with his load. Ashlon silently followed.

The night was inky black without moon or stars as the snow continued to fall. Biting cold sucked the breath out of Ashlon as she gamely followed Aaron, who had no difficulty navigating through the white blanketed forest once they'd reached it. As silent as the snowfall, they moved down a sheltered path closed in by bare-limbed trees and towering pines that hissed and swayed with the occasional icy blast of air turning the loose snow into white swirls around them. Ashlon's night vision had definitely improved, easily piercing the darkness as she struggled to keep up with Aaron. Again, a blessing in all this mess. As they progressed through the chilly silence, she grimly resolved that if nothing else, she would get Misha back to her husband so that she couldn't be used as a pawn against him in the battle for ascendancy to pack leader. And, she'd find a way to effectively screw Grady's grandiose plans once and for all. He'd pushed her too far, and she was damned sick of it, ready to do some pushing of her own. And she knew how she'd do it, too—with a little help from GPS.

After what seemed like hours, and Ashlon was shivering under her cold, wet clothes and snow sneakers, her stiff, frost-nipped hands tucked into her warm armpits, the trees began to thin and the path opened to a small parking area with a wooden railing fence at its head. Aaron headed to the east side of the lot. Ashlon immediately spotted her Jeep, its orange exterior glowing through a snowy mantle. Aaron approached the passenger side and opened the door, setting a shivering Misha onto the seat, and then closing the door. Ashlon grabbed his arm and let him lead her to the driver's side, and then helped her into the driver's seat. The keys were still in the ignition as he'd said. Hot-wiring her ignition with stiff fingers in the near dark would've eaten up too much time.

Aaron stood back, gazing blissfully at Ashlon as she reached over Misha and opened her glove box. Feeling around inside it, she found what she was looking for: a small, round, flat disc with a red light glowing eerily through the darkness. Prying it off its mounting, she grimaced hard with the pain that one small movement had created as she turned and slipped out of the Jeep, approaching Aaron.

"Open your hand," she directed. He readily complied, and she dropped the tracer into it, closing his fingers around it.

"Take this back to the cabin and put it under the mattress. And then, because you were so good to help us tonight, I want you to leave this place as fast as you can. Don't linger. You must immediately leave the area. Do you understand what I've told you?"

Aaron nodded. Ashlon barely touched his face again, sending a visible shiver through his body. Then, as an afterthought, she reached behind her seat and lifted her black bag onto the seat and opened it. She pulled up a corner of the lining at the bottom, recovering another one of the red discs and then returning the bag to the floor behind the seat. Misha watched Ashlon give the second disc to Aaron with a few brief instructions. Then, she sent him on his way. Aaron happily moved back to the path and disappeared into the cloaking forest.

Ashlon propped her backside on the edge of her seat. Using the arm on her good side to assist getting her back into the Jeep, she braced her feet on the doorframe and pushed with them as she pulled herself up and settled in behind the steering wheel. She sat there for a few minutes, taking deep breaths and fighting off the pain-filled curtain that kept threatening to drop over her eyes and brain. Then, she closed her door, fired up the vehicle, and slowly backed out of the parking place. She turned the vehicle toward a wide opening in the trees and carefully headed toward it without her headlights. They soon reached a T-intersection. Gradually breaking her progress to prevent sliding on the loose snow, she looked over at Misha and rasped, "Which way?" The girl pointed right, and Ashlon carefully turned in that direction.

Several minutes later, they reached a larger plowed and paved road, and again Misha indicated the direction. There were other cars traveling along this road, so Ashlon turned on her headlamps as she took off in the direction Misha had indicated. Matching traffic speed so as not to draw attention, she widened the mileage gap between them and the encampment behind them.

"Talk to me," Ashlon said hoarsely, swallowing hard.

Misha reached out and lightly touched Ashlon's swollen and bruised face and ran her hand down to her injured ribs. "How did you do that?" she asked.

"How did you make him do what you wanted?"

"It's a talent I've acquired over the past few weeks."

"Amazing!" Misha said, obviously impressed. The heat in the cab was warming her now, and she shifted uncomfortably in her seat, finally sitting back with a resigned sigh.

"How far along are you?" Ashlon said, glancing at Misha's burgeoning mid-section.

"Nearly at whelping time," Misha joyfully replied as she massaged her bulging belly.

I had to ask. Ashlon grimaced painfully as she tried to hold her arm just a little tighter over her injured chest wall and steer at the same time.

"What is your name?" Misha asked, touching Ashlon's arm again.

"Ashlon Isaacs," she said breathily. "Pleased to meet you."

"And I you. You have an honored place within our pack."

"So I've heard," Ashlon grunted as she shifted in her seat to lean on the console a little more.

They hadn't passed any cars for several minutes. Suddenly, out of the gloom ahead, their bright headlights stabbing through the falling snow, three squad cars with lights flashing appeared, speeding from the opposite direction. Ashlon quickly slowed, pulling over to the side as they flew by, and then headed out once more after they had passed. She smiled to herself when she also heard the pronounced, rhythmic thump thumping of a helicopter passing overhead in the same direction as the squad cars. Detective Anderson had pulled out all the stops, it seemed.

"Misha, it's going to be alright now," Ashlon said, panting softly. "Those were some friends of mine going to do some damage." It was getting hard to concentrate on the road, and Ashlon knew she couldn't hold on much longer. "How much farther?" she asked, leaning painfully toward the steering wheel. *I will not pass out, I will not pass out,* she silently chanted with grim determination.

Misha did not answer immediately. She was peering out the windshield, looking for something through the steady, heavy snowfall. They drove on for maybe another 15 or 20 minutes. Ashlon was about at the end of her tether, struggling hard to stay conscious and get them safely through the snowfall. Suddenly, Misha smiled brilliantly and gleefully firmly tapped her arm. "Here! Stop here!"

With a deep sigh of relief, Ashlon slowed and pulled off the road, coming to a stop and turning off the headlamps. After popping the clutch into neutral and fumbling for the parking brake, she rested her forehead on the steering wheel and closed her eyes as the curtain began to descend again. She was beyond trying to hold it back any longer.

Glancing fuzzily over at Misha, she watched as the girl opened her door and lifted her face to the falling snow. From her throat issued a long, high-voiced howl that echoed off the trees around them and penetrated into the very forest itself. She howled once more in the same manner, then pulled her legs inside and closed the door.

Ashlon barely noticed the happy expression on her face as she reached out and pulled Ashlon back against her seat, holding her there as she continued to peer out the windows. Ashlon's vision was dimming, but not before she spotted several large, shadowed forms move rapidly from the forest around them and onto the road, approaching the Jeep. She gasped at the cold rush of air when her door was opened and a gently laughing, familiar voice said, "Well, sugar! You are certainly a surprise."

A strong pair of arms caught her as she fell into the darkness.

Chapter 46

Early morning sun filtering in through curtained windows also penetrated through her closed eyelids. Soft murmuring voices around her sounded rather pleasant after the harshness she'd endured during the night. She took a deep, painful breath and opened her eyes. Several uniforms were standing by an open door. Female voices from nearby drew her attention, and a woman's face looked over her with wide brown eyes and a gentle smile. She looked up and spoke to someone Ashlon couldn't see. "Dr. Yan, she's awake."

Another face, an older Asian man, appeared on her other side. "Miss Isaacs, I'm Dr. Yan." Another friendly voice, thank heaven.

Ashlon slowly nodded. Her head hurt something fierce and she tried to point to it. "Hurts," she whispered huskily.

"Your head?" Dr. Yan said. "It should, young lady. Whoever hit you fractured the lower orbit and your cheek. It's not going to need surgery but you'll be swollen and bruised for a while. And a fractured rib nicked your lung but you didn't need a chest tube. Bet it made it hard to breathe, though. You were bleeding a little into the lung due to the force of whatever hit you. That seems to have subsided. Good thing your friends brought you here when they did."

"Where?" she croaked, glancing around, and then looking back at him. "You're at County General. You're friends brought you in last night when they found you parked on the side of the road. I understand you were assaulted and kidnapped yesterday afternoon."

Ashlon barely nodded.

"There's a detective outside wants to talk to you. And several friends who refused to leave when you were brought in. They stayed with you through the remainder of the night, and then switched with some others when the sun came up." The doctor sounded irritated by this fact. But, Ashlon knew they were pack members there for her protection. She was vulnerable now, and until told otherwise, they wouldn't leave her unguarded. A very comforting gesture.

A tall, dark-haired, powerfully built man approached the bed, moving soundlessly next to the nurse. Startled, she quickly backed away and disappeared from the room. Ashlon knew who he was from her dream. She tried to sit up, but he placed a large hand on her shoulder and gently shook his head. The voices in the room suddenly became silent.

"I owe you more than I can ever repay," he said, his voice ringing of ancient forests and open hunting grounds, deep and full of gratitude. He bent down close to Ashlon. He looked a little like Bowen, but with piercing amber eyes, long black hair, and a deeply tanned complexion. "Misha told me everything." He lightly kissed her on the forehead and then straightened once more. He looked off to one side and motioned with one hand. Misha appeared next to him, her fresh, pretty face expressing her happiness at once more seeing her rescuer. The man stepped back and allowed her to move in closer to Ashlon, his large hand on her back as she bent over and kissed Ashlon on the forehead. "I will name our cub after you. Male or female, so will its name be."

Her husband nodded his approval and then moved off again with Misha. Ashlon watched them leave the room. She was tired again and needed to shut down, but one more visitor, the large blond man, appeared by her bedside and looked down at her with smiling, light brown, gold-rimmed eyes and a half grin.

"Hiya, sugar," he said softly and bent to kiss her as well. However, his lips lingered just a little bit longer than they should have, and Ashlon honestly didn't mind at all.

"I want to apologize for not getting to you sooner. But your boyfriend kinda helped more than we figured he would."

Ashlon's brow furrowed as she looked at him with a puzzled expression.

"We followed him to the camp. We figured he'd be able to lead us to it because of you. When we got there, we found he'd torn the place apart along with a couple of Grady's buddies." He saw an alarm appear on Ashlon's face as she mouthed Aaron's name. Raising a hand, he shook his head.

"Don't worry, he wasn't there. We found him in a sort of daze on our way in. He couldn't remember what had happened. However, he did say something about 'green eyes'." The blonde man gently laughed as he stroked Ashlon's cheek. "Damn decent of you. He'll face the pack justice now, but we'll go easy on him."

"Helped us," Ashlon whispered. The blond man nodded again.

"The place looked like it had been hit by a tornado. Your boyfriend was in the middle of it with his mouth on the throat of one of Grady's friends. We let him finish him, and then went looking for you and Misha. But you both were already gone, and so was your Jeep. It was getting close to sunrise so we promised him that we'd find you and get you to safety. He had no choice but to trust us."

Ashlon nodded again and managed to barely whisper, "Thank you", as she closed her eyes again. The man bent over Ashlon again and kissed her once more.

"I sure do wish ...," he said wistfully, touched his forehead to Ashlon's, then turned and left the room.

Later that day, she opened her eyes again and spotted Detective Anderson sitting in a chair under the window. He was dozing, but stirred when he heard Ashlon moving in her bed. He stood and stretched with a big yawn, then moved to Ashlon's bedside. She felt more rested now and managed a wan smile as the bristle-faced policeman frowned down at her.

"I'm not going to pretend I know what the hell this is all about," he began, "but I need to know that I'm not imagining any of this either."

"What's that, Detective?" Ashlon grunted as she pushed herself up on her pillows with a painful grimace. Her voice was still a little hoarse, but definitely stronger than it had been earlier.

"When we traced one of the bugs up to the camp, we found the place had been torn apart. I mean, the cabin was in splinters, and several bodies with their throats torn out were just tossed onto the mess we found there. We found one of your tracers under a shredded mattress in the rubble of the cabin. There were other bodies ... well, the best way I can put it is that they looked like they were changing or half-mutated when they were killed. Two bodies were intact but really pale, almost white. Their throats had been ripped out.

"What about Roberts?" Ashlon grimly inquired. Bowen must have been absolutely enraged to wreak such destruction on that place! It spoke volumes about his worry, his devotion to her. And G-d willing, Grady was history.

Detective Anderson shook his head. "He wasn't among the bodies we found. We have to assume he escaped the carnage."

Ashlon closed her eyes again, resting her head back into the pillows. Damn. So much for wishful thinking. And tonight was the full moon. She had effectively screwed with Grady's challenge for pack leadership in a way he could never have foreseen. But, he'd escaped Bowen's deadly wrath and was still at large. She wouldn't be safe until he was either jailed or dead. However, if Aaron had succeeded in his task, that would have happened in a relatively short time.

She hoped.

"What's going on here, Miss Isaacs?" the detective asked, gazing at Ashlon with a tight, almost frightened expression, his lips a thin black line. "This never was an ordinary murder investigation, was it?"

Ashlon sighed heavily. Her head was throbbing, but she knew he needed answers, something he could understand. But was that really possible? Hell, only a few months ago, she hadn't believed it.

"Detective, I wish I could tell you that you're only imagining the things you've seen. Or, that it's all part of an elaborate role-playing game that got out of hand. But I can't. The fact is, there are people out there who aren't always people, or become other things when it gets dark, or the moon is full, or when they get hungry. We humans are only a small part. The parts we don't see, or choose to ignore, don't fit into our neat preconceptions of what most of us consider 'normal'. But they're out there. You only have to be open to the possibility of encountering them." Too bad the detective didn't have her bubbe when he was growing up. She would have enlightened him considerably.

Detective Anderson closed his eyes and rubbed them.

"I'm too old for this shit," he mumbled as he turned and stalked out of Ashlon's room, breezing past Dr. Yan on his way in.

"He looks distressed," Dr. Yan commented as he stood by Ashlon's bed, paging through her chart.

"He just got a reality jolt right between the frontal lobes," Ashlon dryly commented.

The doctor nodded in a purely perfunctory manner and wrote a few notes on the chart. Closing it, he looked at Ashlon. "I'm going to discharge you, Miss Isaacs. You seem to be doing well enough, and I'll give you prescriptions for pain. I want you to follow up with me in several days, sooner if you have any problems. The nurse will be in to help you get dressed. A friend of yours brought over clothes for you to wear home. They're in the closet there. Do you have any questions for me?" When she shook her head, Dr. Yan nodded once more and departed from the room.

Ashlon wearily rubbed her face. All she wanted to do now was go home and take a hot shower and then just sleep until Bowen awoke this evening. She carefully got out of bed, standing still for a moment until the room stopped spinning. Then, she carefully walked around the bed and over to the closet. She found all her clothes there, she had worn yesterday, cleaned and neatly pressed on hangers, her sneakers brushed, and her socks tucked into one of them. A small sprig of pine was peaking from one pocket of her cleaned leather jacket, her Jeep keys were in the other pocket, and her shoulder bag was hung on a wall hook. She opened her bag and felt inside. Yes, she could feel the outline of a pistol in its pocket near the bottom of the bag. Ashlon breathed a sigh of relief as she removed her clothes from the closet.

She was finally back at her beloved McAnders House, soaking in a healing hot tub with lavender and jasmine scenting the steam around her. The hospital bill had already been settled by anonymous benevolent parties, so Ashlon wasted no time getting out of there and getting her prescriptions filled. She'd wanted to be safely ensconced back at McAnders House when night fell and the full moon rose.

After she'd dressed and dried her hair, her cell phone rang. Now, who could that be? She crossed the room to the bedside stand where her phone was recharging. It was the tearoom number.

At first, she wasn't going to answer it. Then, she remembered that Irma had been off yesterday and was probably calling to let her know she was working today. At least, she hoped it was Irma. Ashlon pulled her cell off the charger and flipped it open. "Hello?"

"Ashlon, it's Mineau!" She sounded frantic, fearful.

"What's going on? What's happened?" Ashlon said, suspecting the worst.

"Mom just called. Grady showed up at the house, and he sounded really mad about something. Blamed her for interfering and was yelling at her! I could still hear him in the background! She's really scared, but I can't leave yet."

"Call the police right now!" Ashlon exclaimed angrily into the phone. "She shouldn't be alone with him!"

Mineau immediately clicked off.

Ashlon looked around the master bedroom, desperately wondering if she should do anything or wait and hope the police got there in time. There was no doubt in her mind that Grady could hurt his mother—he was without a shred of conscience—not to mention he was absolutely out of his mind.

She was out the door with her bag and jacket in hand without thinking twice about it. Yeah, she was an idiot to do such a thing, but at least the police would be there, and she could assist with Irma if Grady had roughed her up.

And maybe, just maybe, this would all finally end.

Chapter 47

Thirty minutes later, she was pulling into Irma's little park-ing area and shut down the engine. Something was wrong. Where the heck were the police? Surely they were on their way, she reasoned as she sat there for a few minutes looking around the area with practiced caution before getting out of the Jeep. She had removed the loaded pistol from its hidden pocket in her bag and tucked it into her jack-et pocket as she sped up the county road toward Irma's private lane entrance. Now, she pulled it out, flipping off the safety and holding it close.

Was this dumb or what? How many times at the movies she and Janey had cringed at the utter stupidity of some dumb broad venturing into a dangerous situation, but went anyway out of fear for (boyfriend, brother, sister, husband, best friend, whatever) and get-ting snuffed in a uniquely violent and bloody manner. At least, Ashlon was armed and knew how to use it. Plus, the police should be here any minute. Right?

Sunset was still about an hour away, the milky sun suspend-ed and obscured by a thin high cloud mantle. The snow at this lower elevation was not as deep as it had been in the higher hills where the former Were encampment had been located. But, the few flurries that were blowing helter-skelter as it grew colder with approaching night-fall promised more white stuff before the evening was through.

Ashlon climbed the wide front porch steps and cautiously ap-proached the front entry. Opening the screen door, she immediately noticed the front door was ajar, swaying slightly with the occasional cold gusting of wind. Not a good sign, but at least her caution radar wasn't beeping danger yet as she slipped inside and closed the door only partway, leaving it open as a 'just in case'.

Carefully, she checked out the dining room, kitchen, and back porch areas. Nothing. Then, she approached the stairs and climbed slowly with her back to the wall, her pistol cupped in both hands. The house was deathly quiet; even the grandfather's clock in the upstairs hallway wasn't ticking anymore, as if time had come to a standstill inside the silence. Ashlon reached the top of the stairs, her chest beginning to burn again and her head aching over the facial fractures. Her last pain medication dosing at the hospital was wearing off, and soon she would have to leave if she didn't want to end up curled in a pain-wrecked ball somewhere away from home. Ashlon paused, listening with tension that made her neck ache, but heard nothing, and then carefully worked her way down the hallway. She cautiously opened each door and checked for any sign of life, not daring to call out and inadvertently alert anyone there she didn't want to see.

The upstairs was clear.

She quickly crossed the hallway and descended the stairs, headed out the front door, and down the porch steps. Only one place left to check, and that was the small barn off to the left of the house where Irma kept her small flock of sheep and goats.

As Ashlon crossed the small area of open ground between the house and barn, she glanced out over the open field next to the house and saw, with sinking consternation and a rapidly beating heart, the rising full moon on the horizon, even as the sun behind her was still glowing above the horizon. Ashlon fairly ran to the barn and flung herself through the open doorway, her eyes quickly adjusting to the semi-darkness inside. The nauseating smell of warm, fresh blood and moist earth assailed her nose, making her stomach roll.

What she saw inside fairly sickened her. The few animals Irma kept had all been slaughtered and lay in grotesque contortions in the blood-soaked dust, their throats and bellies cleanly slashed open, entrails dangling and matted in the dirt beneath them.

Shaken by the carnage, Ashlon fought down the urge to just turn and run. She had to take a chance if Irma was still alive.

"Irma!" she softly called out in a shaky voice. She listened through the suffocating silence. Just when she decided there was no one there, either, she heard a weak moan from a hay stack in a far corner of the barn. Quickly pocketing the pistol, she ran to the stack and found Irma in a crumpled pile, half hidden in some of the loose straw in a dark area behind it. Ashlon cleared some of it away and carefully lifted the older woman until she could see her face. There was a large bruise on one cheek and several scratches on her arms and neck. Otherwise, there didn't seem to be any other obvious signs of injury.

She must have fled here when Grady went berserk, and he killed her livestock when he couldn't find her. But if she was here, where the hell was Grady?

"Irma, it's Ashlon! Talk to me! Did Grady do this?" Ashlon whispered. "C'mon, Irma, we don't have much time!"

Irma stirred, partially opened her eyes, and looked up at Ashlon. "I ... I never meant for you to get hurt," she weakly said. A pained grimace crossed her face; then, her eyes fluttered closed as she went limp in Ashlon's arms. A quick check of her pulse, and Ashlon choked. Irma was gone. Her heart must have given out. Ashlon silently mourned as she gently lowered Irma back into the hay stack.

Bastard! That bastard as good as killed her! She bit her lower lip, choking back tears as she touched Irma's face one last time before lowering her into the straw, and then rose with difficulty to her feet again. She had to get out of there and call Anderson.

With sorrow weighing heavily on her, she left the barn and hastened across the open ground back to her Jeep. She didn't even bother looking back at the house as she opened the passenger door, stuffing the pistol back into her pocket. As quickly as her injuries allowed, she slid back into the driver's seat, sitting there hunched over the steering wheel as tears fell onto her lap. Irma had been complicit all along, was one of them. That's why she lived way out here in this isolated area and kept her property as she did. Ashlon wondered bleakly if she had been involved in everything that had happened these past few months. The murders, Grady's kidnapping her, and maybe even Wyatt's death.

No. No, she refused to accept this. Irma had acknowledged Ashlon belonged with Bowen when they had talked at the tearoom last Saturday, condemned her own son for that disgraceful display at the Mayor's party. And, she had been afraid when they had last spoken, expressing her deep concern about what she had overheard Grady and his buddies talking about at the house after he'd been bailed out. Ashlon was pretty sure Irma was telling her the truth when she said she told Anderson what she'd heard. Irma couldn't know, or didn't want to know, how far Grady would go to get what he wanted. That much was obvious from what she had bemoaned at the Mayor's party.

And now, Irma was dead, Grady was somewhere on the loose, and where the hell were the police? They should've been here by now, shouldn't they? Mineau had called them...

Oh shit. I'm definitely getting too slow on the uptake! Ashlon silently groaned as she frantically jammed her key into the ignition and started up her Jeep. She caught movement from the house and half-heartedly looked, her throat silently clutching.

"Well, well!" a deep, sneering voice rang out as she quickly pulled the door shut and locked it. With jarring fear and anger, Ashlon spotted Grady standing on the porch, leaning against one of the support posts. "Look who's being the Good Samaritan."

Ashlon didn't reply. She put her hand into her jacket pocket with the pistol, carefully extracting it and laying it close to her right leg as she stared back at Grady.

"If you think you're going anywhere, think again, bitch," Grady snarled as he leapt from the porch and cautiously approached the Jeep. "You owe me big time."

In her side mirror, Ashlon saw two large grey wolves place themselves in front of the lane entrance. She had no desire to wreck her vehicle or risk further injury just to run over them on the way out. Besides, even with the repairs on the lane, she'd never be able to go fast enough over it to escape from them. That left only one way out. Ashlon discreetly switched the drive mode over to 4 wheel drive and shifted into first gear.

"You've lost, Grady!" she yelled out her partially open window. "You're an asshole and always will be! Especially an asshole who murders his mom!"

Grady stopped in his tracks, his face twisted with rage. But, like Ashlon, he also heard the distant howls of other wolves approaching. They would be at the house very soon. Ashlon looked in her side mirror again. His wolves were glancing at each other with fearful uncertainty and then back at Grady.

Ah, the main pack had tracked the rogues and was closing in for a reckon- ing now that the present leader's mate was safe. But, Ashlon didn't have time to savor this small victory. A handy escape route had presented itself, and as Bette Davis might say, "Hang on boys; it's gonna be a bumpy ride!"

"Stay your ground!" Grady snarled at the wolves that were looking from him to the darkening woods. "The woman cannot leave!" With his attention distracted, Ashlon immediately reacted.

"In your dreams, pal!" she yelled at him, and floored her accelerator as she let out her clutch, a rain of gravel, dirty snow, and mud spewing over Grady. The Jeep rocketed past the house and flew into the open field next to it. She glanced into her mirror and spotted not Grady, but a huge red wolf charging after her with the others close behind him

"Try and catch me!" she growled through her teeth as she bounced down the hill and across the frozen run at the bottom, down shifting to easily climb the other side in a spray of ice, snow, and water. Once she was on the flat, she pressed the accelerator to the floor and shot across the open snow-flattened meadow, leaving the wolves far behind. Keeping the pedal to the floor, she rap- idly reached a narrow drainage ditch and sailed cleanly across it, just barely skimming its edge on the other side. The Jeep landed on the county road in more or less the right direction as she fishtailed for a split second before the tires caught hold on the wet road surface. Ashlon raced toward town, switching on the fly back to two-wheel drive.

She dug her cell out of her bag and punched in the speed dial number for Detective Anderson. When he picked up, she quickly outlined what had happened, that Irma Roberts was dead, and she was headed back to McAnders House. He actually yelled at her to stay there and no more heroics. He also said he'd send an ambulance and several units to Irma's house right away, and then clicked off. Well, that confirmed her suspicions about Mineau not calling the police. She'd been played and had barely got out with her neck intact. Time to stop playing the good guy and head home for some potent medication and wait for Bowen to rise. She had a bad feeling she would need him before this thing was all over.

Chapter 48

Ashlon's chest was burning like she'd swallowed a lit blow torch, and her headache was getting so bad she was seeing bright spots dancing in front of her eyes. She was tasting blood again, and breathing was becoming just a tad more difficult than it had been earlier. She briefly wondered if she shouldn't have gone four-wheeling earlier. However, other than insulting Grady, it had been a hell of a ride. Ashlon managed a weak grimace as she imagined how Bowen would react when she confessed this little adventure to him. She didn't care. She desperately needed to hear his voice again and feel his arms around her. Only then would she feel safe.

Relatively speaking, of course. Lloyds Corner rose up in front of her like a welcome friend, and she set her sights on home.

Slowing as she drove through town and steered around the town circle, she headed into the residential district. She passed her house, rounding the corner to the next street, slowing more as she drove past the wrought iron gate and fence fronting McAnders' house. Quickly downshifting, she looped around the next corner, finally pulling onto the private drive and parking in the garage next to Bowen's Cadillac, tripping the automatic door closer. She waited until it had completely shut and the light came on inside before leaving her vehicle. Carefully slipping from the seat, she stiffly reached behind it and grabbed her bag off the floor, sliding it over her shoulder, and then shutting and locking the driver's side door. Drawing a long, relieved breath, she departed the garage and headed down the path leading to the back entrance.

The house had been waiting for her—its heavy back door instantly swung open as she approached it. Startled, Ashlon peered suspiciously through the doorway with one hand braced on the frame, but then understood when she felt the warmth under her hand, and picked up all all the homey aromas and noises from inside. She entered into the welcoming warmth of the kitchen.

The door swung shut behind her, the lock engaging with a solid 'click'.

The hanging dragonfly lamp over the table in the kitchen automatically snapped on as she walked through and headed into the foyer, which was suddenly brilliant with dazzling light from the tinkling crystal globes in the chandelier. Ashlon headed for the front hall, which was instantly alight for her passage. She hung her bag in the closet and then checked the front door as she turned off the front porch lights. She was safely enclosed once more in this place she had loved for such a long time, even in its former desperate disrepair.

Ashlon sighed happily, crossing the foyer and heading for the staircase. Only a few more minutes before sundown. She wearily started up the stairs.

Oh, oh! Almost forgot one last critical detail.

She sat on the bottom step as she slipped out of her jacket and reached into the pocket with the pistol. Opening the chamber, she started to empty the bullets from it, intending to secure them in her bag until she could place the weapon back in its secure location.

Suddenly, the house shuddered around her. Every light in the place went out just as Ashlon heard a loud banging coming from the kitchen, followed by the deafening splintering of wood as something heavy hit and broke through the back door. Ashlon grabbed her things and quickly moved off the step and around a lintel into the shadow of the curved staircase. Her hands were shaking as she hastily reloaded the rounds in her hand back into the gun chamber, quietly closed it, and flipped the safety switch to the off position. She pressed the weapon close to her as she crouched low against the staircase. Every nerve in her head and chest was on fire as she licked her dry lips. The growing ache in her head and the sharp stabbing to her side also informed her that the pain medication she'd been given at the hospital had finally worn off. Yet, here she was about to fight for her life again. And not a prayer of any more drugs. Grady must have forced Irma to disclose where she was staying before Irma escaped to the barn, damn him!

Too little, too late.

"Heaven help me!" Ashlon quietly despaired when she caught the sound of soft, cautious padding steps and clicking claws approaching the foyer from the direction of the kitchen.

Abruptly, the deafening shatter of glass, followed by more splintering of metal and wood, erupted from the front hallway. Ashlon crouched even lower into the darkness, beads of sweat forming on her face and under her sweater from the fear that was mounting by the second, as much as the pain in her head and side. Desperately fighting down both of them, she hunched in the shadows and waited.

A large animal cautiously entered the foyer, its head swaying and sniffing the floor and air. It was halfway across the foyer when it abruptly halted, suddenly reeled, its glowing golden eyes fixed on Ashlon with a vicious snarl erupting from its jaws. Suddenly, it bounded toward her, but as it gathered for its leap, Ashlon fired, catching it in the neck. It fell backward onto the floor, where it lay still. Another wolf suddenly appeared from the back kitchen hallway and bounded over the far banister railing, hit the steps once, and leapt at her from the side. Ashlon twisted and fired again, catching the wolf directly in the brisket. It fell right on top of her, the force of its attack sending both of them sliding across the tiled floor and smacking hard into the wall next to the sitting room's arched entranceway. The pistol flew from Ashlon's hand, skittering across the floor back into the shadow of the staircase.

Ashlon pushed the furry body off her and scrambled across the smooth floor on her hands and knees back into the deep curved shadow of the staircase, scooping up the pistol. Dropping to a prone position, she peered around the bottom of the lintel, holding her breath as Grady, back in human form again, slowly, cautiously approached from the dark front hallway into the foyer.

"I can hear you breathing," he called out ominously as he stopped at the center of the foyer under the chandelier and looked around him. The house was creaking and groaning at every joint and crevice, protesting the presence of these offensive intruders and trying to divert Grady's attention. Directly above him, the chandelier swung alarmingly back and forth, bits of ceiling plaster working loose and raining on him as he glanced up and scowled at the light fixture, not quite sure what was going on. "I can make the pain go away if you just come to me, Ashlon."

Now she knew he was crazy! Ashlon bit her hand to keep from groaning both in pain and disgust as she watched the sun slowly disappearing through the shades that were now rising in the music room at the front of the house.

Hang in there just a little longer, she desperately urged herself. Only a little longer.

"Why are you doing this?" Grady called out again, sounding more frustrated now. "You know I've always liked you. I know you felt it that day we went to Boston. Even Wyatt said you'd make a worthy companion, though he didn't want you for himself. Thought he could do better once he'd been turned. I told him he was a fool for leaving you, and decided to take you for my own with his blessing. If you'd just let me take you that night in my truck, we wouldn't be going through all of this, and Wyatt might still be alive."

If that bastard thought he could use Wyatt to hurt her, he was dumber than he looked. Ashlon concentrated her focus on Grady. Yes, Wyatt had screwed up; but he also knew something about her he'd never told Grady. Wyatt must have kept it secret in case Grady betrayed him; she was willing to bet. So maybe it was time to redeem him and reveal it to this schmuck. Put an end to this charade once and for all. She needed for him to hear one last item before she plugged him, one last piece of information that would effectively screw with his mind and vindicate Wyatt before she took him out.

Ashlon braced herself on the lintel as she stood, holding the pistol in front of her as she cautiously moved away from where she'd been hidden. Edging around the lintel, she sidled to the foot of the staircase and squared off with Grady, her expression watchful and calculating. Oh gag! He was absolutely naked, and not even an attractive naked. All that damned hair! No wonder he hadn't been able to keep a girlfriend. Too bad he didn't have a sparkling personality to compensate!

"Wyatt saw right through you," she flatly informed him. "But then, you always were as transparent as plastic wrap."

"He was an idiot who followed me because he thought he could acquire more authority in my company," Grady sneered as he warily eyed the pistol pointed directly at his heart.

"We all have our little agendas. But he must have realized how much of a loser you really were when the bodies started piling up, something he hadn't counted on. He probably started feeding you suggestions about me when you pushed the ascension challenge and hadn't attracted a suitable mate." Ashlon watched Grady's face darken—her observation had hit home. "So when you learned I didn't have any impediments anymore, like my daughter, you decided to listen to him. Especially when I reconnected with your mom. Stop me if I'm wrong."

She paused, but Grady said nothing, only closing and opening his hands as his expression grew more menacing by the second.

"But, you just couldn't break old habits, could you? At the Harvest Ball, you came on so charming and confident, and for a nanosecond, I thought maybe you might've changed. But no! There you were with Cherlyn, who wound up dead later because you found out she was going to leave the pack and take her group with her if you challenged."

"Shut up!" Grady snarled, but remained where he was standing. The house had become very quiet, and the chandelier had stopped rocking back and forth. A sudden air of expectation had risen and was prevalent all around her.

He's waking! Ashlon's breathing quickened, and her pulse began to race. Only a few more seconds!

"The other two, and how many others, you and your friends murdered for similar reasons. And still you tried to worm your way into my good graces after that day we spent in Boston. But, you screwed yourself again, became impatient and tried to rape me in your truck. Your late victims disrupted your assault by attacking it. They saved me from winding up with you."

"It's not over yet!" Grady shouted as he fell onto all fours and started to gasp and tremble. "The moon is up and the ascension battle hasn't been fought yet." How could someone be so damned clueless? Ashlon shook her head with disgusted dismay and leveled her final revelation at him.

"Oh, by the way, Grady," she spat at him, working to delay a few more precious seconds. "Just to let you know that Wyatt got his revenge before he died, he kept a little piece of information from you that went with him. I suppose he suspected you might screw with him after he'd been turned and was working with the Forest Service. Even if you forced me to be your mate, you'd still be a loser, because I can't have children. That's a requirement, isn't it? At least that's what I gathered from Misha after we escaped from your cabin. Wyatt never told you our daughter was adopted, did he? Just thought you should know."

Grady's eyes widened and his face contorted with wild rage, growling and trembling and sweating in front of Ashlon, who was now utterly terrified. In less than several heartbeats, he rapidly transformed into the rogue red wolf she'd seen in the field as she'd driven away from the Roberts' house. Without thinking twice, she automatically dropped to one knee and lifted the pistol in front of her. If she was going to die, she'd take him out with her.

The huge animal crouched, ready to spring as it snarled and snapped menacingly only a few feet in front of her. Suddenly, he looked over her and backed away, still snarling, but with a new look of—fear? And then, Ashlon felt a large hand gently squeeze her shoulder as a tall form silently moved beside her. Bowen McAnders glared balefully at the wolf, his amethyst gaze filled with unblinking loathing, his deadly fangs bared, and his hands lethal talons curling and opening as if inviting something to happen. Ashlon could have fainted with the relief that swamped over her, but this was no time to get weak-kneed.

"Grady!" she called out, her deathly pale face glowing in triumph. "This man is Lord Bowen McAnders, master of McAnders House, and my betrothed."

Grady attacked. As he bounded toward Ashlon, Bowen flew forward and caught his charge in midair, slamming the wolf's body onto the floor, his arms wrapped around its neck. Grady twisted and furiously pawed at Bowen's arms and face, snapping his powerful jaws and catching one arm, flipping them both over. Grady wormed his way out of Bowen's iron grip and slid across the floor toward the darkened front hallway. But, instead of trying to escape, he again turned and charged toward Ashlon. Bowen recovered and flew at the wolf, hitting it from the side and slamming them both into the wall next to the music room archway. Plaster and paint flew from the impacted area, and Ashlon spied a large dark indentation where their mass had impacted. Again, the two combatants were a tangled mass, snarling and ripping furiously at each other with bared fangs and claws rending large, deep wounds, bearing raw flesh and sinew. The tiled floor was smeared with blood as the battle raged in front of Ashlon, who held her weapon raised and leveled, following each lightning movement as she desperately tried to draw a bead on Grady, waiting for an opening when he might be exposed to a clean shot. For several long, terrifying minutes, she desperately scanned through the darkness, at the combatants remained locked together in their furious battle. But, her vision was clouding, and she knew she couldn't hang on much longer. She needed an edge if is she was going to help Bowen bring this to an end. He and Grady were too evenly matched. Besides, Grady owed her for all the crap he'd put her through, and she wanted payback. Desperately looking up and around her, she shouted, "Please! Give me more light! Help me help him!"

The response was instantaneous.

Overhead, the large chandelier blazed to life, as did every other light on the first floor. Grady, dazzled and confused by the sudden blinding brilliance all around him, abruptly broke free of Bowen's hands circled around his neck, backing away in startled bewilderment as he stared wildly around him.

Ashlon drew a bead and fired, hitting Grady squarely in the chest above his left front leg.

"You sonuvabitch!" she screamed at him, her nostrils flaring with both her black anger and her ragged breathing effort. "Eat silver!"

Grady staggered to one side but didn't go down. He glared balefully at Ashlon then charged at her one more time. She fired off another shot, targeting his large head between the eyes. He went down immediately as the bullet found its mark and didn't move again.

Ashlon collapsed backward onto the bottom step, panting hard as she slid with difficulty to one side and leaned on the lintel. Closing her eyes with her head pressed to the cool marble, she breathed a pained sigh of intense relief. "Thank you. Thank you," she whispered.

A shadow fell over her. With difficulty, she opened her eyes and looked up, trying to focus on who was there. "Bowen?" she rasped. Detective Anderson knelt in front of her, bringing his face close to Ashlon's, and he was actually smiling.

"Looks like you've been busy, young lady," he commented as he took the pistol from her with a cloth-covered hand and opened the chamber. "Four rounds missing and accounted for. I got here just in time to see you take down that red one. Very impressive, I must say."

Ashlon licked her dry lips and drew in a shallow breath. "Where's Bowen?" She painfully whispered as she tried to look past Detective Anderson.

The policeman looked around, his expression puzzled. "Was he here? Try to be still. I've called an ambulance."

Several uniforms were looking over the bodies scattered in the foyer as they waited for the county coroner and animal control. Ashlon vaguely heard Anderson says something about one of the bodies being a dark-haired woman, the one who owned the lunch shop. Mineau. So, she had been involved, too, Ashlon concluded as she closed her eyes and sagged against the lintel. Mineau had been a mover behind the scenes. Probably even let Grady into the mayor's party to get another shot at Ashlon. But he'd screwed up again and got arrested. His sister's disgust had been evident that night. And then, the call tonight, that had drawn Ashlon to Irma's place, was another ploy to get her into Grady's clutches. They must have been really desperate to pull that one. Well, Ashlon had sworn she'd see him dead first, and that's what happened, thanks to Bowen.

There was hardly any pain now as she let go and fell into a deep, dark, comforting void, hoping he was somewhere close to catch her.

One of the policemen called out urgently to Detective Anderson. "Uh, chief? You better come take a look at this. Like now!"

Detective Anderson worriedly checked Ashlon's eyes and pulse, cursing silently as he stood and turned, moving to the group surrounding the spot where the red wolf had fallen. Their faces were pale with abject disbelief as they witnessed it gradually metamorphose into the human Grady Roberts with two neat gunshot wounds where the policemen had seen them on the red wolf. They stared at each other, waiting for someone to say something.

Anderson looked around at all of them. "As far as our reports are concerned, gentlemen, these three individuals were involved in some sick, twisted game and broke into this lady's fiancé's house with the intent to harm. She and her fiancé acted in self-defense and killed all three of them. Is that clear?" Tense nodding and murmured agreements. "I want to impress on all of you the need to maintain this story, or so help me G-d, I will discredit whoever doesn't and you'll be job hunting over the holidays. Am I clear on this?" Again, murmured agreements all around, and then the uniforms quickly departed as the coroner's representative appeared. One of the uniformed cops called animal control to cancel the call, telling the dispatcher it had been mistakenly phoned in.

Detective Anderson turned back to the staircase and nearly jumped out of his skin when he spotted a shirtless Bowen descending toward Ashlon. He kneeled, gently gathering her into his arms and then standing again, holding her close and gazing down into her face when she weakly cried out. Bowen lowered his lips to hers and softly whispered. Detective Anderson watched with amazement as Ashlon's pained moaning subsided, her body visibly relaxed in Bowen's embrace, and one arm slid down to dangle at her side.

"There's an ambulance on its way," Detective Anderson warily informed him.

The house suddenly shuddered and rattled with a rhythm that sounded almost like laughing. Anderson looked fearfully around him, nervously licking his lips. He backed away toward the entrance hallway, keeping a steady eye on Bowen, whose gaze followed him with a calm, detached expression. He clutched Ashlon protectively close against his bare chest. That's when Ander- son noticed several long, deep scratches around Bowen's shoulders, arms, and upper chest, but bit his tongue when he almost asked where he'd gotten them. "I will take care of my lady, Detective. You clear this refuse from our house and I will be satisfied," Bowen curtly informed him. "If you need our statements, please come by Thursday evening, when she is better able to speak with you about tonight's events."

Detective Anderson nodded and hastily turned to his business with the coroner. Bowen ascended the staircase to the gallery with his precious load, crossing it and disappearing from view.

Callous prick! The detective mused darkly as he watched Bowen's departure. She'd be dead by morning, and then he'd nail his ass for failure to procure medical treatment.

As if in response to its master's departure, lights in the side rooms and back kitchen hallway suddenly went out, leaving only the foyer and front hall light on for the forensics team to work. They nervously took that as a cue to hurriedly wrap up their work and get the hell out of there. Detective Anderson posted patrols to watch the house front and back until repairs could be made to the damaged doorways, but for some reason, he sincerely doubted anyone who might be stupid enough to wander into that place would want to stay long anyway.

Chapter 49

Ashlon abruptly woke with Emma's name on her lips. The bedroom was dimly lit with a banked fire in the hearth and only one dragon sconce candle flickering above the bed. Bowen lay next to her in deep repose. His arms were around her, keeping her locked protectively against his body, his one leg lying over hers. She was surrounded by him, absolutely safe and warm for the first time since leaving the hospital that morning. Had it only been that morning?

There was a strange metallic taste in her mouth, mildly salty and thick. Ashlon couldn't think what it might be since she hadn't eaten anything since breakfast. However, she did notice her head didn't hurt as much, and breathing was easier. She felt only somewhat bruised and sore, now.

However, she had hovered on that precipice between life and death, where she had seen Emma in a light of such brilliance and purity, she wanted to become a part of it more than she'd ever wanted anything else. But her beloved daughter had said she had to go back. Go back for Bowen's sake. What was it Emma had said? Let his love grow with her? Help him see the light?

Ashlon closed her eyes and sighed, relaxing into the sheets and Bowen's arms. The answers would come in time. The threat that had hung over them was gone, and the peace of mind that alone generated was enough to make her smile as she looked into Bowen's peacefully composed face. Emma was right. It was time to start living for him again and give him what he wanted most.

But how would that help him see the light, she wondered as she nestled against him and fell back to sleep again.

Late Thursday afternoon.

Detective Anderson was not a happy man as the car pulled up in front of McAnders House. The plainclothes policeman sitting next to him, Lieutenant Amaya watched the detective chew nervously on the end of an unlit cigarette dangling from his mouth, his face screwed up with an expression of 'don'twant to be here.'

Amaya had arrived at the crime scene Tuesday evening in time to see this darkly glowering, deathly pale giant carrying his injured girlfriend up the staircase, and Detective Anderson shooting poison knives at his back and looking like he wanted to shoot the guy on the spot. Then, there was the house and the way it kept groaning and creaking, giving the investigation team the creeping jeebies as they cleared out the three bodies in the foyer. The house noises had stopped almost as soon as the stiffs were off the premises! What was that all about, anyway? Anderson said in a kind of off-handed way it had something with to do with that McAnders guy.

Amaya wasn't convinced, but he wouldn't say that to Anderson. The guy was too wired to take any suggestions at this point anyway, other than he needed a long vacation after this was done and filed.

The two men got out of the car and passed through the front gate, heading up the front walk to the ivy-covered archway. The doors had been replaced, Anderson noted and the frame was once more intact. The door styling was different. The tempered glass inserts were certainly unique, with multi-colored stained glass designs in each panel. Anderson also noted that on the right side of the door frame, an ornate metal cylinder with some strange script had been placed at an angle just at eye level with the bottom tilted inward. Anderson pointed this out to Amaya as he rang the doorbell and waited.

Something is very different, Anderson thought to himself as he pushed the doorbell again.

The door opened, and a well-dressed older man appeared in the doorway, smiling congenially at the policemen. "Good evening, gentlemen," he greeted them pleasantly. "Please come in. Lord McAnders is expecting you."

The clouds behind them suddenly cleared, and a brilliant late afternoon sun lit up the entrance hall as the policemen went inside. Mr. Stanley stood in the orange and yellow light for only a moment, basking in its mid-November richness. Thanksgiving would be in a few days. This year would truly be one of such thanks and blessings, or as Miss Ashlon would say, something to kvell about. He closed the door when a slight chill rose once more in the air. Didn't want to become ill just before the holidays!

Mr. Stanley showed Anderson and Amaya into the study, where they found Lord McAnders tapping away at a laptop computer and sipping from a steaming mug. He looked up when they entered and motioned for them to sit in a couple of chairs that had been moved in front of his desk for them. The sun filtered in through partially shaded windows and softened his stern features in its mellowed autumn glow. He was still a pale-looking stiff, but not like what Anderson and Amaya had seen two nights ago. For that matter, he looked very content.

"Thank you for returning this evening to speak with my wife and me about Tuesday evening's events," Bowen said as he rose from his large leather chair and walked around the desk, propping himself on its edge with his hands folded in his lap, gazing placidly at the detectives.

"Your wife?" Anderson said. "When did that happen, if you don't mind my asking?"

"This morning," Bowen said warmly. "We drove to Boston after my lawyer arranged with a justice of the peace to marry us. We will have a more formal ceremony when we return to my estate in Scotland next month. We would leave sooner, but Ashlon wants us to stay for Thanksgiving. She and her friend, Janey Villarreal, and Mrs. Stanley are planning a feast at the Stanleys' house. This will be a first time for me. She calls it the All-American Glut Fest, whatever that means." He shook his head with the shadow of a smile lighting his otherwise dour expression.

The two policemen glanced knowingly at each other.

"So, Miss Isaa—uh, your wife is better, I take it," Detective Anderson said, clearing his throat. "She was pretty banged up Tuesday night, wasn't she?"

Bowen's eyes narrowed, but not in an unfriendly way. "I understand your concern, Detective," he said. "My lady is better, thank you. Her previous injuries were not worsened for her encounters that evening, but she still requires a small amount of the pain medication given to her by her physician when she was discharged from the hospital Tuesday. She has admitted to me, however, that she had to make an expedient departure from Roberts when his friends blocked an access road from his house and further aggravated her injuries. I am afraid Ashlon likes to take risks in that vehicle of hers."

Bowen shook his head with genuine dismay.

Detective Anderson was grinning. "That explains the tracks we found in the field behind the house heading for the county road. Funny, though, that we didn't see any through the drainage ditch, but there were tire marks weaving on the other side before the road." Realization dawned on him. "She must have cleared that damn ditch."

Amaya looked at his partner in amazement, and then back at Bowen who only shook his head again.

"As I said, gentlemen, she takes risks."

"What I can't figure out is how she managed to plant those tracers in the cabin and on Roberts," Anderson said.

It was Bowen's turn to look surprised. "The ones you had informed me were in her vehicle and her personal handbag?" he said with a deep frown.

"Those are the ones. We found one of them in what was left of the cabin at that campsite, and the other firmly planted on Roberts in the hair on his back. Like someone had patted him on the back or given him a firm slap there. That's how we were able to track him here."

"I would be most interested to know this as well, gentlemen," Bowen said with genuine interest as he moved to the study door and left the room for a moment.

The detectives heard him talking softly with the older gentleman who replied with something. Bowen returned to the study. He sat once more on the edge of the desk. "My Lady will be down presently. She was resting after our return from Boston, and Mr. Stanley has gone up to inform her of your arrival. Please accompany me to the sitting room, gentlemen," Bowen said, moving to the doorway again. "Ashlon may be more comfortable there by the fire." He departed the study, followed by the detectives. They moved across the foyer to the larger sitting room where a crackling fire was burning in the hearth. A book was open on the coffee table, and a steaming cup of hot tea had been placed on a coaster next to an autumn-decorated dessert plate holding several cookies.

As the detectives sat in two chairs between the sofa and the fireplace, Mr. Stanley entered with Ashlon, who sat next to Bowen on the couch. She was wearing her favorite dead munchkin slipper socks, a well-worn pair of painter's jeans, and a soft black mock turtleneck jersey. She folded her legs under her, leaning on Bowen. He circled her shoulders with one arm, holding one of her hands in his. She looked much better than she had Tuesday evening, Anderson observed.

"Detective Anderson," she greeted him with a warm smile. "It's nice to see you again. Who's your partner?"

Always direct, Detective Anderson mused. "Detective Amaya, I'd like you to meet the lady I've been telling you about."

Ashlon reached out and clasped Amaya's hand in hers. "After

what Grady's guys did to me, I'm healing, but it's still a little painful sitting up for very long without drugs." She reached over to the plate of cookies, offering them to the policemen. When they declined, she lifted one off the stack, taking a small bite from it. "So, where do you want to begin?"

Bowen smiled down at her, idly caressing her hair as she spoke with the two policemen. His mind was somewhere else as he listened with detached interest.

He was still at a loss to explain what had transpired Tuesday night, but it had happened, nothing less than miraculous when he thought back on it. Perhaps someone had finally decided they were overdue for one.

He'd carried her up to their room, laid her carefully on the bed. She had been injured in the kidnapping, but he suspected her injuries had worsened when she was jumped by the one werewolf and slammed into that wall next to the sitting room. He'd sensed it, but was unable to do anything as he lay there in his sanctuary, waiting in quiet desperation for the sun to set. She probably hadn't felt the extent of the damage, either, until she had been sure Roberts was dead. Her hand holding the weapon was shaking badly as she faced off with him, and Bowen knew she would have perished if he hadn't appeared when he did. It fed his killing rage as he attacked, the only thing that kept Grady from getting the upper hand until Ashlon had fired off the fatal shots. Unfortunately, he'd also heard the police arrive and vanish temporarily.

After he disposed of his shredded shirt and was sure his wounds were nearly healed, he'd interceded between her and Anderson's probing, taking her away from the terrible pain as he carried her from that scene of death and destruction, leaving it for the police to clean up.

She was falling away into the abyss. Bowen could see only one course open to her now. He had removed her soiled clothes, then stretched out beside her, locked her into his embrace, kissed her tenderly, and then pressed his lips to her throat, biting into it and firmly sealing his lips to her soft skin. Her mortal journey would end, and he'd waken her to a new beginning with him as her guide, their love continuing through an eternity of awakenings.

She had weakly struggled against him even as death descended. But, Bowen was determined, holding her firmly as his fatal kiss drained away her life. Her faint breathing diminished, her heartbeat slowed to nearly nothing, and she wilted in his arms, becoming deathly still. Bowen lifted his head, gazing into her deathly pale face as he then carefully bit his tongue. He bent his head as his lips parted, easily opening her mouth with one hand pressing on her chin, and then firmly but gently pressed his lips to hers, thrusting his tongue into her mouth. He milked it and filled her mouth with his warm blood, gently stroking her throat to make her swallow it. She did once, twice. With a final loving kiss, he raised his head again. Her lips were ruddy with the force of his passionate kiss and the treasure he had imparted between them. And they were warming with their new life.

It was done. Bowen laid her head back on his shoulder. Lowering his face until it almost touched hers, he spoke softly, calling her to him, reaching through the darkness to touch her, guide her back to him. She would awaken to his calling again the following evening, and then they would leave this place for his ancestral home in the Highlands.

And so, he settled in beside her, withdrawing into his sleep-like state with Ashlon securely wrapped in his arms, his one leg thrown over hers. Now we are truly one, beloved, he silently declared as he kissed her lips one more time. And then, he closed his eyes. He would stir with the dawn and leave her for the day, returning after sundown to waken her to her new existence.

But then, something extraordinary happened, something that he hadn't experienced in over 400 years.

He dreamed.

Ashlon was running through the hills of their home in the cool, bright daylight, a joyous smile lighting her beautiful face as she chased a dark-haired child toward his manor house. He stood in the courtyard next to a sparkling, bubbling fountain he'd built for his mother centuries ago, watching the child nearing the house. He moved around the fountain to crouch with his arms open, snaring the running child in them, holding him and whirling him around, then turning him upside down as the child giggled for daddy to stop tickling him on his tummy. He righted his son, kissed him, and sent him inside with a pat on the bottom as Ashlon joined him, mildly winded but laughing. He took her in his arms and she hugged him close, but not too close because her belly was swollen with another child, his child, growing inside her. He lovingly caressed his hands over it, bent to kiss it, and then held her as they walked together into the house.

Startled, he opened his eyes. Ashlon was standing next to the bed, bathed in a light from some unseen source, breathtakingly beautiful in its glow, looking like an angel to him. She was wrapped in his robe after cleaning up in the shower. She smelled wonderful, and he smiled up at her. However, his angel stared back at him with a wide-eyed, absolutely amazed expression.

"What is it, my love?" he asked sleepily. "Is that the moon? It is so brilliant." She reached out, almost hesitant as she touched his face, which was bathed in that same soft golden glow. It bathed her hands as her fingers stroked his forehead and down the sides of his face. Her expression was filled with awed wonder as she hesitantly said, "Bowen, it's ... it's after sunrise. Look." She turned his face toward the window and slowly smiled as the sun hit him directly.

Absolutely horrified, he cried out a terrible, strangled scream as he threw his arms over his face and eyes, desperately turning away, miserably anticipating his inevitable fiery dissolution in the purity of new daylight. This could not be possible! After everything they had endured, to be cheated by this unspeakable quirk of fate, taking him away from the love he had finally found and won. Why was this happening? Why hadn't he felt the coming of day as he had all these interminable centuries? A deep groan of utter empty desolation escaped from his throat as he curled away from the light, awaiting the inevitable burning agony, trapped in its merciless cold glare.

Ashlon quickly sat on the side of the bed and wrapped her arms around him, cradling him with his head burrowing into her lap, his deep anguished moans tearing at her heart.

"Bowen! It's alright!" she soothed gently and insistently, holding him close as she rocked him back and forth. "Look at me, Bowen!"

And, finally, he heard her. Bowen was calming, reluctantly unfolding his arms, comfort flowing into him from Ashlon's softly spoken words, the protection of her loving embrace, and the early morning sunrise. With stark disbelief, he turned his face into it again as the shades muted the morning glare. The light was gentle, almost caressing, as he looked up into Ashlon's face, made all the more breathtaking in its richness. Dear heavens, he'd never seen anything so beautiful! He reached up with one hand and touched her face.

"I meant to bring you to me, to close the circle," Bowen whispered. "I kissed you, took your life, gave you my blood to bring you back to me. I called to you and beckoned you to come to me, to follow my voice back from the void. I wanted you back with me for all our nights to come." Bowen wrapped his arms around her, pressing his face into her breasts, and heard her strong heart beating a steady rhythm. Suddenly, he desperately wanted to tell her his dream. He tried, but the words wouldn't come; the power of his vision simply too much for him to describe. Perhaps it was because it had been his own personal dream, one he had wanted before becoming one with the night; and now, one he could once more make into something real. He realized, with absolute joy and certainty he had not experienced in a long time, he had that choice again.

A faint tremor coursed through him. Bowen was utterly overwhelmed. She gently rocked him, making a soft shushing noise that calmed and comforted him. Bowen eventually looked up again, his amethyst eyes glistening. Ashlon stroked his face, his spent tears moistening her fingers.

"How has this happened?" he said as Ashlon pressed a kiss to his forehead and continued to caress his hair, his face.

She shook her head. "I don't know," she readily admitted. "I had a dream, Emma told me I couldn't stay with her, that I had to return to you. She told me I would show you the light, and your love would grow with me. At least, part of that I understand now." Ashlon's expression was absolutely overjoyed as she smiled down at him.

Bowen pressed his forehead to Ashlon's heart, thanking with deep gratitude whatever power had intervened, thanking it for sustaining him through the centuries of his lonely night-shrouded existence, thanking it for finding Ashlon and then helping him win her and awaken a part of him he thought long dead.

As for his love growing with her, Bowen was now assured that it, too, would manifest itself in time if his dream was any indication. Maybe someday he would tell her of it as it unfolded before them into blessed reality.

Ashlon confirmed Bowen's and Detective Anderson's suspicions about her escape from the campsite, which included a somewhat altered explanation of how she had convinced the doctor to free her and the girl, and then planted the tracers in the cabin and on Grady Roberts.

Yes, she escaped through that field behind the Roberts' house because several of his guys were blocking the lane entrance. She had been going fast enough to clear the ditch instead of slowing down to go through it. She'd fish-tailed on the road, but nothing she couldn't control. She'd owned that Jeep for a long time and knew what it was capable of. No big deal.

Detective Anderson continued to question and probe about Grady's motive in pursuing Ashlon, and she had to explain her ex-husband's power fixation that had made him desert her; and how he'd been lied to by Grady. So, when Grady was looking for a likely companion in his leadership quest, Wyatt had suggested Ashlon since he knew of Grady's past attraction to her. If Grady couldn't win her by persuasion, he'd take her by force. But, Wyatt had withheld information about her inability to bear children, a requisite for the leadership position Grady had coveted at the expense of so many lives.

Yeah, she supposed it was some kind of cult thing, but then Grady had always had a screw loose anyway as long as she'd known him. She suddenly became silent as she leaned against Bowen and rubbed her temples.

Bowen watched her face tighten and her stomach audibly rumbled. Frowning at Detective Anderson, he flatly said, "My wife is tiring, gentlemen, and needs to have a meal. I think we have answered enough questions for one evening." His expression informed them he would harbor no argument, either.

Detective Anderson, however, wasn't finished yet. Turning to Detective Amaya, he spoke to the man and sent him from the room under the pretext of getting something from the car they'd driven to the house. After Amaya departed, Detective Anderson leaned once more toward Ashlon. Bowen's impatient glower was tempered by Ashlon's hand on his cheek.

"Tell me something," Anderson said in a lower voice as she gazed at him. "You dressed up your narrative. There's more to this than you've told us. I know what my men and I saw happen to Roberts Tuesday night right out there in the foyer."

Ashlon shook her head in dismay and pressed her head against Bowen's shoulder as he held her closer to him.

"You know there is more, Detective," Bowen curtly said. "Ashlon has given you what you need for your report. The other details are not relevant. Those would only complicate your job and make it impossible for you to submit your report and have it believed. I heard what you told your men Tuesday night, so I suggest you adhere to your own advice and let the other details drop. I wouldna want your credibility destroyed. You are too good a policeman, and I shouldna like to see that happen."

Anderson sat back, frowning with frustrated consternation. He huffily stood when Mr. Stanley appeared to escort him out. Bowen nodded to Anderson as the policeman left the room without saying anything more.

"I have the distinct impression he is not pleased," he said, looking down at Ashlon.

"I tried to explain a few things to him at the hospital on Tuesday, but he's just not ready to admit that humans aren't the only dominant life forms on this planet." She sat up, reaching for her cup of tea and another cookie.

Bowen rubbed her back. "Are you sure you do not want to leave for Scotland until next month, love? I feel the need to put some distance between us and the detective."

Ashlon turned, eyeing him thoughtfully. "I'll make a deal with you. We stay for Thanksgiving, but leave directly on the weekend."

Bowen gently smiled. "Most fair," he said with a nod. Ashlon stood up and stretched after finishing her tea.

"I'm feeling better now with him gone. I think I'll go for a short walk and check on my house. We can have dinner when I get back." She started out of the room into the foyer, but Bowen quickly caught up with her, lifting her off the floor and unceremoniously throwing her over one broad shoulder.

"I do not think so, wife," he firmly declared, resolutely clamping his arms over her as she squirmed and protested. He smacked her soundly on the bottom. Utterly shocked, Ashlon became silent as she looked around at him with stubborn consternation.

"Tonight is our wedding night, and we have an obligation to fulfill," the lord of the manor declared. "Dinner awaits us in our room, as does our nuptial bed." And a future to create, he added happily to himself with a lusty gleam in those amethyst eyes that Ashlon knew only too well.

She snorted, resigned inside Bowen's iron grip as he easily mounted the stairs to the gallery.

Mr. Stanley, who was pulling on his coat and hat, laughed heartily as he watched them cross the gallery. Fortunately, he had put their dinner on warming plates with covers before setting it in their bedroom. It might be some time before they got around to eating it.

"Goodnight, sir and lady," he called out with a laugh. Ashlon managed a wave to him before they disappeared down the hallway to the master bedroom. Mr. Stanley listened until a distant door slammed, and then looked around him one last time before leaving. He could feel it in his bones—the house was content, made whole again by a love that had transcended adversity to find its expression in the union of these two remarkable people, kindred spirits who had finally found happiness together.

And that, Mr. Stanley concluded as he walked down the hallway and exited McAnders House is the way it should be.

How he loved happy endings!

END

Author's Note

TAPS is The Atlantic Paranormal Society, an independent consulting firm located in Warwick, Rhode Island. It is dedicated to the investigation of paranormal activity, including hauntings and poltergeist activity. Some of its more notable investigations can be seen on the Sci-Fi Channel Wednesday evenings. They also have an excellent website at www.TAPS.com. Their investigations are conducted using a wide variety of instrumentation to objectively measure and scan affected areas for ghostly activity and other paranormal phenomena.